French ESCAPE

ESCAPE

COLLECTION

April 2017

May 2017

June 2017

July 2017

August 2017

September 2017

French ESCAPE

Barbara MCMAHON *Christy* MCKELLEN *Robin* GIANNA

Published in Great Britain 2017
By Mills & Boon, an imprint of HarperCollins*Publishers*
1 London Bridge Street, London, SE1 9GF

ISBN: 978-0-263-93104-4

09-0817

Our policy is to use papers that are natural, renewable and recyclable products and made from wood grown in sustainable forests.
The logging and manufacturing processes conform to the legal environmental regulations of the country of origin.

Printed and bound in Spain
by CPI, Barcelona

FROM DAREDEVIL TO DEVOTED DADDY

BARBARA McMAHON

Barbara McMahon was born and raised in the south USA, but settled in California after spending a year flying around the world for an international airline. After settling down to raise a family and work for a computer firm, she began writing when her children started school. Now, feeling fortunate in being able to realise a long-held dream of quitting her 'day job' and writing full time, she and her husband have moved to the Sierra Nevada mountains of California, where she finds her desire to write is stronger than ever. With the beauty of the mountains visible from her windows, and the pace of life slower than the hectic San Francisco Bay Area where they previously resided, she finds more time than ever to think up stories and characters and share them with others through writing. Barbara loves to hear from readers. You can reach her at PO Box 977, Pioneer, CA 95666-0977, USA.

CHAPTER ONE

THE SOFT SIGHING of the sea as it kissed the shore should have soothed Jeanne-Marie Rousseau, but it did not. She stared at the expanse of the Mediterranean sparkling in front of her. The sun was high overhead in a cloudless sky. The sweep of beach at her doorstep was pristine white, dotted here and there with sun worshippers on colorful towels. To a stranger, it appeared a perfect relaxing retreat. Off the beaten track, St. Bartholomeus was an ideal spot for those seeking respite from the hectic frenetic pace of modern life. To live here year-round would be the dream of many.

To Jeanne-Marie, it was home. Sometimes joyful, but today it held a lingering hint of sadness.

Today was the third anniversary of her husband's death. She still missed him with an ache that never seemed to ease. Intermingled with that was anger, however, at the careless way he'd treated life—risking his safety every time he went climbing. Now, not even thirty, she was a widow, a single mother and the owner of an inn in a locale that was thousands of miles from her family. She shook her head, trying to dispel her melancholy thoughts. She had much to be grateful for and her choice of residence was hers to make. She shouldn't second-guess her decision over and over. But sometimes she just plain missed American food, family discussions and longtime friends she saw too infrequently.

Yet this small strip of land reminded her so much of Phillipe, she couldn't bear to leave it. They'd spent several holidays together, enjoying the sea and exploring the small village. Or just sitting together on the wide veranda and watching the sunset, content to be together, never suspecting it wouldn't last forever.

And for him there had been the added attraction of Les Calanques, the cliffs that offered daily climbing challenges to men and women from all over Europe.

Her son, Alexandre, was napping. She was alone with her memories and homesickness. She took a moment to sit on the veranda, remembering happier days. The worst of her grief had long passed. Now she could think about their life together, mourn his death and get on with the practicalities of living.

She would have returned to America after Phillipe's death, but she wanted her son to know his grandparents. Alexandre was all Phillipe's parents had of their only child, except for the photographs taken through the years. Her own parents came to visit annually. They spent lots of time via computers between their trips. And they had six other grandchildren. The Rousseaus only had Alexandre.

And it wasn't as if she didn't love France. It had been her lifelong desire when younger to attend school here and maybe even work for a while. She'd not planned on falling in love with a dashing Frenchman. But love had won out and she'd been living in France for more than a decade now. Those first years of marriage had been so marvelous.

What prompted a man to risk limb and life time and again just for thrills? she asked herself for the millionth time. Challenging himself, he'd so often called it. Scaling mountains with flimsy ropes and gadgets to minimize damage to the rock. As if a mountain would care.

Living with a loving family was enough for her. She'd never understood Phillipe's passion, though he'd tried often enough to enlist her in it. Idly she remembered the trips around Europe, always with a mountain to climb as the destination. The few times she'd tried it, scared and inept, but wanting so much to be with him, she'd only caused him to become impatient and demanding. It had ended up being better for him to go on his own and leave her to her own devices.

She swung her gaze to the right—Les Calanques, the limestone cliffs that afforded daily *challenges* to those who liked free climbing. The spectacular scenery of the sea and coast viewed from the cliffs added to their attraction. Of all the places for her to end up—where rock climbers from around the world came. Or at least those who didn't want to stay in Marseilles for the nightlife. It was quiet as a tomb in St. Bart most nights.

Phillipe had been a dedicated climber, not for him the wild parties that could impair performance the next day. Many shared his philosophy.

She was grateful for that, she thought, idly studying the play of light and shadows on the nearby cliff. Not every single mother had the means to earn a living and remain with her son full-time. And realistically she knew not everyone who went climbing fell to his death. It still remained a mystery to her why people dared life and limb to scale a cliff.

Well, there were other things in life she didn't understand. Her moment of introspection was over. Now it was time to get ready for the influx of guests arriving in the next few hours. Seven new reservations would fill her small inn. Business boomed in the summer months, with rarely a single room vacant more than one night. She was frugal and thrifty and managed her money well. While not wealthy by any means, she and her son were definitely comfortable.

She wanted fresh flowers in each of the rooms when her guests arrived. And she'd replenish the flowers in the rooms of those who had already checked in a couple of days ago. All the rooms had already been cleaned and made up with fresh linens. Last-minute touches remained. She'd deal with bittersweet memories another time. She had guests to prepare for.

Two hours later Jeanne-Marie perched on the high stool behind the mahogany counter at the side of the lounge and looked across the open room. Comfortable sofas and chairs were grouped for conversations. Her son played happily in the sunny spot near one of the open French doors. His two small cars and toy truck gave him endless hours of entertainment. Later, after the last guest had checked in, she'd take him for a swim. The sun was lower in the sky now, flooding the front of the inn, making it just a bit too warm, but she had not yet lowered the outdoor curtains that shaded the wide veranda. She wanted the guests' first impression of the inn to be the best and it looked beautiful when lit by the sun. Every speck of wood glowed with polish. The marble floor gleamed without a trace of the sand that was the bane of her existence. The comfy furnishings begged for travelers to sit and rest. The lounge chairs on the wide veranda in front beckoned with the view of the sea.

She heard a car and looked expectantly to the front. Only her solo male guest remained to check in. Once that was taken care of, she'd be fairly free for the rest of the day.

Glancing out of one of the floor-to-ceiling French doors that lined the front of the inn, she waited. Several were open for the afternoon breeze. She could hear the car door shut, the crush of footsteps on the gravel.

He stepped into view, but instead of coming directly into the inn, he turned on the veranda to survey the sea, then the cliffs that rose to the right.

The counter was set to one side, unobtrusive, not easily seen from the veranda—but offering her a perfect view of the man. He carried himself with an arrogant assurance that usually rubbed her the wrong way. Frenchmen thought highly of themselves. Though this man had reason to. He was a bit over six feet, with broad shoulders, long legs. His dark hair shone in the afternoon sunshine; cut short, it still couldn't disguise the hint of curl. She'd bet he'd been adorable as a child—and all the fawning over him had probably gone straight to his head.

She checked her reservation information. No wife or child with him. Was he married? Or too busy being the superlative male to settle for any one woman? From her vantage point, she could admire as long as she wished. He wouldn't see her.

The soft-sided suitcase he carried wasn't large. He had booked the room for a week. As she watched him turn to study the cliffs along the sea's edge, she knew with certainty he'd come to scale them. She could picture him on the cliffs—his fit and trim body easily meeting the demands of muscles and sinews as fingers lifted his body, toes found infinitesimal crevices to wedge in until he stretched out for another handhold.

She straightened the sign-in card, placing the pen

across it, and waited. Despite her best intentions, she couldn't look away. His shoulders were wide, his arms looked well defined. Upper body strength was a must for those who challenged the face of unforgiving stone. When he turned to step into the inn, she caught a glimpse of his firm lips and strong jaw. His dark eyes scanned the area and rested for a split second on her son. With a hint of a frown, he looked around and found her.

The assertive way he strode across the lounge held her attention. Confident, assured, here was a man used to dealing with life and coming out on top. His clean-shaven jaw was firm, hinting at stubborn determination. His dark eyes flashed appreciation when he saw her and she felt more conscious of being a woman than at any time in the past several years. She wished she had taken time to brush her hair and freshen her lipstick.

Foolishness, she chided herself as she watched him approach. A small skip of her heart surprised her. He was just a guest. No one special. Just amazingly handsome. Curiosity rose. She wondered what he did for a living—he could have been a film actor or male model—except he looked too unaware of his looks to trade on them.

"Bonjour," he said.

"Monsieur Sommer?" she asked, refusing to let herself be captivated by the rugged masculinity, the deep voice or the slight air of distance that enveloped him. When he met her gaze, his dark eyes hid secrets, hinted at pain. That surprised her. Who was he? She wanted to know more.

"You have my reservation," he said. His voice was melodious, deep and rich.

Looking down she couldn't help imagining that voice in her ear at night, telling secrets or talking of love.

"Of course." She slid the card forward for him to sign as every sense went on alert. She was not a woman to have fantasies. Where were those images coming from? She caught a whiff of his aftershave and it caused an involuntary reaction of longing. Too long alone, that's all. Squelching her reactions, she kept her gaze on his hands as he boldly scrawled his name. They were strong, scarred here and there, which only made him more interesting. His attire suggested a businessman, his manner a wild and freely roaming adventurer. Curiosity rose another notch despite her best intention. She usually had little curiosity about her guests. But this man had her intrigued in spite of herself.

"Can you recommend a good place for dinner?" he asked, laying down the pen.

"Le Chat Noir," Alexandre said, coming to stand near the man. "Hi, I'm Alexandre. I live here."

Next to him, her son looked so small. He was already five and growing like crazy, but had a long way to go if he would ever be as tall as Matthieu Sommer.

He looked down at Alexandre, staring for a long moment before saying, "And is that a very good place?"

Her son smiled and nodded emphatically. "Whenever we go out for a treat we eat at Le Chat Noir. It's Mama's favorite."

"Then it must be good. The women, they always know the best places," Monsieur Sommer said gravely.

Alexandre beamed at his response.

Jeanne-Marie was pleased that the man had made the effort to take her son seriously. Alexandre was definitely in need of a male role model. She wished her brother Tom lived nearby. Or her father. Or her cousins. He had his grandfather, of course, but he was so much older and beginning to find a small boy taxing to be around for long.

Matthieu looked back at her. "So, your favorite?" he asked.

"*Oui.* It is excellent and affordable. You might wish to try Les Trois Filles en Pierre. It has a magnificent view of the three stone formations they call the maidens. I assume you're here to climb." She tried to keep her tone neutral, but knew a hint of curiosity crept in.

"I am. I hear the cliffs are challenging and the views incomparable." He studied her for a moment, his head tilted slightly. "Any recommendations?"

She shrugged. "Don't kill yourself."

"My dad fell off a mountain." Alexandre obviously wanted to chime in. Jeanne-Marie wished she hadn't spoken. "He would have taught me to climb mountains. Do you know how?"

"It was a long time ago, Alexandre. I'm sure Monsieur Sommer will be extra careful. We don't tell our guests our family situation," she said gently.

Matthieu Sommer inclined his head once, his gaze moving from her to her son and back again. She wondered what was going through his mind.

"I've given you room six. It's a corner room with a view of Les Calanques." She handed him a key and gestured to the wide stairs along the wall. "To the top and left," she said.

"Merci." He lifted his bag with no effort and soon was lost from sight.

Jeanne-Marie sighed a breath of relief. Meeting her disturbing new guest had caused dozens of emotions to clamor forth. She preferred families with small children to sexy single men who believed they could conquer the world. Especially when just looking at them affected her equilibrium. Too long alone, that's all.

What caused the pain that lurked in his eyes? Why had he come to quiet St. Bart when she'd expect a man like him to choose a luxury place in Marseilles?

She studied the registration card for a long moment, as if his name and address could give her any insights. Sighing in defeat, she filed the card and tried to put her latest guest out of her mind.

Rene, the student who worked evenings, would arrive soon. She'd give him an update on their guests and then be free to take Alexandre for that swim. As she waited for Rene to arrive, her thoughts returned to Matthieu Sommer. He looked to be about thirty-five. Too old not to be married. Maybe his wife didn't share his climbing enthusiasm. That Jeanne-Marie could understand. But when Phillipe had gone climbing, she usually went along and stayed in the village or town nearest the mountain to enjoy the local amenities and be near him when he wasn't climbing. So, was the delectable Frenchman single or just vacationing solo?

Matt Sommer entered room six and glanced around as he tossed his bag on the bed. It was spacious, with high ceilings, windows that went to the floor and a view that didn't quit. Fresh flowers brightened the dresser. He took note of the efforts the innkeeper had gone to, but she could have saved her time. A room was merely a place to sleep for him. When he could sleep, that was.

He crossed to the window and gazed at the cliffs he'd come to climb. A friend had recommended they challenge themselves with Les Calanques, but Paul had wanted to stay in Marseilles, and Matt knew that meant constant party time at night, not at all conducive to serious climbing in the morning. Man against nature, with unforgiving demands that allowed no room for error. He did it to escape. For a short while, his mind freed from the past, he'd pit his skill against the rocks. Brief respites from the unrelenting memories. He was prudent enough when climbing to know he wasn't trying to get killed. But if something happened, so be it. It would be no more than he deserved.

He'd booked the room in this quiet village for a week and planned to do some free climbing with or without Paul. His friend was welcome to the nightlife in Marseilles. Spring was a quiet time at the vineyard. For the next week he was on his own. No one from his family knew where to find him. He'd instructed his PA to contact him only in the case of an emergency—a real emergency.

He studied the rocky crags for a long moment, then turned to survey the space he would inhabit for the next few days. Clean and fresh were the adjectives that sprang to mind. The bed was piled with pillows and a duvet with a pristine white cover. The sheers at the windows billowed slightly in the sea breeze. He could leave the windows open at night and hear the soft lapping of waves. The sun shone in, below the angle of the roof. It could get warm if closed up, but the proprietress obviously knew how to cater to her clientele. The room was charming with local artwork on the walls and two comfortable chairs near the side windows. He sank into one chair and regarded the bed for a moment. If he let himself, he could imagine what Marabelle would have thought of the room. But he wouldn't give in. She was gone. Yet he knew she'd have found the place charming and been delighted to be staying by the sea.

Pushing himself up, he made quick work of putting

his clothes away in the armoire against one wall. Time to explore the small town and maybe pick up some information on the best climbs. The small village nestled in one of the inlets of Les Calanques had appeared quaint enough as he'd driven through. Originally a fishing village, it had opened up to tourists some decades ago, yet still retained its roots. The main part of town flanked the marina and hugged the curving inlet.

The inn was older than he'd expected. How had the young widow become its owner, he wondered. She was pretty and friendly enough. A necessary attribute of an innkeeper, he was sure.

Madame Rousseau seemed far too young to be widowed. Not that there was a certain age that made it suitable. Her son was cute. Did she realize how lucky she was? He'd give anything if his son were still alive.

Matt's own son had burned in the car crash that had killed both him and his mother. A car Marabelle had been driving when Matt should have been at the wheel. He fought the anguish. Nothing would ever ease the pain. The rest of his family had rallied around, but couldn't get through to him much as they tried. No one understood. They offered platitudes, but no one had experienced the same kind of loss. The kind that ripped a heart into shreds and never relented.

The woman downstairs might understand. To a degree. How did she cope?

He wondered if the innkeeper's family had offered the same platitudes when her husband had died. Had it helped? Or had she just wanted everyone to go away and leave her alone with her grief?

Not that he cared. So she was pretty. Marabelle had been beautiful. Love had come swiftly and ended in an instant.

He was here to try the kind of activities he'd once loved—and to forget, if only for a few hours at a time.

"Time to get ready for dinner," Jeanne-Marie called to Alexandre later in the afternoon.

"I don't want to," he said, scuffing along at the water's edge. His small footprints on the wet sand made her smile. One day he'd be taller than her and his footprint would be larger, too.

She joined him and ruffled his hair. "Too bad. We need to eat soon or you'll be finishing dessert in your jammies."

He laughed, clutching his cars close. "We can't eat in our jammies. Can we eat at Le Chat Noir? I'm hungry for some of their food."

"I had planned salad and soup for dinner." Jeanne-Marie gathered their towels, slipping on the cover-up over her bathing suit for modesty's sake. She didn't bother with her shoes; they'd brush their feet off on the veranda and scoot to their quarters.

"Please, Mama. It's a special day. The inn is full, I heard you say. And that's always a good thing."

It was her turn to laugh at his mimicking what she'd said to her friend Madeline. "Yes, it is a good thing. So perhaps we could celebrate with dinner out. But not until you wash that sand off your feet and change into dry clothes!" He didn't even know it was the anniversary of his father's death. She was glad in one way, but mourned how little Alexandre would ever remember about his father. Phillipe had loved him so.

With a yell of glee, he took off running toward the inn. Jeanne-Marie followed, keeping enough behind to let him win. They stomped on the veranda and brushed the worst of the sand from their feet. Alexandre scampered into the lounge and through to the back where their quarters were. She wished she could motivate him this way all the time. She nodded to the student staffing the front desk. Jeanne-Marie relished the few free hours each day Rene's being here gave her.

"Everything okay?" she asked.

"Quiet as ever," Rene responded. He was a bit of a bookworm and always had some book in his hand. Yet he could handle requests with efficiency and expediency. Probably to keep time away from reading to a minimum.

"We're going out for an early dinner," she said.

He nodded, returning to his book.

By the time Alexandre had had a quick rinse and was into fresh clothes and she'd showered, it was after six. Most people in town didn't eat this early, but she liked him in bed by eight, so an early dinner was their norm. Walking down the sidewalk to the heart of the village, the sea to their right, she relished the lingering warmth of the afternoon. It was only early May, but warm enough to swim or lie in the sun as the tourists did. Their little town would fill up before the end of the month. Then for the rest of the summer the town would be transformed from the sleepy fishing village to a fast and furious tourist spot as it expanded to its limit with visitors from all over.

When they reached Le Chat Noir, Jeanne-Marie reached for the door handle just as Alex yelled, "There's one of our guests!"

Glancing up, she saw Matthieu Sommer almost upon them. She caught her breath again at the sight of him. He was definitely walking their way. Tentatively she smiled as she pulled on the door. He'd obviously taken Alexandre's recommendation.

He reached around her, put out his hand to catch the door and gestured for them to enter ahead of him.

"I'm taking your advice and trying this place for dinner," he said as they stepped into the restaurant.

After the sunshine, it took a minute for her eyes to become used to the dimmer illumination. She nodded while holding on to Alexandre's hand. "I think you'll enjoy it."

"Are you going to eat with us?" her son piped up.

"No," she said quickly. Then realizing how rude it sounded, she gave Monsieur Sommer a shaky smile. "I'm sure Monsieur Sommer would not be interested in sharing a table with a five-year-old."

He inclined his head slightly. "I'm not the best company," he said.

Jeanne-Marie nodded and turned to the maître d' as he greeted her.

"Just you and Alexandre?" he asked.

"Oui." She glanced at her guest. "Enjoy your dinner." She was not disappointed he chose not to eat with her. She and her guests rarely mixed. And a businessman here to climb would not be interested in the chatter of a little boy. Still, she wished he'd overridden her comment and said he'd like to eat with her, with them. Though, she'd have been a nervous wreck before the first course.

She and Alexandre were seated at one of the best tables on the patio, the place almost empty. Only two other tables were occupied and far enough away that Jeanne-Marie couldn't hear the occupants, who were talking quietly.

Opening the menu, she took a moment to study the items, already knowing what she and Alexandre always ordered, but looking anyway.

A moment later Matthieu Sommer was seated at a table nearby. Suddenly aware of his presence she tried to keep her eyes on the menu. Fortunately he'd been seated with his back toward her, so she wouldn't have to look up and find him watching her. But she couldn't help taking a glance his way now and then. What was it about him that intrigued her so much? He wasn't particularly friendly. *Keep your distance* was more like the vibe he sent out. Granted, he was a handsome man, but arrogant. She didn't know if she liked him or not, but he certainly had captured her interest.

"I want the chicken," Alex said, kicking his feet against his chair.

"As always. And I'll have the quiche."

"As always," he mimicked, grinning up at his mother.

Jeanne-Marie closed the menu and put it on the table. She glanced at Matthieu Sommer studying his menu. Wistfully she wished she'd asked him to join them. Not that he'd want to spend his meal with strangers. But during the meal she might have discovered more about him. And even realized they had nothing in common so this aberration of interest would fade.

Had he joined them she would probably have ended up as tongue-tied as a teenager facing a major crush. Yet, it must be lonely to eat alone. She debated asking him to join them now, but in the end decided to leave things as they were.

When their order had been taken, Alexandre brought out his small cars and began playing with them on the table. Jeanne-Marie was glad of the distraction. She had to stop staring at her newest guest. Once his order had been taken, he began to look at brochures he'd brought with him. She suspected they were the ones offered at the inn. One touted the shopping in the little fishing village, tourist places all. Another gave an overview of Les Calanques. And a third was one from a local sport shop that catered to climbers.

Alexandre looked up. "Will I be able to take my cars when I go to school in September?" he asked.

"Probably not. You'll need to pay attention in class so you learn all you can."

And she needed to pay attention to her son, and ignore the man sitting so enticingly close.

When their meal arrived, Jeanne-Marie devoted her attention to helping Alexandre with his food and eating her own. She couldn't help notice when Matt's dinner was served. And that he finished at the same time they did. The place was still scarcely occupied.

Matt couldn't finish dinner fast enough. The food was excellent, he had to give it that. But he could hear the chatter behind him between the innkeeper and her child. Their laughter sparked memories of happier times—when he and his small family had shared meals together. Etienne would have been seven now. The pain that gripped his heart squeezed again. His adored son, now buried beside his mother in the family plot. He gazed ahead for a moment, trying to blank the memories. Marabelle had scolded their son if he played around too much when out in public. Now he wished they'd let the child do whatever he wanted. He'd lived too short a time.

Madame Rousseau's son was just the age his had been when the drunk driver of the huge truck had plowed into their family sedan and instantly killed them both. He couldn't help thinking his reflexes might have been faster than hers, to escape the crash. Or if he'd been in the car, he would have died with them, and not been left behind with all the pain.

He wanted to tell the innkeeper to cherish her son. But of course he never would. He kept the pain bottled up inside and to the outside world presented a facade belying the constant anguish he lived with. Time heals all wounds, he'd been told over and over. Everyone lied. This wound didn't heal.

Only the challenges of climbing temporarily swept the memories away. Intense concentration was necessary to pit his strength against the walls of rock. And the energy expended ensured he slept most nights without nightmares.

He hoped he hadn't made a mistake in staying at the inn. He hadn't expected a young and pretty innkeeper—or a child.

As he ate he wondered about the widow behind him. Her husband had died from a climbing fall. Yet she ran a successful inn in the shadows of some spectacular day climbs. He was curious about her. His cousins would be delighted to learn that he could wonder about something and not be locked into the past. His uncle would see it as moving on. His aunt might even hold out stronger hopes.

Not that he foresaw much interaction between Madame Rousseau and him except as it concerned his stay.

Climbing was dangerous. He knew as well as the next man, a cliff, a mountain could turn rogue and the one scaling its face could end up injured or dead. Yet the challenge wouldn't let go. To climb a sheer cliff, to scale a mountain too steep and rugged for the average trekker was a challenge not to be missed. The exaltation when conquering each one was a high he had once relished. Man against nature. Sometimes nature won. So far in his pursuits, he'd triumphed. Not that he took joy now; it was just something to do to take his mind off his loss.

He didn't envy the pretty innkeeper. She'd have her hands full raising a son without a father. He knew Marabelle would have had lots of family to rally around if he had been the one to die. His family tried to help out, but he didn't need them. It was easier dealing with everything on his own. It was his own private hell, and he wouldn't be leaving it anytime soon.

Matt heard the commotion behind him as the bill was paid. A moment later the small boy startled him, coming to stand at his side. "Did you like dinner? Isn't this a good place to eat?" he asked, smiling up at Matt. The boy's sunny disposition penetrated his own dark thoughts.

He took in the earnest expression on the child's face and nodded. "It is a very good place to eat."

His reward was another sunny smile the child bestowed. "I like it lots," he said.

"Come along, Alexandre," his mother summoned him.

When Matt followed a few moments later, he spotted the mother and son on the beach. They had removed their shoes and obviously were going to walk back to the inn along the shore.

He hadn't walked along any beach in a long time. He watched them until others exited the restaurant, laughing, reminding him he was standing in the middle of the sidewalk. Giving into impulse, he stepped onto the beach and headed to the packed sand near the water.

The little boy danced at the edge of the sea, running almost to the water, then dancing back when the small wavelets splashed on his feet. His laughter was carefree. How long had it been since he had felt that carefree? Matt wondered. Would he ever again?

CHAPTER TWO

THE NEXT MORNING Jeanne-Marie placed the coffee press in front of the older couple from Nantes. They were both engrossed in their daily newspaper and didn't even glance up. Surveying the small dining area, she was pleased to see her guests enjoying the breakfast she provided. Three couples had requested the box lunch she also supplied to guests. Many liked to enjoy the water sports and didn't want to have to change to eat lunch at one of the establishments in town.

Breakfast, however, was the only hot meal she provided.

Mentally checking off her list, she realized Matthieu Sommer had not yet come down. Or had he left before everyone else while she was in the kitchen preparing the meal? Glancing at her watch, she noted it was almost nine. Surely he would be up and about before now.

Checking to make sure no one needed anything, she slipped back into the kitchen to begin cleaning up. Alexandre sat at the small table at the nook she reserved for their meals. He was playing with his ever-present cars and totally engrossed in his own world. Jeanne-Marie sometimes wished she could go back to being the little girl who had had no thoughts of the future, but had been happy and content in her own safe family life. Her parents were professors at the university in Berkeley, California. She missed the activities of the college town.

She missed her family more and more, but never let them know that when they called. E-mails were easier; she could get the words just right before sending. Truly she was content in St. Bart for the most part. One day she and Alexandre would go to California for a long vacation, but so far it had seemed easier for her parents to come to France than for her to take a small child so far.

She loved France. As she had loved Phillipe. This inn had come to him when his grandfather died. It was a connection she didn't want to sever. Sometimes she dreamed of what their life could have been had he not been killed. That was not to be, and those dreams had come less frequently.

Meantime, once her guests finished eating, she had dishes to clean and preparations for tomorrow's breakfast to start. She baked her own rolls and breads. She liked to prepare a quiche every couple of days, and some of the more English-styled breakfasts for those who wanted them, experimenting with different soufflés and egg dishes.

As she washed the plates and cups sometime later, Jeanne-Marie's thoughts centered on Matthieu Sommer again! She wondered what he'd done upon his return to the inn last night. He'd gone directly to his room. She did not have televisions or radios. She had a small bookcase of mysteries and romance novels, but couldn't see Matthieu Sommer sitting still to read a book. There was a restless energy about him that demanded physical outlets, not quiet reading pursuits.

Had he left early for a climb? Or had something

happened and he had become sick and was still in bed? Maybe she'd run up to check room six. Just in case.

She knew she was being foolish, but it wouldn't hurt. If he had already left, he'd never know she had checked.

At ten o'clock, Jeanne-Marie went to the front desk to work on some of the accounts. Alexandre was content to play with his toys on the veranda, clearly visible through the open French doors. The day was beautiful, balmy breezes came from the sea, the sun had not yet reached its zenith, so the temperatures were still pleasant. She spotted the envelope immediately, and recognized the bold handwriting with her name clearly written across it. Had she seen it earlier, it would have stopped her concern. And the trip to peep into room six.

She took out the sheet of paper, suddenly feeling more alive and alert than before. She quickly read the brief missive. "Wanted a full day of climbing. In case I'm not back by dark, I'm starting on Le Casse-cou climb."

She shook her head and refolded the paper. Just like him to start with the Daredevil climb. No easy warm-ups for him. At least he was smart enough to let someone know where to start looking for him if he didn't return. She shivered, thrusting away all images of what could happen to a solo climber on the face of the cliffs. There would be others around. He might find a group of two or three to join with, each climbing at his or her own rate, yet within yelling distance in case anyone got into trouble.

She tried to imagine putting her life at risk for something as nonessential as climbing. Granted, she could understand challenging oneself, but her most daring adventures were diving in the shallows of the

Mediterranean. Phillipe had loved scaling all different terrains, however. Never tiring, even on climbs he'd done before. So there had to be something to recommend it. That gene had eluded her.

As her guests came and went through the day, she couldn't help growing on edge as the afternoon waned and dusk approached. Matthieu Sommer still had not returned. She prepared dinner for herself and her son. Telling Rene to let her know when Monsieur Sommer returned, Jeanne-Marie didn't fully enjoy her dinner as worry began to rise. The minutes seemed to race by. Shouldn't he have been back by now? What if he'd fallen? What would she do if the police showed up to inform her of his death and collect his things from his room? She almost groaned in remembered agony of when she'd been so notified.

She had climbers all the time staying in the inn. She'd not worried about any of them beyond the normal concern. This was getting ridiculous. He was fine! And it was nothing to her if he weren't.

"The kid at the front desk said you wanted to see me when I returned," Matt said from the doorway to the kitchen.

Jeanne-Marie looked up and caught her breath. He looked hot, tired and a wee bit sunburned. The climbing clothes he wore were dirty and scuffed. He had a small cut on one cheek that had bled and scabbed over. His hair was gray with dust. His dark eyes held her gaze, intense and focused.

She felt her heart skip a beat, then race. Her worry had been for naught.

"I, uh, just wanted to make sure I knew when you returned. So I didn't call Search and Rescue," she said lamely.

"Hi," Alexandre said with his sunny smile. "You need a bath. Then do you want to walk on the beach with me?" His hopeful tone almost broke Jeanne-Marie's heart. It wasn't often he asked anything of their guests. She wished she had found a male friend who would provide a strong role model for her son. He saw his grandfather too infrequently.

"No, honey, Monsieur Sommer's tired and probably needs to eat supper."

"I am hungry," he confirmed.

She nodded. "Did you have anything to eat today?" Climbing took a lot out of a body; surely he knew enough to eat for fuel.

"Got breakfast at the bakery and they made up some sandwiches, which I ate perched on a small ledge with a view that encompassed half the Med. I'm thirsty more than hungry."

She jumped up and went to get him a glass of water, relieved he was safe, annoyed she had even noticed.

She handed him the glass and his fingers brushed against hers, sending a jolt of awareness to her very core. She backed off, wanting him out of her kitchen, out of her inn. He awoke feelings and interests best left dormant. She normally didn't mingle much with her guests. He had already trespassed by coming into the kitchen. Rene could have let her know.

"You can eat dinner here. Mama's a good cook," the five-year-old said.

Matt raised an eyebrow in Jeanne-Marie's direction, a silent question.

She wanted to tell him her inn provided two meals a day, and no one ate in the privacy of her own quarters. But looking at the angelic expression on her little boy weakened her resolve. He asked for so little, was content with life as they knew it. How could she refuse?

"Never mind, I'll get something in town," Matt said, placing the glass on the counter.

"If you want to freshen up first, I'll warm up what we're having. It's a stew that's been simmering all day. I can have a plate for you in twenty minutes." There was plenty—she had planned on it serving her and Alexandre for two days. A plan easily changed for her son's sake.

"Deal. I'll be back in twenty minutes." He left without another word.

Jeanne-Marie let out her held breath with a whoosh. Turning, she went to the stove. The heat had been turned off the stew, so she quickly began warming it. She had fresh bread she'd made that morning. A salad and apple crumble would be a nutritious meal for a man who had expended untold energy pushing his body to the limit scaling a sheer cliff.

And while he ate, she'd let him know it was a one-time meal. She didn't provide dinner. She didn't want him in her space. He'd be gone in a few days, nothing permanent about guests who came and went.

Mostly she felt flustered. Personal customer service was important in running an inn, especially if she wanted repeat customers, but that did not include sharing meals in her private domain. And especially with someone who without effort seemed to turn her upside down.

She and Alexandre had finished their meal by the time Matt returned. His hair was still damp; the cut on his cheek had been taped with a butterfly bandage. Obviously he was used to minor scrapes and had come prepared. His cheeks were slightly sunburned. But the rest of him looked amazingly robust and healthy. Jeanne-Marie was not one to have fantasies about strangers who came to the inn. This aberration had to end!

"I can serve you on the veranda overlooking the sea," she suggested, jumping up and trying to get him out of her private space.

He glanced at their empty plates on the small table. "Since you're finished, that'll be fine with me."

"I can sit with you to keep you company," Alexandre volunteered, clutching two cars against his chest.

Carrying out the plate and utensils, she hoped other guests wouldn't ask for similar service. She worked hard enough without adding an extra meal for all guests into the mix.

She placed his dish on one of the glass tables that dotted the veranda. The sunscreens had been lowered earlier to keep the heat from the lounge. She pressed the switch to raise one to offer a better view, but kept the one directly in front of his table down to shelter it from the last rays of the sun.

"I'll get you something to drink," she said, hurrying back to the kitchen. Normally she kept Alexandre away from the guests when they were eating, but the few moments it took her to get the water wouldn't hurt.

She brought out a pitcher of water and a tall glass. She remembered how Phillipe gulped water as if he were dying of thirst when he returned from climbing.

"Do you need anything else?" she asked.

"No, this looks perfect," he said when she set the pitcher on the table. "I appreciate the water."

"I remember." She sat gingerly on a nearby chair, looking at the sea glowing golden as the sun descended. It would be dusk and then dark before long. Alexandre would go to bed and she'd be alone with her thoughts.

She debated returning to the kitchen. Maybe in a moment. Would it be rude to leave? Did he want privacy or should she act as a hostess?

"You spent a long day on the cliffs," she said.

"I got an early start, then prowled around a bit on the top. The view is stupendous. No wonder it's highly recommended." The words fit, but his tone lacked the enthusiasm she usually heard from climbers.

When he did not elaborate, she said, "The cliffs are so popular the government's concerned about pollution and eco damage. There's talk about closing them down, or limiting the number of people who have access." She glanced at him as he ate. He seemed to enjoy the food. Good. She was an excellent cook. But since her husband's death, she rarely entertained. At first she couldn't face having anyone over. She'd wanted to grieve in private. The first few months after his death, she'd kept busy by closing their flat in Marseilles and moving here and learning the guest services trade.

"I saw some trash and debris while I was climbing. And there was a pile of trash at the top," he said. "People can be thoughtless and careless. Those are the ones to keep out."

She nodded. "Yet how to do that? Ask if someone is thoughtless before permitting them to climb? Who would admit to it?"

He shrugged. "It'd be a shame to close access because of the acts of a few."

"If you eat all your dinner, there's apple crumble for dessert, with ice cream," Alexandre said, leaning against the table and watching as Matt ate. He'd scarcely taken his gaze off the man.

"This is a very good dinner," he told the boy.

"I helped make the bread," he said proudly. "Mama lets me punch it."

"You did an excellent job."

Alexandre smiled again and stared at Matt with open admiration.

"Did you climb a mountain today?" he asked.

"A cliff, not a mountain," Matt replied.

"My dad climbed mountains. I will, too, when I get big. I'll go to the top and see everything!"

"The views from the top are incomparable," Matt agreed.

"Can I go climbing with you? Can we go to a mountain?"

"No. Don't be pestering our guest," Jeanne-Marie said sharply. She didn't like talk about Alexandre's climbing. Too often his grand-père encouraged him by telling him all about climbs he'd done with Phillipe. She didn't think she'd ever like the thought, but realized Alexandre would be his own person when he grew up. If he took up the same hobby as his father, she hoped he wouldn't come to the same end. It scared her just thinking about it.

"He's not pestering me. Actually, I had already taken my son on a couple of easy rock climbs by the time he was Alexandre's age."

"I could go. I'm big now. I'm five." He looked at Matt with a mixture of admiration and entreaty.

Jeanne-Marie felt her heart drop. He had a son. All the more reason to remember he was merely a guest and she the hostess of the inn. And to stay away.

Jeanne-Marie didn't like that look on Alexandre's face. He'd better not get a hero fixation on this guest. Matt was only here another six days. Once before, a year or so ago, Alexandre had latched onto a guest who had been staying at the inn with his wife and daughter and who had kindly included her son in some of their activities. Alexandre had moped around for weeks after their departure, not truly understanding why they didn't come back.

"Alexandre, do you want to help me dish up the dessert?" she asked, standing quickly, anxious to put some distance between her son and guest. He wasn't exactly Mr. Congeniality. She didn't want Alexandre to pester him until he snapped something out that would hurt her son's feelings. Though if he had a son, he was probably used to little boys.

"Sure. We waited for you," he said, placing his cars on the table and running into the house.

Jeanne-Marie hoped Matt wouldn't think she had deliberately waited to be included when he ate the dessert. He was obviously married and with a child. Where was his family? Had they stayed home since he wanted serious climbing, beyond the level of a child? Had they made other plans, separate vacations? She couldn't imagine it, but some couples liked that.

Matt watched as Jeanne-Marie followed her son at a more sedate pace—but not by much. He thought of her that way, seeing her name on the brochure for the inn. He had trouble picturing her as Madame Rousseau.

She certainly hadn't had to feed him; he knew the inn didn't offer dinners. Maybe tomorrow he'd make a later start and sample both the breakfast and box lunch she offered.

Taking another deep drink of water, he watched the brush of the Mediterranean against the white sandy beach. He couldn't believe he'd mentioned his son so casually. The world hadn't ended. The searing pain had not sliced. Instead a kind of peace descended. His son had been so proud climbing the small hills they'd scrambled up together. He could remember his boasting to his mother.

He finished the simple meal and leaned back in his chair. For the first time in ages he felt almost content. He was pleasantly tired from the climb and replete with the excellent stew. And he had liked speaking of Etienne. He never wanted himself or anyone to forget his boy.

His cell phone rang. He glanced at the number and flipped it open to respond.

"Hey, man," his friend Paul said.

"What's up?" Matt responded. He knew—Paul was partying already. He could hear the background noise of a club.

"Having a great time. You should come over. It wouldn't be that long a drive, would it? I've got some hot babes lined up. We can party until dawn."

Over the last year Paul had tried to set him up with several women. His friend felt enough time had passed for Matt to get back into the dating scene. Never having married himself, Paul really didn't understand. There was no magical time to stop grieving. No magical moment when a man said forget the past, marry again. Matt couldn't see himself deliberately putting his heart and emotions at risk. Once shattered, he wasn't willing to take the risk of getting involved again. The fear of another marriage ending suddenly and horribly couldn't be ignored. He'd had his shot at happiness. Now it was time to come to terms with the hand life had dealt.

"Party until dawn and then go climbing?" Matt asked. A sure formula for disaster.

"We could sleep in a little, then hit the cliffs. I got

in a climb today. Beat my own record for going up and back," Paul said.

Even in climbing Paul couldn't lose his competitiveness.

"Did you like the view?" Matt asked.

"What view? Water below me, rock in my face. Hey, I could show you that climb tomorrow, race you to the top."

Jeanne-Marie and her son stepped out onto the veranda, three bowls on a tray. Alexandre proudly carried spoons.

Another time Matt might have skipped dessert, but he was tempted by the novelty of eating with her and her son. Now it also provided a good excuse to end the call.

"You have a drink for me, Paul. I'll skip tonight but be in touch. We'll meet up later in the week and scale something together."

"Ah, man, you'll be missing some kind of fun."

"My loss," Matt said, not believing a word. He flipped the phone closed as Jeanne-Marie placed one of the bowls in front of him. Alexandre solemnly handed him a spoon, then scampered around to sit in the chair across from him. Jeanne-Marie placed a bowl with a smaller serving in front of Alexandre. Jeanne-Marie sat to Matt's right, throwing him an uncertain look as if not sure of her welcome.

He was momentarily taken aback. Giving in with poor grace, he accepted they would sit with him until each had finished their dessert.

The apple crumble was warm and cinnamony, the rich vanilla ice cream a delicious addition. The dessert almost melted in his mouth.

"This is delicious." Even his own cook rarely had a dessert as tasty as this.

"Thank you."

"You should offer dinner to your guests. They'd enjoy your cooking." He had enjoyed it. And the fact he didn't have to leave the inn.

She smiled shyly and shook her head. "I have everything going the way I like. There's such a thing as too much, you know."

"Such as?"

"Trading my afternoons with Alexandre to cook for as many as fifteen people day in, day out would be too much. I try to be creative with my breakfasts, though. You'd know if you try them."

"I plan to sample one in the morning. If I can still get an early start."

"I can provide breakfast as early as six-thirty if I know ahead of time. Sometimes people go diving or out on one of the cruise ships and need an equally early start. I also fix the box lunches for them to take."

"Six-thirty it is."

Matt savored the dessert. He watched Alexandre scrape every bit of it from his bowl and lick his spoon as if hoping more would appear. It reminded him of Etienne. He almost smiled, then felt a pang at his loss. Was that a trait of all little boys? Etienne would have loved this dessert.

Alexandre looked up at Matt, dropping his spoon in the bowl with a clatter. "Can you go for a walk with me now? And can you take me to climb a mountain?"

"Monsieur Sommer is too tired to go walking with us," Jeanne-Marie said quickly. "And there are no mountains nearby."

Truth was he would relish an early night, but the

look of disappointment on the boy's face and the quick way she'd tried to shut him out perversely caused him to agree to the walk. He wasn't sure why he wanted to spend more time with them, but the less she wanted him around, the more he wanted to stay. There was nothing in his room but memories he'd just as soon forget.

"I'm not eighty. A good meal and I'm ready to go. A short walk sounds like just the thing before bed," he said, holding her gaze for a moment in challenge.

"It becomes rocky the closer to Les Calanques we go," she said, glancing at the cliffs, now growing dark and mysterious as the last of the daylight faded.

What was it about her that made him want to spend time with her? Normally he stayed away from people. Was it the novelty of someone not tiptoeing around him that had him interested? Or her quiet appeal that he found intriguing? She didn't flirt, didn't try to sound witty and entertaining. Didn't avoid subjects for fear of his reaction. Of course, she didn't know about his wife and child. That might change matters.

Jeanne-Marie cleared their bowls and spoke to Rene before returning to the veranda. Matt listened to Alexandre talking about his day playing with his race cars and how he helped make the bread and that he still had to take naps, which he didn't need anymore because he wasn't a baby and would be starting kindergarten in the fall. And about how his dad had climbed very high mountains and he wanted to as well.

Matt nodded at Alexandre's earnest conversation and remembered Etienne had been like that. He remembered his son going on and on like this boy did. And he remembered his following Matt around the vineyard, questioning everything. He had had a million questions. God, Matt wished he'd been able to answer them all.

"A short walk," Jeanne-Marie said when she returned onto the veranda.

When Matt stood, Alexandre slipped his small hand in his larger one. He was startled by the feeling of protectiveness that surged toward this small boy. He missed his son. He'd had him until his fifth year. Not nearly long enough. Etienne should have grown up, married, lived a full life.

Instead he was gone.

But for a few moments, Matt would suspend the past and just be with a small boy. And remember the happier days with his own son.

The walk along the beach would have been in silence except for the constant babble from Alexandre. He seemed capable of chattering away forever without comment from either adult. Not that Matt had anything to say. The sea on one side, the last of the establishments on the other and the cliffs ahead. It didn't call for much comment.

Jeanne-Marie looked at him, her expression bemused. "You're doing well with this. I guess it comes from being around your own son. He can talk your ear off."

"He's young, still learning so much. Life is easier at that age." Oddly he was enjoying the walk. It was amazing what a five-year-old had to talk about. The poignant loss of his son was overshadowed by the delight this child had in his surroundings.

"Did you grow up here?" he asked when Alexandre pulled away to run ahead to a piece of driftwood.

She shook her head. It was harder to see her as the light waned. Soon they'd have to be guided by the lights spilling out from the scattered buildings along the beach.

"I was born and raised in California. My parents

are both professors at the university in Berkeley. We lived not too far from the campus. I met Phillipe when I came to France as an exchange student in my junior year. I stayed and graduated from La Sorbonne. When we married, we lived in Marseilles. That's where he was from. His parents still live there."

"So you chose this inn rather than return to America?"

"Phillipe's grandfather left it to him. We had a manager running it when he was alive. But we spent a lot of time here when he wasn't working. After his death, I thought this would keep me closer somehow. Plus it gives me the opportunity to make a living and still be able to spend most of the day with my son. And keep him near enough to see his grandparents. Alexandre's all they have left of their only child."

"It's a charming village. But quiet."

"True. It suits us at this stage in our lives."

He wished he could see her expression. "What do you do in the evenings?"

"Read. Work on the accounts if I don't get a chance during the day. I have a computer and keep in touch with my family and friends. And I have Alexandre."

"He can't be much of a conversationalist, though you wouldn't know it by his chatter tonight. It's captivating, actually."

She smiled, barely visible in the dim light. "He can be funny and wise at the same time—and all without knowing it. I'm content with my life. Why would I change it?"

"To find another husband. It can't be easy to be a single parent."

"I had one. I don't expect a second."

"Men aren't rationed, one per woman."

She shrugged. "How many wives have you had?" she asked.

He paused a second before replying, "One."

"Ah, the contented married man," she said.

"A drunk driver killed her and our son. Two years ago now."

"I'm sorry. How horrible." Jeanne-Marie was stunned. She couldn't imagine losing both Phillipe and Alexandre. Sympathetically she reached out to touch his arm. "I'm so sorry for your loss."

They walked in silence for a moment, then hoping she wasn't making things worse, she asked, "Where do you live?"

"Family enterprise in the Vallée de la Loire."

"Castles and vineyards," she murmured. "Do you have a castle?" she asked whimsically.

He paused a moment. She wished the light was better so she could see his expression.

"My family has one," he finally said.

"You're kidding! How astonishing. Are those old castles as hard to heat as they look?"

Matt was surprised by her question. Most of the time if the castle came into discussion—which he tried to avoid—the first question was how large was it and when could the person see it. "The rooms we don't use are closed off, and those in use comprise the size of a normal house, so it's not as hard to heat as you might suspect."

"Sorry, it's none of my business, but every time I've seen one, I've wondered how in the world it's heated. We don't have such a problem in winter here with the warmer climate."

"Are you a king?" Alexandre asked.

"No. The castle has been in the family for many

generations. But I work for a living like anyone else," Matt said.

"At the family enterprise?" she asked.

"Vineyards and a winery." There. Now see what the woman did with that knowledge.

"*Mon Dieu, vin de Sommer*—I've heard about your wines. They're excellent." She stopped abruptly and looked at him. He stopped and looked at her. The stars did not shed much illumination, so he couldn't see her expression well.

"Are you telling me the truth?" she asked, trying to see him clearly.

"I don't lie," he said calmly. What, did she think he was trying to puff himself up? To what end? He was here for escape, nothing more. He certainly was not out to impress her or anyone else.

"Then why are you at my inn instead of a five-star place in another town?"

"I want what you're offering—peace, quiet and an excellent vantage point to scale Les Calanques." Not the nightlife Paul loved. That he and Marabelle had once loved.

The fact his innkeeper piqued his curiosity was a turn he had not expected. It had been twenty-four months, two weeks and four days since he'd found his interest captivated by anything.

Now that she knew who he was, how long before she changed her attitude toward him? He wished he'd kept his mouth shut! No one needed to know his own tragedy. Sympathy was wasted; it didn't change anything.

"Alexandre, time for bed." Jeanne-Marie calmly took her son's hand when he ran over and began walking toward the inn, cutting obliquely across the sand to reach it sooner than walking along the water's edge.

She didn't say another word to him as he kept pace with them. Once in the inn, she went directly back to their private quarters with only a brief word of good-night.

Matt stood in the lounge watching the closed door for several seconds after she firmly shut it. Of all the reactions he'd anticipated, that had not even been on the list.

"Do you need something, *monsieur?*" the teen behind the desk asked.

"Insight into women," he said.

"Pardon?"

"Never mind." Matt took the stairs two at a time, wondering what exactly had caused him to choose this inn. And why the innkeeper would spark an interest in an otherwise gray world.

CHAPTER THREE

JEANNE-MARIE rose early the next morning to prepare breakfast for her guests—starting with Matthieu Sommer, millionaire extraordinaire and daredevil climber. She knew enough about the wine business, and the Sommer name, to know the normal circles he traveled in were far removed from her family inn. If there was anything further to prove that she needed to keep her distance from this guest, learning that about him provided it.

She'd felt vaguely sad all evening, due to learning about his own wife and son's deaths. How horrible to lose a wife, but even more devastating to lose his son. She didn't know how she'd go on if something happened to Alexandre. Poor man. Truly all the money in the world couldn't bring back a loved one.

The fresh warm croissants waited in a basket, and she pulled the *pain de raisin* from the oven, taking in the delicious cinnamony fragrance as she turned it out onto a cooling rack. Cooking soothed her and brought her joy. She was glad her guests liked her offerings.

"It smells as good as the bakery in here," Matt said from the doorway.

She looked up and frowned. "If you sit at one of the tables in the dining area, I'll bring your breakfast out in a moment." She'd set the tables the night before to save one step in the morning. The two tables by the windows overlooked the garden. As he was first down, he'd have his choice of places in the dining area.

"This is fine." He crossed the floor and sat at their small family table by the windows in the nook. She frowned at his presumption. This was family space. Still, it was early—maybe he didn't want to sit alone in the dining room if she was working here. She could more easily make sure he had everything he needed.

Setting a basket of assorted warm breads and croissants on the table, she asked if he preferred coffee or hot chocolate, annoyed at her rationalization.

"Chocolate. Extra sugar and energy," he said.

Jeanne-Marie brought an assortment of jams and jellies and placed them on the table. "I'll have your drink ready in a moment."

She returned to preparing more bread for her other guests, keeping an eye on the baguettes baking. Timing was not as easy with one guest eating well in advance of the others, but some of the breads would be just as good cold as hot, and she always had plenty left over to use for the box lunches.

She did her best to ignore her unwanted visitor. Normally she had the kitchen to herself. Alexandre didn't waken until eight most mornings. She loved the quiet time preparing the breakfasts and enjoying her own cup of chocolate. Today she felt self-conscious with Matt's dark eyes tracking her every move.

"The more I learn about you, the more I'm convinced you're not making the most of your talent," he said.

She flicked him a glance. "Like what?" she asked.

"Your meals are fantastic. You could make a fortune opening a restaurant."

"I told you, I like my life the way it is. It's not all about making money."

"Money is always helpful."

Stopping for a moment, she looked at him. "Money can buy things. If things are what you want. It can't buy back a lost life."

That was true. He'd give all his fortune for things to have turned out differently two years ago. Had he been driving, would his reflexes have been better than Marabelle's? Could the accident have been avoided?

She couldn't help flicking a glance his way from time to time. His eyes met hers each time. Didn't he have someplace else to look? The view wasn't as good as from the dining room window, but he could see the garden if he sat in another chair.

"So today you again risk life and limb," she commented, wanting the topic to shift from her.

"Hardly. Merely a climb." His eyes studied her speculatively.

Jeanne-Marie felt her heart skip a beat. Frowning, she turned slightly so looking up wouldn't mean she'd instantly meet his gaze.

"If you climbed to the top yesterday, you saw the view. What drives you today?"

"Today I take on a different climb."

She shrugged. "Same view from the top."

"Have you ever seen it?"

She nodded. "Sure, many times. There's an access road that winds along the top of Les Calanques. The scenery is spectacular. And that's a much safer way to see it."

"But not as challenging."

"Perhaps men and women are wired differently. I

have no desire to spend hours clinging to a sheer face of rock."

"What do you like spending hours doing?" he asked.

She looked up, smiling shyly. "I love to bake. And so I indulge myself with homemade breads and rolls and sometimes a special dessert I can serve for special occasions like *La Victoire de 1945* coming up."

The buzzer sounded. The last of the breads was finished. She lined the bread baskets with fresh linen napkins and began dishing jellies and jams into individual serving bowls to place on each table. In twenty minutes, she'd begin brewing the coffee and make sure she had lots of chocolate ready for those who wished that.

Daring to find out more about her guest, she took her own mug of hot chocolate and leaned against the kitchen island looking at him as she sipped the fragrant beverage. "Do you have family who wonders why you climb?" she asked.

"Of course I have family. And a cousin who often goes with me. Not everyone dies who climbs."

"I know that. Phillipe's father actually taught him. It was an activity they enjoyed together. But he wasn't on the K2 climb that proved fatal."

"Lots of people climb for the sheer exhilaration, not just men. And most never have a more serious mishap than scraped knuckles or at worst a broken bone," he said. He rose and carried his mug across the kitchen, ending up close enough to invade her space. For a moment she felt her breath catch and hold. She wanted to move away, but she was hemmed in and didn't want to show how nervous he made her. She was almost thirty years old, far too old to feel this way.

"I'd like the box lunch special," he said, leaning almost close enough to kiss her.

Kiss her? Where had that thought come from?

For an instant the words didn't register. Jeanne-Marie was mesmerized. She could smell his scent, fresh and clean like the forest after a rain. She saw the tiny lines radiating from the edge of his eyes, the smooth cheeks recently shaved. She could feel the leashed energy that was appealing and fascinating in the same instant. And still see that hurt in his eyes. Now she knew what caused it; she'd seen a similar pain in her own.

Suddenly aware of the seconds that had ticked by she slid a step to the side, breaking eye contact. "Of course," she said, turning to take one of the fresh baguettes from the rack. Her hands trembled slightly and her breathing still felt off. Every inch of her skin quivered with awareness. He still stood too close. He unnerved her. Made her aware of her own femininity as she hadn't felt it in years.

Quickly making a sandwich, she wrapped it. Then she assembled the cookies, apple and packaged juice, stashing them in one of her lunch boxes, with a picture of her inn and the sea wrapping around the edges. She turned and thrust it at him.

"Don't litter," she warned. "The conservationists will know exactly where it came from if you do."

"Is that the reason for the picture?" he asked, studying the box a moment, then looking at her again.

"Some people like to take the boxes home and use them for keepsakes—a reminder of their stay here. I had one couple buy a dozen empty boxes to take home to use when giving gifts to family."

"Good idea. I'll see you later." He turned and left without another word.

Jeanne-Marie felt a sudden relief. She was alone again. Quickly clearing his place and rinsing the dishes, she tried to get her mind in gear for the coming day, and erase all traces of her recent guest. But she lingered on the memory of his strong presence. She would make sure if he came tomorrow morning for breakfast to serve him in the dining room!

Matt returned to the inn earlier than the previous day. He'd climbed another ghost of a trail up a west-facing cliff with three others attempting it whom he'd met at the bottom. It was easier than yesterday's climb had been and he'd not lingered as long at the top as the previous day. The lunch Jeanne-Marie Rousseau had made caused him to think about her bustling around her kitchen that morning. He had a cook at the château, but he rarely spent any time there now that he was grown. As a child, he'd loved to invade the kitchen anytime she was making cookies.

Parking his car in the graveled lot, he grabbed his gear—including the trash from lunch which he had packed out—and headed for his room. There were three women sitting in the shade of the veranda. In the middle, Jeanne-Marie. Laughter filled the air when the ladies raised their glasses in some kind of toast. Taking a sip, Jeanne-Marie spotted him.

She spoke softly and the other two women turned to watch him walk toward the wide-open French doors. Then he spotted four children playing in the doorway, Alexandre with his cars, another little boy wearing glasses and two girls—obviously twins. A domestic scene he'd once had at his own home.

"I see you made it through another day climbing," Jeanne-Marie said. He nodded and headed inside.

Halfway up the stairs he heard Alexandre following him. Turning, he looked as the little boy raced up the stairs to join him.

"Can I go with you?" he asked, tilting his back so far Matt was afraid the boy might lose his balance and tumble down the stairs.

"I'm going to shower and change."

"When you go climbing. Can I go with you? I want to learn."

"That's something your mother has to decide."

"I'm big."

Matt nodded gravely. "I can see that."

"She can't take me. She doesn't know how. But you could."

Matt started to turn away, but the pleading look in those warm brown eyes held him. So different from Etienne's bright blue eyes, yet the same trust and faith in adults. He didn't know this child or the mother. But he could recognize yearning. "We'll ask your mother later." He expected Jeanne-Marie would refuse, so that let him off the hook.

"Okay. Do you want to go swimming with me now?" Alexandre asked. "You can change and then you can come play with me in the sand. Mama won't let me go out on the beach by myself. I need a grown-up. I want to play by the water."

"Your mother knows best," Matt said. The little boy looked so earnest. He resumed walking up the stairs.

"She would let me go with a grown-up. Can you be the grown-up? Please?"

Matt hesitated. Children required so little to make their worlds happy. What would Etienne have done had the situation been reversed and Matt had lost his life, leaving his son behind? Who would have spared some time for his son?

"I'll be good and not go into the water unless you tell me I can," Alexandre said, running up three more steps.

Matt looked at the beseeching face and considered the possibility. He'd want someone to be there for his son. A swim in the sea sounded good. He could shower afterward.

"I'll take a quick swim and then if it's okay with your mother, you can come on the sand with me," he said.

Alexandre beamed his smile and raced down the stairs to go ask his mother.

Matt continued to his room wondering if he were losing it. He was here to forget the constant pain; now he was subjecting himself to more? Seeing Alexandre play on the sand would remind him of Etienne. Yet, oddly enough, the ache he normally felt when thinking of his son was not as strong. He was convinced Etienne was in a better place. Another man's son needed some attention. How odd Alexandre had chosen him.

Matt entered his room and quickly exchanged climbing clothes for swimming attire, pulled on a T-shirt and grabbed one of the large fluffy bath towels from the rack before heading back outside. He could hear the women as he descended the stairs but they hadn't heard his bare feet on the wooden steps.

"Honestly, Jeanne-Marie, if you don't explore possibilities, I'll disown you."

"He's just a guest." Matt recognized his hostess's voice.

"If he's taking Alexandre for a swim, I'd say he was looking to make points," the second woman said.

"No, he's only a guest being polite. You know I don't socialize with my guests," Jeanne-Marie protested.

He continued walking closer, unabashedly eavesdropping. So she didn't socialize with her guests. He wondered why. Some might demand more, like dinner in the evening, he thought. Seems as if he had been lucky she'd spent time with him last evening, even though her son was there as well.

Sidestepping around the children, Matt walked out to the veranda. Alexandre spotted him immediately and rushed over. "Mama says I'm not to bother you. I won't be a bother, will I?"

"No. I would not have agreed if I hadn't meant it," he told Jeanne-Marie. Glancing at the other two women, he saw them look first at him and then at their friend, smiles showing.

Feeling like he was on some kind of stage, he walked out to the sand and to the water's edge. He wished he'd heard more about Jeanne-Marie. What was she to do lest her friend disown her?

He pulled off the T-shirt, dropping it and his towel near the water, and plunged into the sea, trying to drive away the thoughts that were coming to mind. He had been happily married. Then torn by tragedy. Less involvement in everything would keep further pain at bay. He went to work, avoiding the long evening walks in the vineyards that reminded him of the times Marabelle and Etienne had accompanied him.

He dutifully checked in with his aunt and uncle and cousins. More to keep them from driving over to check in on him than because he wanted to keep in contact. It was easier to cocoon himself in work and ignore the rest. He would not willingly give his heart as hostage to fate again.

The water was cool and buoyant. He swam some distance from the shore. When he paused to tread water, he studied the village from his vantage point. Fishing boats bobbed in the marina to his far right. There were several establishments that had patios dotted with tables facing the sea, with tourists enjoying the afternoon sun.

It was good to swim after the climb. Later he'd eat in the village and see what activities were planned for *La Fête de la Victoire de 1945* this weekend. He expected the small village to celebrate in a big way. Not that he planned to celebrate. He remembered—then banished the memory from his mind. He would not think of other fetes and how he and his family had celebrated. The year before last had been the worst. The first of every holiday without Marabelle and Etienne had been the hardest, at least that's what everyone told him when he'd growled like a bear in pain if anyone in the family wished him happy. He felt all holidays proved hard now.

Refreshed by his swim, Matt headed for the shore. He had no sooner stepped from the water than Alexandre raced across the sand to join him. Toweling off, he was touched by the child's trust and desire to spend time with him. His cousin candidly told him he was a bear to be around.

If anyone had told him a week ago that he'd be entertained by a small boy at the side of the sea, he'd have called the person crazy. But sitting beside Alexandre listening to him talk was as enjoyable as anything he'd done lately. The child didn't need encouragement; his running monologue continued with only an occasional hmm from Matt.

The self-imposed exile from all things familiar meant he had more time to think than he normally had. Spending time with Alexandre kept thoughts away—except about the child's mother. He looked back, but the women were gone from the veranda. It surprised him she trusted a stranger with her son. Then she stepped out and looked toward them, waving once. So she was keeping an eye on them.

Matt turned back to face the sea. This was a one-off deal. Tomorrow he'd make sure not to return to the inn until too late to be beguiled by a little boy.

"About ready to head back?" Matt asked the boy as the afternoon waned. A quick shower and he'd be back downstairs seeking a good restaurant for dinner.

"Do we have to?" Alexandre asked, looking up at Matt. "This is fun."

"I need to shower and get ready for dinner," he said, pulling his T-shirt back on. He wanted to rinse off the salt water and get into clean clothes. Standing, he looked out at the sea. This trip had been a good idea. While he'd hoped the intense concentration required for climbing would cause his focus to change, being with this boy surprisingly also helped. How unexpected!

Alexandre rose and trotted along beside Matt as they headed back to the inn. When they drew closer, Matt saw Jeanne-Marie with an older couple on the veranda. The woman had brown hair and wore expensive slacks. The older man was dressed casually.

Alexandre stopped when he saw them and grinned. "It's my grand-mère and grand-père! Come on." He began running toward the veranda.

Jeanne-Marie glanced over her mother-in-law's shoulder and saw Matt walking toward them, Alexandre racing ahead. The unexpected arrival of Adrienne and Antoine Rousseau surprised her. They hadn't called, just driven over from Marseilles. Her son had seen them and was running to greet them. Every time she saw them together reaffirmed the wisdom of her staying in France even when her parents urged her to return home.

Adrienne saw her glance for she turned. Spotting Alexandre she smiled, then faltered when she saw a stranger.

"Who's that man?" she asked.

Antoine turned, frowning.

Jeanne-Marie waited a moment until the two were closer. "This is one of my guests, Matthieu Sommer. He graciously agreed to watch Alexandre play by the water."

"Hi," Alexandre said, reaching the older couple. Both reached out to hug him.

By the time Matt stepped on the cool tiles of the veranda, he was close enough for introductions.

"Matthieu Sommer, my in-laws, Adrienne and Antoine Rousseau."

Antoine offered his hand.

Matt shook it, greeted Madame Rousseau and then headed into the inn.

Jeanne-Marie knew she would be questioned by Adrienne. Turning, she smiled brightly.

"Would you like to stay for dinner?" she asked.

"I'll take us all out to dinner," Antoine said, "so you don't have to cook. We wanted to talk about summer plans. We hope Alexandre can come visit sometimes, and give you a break."

"The summer months are always so busy. I remember from when I was a girl and lived here," Adrienne said.

"I'll clean up Alexandre and we'd be delighted to join you. Perhaps you'd like a glass of lemonade while you wait?"

"We'll be fine. We'll sit here on the veranda. Hurry,

Alexandre," Adrienne said. "We want to hear all about what you've been doing."

He grinned and raced into the lounge. Jeanne-Marie caught up with him when they entered their private quarters.

"Can Matt eat with us?" he asked when she took him into the bathroom to give him a quick wash.

"We don't eat with guests as a rule," she murmured. She hoped he wouldn't mention the meal she'd given Matt last night. She also hoped Adrienne and Antoine didn't read more into Matt's watching Alexandre than was there. There was nothing to talk about, and she didn't want her in-laws to get the wrong impression.

Forty minutes later Jeanne-Marie and the Rousseaus entered the town's most elegant restaurant, Les Trois Filles en Pierre. They were soon seated at a round table with a view of the sea. When Jeanne-Marie looked up from her menu, her gaze was caught by Matthieu Sommer sitting directly in her line of sight. She blinked. How had he chosen the same restaurant as they? And beat them here to boot?

"There's Matt. Can he eat with us?" Alexandre asked, waving at the man. "He's my friend. He'll be lonely eating by himself."

"I'm sure he can manage," Antoine said, studying the menu. He glanced up at Jeanne-Marie. "Unless you think he should join us for some reason."

She shook her head. "He's a guest at the inn, nothing more." Good heavens, she did not want her in-laws to think she was seeing the man.

She frowned and bent her head as if she were studying the menu. What would they think if she ever did become interested in another man? It didn't mean she loved Phillipe any less. Still, in all likelihood, they'd feel threatened that someone else was trying to take their son's place.

"Ready to order?" Antoine asked.

She focused on the listings and blotted out all thoughts of falling for anyone. It was unlikely. She thought she was over Phillipe's death, but to make a life with someone else would be too strange.

"Why can't Matt eat with us?" Alexandre asked.

"Really, Alexandre. The man's a paying guest at your mother's establishment. Not a friend," Adrienne said, scolding.

"He is, too, my friend, isn't he, Mama?"

"An acquaintance, at least," Jeanne-Marie said. "But your grandparents want to spend the dinner with you and me, not someone they don't know."

Alexandre got a mulish look to his face and slumped down in his chair, kicking his foot against one of the legs.

"Sit up, Alexandre," Antoine ordered sharply.

"I don't have to," he replied, not looking at his grandfather.

Not wanting to cause a scene, Jeanne-Marie leaned over and spoke softly into Alexandre's ear. After only a moment, he sat up and smiled at his mother. "I'll be the bestest boy in the restaurant!"

Adrienne narrowed her eyes. "What did you tell him?"

"That he's to behave. He'll be fine. I believe I'll have the pasta Alfredo," she said calmly, refusing to admit to bribing him to get good behavior. She wasn't sure how his grandparents would view her tactics. Or even if she could bring about the promised treat if he was good.

She hoped Alexandre didn't give away the secret that she'd said he could ask to walk home with Matt Sommer and not ride back with his grandparents. She hoped she could catch Matt before he left and implore his help. There was no reason for him to do so, but he'd had a son. Maybe he'd take pity on her dilemma and make Alexandre's day.

By the time Jeanne-Marie noticed Matt had called for his bill, she was growing more and more annoyed at her in-laws. They had spent the entire meal trying to talk her into letting Alexandre come for an extended visit and discussing options as if he were not sitting right there watching them with growing dismay. She smiled at him, trying to reassure him with her look, without challenging his grandparents over the meal. She knew they meant well, but he was too young to spend the entire summer away from her.

Feeling a moment of panic at the thought of Matt leaving without her even asking her favor, she jumped up. Both Antoine and Adrienne stared at her in startled surprise.

"Sorry. I'll be right back." She wound her way through the tables and reached the door just as Matthieu Sommer did.

"*Monsieur,* please, I need a huge favor. I'd so appreciate it if you'd walk back to the inn with Alexandre along the beach. I told him I'd ask if he could walk back with you if he behaved during dinner. He ended up acting like an angel. Would you please do that for me? I'll be coming as soon as we settle the bill." She was afraid to turn around, to turn her eyes anywhere but on his.

He looked beyond her at the table she just left.

"You trust your son to me?" he asked softly.

"Aren't you going back to the inn?"

He nodded.

"Then if you wouldn't mind too much, I'd be in your debt."

He looked thoughtful. "Very well. We'll walk along the beach."

"I really appreciate this. I know it's a lot to ask, but he's really taken to you."

"Then perhaps I can ask a favor in return," he said.

"Yes."

He almost smiled. "You haven't heard it yet."

"Anything. I appreciate your help."

"Early breakfast in the morning. I'd like to try another trail that's farther away from St. Bartholomeus, so I want to get an early start."

"That's no problem. I'll be home as soon as I can get there. Once you reach the inn, Rene at the front desk can watch him."

The Rousseaus looked curiously at Jeanne-Marie when she returned to the table. Alexandre looked hopeful.

"Are we leaving?" he asked, looking beyond his mother at Matt.

"After you bid your grandparents good-night," she said.

"Goodbye," Alexandre said with enthusiasm, jumping from the table and giving them each a quick hug. Then he raced across the restaurant and smiled up at Matt with trusting eyes.

"I'm ready," he said.

"So I see." Matt took the boy's hand in his and nodded toward Jeanne-Marie. Then the two of them left the restaurant.

"Whatever is going on?" Adrienne said, annoyance evident. "Why is Alexandre going off with him? Are you seeing that man?"

"No. I told you he's a guest at the hotel. He agreed to walk Alexandre back home," Jeanne-Marie said, resuming her seat. "This gives us some time to talk about Alexandre without him being around. I appreciate your wanting him to visit this summer, and I do think he'd love it. But short visits spaced over the summer, I think."

"You don't even know that man. How can you let Alexandre go off with him? He could kidnap him and we'd never see him again," Adrienne said with concern.

"I have his home address and I doubt he's planning to kidnap my son. He watched him this afternoon by the sea. He lost his own son two years ago. I think being with Alexandre reminds him of his son."

"Alexandre might not understand the attention of a stranger. He could hope for more from a guest passing through," Adrienne said quietly.

"He's used to the transient nature of our guests. It won't hurt him to spend some time with people from different areas."

"He needs a father," Adrienne said sadly.

"He had a father, a wonderful man," Jeanne-Marie said softly.

"Have him come visit us soon. We love having him," Antoine said. "And if not for the entire summer, then for as long as you can let him."

"He'd like that," Jeanne-Marie said. She wanted to get back to the inn. It wasn't that she didn't trust Matthieu Sommer. She did. But she also felt she'd imposed upon him to placate her son.

She refused a lift back to the inn, saying she wanted the walk after dinner. Once she said goodbye to her in-laws, Jeanne-Marie was grateful for the few moments alone as she hurried back home. She'd have to arrange for Alexandre to visit, but right now she was more concerned with how the walk back had gone.

When she reached the inn, she was surprised to see both Matthieu Sommer and her son sitting in chairs on the veranda in the darkness—out of the light spilling from the open French doors.

"Are you solving the world's problems?" she asked, taking one of the chairs nearby. She looked at him, then her son. She was pleased Matt had not gone directly to his room.

"Did you know Matt has horses, Mama? He rides almost every day when he's at home."

"I didn't know that. How amazing." She gave him a look of gratitude.

"Can we go visit? Then I could ride a horse," Alexandre said.

"Oh, no, honey. We live here. Monsieur Sommer is our guest. We're not his."

"I'd like to ride a horse, Mama," Alexandre persisted.

"Maybe we'll find a horse to go riding one day when you're older."

Alexandre thought about it a moment, his face scrunched up. Then he brightened and gave a brilliant smile to the man next to him. "It's later. Now can we ask Mama?"

"Ask me what?" Jeanne-Marie asked.

"Can I go climbing? He can show me how."

Jeanne-Marie frowned. "Monsieur Sommer is here to do serious climbing, not spend time teaching you how to climb."

Matt shrugged. "One afternoon wouldn't hurt. If you'd allow it. There're some very easy climbs he could probably handle. I know what a small boy can do. My son loved it."

Jeanne-Marie looked between the man and the boy. She could see the hope dancing in Alexandre's eyes.

"Mmm, we'll see. Now it's time for bed. We'll discuss climbing another time." She rose and held out her hand. The little boy slid off the chair and reached for her, looking earnestly at their guest.

"We can talk more tomorrow."

"Perhaps." Jeanne-Marie did not want her son pestering the guests. Even though Matt had been kind enough to escort her son home, she was not in the habit of imposing on people at the inn.

After Alexandre was in bed, Jeanne-Marie caught up on some household chores, then went to sit on the veranda. It was nice to relax in the darkness and wait for the last of her guests to return for the night. Sometimes she almost could imagine she was waiting for Phillipe to return from a walk.

Though tonight her thoughts were of Matthieu Sommer. She wished he wanted a last bit of fresh air and would join her on the veranda.

The evening was cool. Settling in the shadows, she gazed toward the sea, dark and mysterious this late. Reviewing her in-laws' visit, she wished they'd spoken about Phillipe more. She missed him. Missed all the family traditions they'd just begun. Like *La Victoire de 1945*. Last year she and Alexandre had gone with her friend Michelle and her family. Alexandre had enjoyed the activities, but she'd felt out of place every time Michelle's husband had swung his son up onto his shoulders so he could see better. Alexandre should have had a father to do the same thing! He was growing so big, it was hard for her to pick him up. Not that her holding him gave him that much extra height.

The last fete she'd attended with Phillipe, Alexandre had been an infant in arms. She remembered the day with a soft smile, startled to realize that the achy pain that normally came when she remembered something done with her late husband was missing. She hoped she'd reach the stage to remember their time with nostalgia and a poignant feeling of days gone by. But for the first time she didn't feel crushed with the weight of grief. Was she at last moving on, as so many had told her she would?

Did meeting Matthieu Sommer have anything to do with that? She almost gasped at the thought.

CHAPTER FOUR

THE NEXT MORNING Jeanne-Marie was in the midst of preparing individual quiches for her guests when Matthieu Sommer walked into the kitchen. She looked up, feeling a spark of delight, which she firmly and immediately squashed.

"I can serve breakfast in the dining area," she said, finishing the last of the crusts and carefully lifting portions into the miniature pie pans she used for the individual servings. Guests usually loved her quiches; her crusts were light and flaky, the warm filling an assortment that so many seemed to enjoy.

"Here's fine," he said, sitting at the same place as yesterday.

"This is a working kitchen."

"Is there a problem?"

She frowned, wondering how to convey how self-conscious he made her without sounding like an idiot. *Please, go in the other room before I lose sense of what I'm doing and just stare at you,* wouldn't go over very well. Sighing softly, she began to make his hot chocolate. Taking the mug to the table, she placed it down in front of him. His hand reached to hold her arm. "Is there a problem?"

The tingling that coursed through her warmed deep

inside. She took a shaky breath. "I guess not. I'm not used to people being in here while I'm working."

There was a definite, huge, mega problem—she was so aware of him as a man, and her own dormant needs as a woman, she couldn't think of anything else. His hand was warm on her arm. The scent of him had her own senses roiling. She'd give anything to be brave enough to sit down with him and forget about the rest of her guests while she learned every aspect about his life she could discover.

"I'll be as quiet as a mouse," he said solemnly.

"Not a good analogy to use in a commercial kitchen," she said, reluctant to pull her arm from his gentle grasp. His thumb brushed against her skin lightly. It sent shivers up her back. With that, she turned away and scurried behind the high counter, doing her best to remember she was in charge of the inn and he was a guest who would be leaving soon. Not a man to get interested in. No someone to start a relationship with.

The thought stunned her. She'd never thought to fall in love again. She'd adored Phillipe. They'd had a wonderful marriage. Too soon over, but she'd never expected to become involved with another man.

Then, she'd never met a man who piqued her interest as much as Matthieu Sommer. Or was as different from Phillipe as he could be. Where her husband had been friendly and outgoing, easily making friends wherever he went, Matt was quiet, kept to himself and seemed to ignore the rest of the world.

"The quiche won't be ready for a half hour. I have some fresh croissants and breads," she said. "I can make you an omelet."

He checked his watch. "I'd planned to leave early, but my friend Paul called last night. He and I'll climb together today. I'm meeting him in Marseilles. We're tackling a cliff on that side. But he won't get up until I pound on his door, if I know him. He was probably up until after two."

Jeanne-Marie looked at him. "So why didn't you stay in Marseilles?"

"This place suits me."

"Mmm." If he'd never come, she'd never have met him. That wouldn't have been all bad. She didn't like the sensations that rose whenever he was near. It reminded her of all she'd lost. And filled her with a vague yearning for things that couldn't be.

Matt watched Jeanne-Marie as she worked. She seemed to enjoy cooking. She could make so much more money if she expanded her meals. Not everyone was so talented or content with less than she might achieve.

Thinking about it, he realized she'd not changed her attitude toward him, either, once she'd learned about his family's situation. She still treated him as any guest, no more sympathy or less than for any other. At least she didn't tiptoe around, afraid to say anything that might remind him of his wife and son.

Jeanne-Marie was that rare individual who seemed genuinely content with life as it was. Too bad he couldn't feel the same way. The raw grief that wouldn't fade drove him. He wanted to escape his thoughts and find some change in climbing, in pushing himself to the limit. Sleep then would be uneventful and deep.

"Here you go. And I warmed a croissant for you," she said, placing in front of him a heaping plate of cheese, pepper and onion omelet, along with a fluffy croissant.

"Thank you. When do you eat breakfast?"

"Before I prepare, or I'd be nibbling all morning."

He began to eat, enjoying the flavors that burst in his mouth. After a moment, he said, "I might eat dinner in Marseilles before returning tonight."

"I won't worry then if you're late back. The center doors are left open for any guest coming in after I go to bed."

"You'd worry otherwise?" Now that was interesting.

She looked up and shrugged. "I'd worry about any guest climbing those cliffs."

He ate, finishing the delicious breakfast she'd prepared. Drinking the last of his hot chocolate, he debated asking for another cup. Instead he put it down and looked at her.

"I could take your son on an easy climb tomorrow afternoon, if you'd permit." He'd thought about it long into the night last night. Being with Alexandre was different from being with Etienne, yet on one level it was the same. Both young boys exploring their worlds. It wouldn't hurt him to spend a few hours helping in that exploration.

"Why would you do that?" she asked, studying his face as if looking for clues.

"For my son."

"Oh." She glanced away and nodded. "Then if you think Alexandre won't be a pest, I guess we could take advantage of your expertise. I don't want him to try more than he can do. But he pesters his grandfather all the time to take him climbing. Maybe trying it once or twice will have him lose interest."

"Or capture his interest even more."

"There is that risk."

"You're a good mother to let him try this when I know you don't approve."

She continued working. "It's not that I disapprove so

much as I don't want him hurt. I think all mothers feel that way. But I'm trying very hard not to be overprotective. If I had my way we'd live someplace totally flat where the most exciting thing he could think of would be to ride a bicycle."

Matt nodded. He remembered Marabelle being concerned when Etienne rode his pony. The boy had loved that pony. And he'd only fallen a couple of times. Nothing to dim the delight he took in riding.

Surprisingly, once they agreed on a time, Matt felt a spark of anticipation. Today's climb would be challenging. But tomorrow's might be more rewarding.

Much as he might like to stay for another cup of chocolate and talk to Jeanne-Marie, he had agreed to meet Paul early. He hoped his friend was ready to climb and not handicapped by a hangover.

Jeanne-Marie watched Matt leave with mixed feelings. He invaded her space, yet when he left it seemed emptier than before. She couldn't figure out how to keep him out of the kitchen. She felt disturbed by his presence. The disruption to her carefully planned life, the extra excitement of being fully alive when he was around made her restless and agitated when he left. She didn't want to come alive, to feel love and then loss. Better to stay in a state that didn't allow strong emotional feelings. It would be safer.

Shaking off her feelings, she tried to draw contentment from her baking. Her life was full, satisfying and suited her and Alexandre perfectly.

As the day progressed, Jeanne-Marie went through her normal routines. Two couples checked out. Another two were due to arrive. When her friend Michelle called to see if they were attending *La Fête de la Victoire de 1945,* Jeanne-Marie was grateful for a break.

"I'd like that. Alexandre has seen the posters I put up and has been plaguing me about when we're going."

"The parade begins at eleven. I thought we could meet at the corner where we met last year."

"Perfect. He'll be thrilled."

The celebration was a big deal in small St. Bart. Phillipe told her how often his parents had brought him to stay with his grandparents for the fete. He'd enjoyed it as a child, much as Alexandre loved it now. They'd only shared one fete here after they married. Now attending each year was special, doing something he'd done. She could tell her son about his father, and continue his memory as best she could.

Her thoughts went to Matthieu Sommer. What would he do that day, another climb? Holidays must be especially lonely for single people, she thought. And especially sad to remember them spent with loved ones now gone. The first without Phillipe had been hard—but she had Alexandre. Matt had no one.

She could invite him to join them.

She caught her breath at the thought. The last couple of years, she'd invited her guests to enjoy the fireworks from the veranda. But she'd never mingled with them during the day.

Late in the afternoon, Adrienne called.

"Antoine and I can come for Alexandre next Monday afternoon," she offered.

"I'll bring him up. I have some shopping I'd like to do in Marseilles. What time works best?"

"Of course we'd like him to come for as long as possible, so early morning, but I know you have things to do at the inn. Come when you can."

"Let's plan on early afternoon, then. Anything special going on I should make sure he has proper clothes for?"

"A swimsuit and sturdy shoes. We'll take a ramble in the park," Adrienne said.

The seaside park in Marseilles was a favorite of Alexandre's.

"He'll love that."

She hung up, happy for Alexandre to have his grandparents so near. Yet she was already missing him for when he left to visit. Usually she let him stay a few days at a time. Every so often his grandparents asked for longer, but so far Alexandre hadn't pushed for any longer visits. And she missed him too much when he was gone to agree.

She finished up her work and went to take Alexandre for a swim. He was going to be thrilled with all the plans.

It was after ten o'clock that night when Jeanne-Marie went to close up the French doors. Rene had left a half hour ago. All her guests except Matt had returned. The last couple had just gone up. How late was he planning to be? Had he decided to stay the night in Marseilles rather than drive back? If so, wouldn't he have called to let her know?

Then she heard the sound of a car on the gravel of the parking area. He was back. She couldn't help the sudden skip in her heart. Every inch of her went on alert and she waited impatiently for him to come in, holding the French door open wide.

He saw her the moment he stepped on the veranda. "I didn't keep you up, did I? I know you rise early."

"No, this is my usual closing time. Did you enjoy

climbing with your friend?" She shut the door after he walked through and turned around to face him. He was growing more tanned each day he spent on the cliffs. He had a rugged masculinity that attracted like nothing else had. She wanted to check her hair and make sure she looked as good as she could. How silly was that? Matt hadn't shown a speck of interest. He was still mourning.

"Paul's driven to competition. Everything has to be a challenge. He made bets on who would reach the top first. Then he wanted to try a different climb down. Racing to be first in both treks, he made me tired just watching him. I didn't come to make everything into a contest."

"Have you climbed together before?"

"Once or twice. I know, I should have expected it. He's always like that. Only this time, I was feeling differently about things. It's the first time I've gone with him since Marabelle and Etienne's deaths."

"Your family?" she asked gently. She hadn't known their names.

He nodded.

"Did they share your love of climbing? Your son must have, if he went with you."

"As long as it was a gentle ramble around hills and lakes. Once serious rock climbing came into the picture, Marabelle always found other pursuits. I had hoped Etienne would like to climb when he got older."

"Phillipe's father taught him. They had lots of treks together. I think it was a bonding time; they were very close."

"Any shared activity would draw parents and children closer. Etienne liked to walk around the vineyard with me. That's what I miss most, I think."

"Tell me about him. Would you like something to drink? Brandy? Coffee?"

He hesitated so long, she was sure he'd refuse. Then he nodded once and said, "I'll take a brandy if you have it."

Jeanne-Marie went back into the kitchen and drew out a bottle of fine brandy and two snifters. She carried them back to the lounge, pleased to see Matt standing near one of the comfortable sofas with a coffee table in front of it.

She set the glasses down and offered him the bottle. He poured them each a small portion of brandy and lowered himself beside her on the sofa once she sat.

"How old was Etienne?" she asked. She hoped he wanted to talk about his son. She often wanted to talk about Phillipe, to remember the good times, to share his life again with friends. It had been hard at first, but now it brought comfort.

"He was five. Alexandre's age. His hair was blond and his eyes blue. Even if he was my own, I thought he was engaging. Funny. Inquisitive."

"What was his favorite thing to do?"

"Follow me around." Matt thought for a few moments, then told her about some of the daily trips around the vineyard, or about shopping at one of the local farmers' markets. Once, he and Marabelle had lost him for a few seconds. He remembered the panic.

As he talked, Jeanne-Marie envisioned the happy family who had thought everything would go on forever. Much as she and Phillipe had done. Her heart ached at the loss of such a sweet little boy. How much more so must he feel?

Matt glanced at his watch. "It's late. I've bored you enough."

"I'm never bored hearing about children." Now or never, she thought. They'd spent almost an hour together, and her interest was as strong as ever. She could do this.

"We will be going to watch the parade for the fete on Saturday. Would you like to join us?" She held her breath.

"I don't think I'm up for celebrating." He put the empty glass on the table and rose. "I'll take off for my room now and let you get some sleep."

She stood next to him, realizing too late how close she stood. Before she could take a step back, however, he reached out and traced his finger down her cheek. "I enjoyed talking about my son. I'll always miss him. He was a part of me that I will never completely get over losing."

"I enjoyed hearing about him. I'm so sorry for your loss. I can't even imagine."

"Most people can't, I guess."

He leaned over and kissed her. For a moment it was the mere brush of lips against lips, but then he moved his hand to the back of her head and held her while his other arm reached around to draw her closer. The kiss deepened.

Jeanne-Marie was caught off guard and before she could protest or push away, he'd released her. She stared up into his eyes, afraid of the tumultuous feelings that exploded.

"Thank you," he said, and after releasing her he swiftly crossed to the stairs and took them two at a time.

She stood still, bemused, confused. "Good night," she said a moment later, feeling stunned with that kiss. She wasn't sure what to think. Had he picked up on her reaction to being around him? He had not shown any particular interest. Why a kiss?

And what a kiss. Did he do that all the time? Slowly she sat back down on the sofa still staring off toward the stairs. Her heart pounded. Licking her lips, she was still shocked. She had not seen it coming.

It had merely been a thank-you for listening. He hadn't meant anything else by it.

Matt went to the window and stared out at the night. He could still feel the imprint of Jeanne-Marie's body against his. She was not as tall as Marabelle had been. But sweet, soft, enticing. How could he have kissed her? There was nothing between them. She'd kindly listened to him talk tonight, that was all. He was lucky she hadn't slapped him silly.

He'd felt a release sharing his son, remembering their normal routines, taken for granted at the time, so precious in memories now. She understood because of her own loss and her own son. She'd shared a few funny incidents involving Alexandre, and he'd been able to counter. The time had flown by.

The room was dark, the night was dark, his thoughts were dark. How could he kiss another woman?

Yet Marabelle was gone.

She wouldn't hold it against him.

He turned and began to strip his clothes in preparation for bed. He'd never thought to kiss another woman, but there was something about Jeanne-Marie that had him momentarily forgetting who and where he was. He'd have to apologize. If she didn't kick him out of the inn first.

Lying in bed a short time later, he threw an arm over his head and clenched his fist. Instead of giving an apology, he wanted another kiss. One in which she kissed him back. How dumb could one man be?

Matt came down for breakfast later than the previous days. He was going to do some exploring around the easy marked trails and then come back for Alexandre's ramble. That is, if Jeanne-Marie would let him. There were some places where the incline was almost gentle enough to walk up. Those would be perfect for a small boy.

He came down the stairs and went to the dining room. Two tables had guests eating. One was still cluttered with dirty dishes and two others were set. He took one to the side and sat down. No sooner had he pulled out his chair than Jeanne-Marie came from the kitchen. Did she have magical powers?

"Chocolate or coffee?" she asked, coming to his table. She balanced a plastic bin on one hip.

"Coffee today." She nodded to the stack of newspapers on the buffet. "Today's papers if you care to read. I'll be right back." Swiftly she stacked the dirty dishes in the bin and carried them out of the dining room. The conversations at the other tables were quiet. He rose and took one of the daily papers from the small stack and resumed his seat.

But he wasn't really interested in the news. He leaned back in his chair and waited for Jeanne-Marie to return.

She did, with a bright smile and a carafe of hot coffee. Also on the platter was a frittata, fresh bread, orange juice and a petite cinnamon roll. She served him, then met his eyes. "Anything else?"

He could hardly ask for her to sit with him. But he missed the companionship he'd had the last couple of mornings. At least she hadn't asked him to leave. She hadn't said anything about the kiss. Were they going to ignore it?

Feeling like he'd won a reprieve, he looked at the meal. "This looks fine," he said.

"Enjoy." She checked on the other guests, then went back to the kitchen.

Alexandre came through a moment later and made a beeline for Matt.

"Hi. We're going climbing today," he said, clambering onto the chair opposite Matt. "My mama said. Are we going now?"

"This afternoon," Matt concurred gravely. "If it's still okay with your mother."

"Will we climb to the top of a mountain?"

"No, we'll start out on a small hill."

"I want to climb a mountain!"

"Climbing is a skill that has to be learned. Everyone starts out on smaller cliffs, then goes on to bigger and bigger challenges. You cannot climb a mountain at five."

Alexandre pouted for a moment. Matt hid a smile behind his coffee cup, taking a drink while the child assimilated what he'd been told. Children wanted everything immediately.

"Can I climb a mountain tomorrow?" Alexandre asked hopefully.

"You can't climb a mountain until you are as tall as I am."

The boy's eyes got big. "I'll never be that tall."

"When you grow up you will." For a moment Matt wondered how tall Alexandre would be. He felt a pang of disappointment that he would likely never know.

Alexandre kicked his foot against the chair. "Are we going soon?"

"After lunch. I have things to do this morning," Matt told him.

"Can I come?"

Matt heard the echo of Etienne's voice. He'd ask just like that. How many times had Matt said not today, when, had he known the future, he'd have taken him every single time?

"I'll be on the phone with work. Then I need to scout out our route for this afternoon. But I tell you what, if your mother approves, once I'm back, we'll start learning about climbing."

"I'll go ask her," Alexandre said, slipping off the chair and running for the kitchen.

Jeanne-Marie came out an instant later and walked right to his table.

"Is Alexandre bothering you?" she asked.

"No. I told him when I finish checking in with work and scouting the climb for later, I'd go over basics with him. He needs to learn a lot to be safe on a cliff. He's still going for a climb today, right?"

Jeanne-Marie nodded her head slowly. "As long as I can go, too."

Matt gave a curt nod. He wasn't sure he wanted two pupils, especially when he had trouble keeping his mind focused when around the pretty innkeeper. Climbing demanded a lot of concentration; he hoped he could remember that.

He met her eyes, seeing the confusion there. But she merely said, "We'll be ready after lunch."

Jeanne-Marie felt almost as excited as Alexandre when she got ready to meet Matt that afternoon. She wore long pants, the cross trainers that offered good soles and a red T-shirt—hoping it would give her courage. Butterflies danced in her stomach. She had gone on some easy scrambles with Phillipe a time or two before she'd gotten pregnant. Easy according to Phillipe—she remembered being in over her head. Maybe a person needed to begin early to master the skills.

She hoped she was doing the right thing in letting her son try this. She knew he had heard so many stories from his grandfather about the climbs he and Phillipe had done, he equated all climbing with his father. She should talk more about Phillipe's work and diffuse the focus on his hobby. His passion, as it were.

Before they left their quarters, she caught Alexandre and held his face between her hands, making him look directly at her. "Listen. You must do whatever Matt tells you, understand? He's the expert. He'll keep you safe, but you have to listen to him."

"I will listen to him," Alexandre promised solemnly.

"If not, we stop and come straight home," she finished.

"Okay. I'll listen." He went racing out of their area into the lounge.

"Matt, Mama says I have to listen to you. I will—really, really hard."

Matt was standing near the French doors. He nodded at Alexandre's comment, then looked beyond him to Jeanne-Marie. She felt the butterflies kick up a notch, but wasn't sure if it was from meeting his dark gaze or the thought of letting her son climb a cliff.

"I thought we'd drive to the trailhead," Matt said.

"Fine, you're in charge." She bid Rene goodbye. The teen had come early to be there when they left.

In no time, the three of them were walking along the rocky trail that skirted the base of Les Calanques. The sea sparkled in the sunshine. The cliffs towered over them, undulating with folds and crevices. The heat of the day reflected from the rock.

"What did you learn this morning?" Matt asked Alexandre as they walked.

The boy began repeating the words of caution and preparation Matt had told him.

"Good memory," Matt said in some surprise. The child had been listening.

Jeanne-Marie was pleased at the effort Matt had made with Alexandre. He had drilled him on the safety features. She didn't know all the ones her son repeated. Phillipe had given her very little instruction, intent more on getting on with the climb.

Was Matt taking extra care because Alexandre was so young? Or was he naturally prudent? She knew from the way Phillipe had talked that he liked taking chances. She suspected Matt got the same adrenaline high from climbing, but took a bit more care to make sure he'd return in one piece.

They reached a sloping hummock that led right to the path. Matt stopped and studied it for a moment, then looked at Jeanne-Marie.

"This is the one I thought he could do."

She nodded. The hill was steep, but not sheer by any means. There were plenty of rocks to hold on to and even some small trees growing from cracks. She could almost walk up it herself without difficulty.

"This would be perfect," she said with genuine gratitude. She wouldn't have to worry about her son on this. Or herself.

"Okay, Alexandre, now listen carefully," Matt said, stooping down to be at his level. "We'll look over the entire hill first. Decide which way we want to go. Then once we begin, we'll look ahead several holds to make sure we always have a way to go. Understand?"

The boy nodded, excitement shining in his eyes.

Matt pointed out rocky protuberances they could use, some sturdy plants, some suspect. Cracks where a foot would find purchase.

Matt rose and looked at Jeanne-Marie. "Any questions?"

"Nope, I'm good to go."

"You're climbing? I thought you just wanted to observe."

"I've been listening. I think I can master this. Maybe I'll find out what all the fuss is about. Like you said, if Alexandre and I have activities in common, we might draw closer."

"Then follow us up. I want to stay near him."

Matt had Alexandre go first. Pointing out handholds and where to put his feet, Matt never was more than a foot or two away from him. Close enough to help out if anything went wrong. Close enough to catch him if the child slipped, yet giving him enough space that Alexandre would think he was doing it all on his own.

Alexandre followed Matt's instructions, climbing up the steep incline slowly and methodically.

Jeanne-Marie waited until they were well ahead and then she began her own ascent, looking ahead like Matt had instructed. It was actually fun to be going from one rock or knob to another, almost like climbing a ladder. The rock was warm beneath her fingers, the sun hot on her head. After a few feet she felt a spark of elation. She had hated the thought of this for so long, but found it was enjoyable. Another place to stand, reach up, hold on and step up.

She might never want to go up a sheer cliff or climb

a mountain, but for a gentle scramble, this was turning out much better than she had expected.

"Mama, I'm climbing!" Alexandre called, looking over his shoulder to her.

"Pay attention, Alexandre," Matt said. "Looking around can cause a distraction. Focus on the rocks."

"Okay." He climbed some more and finally reached a wide ledge. Climbing over to sit on the flat portion, he grinned as Matt joined him. "I did it. I climbed!"

"Yes, you did a great job."

Jeanne-Marie reached the ledge, looking at the two satisfied males sitting there. "I did it, too," she said, scrambling onto the ledge. It was over a dozen feet long and at least six feet from lip to back wall. A shallow cave seemed carved out behind them. Looking up, the next stage of cliff was steeper.

She sat on the edge, letting her feet dangle. They'd come almost thirty feet. Not a huge distance, but she was grateful for the attention Matt gave her son. "This is fabulous. Look how far we can see, almost to Africa." She looked at Matt. "I can't thank you enough. I can almost see what drives climbers."

He nodded. "The more familiar you become, the more you want a bit more of a challenge."

"Maybe. But for now, this suits me perfectly. Alexandre, you did so well! You'll have to tell your grand-père. He'll be proud of you."

"Maybe he will take me climbing."

"I bet he will." She thought about how he'd lost heart after Phillipe's death. But a gentle hill like this one would be perfect for him to spend time with Alexandre.

"Now are we climbing to the top?" Alexandre asked, jumping up and looking toward the rim.

CHAPTER FIVE

"NOT TODAY. We still have to get back down, and it's harder," Matt said. "You have to feel for your toeholds, because you can't see like you can going up."

Alexandre went near the edge and looked over. Matt casually reached out his hand and took hold of the child's arm. "Not too close," he said.

Jeanne-Marie felt another wave of gratitude toward the man. He was patient and alert. She knew Alexandre was safe around him. And this climb had opened her eyes about a lot of things.

In thinking about Phillipe, she knew he'd never have been as patient. He hadn't been with her. Would he have pushed Alexandre beyond what he was capable of? Or left him behind because he wasn't as skilled? Would he have taken time to teach him?

The trip back down was harder. Matt went first, and then coached Alexandre. When Jeanne-Marie looked over to try to plan her descent, she couldn't remember the way she'd come up. It looked steeper than it had coming up. Now she wasn't sure where she could find a toehold or how to make it down without falling.

"You'll do fine. Start a little to your left," Matt called up. He and Alexandre were about fifteen feet below her and to the left. She picked out a couple of places to start and eased over the edge. Reaching down for a foothold, she felt a rock. Slowly she eased her weight on it. It held. Whooshing a breath, she held on with her hands and stretched her other foot lower, moving it back and forth, trying to find a rock.

"Try a bit lower," he called.

She found the rock.

It was slow going and her arms and legs were trembling by the time she reached the bottom. But she'd made it, thanks to Matt's prompting the entire way.

Sitting down on a nearby rock, she wrapped her arms across her chest, hoping they'd feel normal in a bit.

"Wow. It's lots harder going down," she said.

"You did fine. So did Alexandre."

"But only because you were here. I might have made it up okay, but I don't think I ever would have made it down on my own."

"Sure you would. It takes practice."

"And a lot of strength. My arms and legs feel like wet noodles."

"Oh, yeah, I forgot about that." He grinned.

Jeanne-Marie stared at him. He looked ten years younger. It was the first time she'd seen him amused and it made her heart flip over. He was gorgeous. Sadness had robbed him of joy, she knew. But today, going with them, perhaps he'd forgotten for a short time and could enjoy the moment. His eyes crinkled slightly, his teeth shone white against his tan. She could stare at him all day long!

"It was fun, Mama," Alexandre said, jumping up and down. "Can we do it again?"

"Another day. If I live through this one," she murmured.

"We'll walk back to the car and you can rest there."

"Smart move, bringing the car. I don't think I could have made it all the way home otherwise," she said, struggling to stand.

Matt offered his hand and she took it. He pulled her to her feet and gave her hand a quick squeeze. Another flip-flop of her heart. She looked away lest he think she was an idiot. Slowly she started walking to the car. This had been a special day. She had learned more about herself and about the patience some men had. Not that it changed the way she felt about Phillipe, but it did raise questions she'd never thought about. He'd been a man with foibles and drawbacks like any other. Dying young didn't confer perfection.

Saturday dawned a beautiful day. The sky was crystal clear, the temperature moderate and the light breeze steady from the sea. Jeanne-Marie felt a sense of excitement and anticipation she had not experienced in years. She tried to downplay the climb, but it was all she could think about. She shouldn't become involved with anyone, especially a guest who was only staying a couple more days. There was no future in that. But she was still struck by his kindness to her son, and his care of her on the face of the rock.

She'd put the thought of his kiss firmly away. It had been a grateful father's gesture for listening to him talk about his son. Nothing romantic about it. At least not on his part. She would not embarrass herself by making more of it than he had intended.

Today she and Alexandre would spend the day with Michelle and her family, exploring all the booths of the fete, enjoying the parade and ending up in the evening sitting on the veranda to watch the fireworks that exploded over the sea, doubling the enjoyment with the reflections on the water.

Busy in the kitchen, she hoped to finish everything including cleaning up before nine. She'd left notes for her guests saying she would only serve breakfast until eight-thirty. If they didn't come down by then, she would place a cold collection of continental breakfast rolls and biscuits and hot coffee on a serve yourself basis on the buffet.

So far everyone but the couple in room three and Matt had been served. Just as she carried a bin of used dishes toward the kitchen, Matt came down the stairs.

"I'll bring you chocolate in a moment," she said, motioning for him to take a seat at an empty table. Glad for the busy tasks facing her, she hurried to the kitchen. Dumping the plates in the sink, she placed the silverware into a soaking pan and then dried her hands. She made a new pot of hot chocolate and placed it on a tray with the hot breakfast strata, a basket of rolls and jams. Lifting it easily, she carried it out.

He'd taken a seat at one of the tables by the window. She smiled brightly and placed the edge of the tray on the table while she unloaded his breakfast. "I have strata for breakfast today. And assorted rolls and breads. Anything else I can get you?" She did not let her gaze linger. He seemed to be avoiding her eyes as well.

"This looks like all I need. Thank you." He reached for the hot chocolate. "How are you feeling today?"

She brushed her hands over her apron, trying to rein in her racing heart. A quick glance around showed everyone was eating. She wanted to escape. "The bath helped. I feel a bit stiff today, but not sore. Let me know if you need anything further," she said, tilting the tray sideways and walking back to the kitchen. She felt as if she'd run a mile.

Alexandre came running in. "Hi, Mama, is it time to go to the parade?"

"Not yet. I have to get the kitchen cleared first. Our guests are still eating."

"Is Matt there?"

"Don't bother him," Jeanne-Marie warned. She plunged into the soapy water and began washing the silverware.

When she looked up a moment later she was alone in the kitchen. Quickly drying her hands, she went to the door. Alexandre was standing beside Matt, talking earnestly.

Jeanne-Marie hurried across to them.

"Come away, Alexandre. I'll make your breakfast."

"I want to eat with Matt," he said. "Don't you want me to eat with you? If you eat alone you'll be lonely."

"He'll be fine here," Matt said.

"He can eat in the kitchen."

"He'll be fine." Matt looked at her, his eyes narrowing slightly. "Unless there's a reason you don't want him here."

"You'd probably like peace and quiet."

He looked at the little boy. "I think conversation would be best this morning."

Alexandre beamed. He pulled out the chair across from Matt and sat down. "I can eat here, Mama." He looked at Matt. "We're going to *La Fête de la Victoire de 1945* together. There'll be lots to see. Did you want to come with us?"

"No," Jeanne-Marie said. "We're meeting Michelle and Marc and Pierre, remember?"

"But Matt would like them. Marc is big like him.

Then we would all have a friend at the parade. Michelle and Marc, me and Pierre, and you and Matt. It'll be good, Mama."

"I'm sure Matt has already made plans for the day," she said. "I'll get your breakfast. Don't be pestering him."

"Did you make plans?" Alexandre asked when his mother walked away.

"I was going for a climb," Matt said. Truth be told, he had planned to do another climb not as challenging as he'd been doing. He was getting a later start than he wanted, due to a sleepless night.

But as he ate and listened to Alexandre's chatter, he thought more about changing plans and going with the Rousseaus to the fete. Would Jeanne-Marie be amenable? Or would she rather not mingle her guests and friends? She'd gone quickly to her quarters yesterday after they'd returned to the inn, saying she needed to soak in a hot bath.

He'd gone to town to eat and hadn't seen her again until this morning.

Alexandre bounced on his chair. "I love fetes. I like the food and the parades. And all the people. Sometimes I can't see everything because I'm little, but then Mama picks me up to see better. Pierre's dad picks him up really high. Mama can't pick me up so high. You are very tall. You could pick me up highest."

"If I were going with you."

"Can you, please?"

When Jeanne-Marie returned from the kitchen with Alexandre's breakfast, both of them at the table looked at her. "Mama, Matt is going with us to the fete and he'll lift me up high to see!"

Jeanne-Marie's eyes widened and she stared at him. "You're going with us?"

"If you don't wish me to lift him, I won't. But he would be higher, don't you think?"

She nodded, putting the plate in front of Alexandre, trying to understand what was going on. "I thought you were climbing."

"I can climb tomorrow."

Jeanne-Marie didn't know what to say. How would she spend the entire day in close proximity to Matthieu Sommer?

They left the inn just before ten o'clock. Alexandre was beside himself, racing out in front, then running back to urge them on. Jeanne-Marie was careful to keep a distance between herself and the stern-looking man walking beside her. He had not smiled again like he had yesterday. If anything, he seemed to regret it. Still, he was going with her today. She wondered what Michelle would think when she showed up with him.

The small coastal town was already crowded with colorful booths lining both sides of the main street, which had been closed for the day. Everything imaginable was for sale, from fresh warm cookies to scarves, sunglasses, wood carvings, brassware, and original paintings and crafts of every kind. When they began to be jostled by others, Jeanne-Marie took hold of Alexandre's hand so he wouldn't get separated from her in the growing crowd.

The tricolor flew on every lamppost and by each booth. The joy in the day was evident by the happy revelers. It was a perfect day.

Or would be if she could enjoy herself instead of being so very aware of the man walking at her side. She was getting too interested in her guest. Surrounded by the crowd, she still felt as if she and Matt were almost alone. She had to pay attention to what else was going on around her.

Matt studied the scene from time to time, looking wherever Alexandre pointed. They passed a juggler mesmerizing his audience. A small band played near the town center, with people crowding the sidewalks to enjoy the music.

They stopped at every booth. Matt wondered if the entire day was going to be silent, with Jeanne-Marie not speaking. He reached out and took her arm, stopping her.

She turned and stared at him with wide eyes.

"If you don't wish for me to accompany you, please say so."

"Of course you can come with us. You're here, aren't you?"

"And you haven't said one word since we left the inn. Which leads me to surmise you'd just as soon wish I was a million miles away."

She shook her head. "No, I'm glad you came with us. It's just—" She shrugged. "I don't know, I feel a bit funny if you want the truth. This is the first time I've attended anything with a man since Phillipe died. It feels awkward. I know this isn't a date or anything," she rushed in to explain. "But others might look on it as if it were and then I'd have to explain and there's nothing to explain, but it gets complicated."

He nodded. "I get it. This is the first time I've attended anything since my family died, too. It is different. It's not what either of us thought we'd be doing today, but let's give Alexandre a good day. Let others think what they want."

She nodded, relieved he understood. And for her, nothing was more important than letting her son enjoy himself.

Except—today she wanted Matt to enjoy himself as well. He'd lived with heartache too long.

"You and I know the truth, so what does it matter what others think?" he asked, leaning closer so she could hear him. Feeling the brush of his breath across her face, her eyes grew even wider as she stared right back at him. Matt was shocked at the sudden spurt of awareness and desire that shot through him.

His gaze dropped to her lips and she instinctively licked them. He felt another shot of desire deep inside. Time seemed to stand still. Alexandre had nothing to do with the sensations he was feeling now.

Clearing her throat, Jeanne-Marie dragged her gaze away and turned to look at the booth they stood in front of. "This is a fine example of local wood carving," she said, her voice husky.

It took a moment for him to be able to move. He was stunned he could feel anything after Marabelle's death. He took a step back and gave his attention to the vendor, who tried to convince them they needed an assortment of wooden animals. Blood pounded in his veins. He glanced around, but no one else in the crowd noticed anything unusual. No one picked up on his reaction. No one could condemn him for normal male reactions to a pretty woman.

"We don't buy, we just look," Alexandre said. "Too much stuff to carry," he said gravely.

Glad for the boy's comment, Matt drew in a deep breath, avoiding looking at Jeanne-Marie. "Maybe on the way home we can find a memento of the day," Matt told the boy. Keep things impersonal. And keep

Alexandre between them. He'd focus on the little boy and make sure he had a good time.

They met Jeanne-Marie's friends at the designated corner shortly before the parade was to begin. Michelle couldn't hide her surprise when she saw Matt accompanying Jeanne-Marie and Alexandre, but she tried to cover it up, rushing to introduce her son and husband. Alexandre and Pierre were friends and began talking about what they hoped was going to be in the parade.

When more and more people pressed in around them, Matt knew the parade was about to begin. He lifted Alexandre into his arms so he could see more than waists and legs. As a defense mechanism it wasn't foolproof, but it kept his attention focused on the parade and the boy and not the woman standing beside him. When others moved to crowd into the remaining space, Jeanne-Marie had to step closer. He could smell her perfume, light and airy, and as much a part of her as her dark hair. She was no longer so distant, and he wasn't sure if that was good or bad. At least when she wasn't talking to him, he had been okay. Now he grew more aware of her every second.

"I'm up high," Alexandre said gleefully, leaning over to see Pierre, whose father had also lifted him.

"Me, too," Pierre said with laughter.

The first entry in the parade was an eclectic band, the national anthem played at the midway point of the parade route. Then the musicians played marching music as they continued down the street.

Following were homemade floats, decorated cars with people waving, a dancing group from a local school. A high school band, and assorted veteran companies dressed in uniform, cheered by the spectators. A fire truck followed, blowing its siren from time to time and spraying the crowd with a fine mist of water.

When the parade ended forty-five minutes later, Michelle and Marc invited Jeanne-Marie and Matt to join them for lunch.

"No. I need to get back to the inn," Jeanne-Marie said.

"Why?" Michelle asked. "You have Rene to keep an eye on things, and all your guests are surely here."

Jeanne-Marie turned slightly so Matt couldn't see her face and rolled her eyes in his direction.

Michelle grinned and leaned closer. "To be alone with him?"

"No!" Jeanne-Marie said, horrified. This was just the kind of conclusion she was afraid her friend would jump to. "I can't tie him up all day," she said softly.

"I want to ride the merry-go-round," Alexandre said.

"We usually do let the children ride," Michelle said, her eyes dancing at Jeanne-Marie's discomfort.

"Is there a carousel?" Matt asked Jeanne-Marie. She turned and nodded, giving up on her plan to flee back to the inn and barricade herself into her private rooms.

"There's a traveling carnival at the edge of town, in one of the lots set back from the sea. It'll be jammed with kids, though."

"I'm a firm believer in letting children enjoy life as much as they can while they can." And it would delay return to the inn. He would spend the entire day surrounded by the crowd if he could. He did not want to be alone with either Jeanne-Marie—or his thoughts.

"Okay, thank you, he'll love it."

Time passed swiftly. Despite his best efforts to remain distant, Matt caught himself darting glances her way. Her laugher was contagious. Her delight in mundane things had him looking at the world in a new light. Everything seemed lighter than before, more colorful. Even the heightened sense of awareness that did not diminish as the day went on. He wondered if she picked up on it. She was careful to keep out of touching distance. Though once or twice the crowded walkway jostled her so she bumped into him. He let his fingers linger just a second when steadying her. Her skin was soft as silk.

Jeanne-Marie knew most of the people in town and was frequently greeted. She in turn introduced Matt, mentioning only that he was visiting to climb Les Calanques. She ignored the occasional look of speculation.

By three o'clock Alexandre was definitely tired. He rested his head on Matt's shoulder and stopped talking.

"You all right, Alexandre?" he asked.

"I'm tired," he said.

"He usually naps most days. I'll take him back to the inn. It's been wonderful. I haven't had this much fun in a long time. Thank you, Matt, for seeing it with us. I hope you enjoyed it as well," she said, her eyes darting to his, then back to Alexandre.

"I'll go back with you. This little guy isn't going to be wanting to walk and he's too heavy for you to carry all that way." There was still time to get in a short climb. Preferably very steep and strenuous. Something to take his mind off the woman at his side.

"Thank you."

The three of them headed for the inn. To a casual observer they probably looked like a young family, husband, wife and child. For a split second Matt felt a pang that it wasn't so. Then reason returned. He was not looking to replace his family with another. He was not going to fall in love again. Life was too uncertain to risk everything by falling in love, having his life on edge awaiting another fateful outcome.

When they reached the veranda, Matt let Jeanne-Marie take Alexandre, who was almost asleep.

"Thank you," she said again.

"No problem."

He handed off the boy. When she went to their quarters, he took the stairs to his room.

Quickly changing into climbing clothes, he headed out.

She was talking to Rene when he descended. She looked up.

"Going for a climb? Isn't it a bit late?"

"I'll find a short climb, check out the view from another vantage point," he said, and kept walking. He would drive himself to the point of exhaustion so he'd sleep. And he'd get his head on straight. He might find some physical attraction to the pretty innkeeper, but he wasn't going there. She was a forever-after kind of woman, and he'd not risk his very soul again on ephemeral love.

Jeanne-Marie watched as he left, a spring in his step, his look anticipatory.

She brushed her fingertips across her lips, remembering their kiss. She'd pushed the thought away during the day, but now the memory returned. She had felt a pull of attraction that was as strong as any she'd ever had for Phillipe. Once when he'd leaned over her to say something, she'd thought he was going to kiss her again.

But she'd misread the situation. Matt had turned away

and the moment had been lost. Not that she forgot it. Doing her best to keep her distance the rest of the day, she still felt an awareness that bordered on the edge of obsession. He was the perfect tall, dark and handsome man romance novels so loved. His body was honed to perfection. His smile didn't reach his eyes, but still had the ability to stir her heart.

"Which is foolishness," she said aloud, to Rene's confusion.

"Pardon?"

"Rien." Shaking her head, she went to prepare a pitcher of lemonade and then to sit on the veranda. She'd enjoy the rest of the day no matter what! Alexandre would probably sleep till dinnertime, which was good, so he would keep awake for the fireworks. Softly she sighed as she looked across the beach to the sea. Spending the evening on the veranda and watching the pyrotechnics from the comfort of the inn was the perfect way to end the day. The fireworks were shot over the water, so the veranda offered a perfect vantage point. Since she had taken over running the inn, Jeanne-Marie had invited all her guests as well.

It was a nice tradition, she thought, and kept the memories of Phillipe alive.

It had taken a while, but now she knew she wouldn't fall apart if she remembered happy times with him. More often than not, now she was angry at his taking foolish risks and leaving her and Alexandre behind. She knew her loss and his couldn't be measured by how or why. Only the aching emptiness where love once flourished.

She felt restless, and sitting still had all sorts of thoughts crowding her mind. Ones she didn't want. Again her thoughts went to Matthieu Sommer.

This had to stop.

She popped in to tell Rene she was going for a walk and would be back soon.

Stepping off onto the sand, Jeanne-Marie took off her sandals and looped them through her fingers, heading directly to the sea and the packed sand where the water kissed the shore.

Then, as if unable to stop herself, she turned to walk toward Les Calanques. It wasn't that she expected to run into Matt on his return, but if she did, then they could talk as they walked back to the inn.

She studied the crags and cliffs ahead of her. How Phillipe had loved them for the short climbs he could take on weekends. And she'd enjoyed spending time with his grandfather while they waited for him to return.

Yesterday had been amazing. She'd actually climbed a cliff. Granted, it wasn't very high or steep, but it was more than she'd ever done before. And Alexandre had loved it. He'd talked about it all last night. And had regaled Pierre today when they were watching the parade.

She knew Alexandre wanted to climb mountains one day. She hoped he'd outgrow the idea. But if not, could she stop him? She didn't want to coddle him. But the thought of him scaling a sheer face of rock had her almost in a panic. She wanted him to be proud of his father. Yet she didn't want him to necessarily follow entirely in Phillipe's footsteps.

By the time she reached the rocky area that led to the base of the cliffs, Jeanne-Marie knew she had to turn around. She needed to be home when Alexandre awoke. Just as she was about to turn, she saw Matt in the distance, gazing out to the sea. She stopped. Her inclination was to continue until she reached him. But he looked so intent, she didn't know if she should intrude.

She watched for a long time. Giving into temptation, she scrambled over the rocks and found the faint path at the base of the cliffs. Following it, she would reach him in no time. Then what would she say?

He saw her and turned to walk toward her.

"Out for a walk?" he asked when he was close enough to be heard.

"Alexandre's sleeping, so I thought I'd have a bit of time to myself."

"Ah, then I'll leave you to your walk."

"No. That's okay. I'm ready to head back. You looked like you were lost in thought gazing out at the sea."

"I was thinking about sailing around the world."

"Oh, wow, that's ambitious. I didn't know you sailed."

"A totally unrealistic thought since I've never sailed by myself. I think I'd like a competent crew and big boat that could handle anything the sea throws at us. Then maybe."

"Have you done any long distance sailing?"

"Around the Med a few summers ago as part of a crew. But my father was living then and in charge of the winery. Now, it falls primarily to me. The appeal of being on the water would be the total lack of communication. And that's unreal—decisions have to be made, plans implemented."

"So work up to a sabbatical like professors have," she said, falling into step with him.

"Hmm. In the meantime, climbing's a strong leader for most desired escape."

She laughed. "What happened to quiet, safe hobbies

like stamp collecting or photography?" She felt almost giddy around him.

He tilted his head slightly. "I might consider taking a picture from the top of a climb."

"If the camera didn't get banged up on the way."

"Never happen."

"Have you ever fallen?" she asked.

"Slipped a few times. No harm done."

"That's a blessing."

"Not all climbers fall," he said.

"I know that. But there have to be less scary hobbies."

"Sure, but what could compare?"

"Travel, for one."

"Where would you like to travel?" he asked.

"London," she answered promptly.

"And what's there?"

"Everything. From Westminster Abbey to the London Eye."

"Would you be brave enough to ride in it?" he asked.

"Hey, I'm adventuresome. I came to France from America, didn't I? I climbed a cliff yesterday. I imagine the view from the top of the Eye would be spectacular."

"Probably. The view from the top of the cliffs is spectacular. I'd hardly call what you scaled yesterday a cliff."

The teasing tone in his voice startled her. She looked at him suspiciously.

"Are you making fun of me?"

"No." But his lips twitched.

She remembered the grin he'd given her yesterday when she'd complained about the strain on her arms and legs. It would be worth being mocked to see him laugh.

The walk back took far less time than she expected. Alexandre was playing on the veranda and jumped up to run to her when he saw her.

"I'd like to take you and your son to dinner," Matt said just before the child reached them.

"What? You don't have to take us to dinner," she said quickly. Her interest couldn't be that blatant, could it?

"If you knew me better, you'd know I rarely do things I don't wish to. It would be a…a good ending to the day," Matt said as if choosing his words carefully.

"Mama, where were you? Rene said you'd be back but you've been gone a long time," Alexandre said when he reached her.

"I went for a walk. I thought you'd still be asleep. Now I'm back. Matt asked to take us out to dinner. Won't that be fun?"

"Shall we leave in about a half hour? That'll give me time to clean up a bit."

Jeanne-Marie nodded. She wanted to clean up a bit herself.

Once in her room, she debated what to wear. She loved the way her blue dress fit and showed off her figure. But was it too much when she'd been wearing khakis all day? Maybe the pink top, which gave color to her cheeks. She stared at herself in the mirror for a long moment. Who was that staring back? A widow living without her husband. A mother who loved her son.

But, just maybe, a woman on the brink of something different. Would it be wonderful or end up leaving her mourning what could never be? Funny, she hadn't thought about making a life with any other man. She'd loved Phillipe. She was trying to make her life what she thought he would have wanted. But he was gone. Maybe it was time to look for other ways to spend the future. Alexandre wouldn't be with her forever. He would grow up, go off to college and marry. He could live on another continent as she did, so far from where she grew up.

What would the years after that hold?

Right now was not the time to grow philosophical.

She chose the pink top to go with the khaki slacks. She would wear nicer shoes. Every restaurant would be mobbed because of the holiday. Casual was the dress of the day.

The excitement shining in her eyes couldn't be ignored. Was she ready for this?

"Do you like growing grapes and making wine?" Jeanne-Marie asked once they were finally seated in Le Chat Noir. The wait had seemed interminable, with Alexandre complaining every two minutes he was hungry. Most of the people waiting, however, had been in high spirits. The festive air permeated the village. Matt hadn't minded the wait. For the first time in a long while he felt connected with others.

"Is that something you always wanted to do?" she added.

"Ever since I was a kid, I knew this was my role in life. I enjoy it. And when I can take a vacation, it seems the best part is returning home. I can't imagine anything else I'd rather do. I suspect you never yearned to be an innkeeper." He thought of the acres of vineyards, the constant worry about the weather or pests. The heavy, laden vines just before harvest, the purple grapes looking almost frosted. He missed being there.

She laughed. Matt was struck again by the sound of her laughter. He let his gaze settle on her for a moment.

She looked lovely tonight with color in her cheeks and a sparkle in her eyes. He would like to hear that laughter more. He suspected that she didn't laugh nearly enough.

"Not at all. Before I met Phillipe, I planned to be an art historian, maybe teach. I enjoyed my classes at university and wanted to have others find the same delight in studying paintings by the masters. But once I fell in love, all I wanted was a family and a happy life. Strange how things worked out. Phillipe hadn't wanted to run the inn, but refused to sell it when his grandfather died. Even his mother suggested selling and it had been her childhood home. I never expected to own it myself and run it. Still, look how fortunate I am."

"Indeed." Making the best of the situation. Which he struggled to do as well.

After their order had been taken, he leaned back as Alexandre chattered away, talking about his day, the rides he'd gone on and the fact he'd seen all the parade since Matt had held him so high.

"Definitely a wonderful thing," Jeanne-Marie said, wishing Phillipe had had more time with his son. Alexandre had been a baby when he died. He'd never known the joy of his conversation, his enchantment with life. And Alexandre would never know his father except by what Jeanne-Marie and his grandparents told him.

Matt leaned forward slightly. "No time for sadness. This is a celebration."

She looked up. "I'm sorry, I was thinking about his father and how much he missed. I really appreciate your coming today. Look how much he liked it."

Matt looked at Alexandre. "My son was that age when he was killed. Think of all he missed."

"Oh, you're right, this is not a time to grow melancholy.

Thank you for inviting us to dinner. Afterward, we'll head back, grab a good seat on the veranda and watch the fireworks. They are the highlight of the day for me. You'll love them."

Matt pushed away thoughts of another woman, another fete, and focused on the woman with him tonight. One evening didn't mean he'd forgotten his family any more than Jeanne-Marie had forgotten hers. They were both alive. Life was meant for the living.

Several of the guests at the inn were seated on the veranda by the time Jeanne-Marie, Matt and Alexandre returned. A few chairs were empty, which she asked him to stake out for them while she went to get the cookies and cakes she'd prepared earlier in the week for just this occasion. Soon everyone on the veranda was sipping iced lemonade and munching on the desserts.

The bursting of colorful fireworks was the perfect ending to the celebration. Jeanne-Marie couldn't remember a happier day since Phillipe died. She was growing more comfortable around Matt and appreciated his attention to her son. He must have been a great father to his own child. Would Phillipe have been as attentive and involved? He'd worked long hours, and gone climbing every chance he got. He hadn't curtailed his activities after Alexandre had been born, but as an infant, he wouldn't have been much company to his father. As he'd grown older, would Phillipe have included him?

No sense worrying about what might have been. Phillipe was gone. Never to return. And Matt? He was here today. Beyond that, she didn't care to look.

CHAPTER SIX

JEANNE-MARIE put Alexandre to bed, but she felt too restless and keyed up to sit quietly after the fireworks. She went back to the common area, straightening cushions and pillows here and there. Rene had taken off and she'd close up in another hour or so. Several of the guests had gone back to the village to enjoy dancing at one or two of the places that offered a band.

Wandering out onto the veranda a few minutes later, she was surprised to see Matt still sitting there. Feeling her heart lurch a bit, she went to join him.

"Not going back to town?" she asked as she sat beside him.

"Nothing there for me. Does the town always have such an amazing display of pyrotechnics?"

"A lot of the annual budget goes to them. Fabulous, I think."

There was a muffled boom in the distance and a faint glow in the sky.

"Marseilles is finishing up," she commented. "I remember a few years ago we were amazed with their display. But this suits me fine. I like not being in the midst of a huge crowd," she said, gazing out across the dark sea. In the distance a ship's lights could be seen, gliding toward the east.

"Do you go to Marseilles often?" he asked.

"Not as often as I probably ought to. Alexandre's grandparents live there and he visits them from time to time. I'm taking him over on Monday for a couple of days. I'll do some shopping while I'm there, but pretty much St. Bart suits all our needs."

"What time are you taking him?"

"In the afternoon. Why?"

"I could drive you both and then take you to dinner."

Jeanne-Marie tried to see his expression in the faint light spilling from the French doors. But his face was in shadow. Another dinner? She swallowed hard. They would drop Alexandre off at his grandparents. It would just be the two of them. No matter how she thought about tonight, a dinner in Marseilles, just the two of them, would be a date.

A touch of panic. Was she ready for such a step? Not that it meant more than two people enjoying a meal together. He hadn't asked her to run away with him.

"Why?" she blurted out.

"As a thank-you for your hospitality."

"I'm an innkeeper, you're a guest. Nothing beyond payment for your room is needed." She felt deflated. It was merely a thank-you. She'd thought he meant more.

"Then, because I'd enjoy sharing another meal with you. I'd like to spend a bit more time together before I head for home."

Her heart sped up a little. "Just you and me?"

"Unless you wish to take Alexandre to his grandparents later. Then he could eat with us," Matt said easily.

It would be less like a date if Alexandre were with

them. But—there was nothing wrong with having a meal with a guest. Especially on his last day. She would view it as the thank-you gesture he said initially.

"He should go to his grandparents first. And yes, I'd like to have dinner with you." The minute she said it, she wished she could snatch back the words. It was a date! She hadn't dated in years. She never thought she would again, at least not until she was over Phillipe's death. Which she wasn't. Yet. Or was she?

"Maybe I'll extend my stay another few days," he said.

She tried to remember future reservations. "I think I'm booked," she said finally, feeling disappointed. This seesaw of emotions confused her. Did she want to see where a relationship between them could lead or not?

She did. She'd have to double-check reservations. If there was a way to keep a room for Matt, she would find it.

"Ah, I hadn't thought about that. Maybe I'll have to look for something elsewhere in the village."

"I can double-check." She made a move to stand, but his hand caught hers and tugged her back down. The tingling that shot through her arm was pleasant, tantalizing. She looked at him, feeling his hand imprinted as if she'd never forget.

"Time enough in the morning. Let's just enjoy the evening. If the rooms are all booked, so be it. I'll take you to dinner and then head for home."

"That would be so late."

"Or we could get rooms in Marseilles and I'll drive you back in the morning and then head for home."

That raised all sorts of concerns. Jeanne-Marie took a deep breath and shook her head, much as she was tempted. Not that he was suggesting a single room. She caught her breath at the thought. His kiss had knocked her off her senses; what would making love be like?

She grew warm thinking about it, glad for the darkness to hide her face. She was probably beet-red by now.

"No, I have to prepare breakfast for my guests. I have to return home Monday night, no matter how late."

"Of course."

It was a beautiful evening with a soft breeze blowing from the sea and she was sitting with a gorgeous man. His hand had slid down her arm and now held her hand loosely in his. The focal point of her existence was on their linked hands. She couldn't think about anything else except Matt and the wild feelings that exploded in her when he touched her. A million women would trade places with her in a heartbeat. How had she been so lucky?

In a desperate attempt to stop thinking about unlikely possibilities, she asked, "What was your favorite part of today?" Her entire body seemed attuned to Matt. She could stay here forever. The darkness sheltered them. The gaiety in the town was a sweet background melody that mingled with the soft sighing of the sea as it brushed the sand. For a time, cares seemed forgotten. The past faded away, the future was unknown. She had only this moment.

"The food. I bet we sampled two dozen different dishes. How that boy of yours kept eating is amazing to me."

"He has his moments. I hope it all goes to making him a tall man. My father isn't very tall. I want Alexandre to be tall like his father."

"Tell me about Phillipe," Matt invited.

She hesitated. She disliked the way people tiptoed

around the subject, but now that it was broached, what could she say? She didn't want to talk about him to Matt. Yet, he was such an important part of her life. "He was tall, with brown hair, looked a bit like his father, whom you met. He had the most amazing vitality. He was always on the go. I used to wonder how he had the patience to scale the sheer cliffs he did. It takes careful study and patience to pick out the best route. He always seemed antsy, always looking for things to do. He didn't sit still very often." She didn't bother to reveal he had also been a bit of a show-off, talking about exploits he'd done, bragging about future climbs he planned. The more daring, the more he liked talking about them.

"Did you two have a house?"

"No, a large flat near the water in Marseilles. He made a good living and supported us well. The place seemed so empty after he died. I sold it when we moved here."

"What was your favorite holiday?"

Jeanne-Marie thought about it for a moment. Did none stand out? "We usually went wherever he was going to climb. I don't climb, as you saw the other day, so I found things to do in the towns or villages where we stayed. I liked Italy. He climbed in the Italian Alps one time and I enjoyed the village he used as base. He never wanted to spend the time sightseeing when he could be climbing."

"And that suited you?"

"Well, a real dream holiday would be pampering, breakfast in bed, then a day of shopping, maybe a play in the evening or a fabulous dinner somewhere with dancing," she said dreamily. "But for the time being, I think Alexandre and I will be content to stay here. You have to admit, it's beautiful right on the sea. I do love living by the water."

"You should come visit the Loire Valley sometime. Especially in spring. It's beautiful, as well."

Matt hoped when she checked the reservations tomorrow that he'd be able to stay. Paul would be returning home soon. Not that it mattered much to him. The one climb they'd done together hadn't been as relaxing or challenging as the others this week. Paul's idea of recreation was more clubbing and less climbing.

He thought about Jeanne-Marie's husband. Granted, he understood the appeal of taking vacations to climb. But surely at one point in their marriage he would have wanted to go where she wanted. Not that Matt was going to pass an opinion on their marriage. Jeanne-Marie had loved the man and grieved his death.

Not liking the trend of his thoughts, he glanced at her. She seemed so serene. He liked that the most about her, he thought. Not that her laughter wasn't infectious. Or the special way she looked at a person when he talked, like he was the only other person in the world. Her hand was smaller than his, felt delicate and warm in his. Contentment seeped in. It was comfortable sitting on the veranda in the dark.

Then the thought of kissing her rose and wouldn't be pushed away. Would she be willing? One way to find out.

He gave her hand a gentle squeeze and released it. "I'm heading for bed. I'm making another climb tomorrow. You can let me know when I get back if I can stay another few days."

She jumped up, almost pressing against him she was

so close. "I'd better get some sleep myself. Dawn comes early and breakfast doesn't make itself."

"Before we go in..." he said, drawing her into his arms, slowly so as to give her time to back out if she wanted. She didn't.

When his mouth found hers, her kiss was sweet. Her lips were warm, opening to his without hesitation. Deepening his kiss he felt her response, passion with passion, pressing against him with her body as if wanting to get as close to him as he wanted to get to her. Desire spiraled, senses went into overload. Her curves inflamed him. Her softness made him that much harder. Matt could only feel the hunger increase. He wanted her. She was all he wanted right now. The rest of the world faded until only the two of them existed in the darkness. Would she come to his room with him?

The thought shocked him. He pulled back, trying to see her in the faint light. She gazed up at him, her expression impossible to read. Kissing her on her cheek, trailing down to her neck and back up the other side to that cheek, he breathed in the scent of her, tasted that soft skin, heard her ragged breathing as she held him tightly in her embrace.

Reluctantly he rested his forehead against hers. He didn't know what he wanted. Making love with her would take him in a direction he never thought to go. Was it too soon for him? For her?

He'd vowed never to be a hostage to fate again. The solo path was safer. If he could only clamp down on the roiling desire that rose.

"I need to go in," she said softly, her fingers brushing against his cheek. "I had a wonderful time today." When she pulled away, he let her go. And watched her walk into the inn.

He stared after her long moments after she left. His own breathing slowed.

He'd kissed her again, over and over, actually. And she'd responded.

Had she ever!

With a groan, he relived every second. She'd felt so feminine and utterly desirable. He'd thought that aspect of life was over, but her kisses proved him totally wrong.

Matt was down the next morning before the sun rose. The kitchen was still dark.

He continued on to his car, not wishing to meet up with Jeanne-Marie this morning. He needed some time to get his head on straight. He stopped by the bakery on his way to the base of the cliffs. Once the car was parked, he quickly walked along the path until he came to the one he planned to try. He paused at the base and scanned the face. No other climbers out yet, which could make the climb more dangerous in case of trouble.

Yet wasn't that why he pushed himself? Taking harder and harder climbs as if determined to triumph in one area of life. If fate had a different ending in mind, it would only end the sorrow that much sooner.

Dipping into his resin bag, he coated his fingers. He didn't feel as driven today as the previous days. A challenging climb, not a dangerous one, was what he was seeking today. The pamphlets he'd obtained from the inn and the sports shop in the village rated the climbs. This one promised to be only moderately difficult.

Reaching for the first handhold, he thought about Jeanne-Marie. Would last night's kisses have changed things between them? Did he want them to?

Pausing for a moment between reaching for handholds,

he leaned his forehead against the cool stone. He was not getting entangled with anyone ever again. He'd made that vow when he'd buried Marabelle and Etienne. So what was he doing kissing Jeanne-Marie?

The sun hadn't yet risen high enough to show every nook and cranny of the cliff face, but there was more than enough light to choose the best way up the seemingly flat face. He wanted a short climb, to get back to the inn. See her again.

Climbing took concentration, an awareness of where he was and what his next move would be. Forcing other thoughts away helped him remain focused. Yet from time to time his attention lapsed and he wished he'd found out before he'd left this morning if the room was available next week. If she would have been glad to see him, or was feeling awkward.

This was as bad as being a teenager with overzealous hormones. He kept thinking about Jeanne-Marie. Last night had not been enough. He wanted more.

Reaching the summit sometime later, he lay back on the warmed rock and closed his eyes, immediately seeing her face. Maybe staying longer wasn't the wisest move he could make. But for the first time in a long while he felt alive. He didn't want to cut it short. The aching pain of loss had diminished. He would never forget, but he could move on. Just like people had said.

He remembered some of the comments Alexandre had made at the fair and laughed out loud. Then he remembered kissing Jeanne-Marie and almost groaned. Just thinking about her had him longing to get back to the inn to see her. He sat up and began eating lunch, gazing across the sparkling blue of the Mediterranean.

Despite his best intentions to segregate himself from the world, Matt was being brought out of the past and into the present. Each time they were together, Alexandre said something funny. And the hero worship he had was special. Matt dared not do anything to tarnish that. It was healing to find he could be a role model to an impressionable child.

It was Jeanne-Marie who had him thinking of kisses and caresses and wanting to spend time together, at dinner, sitting on the veranda. Wherever she was.

Jeanne-Marie sat at the desk, totaling all the figures for the past week. Three couples had checked out. Two more were due to arrive before dark. And the couple in the suite had left a huge tip, which she put right into Alexandre's college fund. When he grew up there'd be money for university, or whatever else he might wish to do. In the meantime, they were comfortable.

The numbers blurred and once again she was on the veranda reliving the kisses she and Matt had shared last night. Looking up and out to the sea, she again felt the sensations that had swamped her. Desire, heat, longing. She loved his kisses. She loved the feelings she had when he held her. Feeling as if she'd wakened from a long sleep, she relished every tiny aspect. She had thought about those kisses far into the night, unable to sleep as she fretted about her reaction. She'd been late with breakfast, barely having the first batch of warm bread out of the oven when guests came to the dining room.

Now she was alone and again the memory of his warm lips demanding a response from her captured her thoughts and wouldn't turn loose. She was still surprised at the delight that had splashed through her. Unable to wrap her mind around her own response, she brushed her fingertips across her lips. Was she ready to look beyond her life with Phillipe and into a different future than she'd once thought she'd have?

She heard a car in the parking lot and involuntarily her heart rate increased. Was it Matt? Wiping her hands on her khaki slacks, she watched the corner of the veranda, anticipating the moment she'd see him again. She'd missed him that morning. Almost laughing at herself, she remembered going straight to the reservation book before even starting breakfast.

He came around the corner onto the veranda and strode toward one of the open French doors. Stepping inside, he spotted her instantly. Jeanne-Marie caught her breath, forced herself to exhale and then smiled. The memory of their kisses sprang to the forefront. It was all she could do to bravely meet his eyes. He didn't have second thoughts, did he? She didn't know what to think when she realized he'd left this morning before she could see him.

"Good climb?" She was pleased her voice sounded normal. She hoped he didn't see signs of her rapidly beating heart.

"Excellent. Did you check reservations?" The intense way he looked at her convinced her he was also thinking of those kisses. No second thoughts. His dark eyes searched hers, his gaze touching on her lips.

She licked them nervously. "Yes. I was booked, but amazingly, around ten this morning, one of the reservations was canceled. You can stay another few days if you still want to."

He walked to the counter and leaned over it slightly. Jeanne-Marie saw the tanned face, the dark eyes focused on her with faint lines radiating from the edges. She could smell sunshine on him. Was he going to kiss her again?

"I do want. And we're on for tomorrow night?" His voice was low and vibrant. His gaze held hers and it was all she could do to respond to the question. Her fingers ached to reach out and trace those firm lips, test the strength of that strong jaw, feel the warmth of his suntanned skin.

She nodded. She had to clear her throat before she could speak. "I thought we'd leave around three, drop Alexandre off and then have an early dinner?"

"Works for me. Where is he?" He surveyed the room, then glanced out to the beach.

"He's at Pierre's house for the afternoon. Michelle and I trade back and forth having the kids. Today they're building a ramp for their cars to race. Marc's into woodworking and said he'd help the boys. I suspect it'll be more he'll do it and they'll be the ones clamoring to help."

"He likes those cars. Think he'll be a race driver?"

"I want him to be an accountant or something," she murmured. She couldn't look away. His eyes still held hers. She wished she didn't have the counter between them.

He laughed and her breath caught again. His laughter was rich and masculine and made him look younger, definitely happier. It was the first time she'd seen him laugh. Her heart ached to think how little he'd had to laugh about in the last two years. She smiled in delight, hoping he would find more to bring happiness in the future.

"He'll be what he'll be," Matt said. He reached out and touched her nose. "You can't keep him from doing what he wants, even if it's racing. If that makes him happy and being an accountant doesn't, which would you choose?"

"I want him to be happy. But preferably happy for a long, long time." She liked Matt's familiar touch. It made last night seem less like an aberration and maybe the beginning of something.

Two of the new guests arrived on the veranda. Jeanne-Marie could have screamed in frustration. Matt glanced over his shoulder, then told her he'd see her later and took the stairs two at a time. Jeanne-Marie turned to watch him before she greeted her guests. She wished she could shift into full innkeeper mode. But part of her couldn't let go of Matt.

She walked over to Michelle's house to get Alexandre before dinner. Visiting briefly with her friends, she and her son then walked home, with him talking a mile a minute about the ramp Pierre's father had built for their cars.

"And mine won almost every time. Pierre's going to get a new one so he can beat me, but today I won," her son explained on the way home.

"That's good. Next time maybe Pierre will win."

"Is Matt at home?" Alexandre asked when they reached the inn. "I want to tell him about the ramp."

"Yes, he's back from climbing." She wondered what he'd been doing since he returned. He had not come back downstairs after she'd checked in the new arrivals. "He's in his room, but you wait until he comes downstairs before talking to him. Do not disturb him in his room," she said.

"I won't 'sturb him, but he'll want to know about my ramp," Alexandre said earnestly.

"Nonetheless, you wait for him to come down."

Alexandre pouted and walked over to flop on one of the sofas in the lounge area.

CHAPTER SEVEN

JEANNE-MARIE prepared a thick soup and crusty bread for their dinner. By the time dinner was ready, Alexandre was in a better mood, but still impatient to see Matt. For that matter, so was she. She hoped it didn't show as much as it did with Alexandre.

"Tomorrow you're going to your grandparents' house for the night," she said as she set the small table in the alcove for their dinner.

"Can I take my cars?"

"Of course. Your grandfather will want to see them race side by side."

"Maybe we can go climbing. Do you think Matt would take me again?"

"Maybe." She wouldn't mind trying it herself again, as long as it was with Matt. Who would ever think she'd find anything redeeming in climbing rocks?

"Matt!" Alexandre scooped up his cars and ran to the kitchen doorway. "We builded a ramp and our cars went really fast." He hugged the man's leg and looked up at him, his eyes shining.

Jeanne-Marie looked as well, wondering if she had that same look of adoration her son wore.

"Fantastic, I want to hear all about it," Matt said,

stooping to be on eye level with Alexandre. "Did yours win?"

"Yes. But Mama said next time maybe Pierre's will win. But mine's really fast."

"Life is not always about winning, but it's great when we do," Matt replied, his gaze moving to Jeanne-Marie.

"We're having soup and bread for dinner," she said. "There's plenty if you want to eat with us." She held her breath, hoping he'd say yes.

The faint flush of color on her cheeks could have been from the stove's heat, or it could mean something else. Matt nodded and rose, walking with Alexandre to the small square table, three chairs on three sides and the fourth side pressed to the wall beneath the window that overlooked the garden.

In only moments, Jeanne-Marie had served them all and sat down opposite Matt, Alexandre in the center.

The boy talked as fast as he could until his mother said, "Enough. Eat before the soup gets cold. Then you can finish telling Matt about your racing adventures."

Alexandre scowled but picked up his spoon. "But Matt needs to hear."

"When you're done eating," Matt said. He looked at Jeanne-Marie. "Are you full again? I heard people climbing up and down the stairs."

"More than full. One couple has a baby they didn't tell me about. I hope it doesn't cry in the night."

"Do you not let rooms to babies?" Matt asked.

Jeanne-Marie nodded, watching to see if he liked the meal. The soup had been simmering all afternoon, so thick with vegetables and beef it was almost a stew. The fresh, crusty bread had been made that morning. It was a simple meal, but one she took pride in. He seemed to like it.

"If I know in advance, I usually give families with small children the end room above the kitchen. There's a small storage room separating it from other rooms in the back, so crying babies aren't so noticeable. But they have the room smack in the center of the front, flanked by two other rooms." She shrugged. "I'll have a better idea if it's going to work by tomorrow. Here's hoping the baby sleeps through the night."

"I'm all done," Alexandre said, tipping his bowl slightly so his mother could see it was empty. "Now can I talk?"

Matt smiled at his impatience. Just like Etienne had been. He flicked a glance at Jeanne-Marie, raising an eyebrow in silent question.

She nodded solemnly. "Now you may talk."

"I have to go to my grandparents' tomorrow," he said, almost bouncing in his chair. "Will you still be here when I get back? We could walk along the beach again. Or I could go climbing with you," he ended hopefully.

"Yes, Matt will be here when you get back," Jeanne-Marie said.

"You'll have fun at your grandparents', right?" Matt asked.

"Sure, we'll go have ice cream and play in the park and watch movies on television. They have a television. We don't. Do you have a television?"

"I do."

Alexandre's eyes widened. "That's cool. I wish we had a television."

"Think what a treat it is when you go to your grandparents'," his mother said.

"She says I look like my dad," he told Matt.

He looked up at Jeanne-Marie, a question in his eyes.

"He looks a lot like Phillipe did at that age from the pictures I've seen. I'm sure Adrienne is constantly reminded." She looked at her son and Matt knew she was constantly reminded of her husband as well when she looked at him.

Which was worse, to have purged his house of reminders or to be constantly reminded by just looking at her son?

"Maybe they can take me to ride horses so I can learn. Then I can come visit you, Matt, and ride your horses."

"Maybe."

Jeanne-Marie threw him a look that was difficult to interpret.

"What?"

"We're not coming to visit, so don't raise his hopes."

"You'd be welcome," he said. Thinking about it for a moment, he realized he'd like to have her and her son come to see where he lived, where he worked. What would they think of his family's enterprise?

"Do you want some more soup?" she asked, clearly changing the subject.

"Yes. And more of that delicious bread."

After dinner Matt suggested a walk along the beach. While he saw no benefit from lying in the broiling sun all day, he did like being by the sea. The air was fresh and invigorating. She wouldn't go without her son, which suited him. Matt was surprised to realize he enjoyed Alexandre's company.

"A short walk, perhaps. We have to get ready for Alexandre's trip," she said, hesitating.

"Instead of going later, shall we leave in the morning

and have lunch together in Marseilles before dropping Alexandre off at his grandparents'?" Matt asked.

Alexandre looked at him. "Are you going to Marseilles, too?"

"I'm driving you to your grandparents' place," Matt said.

"Yea!" Alexandre danced around. "And will you pick me up, too?"

"If it's okay with your mother." And with that, Jeanne-Marie knew nothing could be better.

"We need to return soon so Alexandre can take a bath before bed," she said an hour later when they reached the marina. Twilight was near. It would take a while to walk back along the curving beach to get to the inn.

"If I swim in the sea I wouldn't need to take a bath," the little boy said, running ahead, then running back to be with them.

"Would you read me a story tonight?" he asked Matt, slipping his hand into the man's larger one.

It was startling. The child was without pretension. He said whatever came into his mind. Holding his hand, Matt was swept away with a feeling of protectiveness toward the little boy. How unfair life had been, losing his father when so young. Who would teach him how to be a man?

The sun had set only moments before. Twilight afforded plenty of light to see. The soft murmur of wavelets against the sand was soothing. Stars had not yet appeared but undoubtedly would before they reached the inn.

With Alexandre between them, each holding one of his hands, Matt thought how like a family they must appear. The thought came more and more frequently. He railed against it. He was on holiday. That was all.

Looking over at Jeanne-Marie, he was struck by her air of serenity. Content with her life, happy with her child, she cast a spell over him. He wanted that serenity, that contentment.

"Can we go swimming after dark?" Alexandre asked as they approached the inn.

"Not safe," his mother replied.

"Not dangerous, either. It could be fun," Matt said. He'd love to go swimming with Jeanne-Marie, to see her sleek body in a swimsuit, to touch her, to kiss her again. To feel her body against his, skin to skin.

He took a breath and shook his head trying to dislodge the images.

She looked dubious. "Maybe."

"Can we?" Alexandre was thrilled at the thought.

Matt looked at Jeanne-Marie. "Why not?" He could think of a dozen reasons to go, all starting with his motivation for the swim.

"Okay, let's do it."

"Yippee!" Alexandre yelled and took off running for the inn.

In less than ten minutes they had changed and were at the water's edge. Suddenly shy, Jeanne-Marie hesitated to take off her cover-up. The swimsuit she wore was the one she wore all the time. It maintained her modesty, but she felt exposed wearing it in front of him. She knew she was self-conscious because of Matt. Good heavens, it was almost pitch-dark out.

"Hurry, Mama," Alexandre called, already up to his knees in the water.

"Last one in's a rotten egg," Matt murmured, dropping his towel and walking toward Alexandre.

In one movement, she drew off her top, dropped it and ran by Matt, splashing into the water seconds before he did.

She kept going until the water was up to her waist.

"Wait for me, Mama."

Alexandre swam out to her and grabbed hold of her shoulders. "This is fun."

There was enough light now from the stars and the establishments along the shore to give some visibility. It was an adventure, however, to find the water so dark. Normally it was as clear as crystal with the bottom clearly visible.

Matt walked over. "Refreshing."

"Cold, you mean," she said. It was cool, but pleasant. And the delight of her son made it well worth it.

"Since he can swim, why don't we paddle a little out and then back?"

"Okay."

"I want to swim next to Matt," Alexandre said.

Me, too, was Jeanne-Marie's immediate thought.

They swam a short way, and because of the gentle slope Matt could stand when they stopped. Alexandre clung to him while Jeanne-Marie trod water beside him.

"If you get tired, you can grab hold of me," he offered.

She was tempted.

"It's scary out here," Alexandre said, looking around.

"No different from being here in the daytime except we can't see," Matt said.

Jeanne-Marie brushed against Matt's arm as she was moving around. He caught her and pulled her close. Resting her hand on his shoulder, she felt the warmth of his skin even though the water had cooled the surface.

Clinging, she smiled at her son.

"We've never done this before, have we?" She dared not look at Matt for fear she'd forget Alexandre was here and be caught up in Matt's spell. Would he kiss her again?

"I want to go back," Alexandre said.

When Matt put his arm around Jeanne-Marie's waist, she gasped. He drew her against his sleek body, the cooling effect of the water evaporating. She stared at him, wishing she could see him better. Her heart pounded as every inch of her became attuned to him. Heat matched heat and had her aware of him like never before. Her hands skimmed against his bare chest, feeling the muscles, his skin heating when she rested her palm against him.

For a moment she wished Alexandre was home in bed and just she and Matt were swimming in the darkened sea. Touching, kissing.

"We should go back," she said in a low voice. If it had been the two of them, she knew nothing would have stopped kisses and caresses.

So slowly she knew it was an effort, he released her, trailing his fingertips across her bare back, sending shivers up her spine.

"Race you, Alexandre," she said to cover her confusion. In a moment she was splashed by the little boy's wild swimming technique. This was her reality.

When they reached the shore, Matt right beside them, Alexandre ran onto the sand. "I beat!" He danced around and laughed. "That was fun!"

As Jeanne-Marie slowly climbed out of the water, heading for her towel, she could feel Matt's gaze on her and wished she dared turn around to feast her eyes on him. A spotlight on the beach would have been perfect. But first things first. She had her son to think about.

"No warm sun to dry us off," Matt commented, standing near her, watching her as she toweled off her body. She glanced his way, captivated by what she could see of his broad chest and muscular arms. He needed a lot of upper body strength to lift his body by his hands on climbs. She wished she had the courage to reach out and feel that strength. She looked away, yearnings firmly squashed.

"Can we do that again?" Alexandre asked.

"Not tonight. Time you got to bed. Tomorrow will be a big day," she said, pulling on the short cover-up. She wrung water from her hair and then looked at Matt again, vaguely disappointed he'd pulled on a T-shirt. So much for fantasies in the moonlight.

The next morning Alexandre bounced on the backseat of Matt's car. He seemed almost more excited to be in Matt's car than about his visit. Going to Marseilles with Matt felt like a big adventure to her, so she could empathize with her son's excitement. They'd deliver Alexandre to his grandparents after lunch and then she'd spend the rest of the afternoon and evening with Matt. Anticipation built. She wanted to rein it in, but no matter how much she tried, she couldn't squelch her excitement.

It was not a date. Not precisely. They'd have Alexandre with them for part of the day. It was the kindness of a guest to his hostess.

She didn't believe that for one second.

After lunch at a family-style restaurant, they arrived at the small home on the outskirts of town where the senior Rousseaus lived. Matt parked in front.

"Shall I carry his bag in?" he asked, turning slightly in the seat to look at the house.

"No. I'll just be a minute," Jeanne-Marie said. She could just imagine what spin Adrienne would put on seeing her with Matt. She didn't want to force her into acting like a gracious hostess. She'd deliver Alexandre and let his grandparents spoil him. While she went on her own adventure. "Tell Matt goodbye."

In seconds she took her son's hand and headed up the short walkway to the front door. She rang the bell. When she and Phillipe came to visit, he'd always walked right in, but she didn't feel comfortable doing that, though the Rousseaus had told her time and again she didn't need to stand on ceremony.

"Ah, Alexandre, you're here!" Adrienne threw open the door and greeted her grandson with a bright smile and big hug. "I thought you might be here earlier. I called the inn to get an exact time and your clerk said you'd already left."

"We ate lunch with Matt," Alexandre said, turning to wave at the car.

Adrienne looked beyond them to the car, her smile fading. "I see. I thought he was a guest at the inn." She looked at Jeanne-Marie with worry in her eyes.

"He is. He offered to drive us here today. He has a friend in Marseilles also vacationing," Jeanne-Marie said, feeling guilty.

"So you don't wish to come in," Adrienne said.

"I don't think I should keep him waiting," Jeanne-Marie said. This was more awkward than she'd anticipated. What if Adrienne thought she was dating again?

In a way she was.

Her mother-in-law looked at the car again and then

shook her head. "Well, we've planned such fun things to do, Alexandre. If your mother's made other plans, we need to tell her goodbye."

Jeanne-Marie looked at her closely. "It's not a date," she said, not wanting to hurt her mother-in-law. She did, however, have the right to see anyone she wished. And if she did start dating again, it didn't mean she'd ever forget Phillipe.

Jeanne-Marie heard a car door shut and she looked back to see Matt standing by the car. She drew in a breath. This was harder than she wanted.

"I'll pick him up tomorrow around four if that's a good time for you," she said.

"Yes. Do you want to stay for dinner tomorrow?"

"Thank you, but I'd better return to the inn. It's full and I've already taken today off." Jeanne-Marie leaned over and gave Alexandre a hug and whispered she loved him in his ear. "Be good for Grand-mère," she admonished. She'd miss this little guy. But it was important he visit often. She started back for the car.

"Bye, Mama," Alexandre called. She turned and waved.

Adrienne urged Alexandre into the house and shut the door.

Matt opened the passenger door for her. "You okay?"

"I should have thought this through. I expect she has me married off with a bunch of other children, just seeing me in the presence of another man. It was harder than I thought. I don't want her to get the wrong impression."

Once he was behind the wheel again, he looked at her. "Would that be so bad? If you married again? You're young, could marry and have more children."

"She'll have no other grandchildren but Alexandre," Jeanne-Marie said. "Though if it ever did happen, she'd still have a part in Alexandre's life. I would never take him away from them—that's one reason I'm still living here rather than back in the States. I hope she'd love any other children I had. A child can't have too many people love them."

"She probably only sees the potential of your moving away, taking her only link to her son with you."

"That's the very reason I didn't return to the States when Phillipe died. I wanted to stay where he'd lived, let Alexandre know his father's family. And mine. But mine are more likely to come to visit here than the Rousseaus are to venture to America. Anyway, I didn't mean to burden you with family situations."

"It's still early—want to stroll through the Prado Seaside Park?" he asked.

"Yes. Fresh air and no worries." It had been a long time since she had had a day solely devoted to her own pleasures and she planned to enjoy it. And her companion.

They walked along the broad pathways, dodging in-line skaters, dogs and kids running and yelling. The park felt festive with colorful awnings and canopies, all manner of items for sale at the edge, from clothes and jewelry to fresh fruit and fish. Exploring each stall didn't give time for introspection or much conversation, which suited Jeanne-Marie perfectly. By the time they were ready to find a restaurant for dinner she was feeling carefree and happy.

Waiting for a table, she glanced around. She'd never eaten in this establishment, no memories to detract from her time with Matt. Soaking up the atmosphere, she committed it all to memory—to pull out in the winter months when she might be feeling blue. She'd have this happy afternoon to remember.

The maître d' seated them at a small table to the side. Perusing the menu, Jeanne-Marie was delighted with the choices of fresh fish. She loved fish, but didn't especially like the cleaning necessary to serve it at home. She smiled when she looked at Matt.

"What's that for?" he asked, putting down his own menu.

"You've given me a wonderful day. One to remember down through the years. Thank you."

"Nothing much."

"But perfect as it was."

"Perfection is hard to reach in this day and age."

"Not always. Where will you go next on holiday?" she asked, not wanting to dwell on the future, but curious if he'd say he'd come back.

He was staying another day or two. Then he'd be returning home. Next time he took a vacation, it likely wouldn't be to a sleepy town along the Med.

"I'll go skiing this winter in Gstadd," he said. "Do you ski?"

"I used to, but haven't since Alexandre was born. I was pretty good. Skiing's popular in California."

"I enjoy it."

"No desire to climb the peaks instead of skiing down them?" she teased.

He caught her gaze and held it. "I'm not completely devoted to climbing as I think Phillipe was. I like a variety of sports. Besides, climbing in winter could be very dangerous."

"Instead of only sort of dangerous?" she asked.

"Exactly." He shrugged and leaned back slightly, his gaze firmly on her.

The waiter came to take their order. When he left, Matt asked about her own plans for the rest of the summer.

"I have full bookings through August. Once school begins, visitors taper off. Until the Christmas break."

"Will you take a holiday in the fall?" he asked.

"Maybe, but just for a weekend. Last year we went up to Paris. I wanted to show Alexandre where his mother and father met. Now I'll be one of the families limited to traveling around a child's school schedule."

"Tell me your favorite place in Paris."

She smiled and told him about the Tuileries Garden and how often she and Phillipe had gone there. How last fall she'd shown her son all their favorite spots so he'd have some knowledge of his father's life. That led to reminiscences about their respective childhoods. The meal was served. The conversation continued, with each learning more and more about the other.

When it was time to leave, Jeanne-Marie did so with reluctance. Her special day was ending. She wished she could hold back time.

The drive back to St. Bartholomeus was quickly made, with little traffic on the highway. The inn looked especially welcoming with lights spilling from the large French doors onto the veranda. Her student employee had his nose in a book, as usual, when they walked into the lobby.

Rene looked up, blinking as if not sure where he was. "Home already?" Glancing at the clock, his eyes widened slightly. Jeanne-Marie looked as well; it was almost midnight. Much later than she expected.

"I'm sorry we're so late. No problems?"

"None." He put a bookmark between the pages and stood.

After he left, Matt looked at her. "I'll be leaving early on one last climb tomorrow. Breakfast at six-thirty?"

"Yes. Thank you again for a lovely day."

"I enjoyed myself, as well," he said. Then he kissed her.

She had been half expecting it—or hoping for it? She hoped all her guests were already in and not likely to walk through the lounge as she moved closer, thrilled when his arms came around her to draw her against him. His hard body pressed against her while his mouth wreaked havoc with her senses. She encircled his neck and kissed him back, reveling in the sweet sensations that seemed to lift her from the present into a dream time. A wonderful ending to a wonderful day.

She would not think about tomorrow being his last day. She would not think about the empty days ahead. She would not think about anything but the way his kisses made her feel.

Time seemed to stand still. The lights in the lounge faded. She was floating on passion and desire, hungry for more, buoyed by the waves of ardor of his kiss and the fervor of her own.

When he pulled back a scant inch, it was to ask, "Do you have to go to bed right now?"

She looked up at him. "What do you have in mind?" Her heart pounded. What would she say if he asked her to his room? She wasn't sure she was ready for that. Yet the way she felt, she was equally uncertain whether she could refuse.

"A midnight swim?"

The cool sea might be what was needed to keep her blood from boiling. This time there would be no little boy to chaperone. She smiled dreamily. "I think that sounds very daring and unlike me. Twice in a week! Yes, I'd love to join you there."

"Meet me back here in five minutes." He gave her a quick kiss.

"Okay." Another quick kiss.

She stepped back but he wouldn't let her go until he'd given her another kiss.

"Hurry," he urged.

Jeanne-Marie didn't need any encouragement. She didn't want to miss a minute with Matt.

Wading out into the water a few moments later, she felt young and carefree. Around the curve of the beach, close to the heart of the village, other revelers were playing in the water. Their laughter and shouts could be heard in the otherwise silent night. All the establishments along the beach were brightly lit as the celebration continued far into the night.

They swam side by side until the sound of the merriment in town faded. The gentle breeze refreshed. The water was cool, but not unduly so. It felt silky against her sensitized skin. Every sense was heightened just being with Matt.

"I don't have this at home," he said when they stopped swimming, lazily moving their arms to keep upright in the buoyant sea.

"And I don't usually come out after dark. It's magical. I love looking at the lights on shore and seeing them reflected on the water."

"You make the evening magical," he said, swimming closer.

Tentatively she reached her foot down. It was too deep to stand. If she could, would he kiss her again?

"Let's head back," she suggested, hoping when they

reached standing depth he'd want to do more than return to the inn.

They swam toward the beacon of the inn. When she reached waist-high water, she stood up and began wading toward the shore, leaning to one side to wring the water from her hair.

When she straightened, Matt was there. He brushed some of the hair back from her face, then cupped it and leaned in to kiss her. His palms were warm against her cheeks and his mouth a delight against hers. Stepping closer, she pressed against him, feeling the coolness of his skin heat where hers touched until it instantly turned hot. He wrapped her in his arms and held her closely. Skin to skin, mouth to mouth, she was in heaven. She felt the gentle movement of water move to shore and retreat, but only in an abstract way—her entire being was enveloped by Matt.

Longings and desire rose. She wanted this man. She didn't question falling for someone so fast. She could easily fall totally in love with Matt and be heartbroken when he left. But she couldn't stop their kisses if she tried. She couldn't stop her heart from opening to him, and wanting him with an intensity that startled her.

His mouth trailed kisses along her jaw and she tilted back her head to give him access to her throat. Hot kisses along the pulse point at the base, then back up to her mouth again. Her tongue danced with his. The heat seemed to escalate until she vaguely wondered if the sea temperature would rise.

His chest was muscular and hard against hers. His arms held her securely, firmly, lovingly. He was no more immune to the passion rising than she.

A passing speedboat raised a wake that washed them up to their shoulders, breaking the moment as they struggled for footing against the water's surge. She stepped back, laughing and breathing hard. Trying to see him in the dim light was difficult. He was merely a silhouette. But she knew he was there. Where did they go from here?

"I should go in." She needed to get ready for the morning. But she didn't want to leave him. Yet she knew she was not ready for the next step. Not that he'd said anything to indicate he wanted a next step.

"Morning comes early, I know." He turned and started walking toward their towels.

Disappointed, Jeanne-Marie followed. She dried off, wrapped her hair in the towel and donned her cover-up.

He had toweled off as well and pulled on a T-shirt.

Taking several steps toward the inn, she realized he wasn't going with her. She turned. "Good night, Matt. Thank you again for today."

He stood near the water's edge, barely visible.

"Good night, Jeanne-Marie. It was a good day, wasn't it?"

She caught the hint of surprise in his voice. "It was." She turned and walked back to the inn and straight through to her private quarters, her heart racing. She licked her lips, tasting salt water and Matt. When she shut the door behind her, she shook her head trying to dislodge the desire that simmered. They had no business kissing like that. She knew there was no future with them.

But, oh, for a moment she could dream of them sharing kisses well into the future.

Matt watched her go with some regret. He clenched his hands into fists, wishing he knew what was going on.

Her soft body inflamed him. Her guileless gaze when she looked into his eyes caused his own common sense to flee. Her mouth was sweetness and passion.

He had enjoyed the day. That was a minor miracle in itself.

Kissing her had driven all thought from his mind. Now sanity returned.

She was nothing like Marabelle, but she was gradually pressing out his memories of his wife.

Panicked, he turned and began walking toward the cliffs, leaving the inn, the town and the partygoers behind. The faint moonlight of a waxing moon gave enough illumination. His thoughts were torn. He couldn't forget Marabelle. She'd been his life's love. And his son. The ache of their loss would never go away.

Yet as he walked, he could hear the echo of Jeanne-Marie's laughter. See the way her eyes sparkled when they dodged that one kid on the bike who'd almost ran into them. She hadn't gotten angry, but excused him for his youthful exuberance. And commented on how agile they'd been. She'd been enthusiastic about the entire day, including the meal they'd shared before returning to St. Bart.

It had been a good day. Not what he'd expected when he'd come to climb the cliffs. For two years he'd lived in a kind of limbo. Today, he'd been involved.

When he reached that section of shoreline where rocks tumbled from cliffs above him, he turned to retrace his steps. He'd take one last short climb in the morning, then head for home.

Thoughts of home, of the work awaiting, began to crowd in. The break had been welcomed, but he had the company to run. It was time to end the holiday and return to his life.

* * *

Matt entered the kitchen the next morning, his mouth watering at the aroma that filled the air. Jeanne-Marie was baking cinnamon rolls and he could almost taste them from the cinnamon scent alone.

"Good morning," she said, scarcely looking up when he walked over to the counter where she was filling another pan. "Hot chocolate will be ready in a moment," she added.

"Good morning to you. I can pour my own hot chocolate if you like," he said, watching her. He'd like to kiss her, but wasn't sure if she'd welcome the gesture in the midst of working. If they didn't stop at one kiss, breakfast could be seriously delayed.

At her nod, he reached for a mug and poured the hot beverage. Leaning against the counter he studied her as she worked. It was like poetry in motion. Her hands rolled the dough, then swiftly cut it into strips to coat with the cinnamon spread and roll into tight wheels. They would expand when baked. Her concentration was complete.

"Can I help in any way?" he asked.

"No. Sit. I'll bring you a roll as soon as the first batch comes from the oven in about three minutes." With that she darted a glance in his direction, then looked instantly back at the task at hand.

"It's supposed to rain this afternoon," she said. "I would suggest being off the cliffs when the storm comes."

Matt nodded. He knew better than she how dangerous wet rock could be. If lightning was in the mix, storms could become lethal.

Despite his best efforts, she would not be drawn into conversation, remaining firmly behind the counter preparing the rolls, then moving to another kind of bread.

At that rate she'd have enough bread to feed the entire town of St. Bart.

Feeling vaguely dissatisfied, and yet unable to pinpoint exactly why, he left once he'd finished eating. She'd prepared him another box lunch, which he stuffed into his backpack before he headed out. The dawn sky was luminescent in pale pink. He found a short route to a ledge he'd try for today, eat one last time on Les Calanques, then pack and head for home.

The appeal of climbing had waned, he admitted as he stood at the base of the faint track left from previous climbers and considered the best route up. He would rather have spent the day with Jeanne-Marie, even if they just sat on the beach and talked. Though if it were to rain later, that probably wouldn't be feasible. Sitting together in the lounge, maybe lighting a fire in the fireplace to chase away the chill, talking, learning more about her wouldn't be bad, either.

"Forget it," he muttered, reaching out for the first protrusion and raising his body up with fingertips and toeholds only.

It took less than three hours to reach the ledge. An easy climb, just as he'd wanted for this last day. He stretched out on the narrow lip and pulled out the lunch she'd made. Still early to eat, he nevertheless munched the fresh bread, cheese and grapes. Already he was changing from vacation mode to business mode as he began to itemize all the things he needed to look into upon his return to work.

He looked toward St. Bart. He couldn't see the inn from this vantage point, but could see the farther end of town as it curved into the sea. Boats sailed in the water, which was more a steely-gray today than the normal blues and aquas. He studied the overcast sky. It looked as if it would start raining earlier than predicted. Finishing rapidly, he made sure he left no trace and began to descend, trying a different route for variety.

The first raindrops hit before he was halfway down the face. Seconds later a deluge poured down on him, water running down the face of the cliff, running into his own face, blinding him as it splashed into his eyes. Dusting his hand with resin only to have it turn to paste when it got wet did not give him the secure purchase he needed on the rock face. He made an extra effort for speed while not sacrificing safety. Maybe he should have remained on the ledge until the storm had passed. Waiting would ensure water wouldn't be sheeting on the rock, making each hold more treacherous than before.

Not able to wipe the water from his face, he shook his head again and again to clear his vision. Not that he saw much—wet rock, gray skies and, if he glanced down, the waiting rocky ground.

When he was about twenty feet from the base, he lost his footing. For a moment he hung by his fingertips, searching for a toehold to keep him in place. One foot found a tiny knob. Adrenaline spiked. He took a breath, feeling his fingers slip. The knob gave way. For an instant he stared dumbfounded at the rock face, slipping past him at an astonishing rate.

A split second of pain, then blackness.

CHAPTER EIGHT

THE RAIN CAME so hard it almost obliterated the sea as Jeanne-Marie sat at the registration counter catching up on bills and receipts. Once it began, it was as if the storm settled in over St. Bart. It poured for hours, a hard driving deluge. She hoped Alexandre was enjoying his visit and wondered briefly what his grandparents would do with him in the rain. From time to time she glanced up, wondering where Matt was. He couldn't still be climbing. He was too experienced to try it in this downpour, so he was probably holed up somewhere to wait out the rain.

It was almost time for her next guests to arrive. Too bad they were coming on a day like today. The beauty of the village and sea were hidden in the rain. It looked close to twilight, though it was still midafternoon. She would be leaving to pick up Alexandre as soon as Rene arrived.

She heard a car on the gravel of the parking lot and checked things around her. Everything looked warm and welcoming with scattered lights on. She took a registration card from the stack and placed it and a pen on top of the counter.

To her surprise a police officer entered. Suddenly her heart dropped. She blinked as fear flooded. She'd been through this once before. Mesmerized by the officer's solemn look, she tried to breathe but felt her breath catch in her throat. Matt—something had happened to Matt. No, please, not that!

"Madame Rousseau," the police officer greeted her. "One of your guests is a Matthieu Sommer, *n'est ce pas?*"

"Yes. He has a room here." She couldn't say anything else as her heart raced. *Please don't let him tell me Matt died,* she prayed.

"He was in an unfortunate accident today—he fell while climbing. He's being transported to a hospital in Marseilles. He asked to have you notified."

Her worst fear—yet not quite. He had not died from the fall. She had to catch her breath.

"Ah, then he's alive."

"*Oui,* and not happy from what I heard. But he did not wish you to worry when he didn't return today."

She gave a brief prayer of thanks and tried to smile. But the fear that coursed through her had her blinking back tears instead. "Thank you for letting me know. Is he badly hurt?" she asked. How far had he fallen? What had happened?

The man checked the small notebook in hand and nodded. "Broken arm plus scrapes and bruises and a concussion. He won't be climbing again for a while."

"Thank you for letting me know," she said to the officer. Her fear diminished only slightly. A concussion wasn't good. And a broken arm would slow him down. She couldn't imagine him injured. He was in such great shape.

The officer touched the brim of his hat and turned to leave. Then he turned back. "St. Mary's Hospital. On Girard Street."

"Thank you."

The police officer was crossing the veranda when the new guests showed up. Looking surprised and curious, they entered the inn. It took only a few moments to explain his visit, register them and show them to their room. Jeanne-Marie went through the motions like a zombie. Her every thought was with Matt. She had to go see him, to verify for herself that he was alive and going to recover. She didn't question why she felt that compulsion; she just knew she had to see him.

When she came back downstairs, she yearned to pick up the phone and call the hospital. It was highly unlikely they'd tell her anything. She needed to see him for herself. But she couldn't leave before Rene arrived.

Matt's fall was her worst fear. Made more immediate with the feelings that were growing. She didn't want to care for anyone the way she had Phillipe, but Matt had become so dear to her, so important, now she knew love had slipped in unawares. She pressed against the ache in her chest. Every instinct urged her to his side. Damn the responsibilities she had to see to first. She could hardly think of what they were, so intent was her longing to get to him.

She wanted to see him, touch him, reassure herself he was alive and would be all right. Looking at the clock she seethed with impatience. Rene wasn't due for another forty-five minutes. She didn't know if she could wait that long. Her poor Matt. She hoped he wasn't in much pain. Surely they'd give him some medication for any pain. How could there not be pain, he'd fallen off a cliff!

Or could they medicate with a concussion? She didn't know—only that she had to get to him as soon as she could.

Rene arrived promptly at three.

Two minutes later she relinquished the front desk and hurried to her car. She was going to see for herself that Matt would be all right.

The drive to Marseilles seemed to take forever. Each mile mocked her with the distance between them. It was nothing to the distance once he returned home. She'd deal with that later. Right now she needed to see him.

When she reached St. Mary's, she dashed in and asked for his room.

"He's still in surgery," the receptionist said after checking. "They had to pin the arm and stitch up some cuts. He'll be in recovery soon. Are you a relative?"

"No. But a very concerned friend," she said. "I really need to see him."

The receptionist nodded. "Second floor, west. There's a surgery waiting room there and you'll be called when he's conscious again."

She was closer, but still not with Matt. Jeanne-Marie took a chair in the waiting room, staring dumbly at the television that played softly in the corner. She saw nothing but images of Matt lying at the bottom of a cliff. She wanted to see him!

Who had found him? How had they gotten him to an ambulance? How badly was he injured if he needed surgery? The minutes seemed to drag by. Questions flooded. There was so much she needed to know.

"Madame Rousseau?" A nurse stood in the doorway.

"Yes." Jeanne-Marie jumped up.

"You can see Monsieur Sommer. In fact, he's asking for you."

She followed the nurse to Matt. He was hooked up on tubes, his right arm in plaster, cuts and bruises all over his skin, with a white bandage across an area from above his ear to above his left eye. A couple of stitches on his cheek and another set on his left arm.

"What happened?" she said, going to stand right by his bed, reaching out to take his free hand, gripping it in her need to feel him, to know he was alive. "That police officer scared me to death. I thought for a second—" She wasn't going to say it. He was alive. He would be all right eventually.

"Sorry." He was slightly groggy, staring at her with eyes darkened with pain.

"I'm just glad you're going to recover. You are, right?"

"So they tell me." He frowned. "I didn't mean to fall. I didn't. Maybe I wouldn't have cared a year or so ago, but not now. I didn't mean to fall."

She squeezed his hand gently, nodding. "Of course you didn't. It's okay. You're going to be all right and back to climbing in no time." Her heart squeezed in sorrow. She knew how hard it was to go on when a loved one died. She would never ever think of Matt trying to end his life. But he might have felt that if chance had him falling, it was meant to be. She was so glad he no longer felt that way.

He closed his eyes a minute, then opened them. "My head hurts, my arm's throbbing, I ache all over. I banged up one knee."

"But you're going to be fine, give it time."

He closed his eyes again.

"I'll leave you to get some rest," she said, not wanting to go, but knowing he needed rest to heal. She could leave, having seen him. She didn't want to, but she could.

His hand gripped hers tighter. "No, don't go. It's just

I'm seeing double, so it's easier not to have my eyes open." He looked up at her. "I don't think I'll fall asleep just yet. They just woke me up from the anesthesia."

"Five more minutes, then we're taking him to his room. You can visit there," the nurse said, coming to his bed and reaching out to gently dislodge Jeanne-Marie's hand so she could take his wrist in her hand. "How do you feel?" she asked, checking his pulse.

"Like I fell off a cliff," he muttered.

Jeanne-Marie hid a smile. Grumpy she could handle. Some of her fears eased. She wanted to believe he'd be better in no time. Or as long as it took for his arm to heal. She hoped there would be nothing lasting from the fall. She couldn't bear to think of him as incapacitated in any way.

When the nurse left, Jeanne-Marie took his hand again and squeezed it gently. "Oh, Matt, you could have been far more injured or worse."

"Hey, I could have but I wasn't. The storm came in earlier than I expected. I was almost to the bottom. Short fall. I didn't mean to, truly!"

"I know."

He stared up at her for a moment. "It's important you know that."

"I do know it. Close your eyes and rest. I'll stay a bit longer."

While Matt was being moved to a private room, Jeanne-Marie went to call the Rousseaus to let them know she would pick Alexandre up later than originally planned. Then she went to find Matt's new room.

She peeped around the door and saw him lying in the hospital bed in the pristine room. The rain continued outside the window. His precious face was battered, scraped and bruised. His right wrist had a bandage around it. When he turned to see who had entered, she saw both eyes were growing black.

He smiled when he saw her and her heart flipped over. He looked as if he'd been in a fight—with the other guy winning.

"You stayed," he said.

"I said I would," she replied, coming in, pulling the visitor's chair near the bed and sitting. That put her slightly below him. She hungrily searched his face, noting the damage, thankful he was still alive. Unwilling to examine feelings that had been on a roller coaster since she received the news, she smiled and asked, "Feeling any better?" Wishing she dared reach out to touch him as she had earlier, she clenched her hands in her lap. To Matt, she was merely a friend nearby when he was injured.

"Worse than before, actually. The more the anesthesia wears off, the more I feel every inch. And all of me aches to one degree or another," he said with a wry smile. His gaze never left hers. It was as if he were drawing strength from her.

"What does the doctor say?"

"The doctor says the headache will go away and so will the double vision, but they're not sure exactly when."

"Close your eyes. You can talk with them closed."

He gave a half smile. "Guess I can," he said, closing both eyes.

"So when can you be released?" she asked.

"In a couple of days, depending on what happens with the concussion. And then only if I have a place to go where someone can watch me. Damn inconvenient, if you ask me."

"So you'll be going home?" Of course he would. Sick people liked the comfort of their own homes while recuperating.

"I don't know. It'd be a long ride. Right now I don't feel like sitting up, much less doing it for hours on end."

The silence stretched out. He was so still, she wondered if he'd fallen asleep. She didn't want him to return home. She wanted him to stay with them.

Then she said, "You could stay in Alexandre's room. He has twin beds, not the biggest in the world, but I think you could manage."

"Thanks for the thought, but I don't think I'm going to be the best patient in getting well."

She laughed. "What man is? Still, it might be better for you than going home alone. I mean, if you want to. I know Alexandre can be talkative, but I could keep him away. And you could sit on the veranda during the day and see the other guests. Read. Do whatever you want until you feel up to the long ride home."

He opened his eyes and looked into hers. "I'd be an extra burden. You said you had your life just as you liked it."

"It wouldn't be that much. I'd be happy to do it." Her heart began to race knowing just how happy she'd be to do it. She loved him. Anything to help would be a joy. And he'd stay just a little longer. She wouldn't have to say goodbye so soon.

She stared at him, her heart pounding. She loved Matthieu Sommer. Oh dear, when had that happened?

"I'd have to pay my own way."

Jeanne-Marie recognized pride when she saw it. "Fine. Maybe I'll charge in a bit extra for the waking service." She was on tenterhooks in case he realized her feelings. Had she given herself away? Only by dashing to his side when he was hurt. Please let him think of that only as a kindness.

She loved Matthieu Sommer and he had never given her any encouragement—except for those hot kisses, the joyful days at the fete and in Marseilles, and being so kind to her son.

Closing his eyes again, he nodded. "Works for me."

She considered that, knowing she'd never charge him for anything she could do for him. "What arrangements will you need?"

"I'll check with the doctor as to when he'll release me and for any special instructions. Probably say I shouldn't go climbing again for a while."

"Wise advice," she said. Why was she destined to fall in love with men who risked life and limb for a fleeting challenge of rocks and height? She looked at him and her heart melted. She caught her breath, realizing if he'd hit his head harder, if he'd fallen from a greater height, she could have lost him forever.

Not that she had him. He would be returning home as soon as he was able.

Then what was she going to do?

He opened one eye. "Thank you for coming, Jeanne-Marie."

She smiled, her heart turning over. "I wouldn't have stayed away for anything." And she hoped he never knew the full truth of that.

Just then a man knocked on the half-opened door and entered.

"Whoa, surprise, surprise. I rushed over here thinking you'd be at death's door, and here you are entertaining a pretty woman. Maybe I should fall off a cliff," he said, smiling at both Matt and Jeanne-Marie.

"Paul, what are you doing here? I thought you left for home already," Matt said.

"Couldn't resist the nightlife here, plus we only did one climb together. I called to see if you wanted to do another together before heading home and learned you were here. I couldn't head for home until I made sure you didn't need anything. I see you don't." He grinned at Jeanne-Marie.

"This is Jeanne-Marie, hostess of the inn I'm staying at. Jeanne-Marie, my climbing buddy, Paul Giardanne," Matt said.

"Explains why you didn't bother staying in Marseilles. *Enchanté, mademoiselle,*" Paul said.

"It's Madame Rousseau." Jeanne-Marie rose and nodded to Matt. "I'll call later for an update. In the meantime, rest and get better. Nice to meet you, *monsieur.*"

"Wait. Paul won't stay long." Matt glared at his friend.

"Not at all. Just wanted to make sure you were alive and kicking. Which I see you are. I'll be in town a couple more days. Do you need anything?"

"No. I'm good. Or will be once my arm heals."

"And the assorted scrapes and bruises. Man, did you slide down the face?"

"Feels like it."

Jeanne-Marie didn't know whether to stay or go. He'd asked her to stay, but if his friend visited for long, she wouldn't be needed.

"Okay, then. I'll check back tomorrow. I'll come when you don't already have company. Take care, man. *Madame.*" He bid them both goodbye.

"I could have left and let him visit with you," Jeanne-Marie said, standing by the bed.

Matt reached out to take her hand in his left one.

"I'd rather visit with you. What time are you picking up Alexandre?"

"Later. After I leave here."

"How did you fare without him around?"

"I missed him, of course. But he was only gone overnight and last night I had plenty going on." Had it only been last night they'd gone swimming in the sea, kissed in the shallows?

She sat gingerly on the edge of the bed, conscious of his hand holding hers, his thumb tracing patterns against her skin. Her heart skipped a beat. She watched him as he closed his eyes again, wishing she could soothe his headache, erase all his pain. She'd be devastated if anything happened to him. She couldn't go through something like that again.

"So tell me what exactly happened," she said.

Listening to him talk about the slippery rock and how close he had been to the bottom did nothing to alleviate her fear. When he talked about how short a time he estimated he lay at the bottom until other climbers found him, she gave up a prayer of thanks. He could have been lying in the rain for hours if they hadn't arrived.

Learning of Matt's accident had scared her to death. Maybe it was best for him to return home. At least she could always think of him alive and well and not be hurt herself when he hurt, not be worried about him if he was late coming home.

Jeanne-Marie did not tell the Rousseaus about Matt's fall and her visit to St. Mary's. They welcomed her as they always did, and Alexandre was full of talk about his playing in the room that had once been his dad's and the ice cream cone Grand-père had bought him when they went out. He could talk nonstop, she knew. But better to fill the time with that than have them question her about Matt. She would always consider them dear relatives, Alexandre's grandparents. But she also realized she was a separate person, who would have to live her life on her own terms, not those of her in-laws.

They wouldn't understand her falling in love with someone else. Not yet. Maybe never. So she kept that secret to herself.

Soon after stopping, Jeanne-Marie and her son were on their way back to the inn. It was during the car ride that she told him Matt had been injured and would be coming to stay with them a short time until he felt better.

How long did a concussion take to heal?

Alexandre was concerned about the fall and peppered her with questions. He wanted to go see him, but they were almost home by then.

"You'll see him when he comes," she ended, not able to answer more than half his questions. "He's going to share your room, so you have to be extra careful to be quiet when he's sleeping. And don't leave your toys on the floor where he can trip over them."

"I will be the bestest boy ever!" he vowed.

She laughed. "You already are."

Two days later Matt called to say he could be discharged if she was still willing to have him stay. Jeanne-Marie insisted she was. They had spoken on the phone a couple of times each day, but she had not returned to Marseilles. There was too much going on at the inn to take another day away.

She'd gone back and forth in her mind over the last two days, worried she was going to get involved more than was wise if he stayed. Yet how much more in love could she fall? She'd savor every moment together. She wanted to see him.

His room had been cleared and was now occupied by an older couple from Nantes. She already saw him in her mind every time she walked into the kitchen. Staying with them for a while—how long, days? Weeks?—would leave lasting memories of every space in the inn. Still, he'd be there a little longer. Right now, that's all that mattered.

Matt made the trip to the inn that afternoon without much discomfort. He wished he could have made it in a car, but the ambulance was comfortable and he knew the driver and paramedic would be able to convey him to the inn with minimum effort. His arm ached and his headache was relentless, pounding in time with his heart. He had trouble eating with his right arm in the cast. Closing one eye helped in the vision department, but with both closed he only felt a slight dizziness. He needed his head to heal first! This was driving him crazy.

But none of it mattered. He was going to Jeanne-Marie's until he was better. At least until the concussion healed. Which one doctor estimated might be as long as a couple of weeks. Two more weeks to hear her laugh, see her brown eyes look into his. And in the evenings after Alexandre went to bed, who knew what might happen?

The men got him out of the ambulance and into the wheelchair he'd be using until his balance stabilized. He wore a new set of clothes Paul had brought for him. A bag held his climbing gear. The gravel parking lot was bumpy, but once on the stone pathway the ride smoothed out. He wasn't complaining; at least he was away from the hospital. And almost home.

He smiled wryly. This wasn't his home. But it felt

the closest to anything home should feel like in a long time.

Entering the lobby, Matt looked around and felt a pang of disappointment. Rene was behind the desk. He looked up, startled to see the paramedics pushing the wheelchair.

"Wait there," the young man said and swiftly ran around the counter and back to the door to the Rousseaus' apartment.

In only seconds Jeanne-Marie hurried out, followed by Alexandre.

"You're here," she said, wiping her hands on the apron around her waist. "I didn't expect you this early." She smiled and went to touch his shoulder. Matt wished she'd kiss him, but with everyone standing around staring at them, she probably didn't feel it was appropriate.

He was surprised at the disappointment.

Alexandre came to his other side, looking at his chair and then at him. "You have black eyes," he said. "Do they hurt?"

"Not as much as my arm," Matt said, feeling a bit better for seeing the little boy.

Alexandre studied the cast, then smiled. "I can draw a happy face on it if you like."

Matt's arm ached and his head pounded so badly he could hardly stand it. Still, he appreciated the boy's thought. "Sure, maybe later, okay?"

The paramedics checked to make sure he had all his belongings, then left.

"Are my clothes up in my room?" He looked at Jeanne-Marie.

She shook her head. "I've already brought them down to Alexandre's room. Maybe you should rest before dinner. I can come get you when it's time to eat. Or would you rather go to bed? I bet the trip was tiring."

The spark of interest at the thought of her helping him dress for bed proved he was not as badly injured as he thought. His mind immediately envisioned the two of them alone by the bed. Only, the clothes didn't get put on, but came off.

He groaned.

"Oh, no, what hurts?" she asked, leaning close to study his face.

He opened one eye and looked at her. Could he pull her into his lap and give her a kiss?

The pain meds were messing with his mind.

"A rest would be good. I didn't realize how bumpy that highway was until I felt every jarring inch of it."

Alexandre patted his arm. "I'm sorry you got hurt," he said.

Jeanne-Marie looked him over with a critical eye. "You look exhausted behind these colorful bruises dotting your face."

"They're purple," Alexandre offered helpfully.

Matt laughed, wincing when the pain in his head upped a notch.

"Your bed's ready now. Lie down for a while. Then we'll see if you want to get up for supper or have it there. I was planning soup again."

"Sounds good to me. I don't have much of an appetite, probably due to the medication. And eating isn't the easiest thing."

"Me and Matt can sleep together in my room," the little boy said.

"I think maybe for the first couple of nights you'd better sleep in with me."

"But I want to sleep with Matt," he protested. "There're two beds. And I'll go right to sleep at bedtime. He wants me to sleep in with him, don't you, Matt?"

"Let him sleep in there, Jeanne-Marie," Matt said,

unable to resist those pleading little-boy eyes. He wondered if he objected, would Jeanne-Marie consider letting *him* sleep in with her? Sounded like a better plan all around.

"We'll see how it goes," Jeanne-Marie said.

"Did you have fun at your grandparents'?" Matt asked Alexandre. Now that the anticipation had worn off, he was tired. He was pushing things, but he wanted to be safely ensconced in bed before letting down his guard. He wasn't sure he'd be able to get up again today.

"Yes. I got to have ice cream and go for a ride with my grand-père. And swinged on the swing in the backyard. I played with my cars and we watched my dad on TV 'cause it was raining."

"Your father was on TV?"

Alexandre nodded. "It's DVDs. He smiled a lot. I like him."

"Of course you do," Matt said, wondering how it would be to have only a DVD of his dad. His father had died only a few years ago. Matt was thirty-two and he still felt he'd had his dad for too short a time. How awful would it have been to lose him before he could even remember him?

"Do you have DVDs of your dad?" Alexandre asked, leaning against his leg.

Matt nodded. "A few, with my wife and son."

"Does your arm hurt? And your face? Your eyes are dirty, they're all black."

"Everything hurts."

"Maybe Mama should kiss and make it better. She does that if I get hurt," Alexandre said very solemnly.

Matt smiled in spite of himself. He looked at her. He wouldn't mind Jeanne-Marie kissing him until he was better. It would take a lot of kisses for him to feel better.

"Let's go. We'll talk kisses later," she said, taking hold of the handles on the wheelchair.

"Deal." Matt closed his eyes as she told Rene she'd be in the back if he needed anything, and then pushed the chair.

"Do you need help getting into bed?" she asked a moment later when she stopped in the middle of the two twin beds in Alexandre's bedroom.

Matt opened one eye and surveyed the distance. Lying down would be a relief.

He made an effort and was prone on the comfortable mattress in only seconds, feeling the tension fade as fatigue won.

"I'll probably sleep through the night."

"Except when I need to waken you to make sure you're not going into a coma. I'll check back around six to see if you want to eat anything."

"Fine." With his eyes closed, he didn't see her leave, but could feel how empty the room was the next minute. Slowly he gave in to sleep.

"Wake up, Matt. I'm here to check on you," Jeanne-Marie said, coming in and dimming the light sometime later.

She touched his forehead, her hand cool and soft. Slowly she trailed it off, then pushed back his hair and reached down to press her cheek against it. "No fever that I can tell," she said. "Are you awake?"

Matt breathed in the scent of her. Too bad he was injured; he could get to enjoy attention like this. When she didn't say anything for a moment, he opened his eyes. She looked worried. He hadn't meant for that.

"I'm awake. I know who the president is," he said.

She laughed softly, brushing his hair back.

"That feels good," he said, eyes closed.

"I'm wondering if I can really let Alexandre sleep in here with you. You'd do better with complete rest."

"Let's see how things go. He'd be disappointed," Matt said. He'd give a lot to keep the boy from ever being disappointed.

"Do you want to eat something? I can bring it here."

"If it's soup, put it in a mug. I can drink it." He lifted the arm with a cast. "It's hard to eat left-handed."

Jeanne-Marie went to get his dinner, wondering if she'd lost her mind offering to let Matthieu Sommer convalesce at her home. She wanted to be more than friends. She wanted him to kiss her again. Maybe even talk about the possibility of seeing each other again. She wanted him to grow to care for her. Maybe not as much as his wife, but something more than friendship.

Was she wishing for the moon?

Alexandre was thrilled to have him stay, but she was playing with fire. Every time she saw Matt—injured as he was, the bruises on his face, the scrapes on his arms—she wanted to hold him close, share her vitality to aid in healing. She wished she could hold him, kiss him, let him know she ached with the fact he was so injured.

He ate quickly and then lay back down.

"I'll wash up and be back with Alexandre in an hour or two. Sleep if you can," she said.

Once the kitchen was clean, she quickly bathed Alexandre and then helped him into his pajamas. "Quiet when we go to your room," she said. "Matt might be asleep."

He was. She whispered to Alexandre as she tucked him in bed.

"Mama, you should kiss Matt to make him all better," Alexandre whispered back.

Jeanne-Marie tousled her son's hair. "I think time will do that," she replied.

"Please, Mama."

"Okay, now go to sleep."

She crossed over to Matt, leaning over to kiss him gently on his forehead. She wished she had the right to do that all the time.

Jeanne-Marie walked through the lounge to the veranda. Hearing the sound of the sea soothed her. She sat on one of the chairs and gazed out where the water was, hoping the peace would penetrate her jumbled thoughts. Too dark to see much, she let the soft breeze caress her as she relaxed and thought about Matt. She was falling more and more in love with him despite her best efforts to resist. She didn't have only herself to consider, but her son. Alexandre didn't miss Phillipe because he'd hardly known him. But he could get attached to Matt, and when he left, it would cause great sadness. She wanted to protect her son as much as she was able.

Yet since the accident, each time she looked at Matt, she saw possibilities. And complications. More complications than she could deal with tonight. Time for bed.

She entered Alexandre's bedroom. Both were sleeping. She went to Matt and shook him gently. "Matt?" she said softly.

He groaned and opened one eye. "What?"

"Just checking on you. Do you know what day it is?"

"The day I wanted to sleep through. I'm fine, Jeanne-Marie. Go away."

She nodded and left.

Once in the night she checked on him again, and found him just as grumpy.

The next morning Alexandre didn't come for breakfast

at his regular time. Jeanne-Marie saw to her guests, then went to his room. She could hear the two of them talking before she reached the door.

"Anyone ready for breakfast?" she asked, knocking on the door before opening it.

Matt had put a couple of pillows behind him and was halfway sitting up. His cast rested on the covers. Alexandre perched on the narrow space between Matt and the edge of the twin mattress. They both looked at her when she entered.

"I'm ready, if Matt is," Alexandre said, hopping off the bed.

"I'm more than ready," Matt said. "I could eat half a dozen eggs. The sleep really helped. And being away from the hospital."

Once breakfast was over, Jeanne-Marie suggested Matt might like to sit on the veranda. It was a pleasant day and she took a couple of moments to sit beside him. Alexandre had his cars and quickly began playing near the sand.

It was an idyllic setting, one that could lead to foolish hopes of them making a family together. Only, they were her foolish hopes. Matt hadn't even tried to kiss her since he'd returned. He'd get well and leave.

And she'd be left alone again.

CHAPTER NINE

MATT HAD MOVED to one of the lounge chairs on the veranda. Sheltered from the hot sun, he could enjoy the warmth without becoming uncomfortable. It felt good to be outside. The sea washed against the shore. Alexandre talked to himself as he played with his cars. Matt turned his head slightly to look at Jeanne-Marie, then couldn't look away. The feeling of contentment slowly faded as awareness rose. Time seemed to stand still. Despite his battered body, he wanted her. He wanted kisses and caresses and to make love all night long. Being around her made his senses soar as they never had before.

Just thinking about brushing his fingertips over her soft cheek had sent spirals of desire coursing through. He wanted to pull her into his arms and kiss her as if he'd never let her go.

Finally looking away, he tried to block the temptation with thoughts of work. He'd have to check in soon. He'd planned to be back by now. The fall had been a wake-up call. He could have died. That would have been tragic. When had he changed his mind from being willing to take his chances with fate to a strong desire to live a long life?

He still missed his wife and son, but Jeanne-Marie had brought him new reasons to embrace life.

Yet one day he would grow old and die. What would happen to Sommer's Winery then? It was a legacy to the future. The Sommer family future. He had his cousins. They would take over if he was out of the picture.

But he'd like a son of his own to pass the land to. He missed Etienne. He'd thought never to have another child, but he was young enough. If he found someone to build a life with. If he dared risk his own heart.

Very quickly a new routine was established. Jeanne-Marie prepared breakfast for her guests each morning. Then she sat with Matt and Alexandre as they ate at the table in the kitchen. After cleaning the kitchen, she'd join them on the veranda where Matt spent most of the day, resting, talking, watching the sea and laughing at the nonsense Alexandre often said.

When he wasn't resting or talking with them, however, Matt was on his phone to his office. The first day he'd been there, Jeanne-Marie had overheard him talking with an aunt, reassuring her he was going to be fine, minimizing the extent of his injuries and promising to let her know when he'd be returning home.

"I need to be able to sit long enough for the drive," he'd said.

And be able to see, Jeanne-Marie thought. But he had not told his aunt that part of his injuries.

Jeanne-Marie came to cherish those hours on the veranda. Often Matt had his eyes closed, but each day he felt stronger, the headaches began to diminish and by the end of the week the double vision was a thing of the past. They talked about everything under the sun. She learned about his cousins, friends, goals for the winery. And he questioned her about her parents, siblings, friends. When he mentioned a favorite food, she made a mental note to fix it for him. When he mentioned he liked blue, she made an effort to wear blue clothes.

Alexandre relished having so much attention. He would come and lean against Matt to discuss some important aspect of his day, or clamor to know when they'd go climbing again.

"I never fall," he told Matt.

"I rarely fall," Matt returned. "It was foolish of me to go in the rain. Remember that."

"It's not raining today. Can we go today?" Alexandre asked one afternoon.

Matt raised his cast. "I can't climb until I get this off."

"And build up your strength again," Jeanne-Marie murmured. "Alexandre, you can go climbing another time. Don't pester Matt."

"I know how," he said solemnly.

"Well, you sure have more experience than you had before. But I'm not sure you know how," his mother said.

"I do. I did good, didn't I, Matt? I didn't even fall."

"You did fine."

Jeanne-Marie did her best each day to deflect the subject of climbing, though with Matt as a constant reminder, Alexandre brought it up constantly.

By the end of the week she was getting tired of his constant pressure to go climbing. It had been a mistake to let him try. Now after one successful—easy—climb, he thought he could tag along with Matt.

"Let's go swimming," she suggested.

"Can Matt go?" he asked.

"Not while he has the cast," she said.

"Then I want to stay here," Alexandre said.

"How about I go walking along the shore, and you can splash in the water and cool off?" Matt suggested.

Twice during the week, Jeanne-Marie had to let them go off without her as she'd had guests to attend to. She'd watched them walk side by side, knowing by his position that Matt was leaning over a bit to hear Alexandre. He was so good for her son.

Despite his own loss, he seemed to enjoy being with the boy.

But it was the nights that Jeanne-Marie loved. After Alexandre was in bed and Rene had left, she and Matt would sit on the veranda and talk, kiss, be foolish together. Twice they'd walked along the shore in the moonlight. His knee was no longer giving him problems, and he'd never injured his mouth.

She felt closer than ever and so in love she could hardly see straight. He'd never said anything, but surely he had to feel something. His kisses were all a woman could want. His caresses inflamed her. His words of passion set her imagination on fire.

If he had been feeling one hundred percent, would he have pushed their involvement further? She wanted more than he gave. Yet maybe he didn't feel the same way and kisses and caresses were enough.

He never spoke of the future.

And she never stopped thinking about it.

On Wednesday Jeanne-Marie received a phone call from her in-laws asking if they could come and spend the next day with Alexandre. She was happy to invite them, but after she hung up she began to worry about what they'd think when they saw Matt. She had not told them about his injuries, or that he was convalescing here.

What would they think when they found out? Keeping

it a secret now seemed awkward. It wasn't that she didn't want them to know, precisely. Well, maybe. But only to avoid any disappointment. They loved their son. She had loved him as well. But life truly did move on. She hadn't thought she would fall in love again. Or have to keep it a secret.

Phillipe had made no secret of his love for her from the first moment they met. Matt was so different.

She didn't like complications. But she was not yet confident enough to declare her love when he had not hinted himself.

Yet, could any man kiss like he did and not feel something?

On Thursday morning Adrienne and Antoine arrived at ten.

Matt was sitting on the veranda when they arrived.

They seemed surprised to see him there, but greeted him cordially. Then turned questioning looks in Jeanne-Marie's direction.

Jeanne-Marie had told him and Alexandre at dinner last night that they would be coming. And she'd admitted they didn't know Matt was convalescing at the inn.

He knew they would be even less happy to see him if they knew the thoughts he was beginning to have about their son's widow.

"We thought we'd walk around the town for a while, then have lunch and spend the afternoon together at the beach. I know he likes to build sand castles. We'll be back before dinner," Adrienne said.

"Do stay for dinner," Jeanne-Marie said.

"Or I'd be happy to take everyone out for dinner," Matt said.

Jeanne-Marie looked at him, then nodded. "That would work, too."

The older couple looked at each other. "I suppose," Adrienne said slowly, searching Jeanne-Marie's expression as if trying to see if there was anything to learn.

Jeanne-Marie gave her son a quick hug. "Mind your grandparents," she said. She smiled at Adrienne. "I know he'll be good."

"Of course, he's Phillipe's son." With that they were off.

Jeanne-Marie sighed. "He's half mine," she said to their retreating backs.

"I think the comment was made for me," Matt said.

She shrugged. She'd tried so hard to act normal around Matt. Had Adrienne picked up on her feelings? She turned and looked at him, her heart skipping a beat. She could look at him all day. And now that he was healing, his amazing good looks were resurfacing. She no longer felt a pang of sorrow at his battered face. He was bouncing back and would be as good as new before long.

The longer Matt stayed, however, the more she dreaded his departure. Could she let him go without telling him how she felt?

And if he ever came to love her, how would she tell Adrienne and Antoine?

"Jeanne-Marie?" he said, coming to stand beside her.

She smiled at him. "We have the day to ourselves," she said. "What would you like to do?"

His expression was serious. He brushed back some of her hair from her face, letting his fingers linger. "I'm going home tomorrow. I've been away too long. I only meant to be gone a week."

Her heart dropped. Clinging to the vestige of her smile, she tried to absorb the news and not wail in denial. "Of course. You do have a vineyard to run." She turned, but he caught her arm, holding her. She kept that insipid smile on her face and looked at him.

"So what would you like to do on your last day?" she asked.

"Walk around the town, maybe have lunch on the patio at Le Chat Noir, dinner at Three Sisters? It'll take me all day to drive, so I need to start early in the morning."

"Early breakfasts are my specialty." Tomorrow morning! Less than twenty-fours hours left. She couldn't bear it.

She had to wring every memory she could from the time left. And pray she wouldn't completely fall apart when he left.

"Too bad we can't go swimming. I liked that," he said, his fingers gentle against her arm. She wanted to lean into him and hold him and never let go.

"Me, too. Let me freshen up and we can take that walk."

She went to her room, closed the door and moaned in the pain. She'd known in her head he'd be leaving. But somehow she couldn't believe it. Now it was time.

Matt stayed on the veranda, gazing out at the sea. Boats sailed across the bay. He glanced at the cliffs. Maybe he'd come again to test himself against them.

He had to return home. His fall had cemented his commitment to life. Granted, he would always miss his family. But there was more living for him to do. He'd work with his cousins and build the winery up to a world renowned producer of fine French wines. He would spend more time with his aunt and uncle. His father's brother was the only link he now had to his dad.

And he would take each day as it came, see what wonders he could wring from it like Jeanne-Marie did. He owed her so much. Her and Alexandre.

He couldn't help but smile when he thought of the little boy. He was charming without knowing it. Precocious sometimes and still just a short time away from being a baby. Matt would miss him.

And he'd miss Jeanne-Marie.

"Ready," she said behind him. She'd changed into a pretty pink top that went well with the khaki pants she wore. She'd donned dark glasses against the sun's glare. He wished he could see her pretty eyes.

"Let's walk down on the sidewalks, have lunch and then come back along the sea," he suggested.

"Fine." She fell into step with him as he headed for the small town of St. Bartholomeus. The festive air from *La Fête de la Victoire de 1945* was missing. But colorful awnings still shaded sidewalk cafés. The displays in the shops were eclectic and enticing. He wanted to visit the sporting store one more time, check out some of the climbing paraphernalia. Not that he would be doing any climbing soon.

He took her hand. She laced her fingers with his. It felt right to be seeing the town one last time with her. Would she ever consider coming to see the winery?

Did he want to continue a relationship with Jeanne-Marie once he left St. Bart? He might not return for many years. There were mountains to climb, other rock formations he wanted to try.

Yet the thought of saying goodbye bothered him.

"You're sure you're ready to drive all the way home?" she asked as they walked along.

"The headaches are completely gone. Every once in a while I feel a twinge. Good reminder to focus on what I'm doing and how worse it could have been."

"Focus?"

He looked at her. "I was distracted."

"I thought the rain made the rock slippery."

"It did. What I lost sight of was how fast the storm was moving in."

"Oh."

He could tell her he'd been thinking about her. But to what end? He found himself thinking about her most of the time lately.

They window-shopped. Entered the sporting shop and browsed the climbing gear.

"Looking for anything special?" she asked.

"No, just looking. For such a small town, this is a well-stocked store."

"Caters to the reasons a lot of people come here—the sea and the cliffs."

He'd enjoyed both.

"Ready to eat?" he asked sometime later.

"Yes."

He glanced ahead; they were near Le Chat Noir. Then he spotted Madame Rousseau sitting at a sidewalk café reading a book.

"Isn't that your mother-in-law?" he asked.

Jeanne-Marie nodded. "Where're Alexandre and Antoine?" She looked up and down the street.

"I don't see them. Maybe in one of the shops?'

When they drew opposite Adrienne, Jeanne-Marie pulled her hand free and went to the low railing separating the café from the rest of the sidewalk.

"Adrienne, where's Alexandre?" she asked as soon as she was close enough for the other woman to hear.

Adrienne looked up. “He and Antoine went off. He was telling us how he could climb and I guess he wanted to show Antoine.”

“They went on a climb?”

“Hardly. I’m sure they went on a gentle ramble. But Alexandre was so delighted his grand-père was here and could see how he could climb, Antoine said he’d go with him. They’ll be back soon, I’m sure. It’s not like he can really climb a cliff, is it?”

“He climbed a short one.”

“He’s only five.”

“It was very easy,” Matt said. “And I understand your husband is an accomplished climber. I’m sure they’ll be fine.” He looked at Jeanne-Marie. “Don’t worry.”

“Easy for you to say. What if Antoine forgets he’s so little, thinks he can do more than he’s capable of?”

“Antoine’s hardly dressed for serious climbing,” Adrienne said. “They’ll be back before long. Hungry for lunch, if I know little boys.”

Jeanne-Marie looked back toward Les Calanques.

“We could walk back and meet them if you like,” Matt said, picking up on her uncertainty. “I’m sure they’ll be fine. His grandfather knows what little boys can do.”

“Antoine’s been climbing for decades and never fallen,” Adrienne said, glancing at Matt’s cast.

“We’ll eat lunch, then if he’s not back, we can walk back along the main trail to meet them.”

“I think we should go now,” Jeanne-Marie said.

“Antoine wasn’t going to climb, just see where Alexandre had climbed and spend some time with him,” Adrienne said, rising and tucking her book into her large purse. “I’ll go with you. We can all eat lunch together that way.”

Jeanne-Marie knew Alexandre's grandfather would never do anything to harm him, but she still wanted to make sure they were both okay.

Matt reached out and she put her hand in his. That seemed so right. She ignored Adrienne's frown when she saw they'd reached for each other. Jeanne-Marie didn't have time to worry about that right now. She wanted to make sure her baby was safe.

"I'm glad you came," she murmured as they hurried down the main street heading for the cliffs.

"He'll be all right." He squeezed her hand slightly and continued their rapid pace.

"He's all I have. I can't lose him, too."

"Don't be dramatic. He'll be fine, and probably as hungry as a bear when we find him," Matt said. He knew she was scared, but he couldn't imagine the older man putting the little boy in danger. He was probably giving Alexandre some special time together by letting him show his grandfather where he'd climbed.

Jeanne-Marie wanted to race across the distance and find Alexandre, assure herself he was fine. Once they left the town behind, the pathway became rocky and uneven, slowing them down. She would not help Alexandre if she sprained an ankle. She looked at Matt.

"Your knee holding up okay?"

"I'm fine."

She couldn't help scanning the cliffs as they approached. Adrienne kept harping that Antoine wouldn't have climbed today, but Jeanne-Marie couldn't help but be fearful she'd see her son halfway up some sheer cliff, already envisioning him falling to his death as his father had. Matt was an accomplished climber and he'd fallen. How easy it would be for Alexandre to fall. *Please, God,* she prayed, *keep my child safe.*

"Where are they?" she asked. The minutes ticked by. They scoured the pathway, looking to the left and right in case Alexandre and his grandfather were off to the side. From time to time they had to scramble over rocks. Where were they? They were quite a distance now from St. Bart.

They passed others hiking back toward St. Bart and asked them if they'd seen the older man and young boy. They had not. Jeanne-Marie was sick with fear.

"Stop." Matt pulled her to a halt and waited for Adrienne to catch up. The older woman was breathing hard and now looking worried.

"I can't believe they would have come this far. We must have missed them," she said.

"We need to think this through and not rush off with no plan," Matt said. "I'd thought we'd run into them by now, but it appears they went farther than I would have."

"Or returned by the sea and we missed them," the older woman insisted, looking behind them as if expecting her husband and grandson to appear.

"Are we at the spot we climbed?" Jeanne-Marie asked. "It all looks the same to me."

"Not quite. It's just ahead."

"Then I say we go on to see if they're there."

"If the hikers didn't see them, either they left the path or they returned home before we left and we've missed them. They could have gone along the sea as Madame Rousseau said and be back at the inn wondering where we are."

"They would've gone back to Adrienne," Jeanne-Marie said. "Antoine would have taken them all to lunch."

Adrienne nodded. "I agree they'd have come for me before lunch."

"I suggest we begin looking off the main path, where there are side paths that have gentle scrambles. We have a man in his fifties and a five-year-old child. He would not take the child up the face, so they have to be somewhere on the flat, but maybe off this path," Matt said reasonably.

Five minutes later Jeanne-Marie recognized the gentle slope they'd climbed a couple of weeks ago. No sign of Alexandre. Where was he?

Then Matt stopped abruptly. "Wait, listen!"

The faint cry seemed to float in the air, directionless. He tilted his head to hear better. Jeanne-Marie almost held her breath. It was Alexandre.

Matt looked up and scanned the cliff.

"*Mon Dieu,* he's there." He indicated a point about thirty feet up the cliff a few yards beyond where they stood. Alexandre peered over a ledge. There was no sign of Antoine Rousseau.

"He climbed it again," Matt said. "I wouldn't have believed it."

"Where's Antoine?" Adrienne sounded frantic as she came up and clutched his arm. She scanned the cliff in all directions. "I don't see him."

"Alexandre, we see you. Wait there, do not move," Matt yelled up. "Wave if you hear me, but do not move from where you're sitting."

The little boy waved his hand. "I can't get down. I don't know where to put my feet. Matt, can you tell me? Grand-père is sleeping."

A small blue object flew from the ledge, bounced against some outcropping and landed at the base.

"My car!" Alexandre leaned over watching the toy bounce down the cliff.

Jeanne-Marie stared in fear. She could scarcely breathe. She wanted to fly to her child, yet her feet couldn't move. "Get back!" she screamed. She looked at Matt. "How did he get up there? How could he? The other day you had to show him every handhold."

"Apparently so did Antoine. It really is an easy climb, Jeanne-Marie. Now I'll talk you up. You've done it before. It's the same place."

"But you were with us. I can't climb this cliff." Her eyes returned to Alexandre. He seemed so little against the immense cliff. She wanted to cry. Instead Matt pulled her along to the area directly beneath the ledge. He was scanning the face, studying the rocks and crevices.

Jeanne-Marie yelled up to Alexandre, "Stay back from the edge, sweetie. We'll come get you, but move back."

"I lost one of my cars," he wailed.

"We'll find it once you get down. Get back!"

Matt needed only a second to plan what to do. "I don't see his grandfather, but something's wrong. He wouldn't take a nap. *Madame,* you must go back to the village to get help."

"No, I need to know if Antoine's all right," Adrienne said. "Alexandre, where is Grand-père?"

"He's sleeping. He won't wake up." The little boy peered over the edge.

"Get back against the cliff," Jeanne-Marie yelled. Her heart pounded with fear, her eyes unable to leave the sight of her precious little boy high above her on a rocky ledge.

"You have to go for help, *madame*. Find the constable

and tell him there's been a climbing accident. He'll bring rescue workers. Go, speed is of the essence," Matt instructed Adrienne. "Be sure to tell them we need a medic. And be careful; we can't afford to have you slowed down by being injured. I think maybe your husband had a heart attack."

"Oh, no, Antoine!"

Matt looked up again, studying the cliff face. "The sooner you bring help, the sooner we can get to him," Matt said with what patience he could muster. It was an easy climb, but still a challenge for a child. Had he been in perfect condition, he could scramble up in five minutes and bring Alexandre right back to his mother.

"I can't climb," he said aloud. "My arm will not hold my weight. You'll have to do it, Jeanne-Marie."

She turned to look at him in astonishment, tears glistening on her cheeks. "I can't climb, I'm too afraid. You have to go. He's so little. Please, Matt. I need you to rescue my son."

CHAPTER TEN

"I WOULD GIVE my fortune to be able to do that, but I can't. Not won't, but physically cannot. It's an easy climb…you've done it already. You can do it again. But it still needs both hands and feet, and my arm prevents me from going. You'll have to climb up, stay with Alexandre and wait until rescue comes. The men who come will be able to get you down with no trouble."

"I can't." She turned and looked at the cliff with horror on her face. Fear pounded through her. All she could think of was how Matt had guided her up and back the last time. She couldn't do it on her own.

He caught her chin and brought her face around to his. "Yes, you can. This is an easy climb—a five-year-old did it. You've done it. I'll guide you every inch from the ground. We'll take it slow and you'll be up with him in no time. You need to check on Antoine, too. When the rescue workers arrive, you two will be the first down. You can do this. Trust me, I would never put you in harm's way."

"If I fall, Alexandre will have lost two parents."

"Look at me. You will not fall. I can see a clear way up from here. I'll tell you every move to make."

"You know what you're doing and you fell. I have

climbed only a few times, never on my own. I could fall and get killed."

"Or you can climb up the way I tell you and be with your little boy."

She stared into his eyes, clinging with hers, as if hoping to draw confidence from his gaze. Tears stopped and a certain resolve took their place.

"I'm scared out of my mind," she said in a wobbly voice.

"I know. But you can do this. Think of Alexandre. He needs you. Trust me, Jeanne-Marie, I would never let anything bad happen to you."

"Mama, come get me," her son called.

Jeanne-Marie and Matt both looked up—Alexandre was leaning over the edge again.

"Get back, I'm coming," she yelled. Taking a deep breath, she looked back at Matt. Recklessly she pulled his head down and kissed him. "For luck," she said when she stepped back. Turning before she could change her mind, she walked to the base of the cliff. Looking up, it seemed endless. She tried to breathe, but fear clogged her throat.

"Move to your right about four feet. See the rocks jutting out from the base?" Matt asked, coming beside her and pointing to the protrusions.

"Yes," she said.

"Look here." He pointed to some others higher up. "Step up there, reach up for this one and hold on with your hand. Okay, good. Now lift your left foot and reach for the rock about ten inches up. Good. Now move your right hand up to grasp that rock a bit to your right."

Step by step he directed her through the climb. It was an easy trail, and as she climbed, she concentrated on the calm instructions Matt called. She'd done this before. She didn't find it fun, but it was not impossible. Slowly but steadily she moved up the slope.

Matt watched carefully, scouring the cliff, looking for the easiest way for her to get to Alexandre. Once her foot slipped and Matt caught his breath. She could not fall. Please God, do not let her fall. She quickly put her foot on the outcrop of rock and found a new handhold. In less than five minutes, she reached the ledge, pulled herself on it and swept Alexandre up in a fierce hug, drawing him back against the cliff that rose so high behind them, away from the edge, out of his view.

Matt turned and leaned against the wall. His heart pounded. He'd never felt such fear when he was climbing, but he worried every second that she would fall and be injured or worse. He felt he'd aged five years in five minutes. Yet she'd done it. He'd known she could.

Pushing away, he walked out several yards to look up. He couldn't see anyone, but could hear her soft voice murmuring to Alexandre.

"Is Antoine there? You two okay?" he called up.

"Yes, but he's unconscious and his color's not good. He's breathing, but his lips look blue—can't be from cold, he's in the sunshine."

Coming down would be harder than going up—especially for Alexandre. On their climb he'd been right beside the boy, ready to catch him in an instant if he missed a step. He wouldn't risk the child or the mother on their climbing down on their own. He had to bide his time until the rescue people arrived to see her safely down. God, it was terrifying when you saw someone you loved in danger.

Loved? He closed his eyes tightly. Loved. He loved Jeanne-Marie. The fear he'd felt for her safety made it all come clear. He'd been reluctant to leave; only pressing business matters had finally decided on his departure in the morning.

Now he didn't want to leave at all. Duty called. His heart had been captured again. He hadn't expected to ever fall in love again. He couldn't realize his love for her only to have her fall from a cliff. The ironic turn almost made him sick.

Her voice came down. "I've loosened his collar, but he doesn't respond when I shake him. It must be a heart attack."

"Yes. He's not in danger of falling over the edge, is he?"

He heard some scraping, then Jeanne-Marie's head peered over the edge. "I moved him back, but I don't think he's going anywhere. You remember how wide the ledge is and it has what looks almost like a shallow cave at the back. I'll try to get him out of the sun, but he's heavy, and I don't know if I'm doing any damage moving him."

"No visible injuries?"

"No. Alexandre said they just climbed up, and Grand-père was breathing hard and then lay down." She looked out across the sea. "I see the same view from my house. There's nothing special about this. I still don't see why people risk their lives."

"We can talk about that when you get down. You did a good job and I know Alexandre will forever remember his mother came to his rescue."

"Thanks to you. I'm still scared out of my mind. They'd better have ropes to get me down so I can keep my eyes closed the entire way."

He laughed, wishing he could have spared her. Wishing he could have been the one to rescue her son. As climbs went, this one was very easy.

Trying to gauge when Madame Rousseau would return with help, Matt sat on a boulder and watched the edge of the ledge wishing with all he had he could be there with them. Jeanne-Marie and Alexandre weren't to be seen, but he heard the murmur of their voices. How long would it take the older woman to convince the local Search and Rescue group to mobilize? He hoped not long.

The afternoon continued. The sun was hot. The breeze from the sea sporadic. His head began to throb again. He was not fully recovered from his own fall. What would he have done if Jeanne-Marie had fallen? He didn't want to think about that.

He wished they'd brought water. Probably Alexandre wished for food. He looked back down the path, but no sign of anyone.

Then he heard the sound of a powerful boat rounding the spit of land separating them from St. Bart's bay. In only a moment he saw several men standing on the large boat. The driver brought the boat close to shore and three men jumped out, coils of rope over their shoulders. A young policeman led the way.

With a few succinct words, Matt outlined the situation and urged them to get the woman and child down first.

Jeanne-Marie peered over the edge.

"You'll be down in no time," Matt called up.

The men were efficient, scrambling up the rock as if it were a walk in the park. And true to his word, in no time Jeanne-Marie and Alexandre were on the ground.

Matt helped them untangle themselves from the ropes that had belayed them down, then swept Jeanne-Marie into a tight hug. His chin rested on her head, his eyes on Alexandre. "You two doing all right?"

"I lost my car," Alexandre said, looking around.

"How's Antoine?" Matt asked, unable to let her go.

"The men were strapping him on the stretcher, then they'll let him down," she said, clinging as tightly as he was holding her.

They watched as the Search and Rescue men began to lower the stretcher on its journey down. Two men held the ropes at the top, one accompanied the stretcher lest it get caught on some rocky protrusion. In no time Antoine was on the ground. Jeanne-Marie and Matt went to stay with him while the other men made short work of descending.

"The boat'll be faster and easier on him," Matt said, watching as they carried the stretcher to the waiting boat.

Once aboard, the SAR men verified the three of them could make it back to St. Bart on their own, the boat pulled back and swiftly headed for St. Bart.

"Thank you," Jeanne-Marie called. "Tell his wife we'll be along as soon as we can."

"I see my car!" Alexandre exclaimed, running a short distance to pick up a blue object. Sadly he studied it and then came back. "It's broken."

"Thank God it's only the car that was broken," she said, hugging him quickly.

"I didn't fall like my dad or Matt," he said, looking up the face of the cliff. "But it was really scary, Mama, to be alone when Grand-père went to sleep. I wanted Matt with me. He's the best."

"He is, but unless he's there, you had better never climb a rock again!"

Matt took her chin in his hand and kissed her. "I was scared to death for you," he said.

"Are you kissing Mama?" Alexandre asked, coming to stand beside them both.

"I am." Matt stooped and hugged Alexandre and kissed the top of his head. "And I'm kissing you because you're safe."

"Oh." He smiled at Matt. "Are you proud of me? I showed my grand-père how I could climb. He said he was proud of me. Only then I couldn't go down."

"Going down is the hard part, remember. You were smart to stay there until a grown-up came."

"Yes, my mama!"

Alexandre reached out for her hand, Matt took the other. For a moment Jeanne-Marie was as happy as she'd ever been.

When they reached the beach, they veered off the path and walked on the damp sand. Alexandre raced ahead.

"No lasting harm, I think," Matt said, watching him.

"Kids are resilient. I may never recover, however," she said.

"Me, either," he said.

She looked at him. "Why's that? As you said, it wasn't that big a challenge. If your arm was healed, you'd probably scramble up it in a heartbeat."

"I have an entirely new perspective on things."

"What do you mean?"

"I'll tell you later." He glanced down at her and squeezed her hand slightly.

"I'm so glad you were here. You knew exactly what to do."

"I'm glad I was here as well."

The inn came into sight. Alexandre was already running up to the veranda, none the worse for his afternoon on the ledge.

"I'll need to call the clinic to see how Antoine's doing. And if he's conscious, find out what in the world he was thinking letting Alexandre climb."

"My guess, he knew the child had done it before, and he was there to supervise. If he hadn't had a heart attack, they'd have been back for lunch with Alexandre thrilled to have climbed with his grandfather. Antoine probably wanted to recapture what is now lost with the death of his son."

Jeanne-Marie called the clinic as soon as she reached the inn and learned Antoine had been stabilized and then airlifted to a hospital in Marseilles. The diagnosis was a heart attack, but he'd been awake and lucid before leaving the clinic. The hope was he'd recover fully.

Putting down the phone, she smiled tentatively at Matt, who hovered nearby.

"He's going to recover?" he asked.

"They think so. This sure isn't the vacation you envisioned, I bet."

"Hey, glad I was here. I would hate to think of you going through something like this on your own."

"I never want to think of going through another day like today."

"I'll take you and Alexandre out tonight. Le Chat Noir's your favorite, I have it on good authority."

"Then a walk back along the beach?"

"Yes." Between now and then he had some serious thinking to do.

Jeanne-Marie bathed Alexandre, then put him down for a nap, citing his busy day and the dinner in the offing that night. He was asleep in less than five minutes. She then went to take a long shower, washing away the grit and dirt, trying to wash away the memories of that horrible few minutes when she saw her son on the ledge with no apparent way to get down. She didn't want to relive the climb. Matt had seen every handhold and toehold and he'd been right; it was easy enough for a five-year-old. Still, it would never rank as a favorite hobby with her.

Matt—he'd been what she'd clung to during the climb. His voice, calm and assured. His vow he would let no harm come to her, his confidence in her ability to reach her son. He'd been there for her at the most crucial time.

She thought about him as she donned a pretty sundress. She owed him more than she could ever repay. And he deserved her best at dinner. She almost wished Alexandre could go and visit Michelle or another of her friends with children for the evening. Then she chided herself for the thought. Her precious son was safe and it would be a long while before she'd feel comfortable with him away from her.

Thoughts spiraled back to Matt. Did he mind that Alexandre would be going with them? He seemed to like him. He was always kind, always had time for him. Not many men would want to spend their vacation with a five-year-old.

There was no question Alexandre adored Matt—especially after their climb together. That had been all he'd talked about ever since that day.

Ready at last, she went out to the lounge area, disappointed not to see Matt there. She walked to the French doors and there he was, sitting on a chair near the far edge of the veranda.

"You look lovely," he said, rising.

"Thank you. I can get us some sandwiches and lemonade for lunch, if you like. To tide us over until dinner."

"Just a snack'll do. I'll come with you but let's eat out here."

They made the sandwiches together, bumping into each other, laughing, working in harmony.

Eating alfresco was a favorite part of living by the beach for Jeanne-Marie. She did it often and was pleased Matt seemed to like it as well.

Finished, replete, the heat of the afternoon making her a bit sleepy, she leaned back in her chair, content with the day and the way things had turned out. Now if she'd only hear her father-in-law was going to recover fully, everything would be perfect. Or almost perfect. Matt was leaving in the morning.

"Jeanne-Marie?"

Slowly she looked at him.

"I was going to wait."

"For what?"

"To ask you to marry me."

"What?" She sat up at that, totally shocked.

Matt rose and came to kneel by her chair. "I was going to wait until tonight when Alexandre was asleep and Rene had gone home. When it was just you and me. I love you, Jeanne-Marie. That became abundantly clear today when I couldn't scale the hill with you but felt your fear and uncertainty. The awful thought came—what if you fell? I couldn't imagine living through a loss like that again. I knew then the feelings I've felt over the last weeks were more than those for a friend. You have captured my heart. I never thought I'd love again. I never wanted to live in fear of something happening to someone else I love. But today proved I don't always get what I want."

"You never said you were starting to care for me. We haven't even dated. Are you trying to protect us or something? Did today make you think I can't cope on my own and need a keeper?"

He laughed. "No, you're the last person who needs a keeper. Today made me vividly aware that I couldn't imagine my life without you in it. I want you for my wife. I don't want to leave tomorrow without knowing you'll be part of my life. I know this is fast. We haven't known each other long. But sometimes it doesn't take long—to find the perfect life partner. I've found her and want to spend all my time with her—you."

She caught her bottom lip between her teeth, trying to assimilate all he was saying. Her heart blossomed. He loved her? She loved him. It was fast. It also felt right.

"I want to see you every day, eat your amazing breakfasts, hear your laughter, see your smile, touch your silky skin. I want you to be part of my life," he said, his eyes holding her gaze, the sincerity shining through. How could she have thought him stern? He was so wonderful she couldn't believe it.

She reached out and touched his cheek, her eyes growing moist.

"Today when you went up that cliff, all I could think of was what if you fell? What if you were hurt worse than I was? What if something happened and you died? I knew at that moment that I couldn't go on if that happened." He took her hand in his and kissed the center of her palm, wrapping his fingers around, relishing the touch of her skin, wanting more than anything to draw her into his embrace. But he wanted her answer first!

"I have a son—"

"Whom I already love. He's a precious child and I would be honored to have a hand in raising him. In the Loire Valley, here, wherever we live. Come, my love, make a family with me, grow old with me. Let me love you until the end of time."

Before she could open her mouth to give him an answer, he pulled her into his embrace and kissed her as they both tumbled to the veranda.

Jeanne-Marie felt like she was floating. She moved closer into his embrace, letting the love she'd kept hidden blossom and shine. She loved this man and he said he loved her.

"Mama, Mama, why are you on the floor kissing Matt?" Alexandre asked, running out from the lounge.

They pulled apart, sat up and looked at the little boy.

"I've asked your mother to marry me and come live with me in my castle. Would you like that?" Matt asked, opening his arm for the child to join them.

"Can I come, too?"

"Of course, I wouldn't take her without you." Matt scooped him up with his good arm and faced Jeanne-Marie. "I'm waiting to hear her answer," he told Alexandre. Both of them looked at her.

She laughed and reached out to touch Matt's face again, free to do so, knowing she could touch him whenever she wanted—forever. "I love you. I would be honored to marry you and come and live in your castle. As long as we can vacation here by the sea. And how many children do you want?"

"A houseful. No onlys for us."

"I think that can be arranged." She looked beyond him at Les Calanques and grew pensive. "I never thought I'd fall in love again." Looking at him, she smiled brightly. "But look what they brought me. How lucky can one person be?"

"Ah, *ma chère,* I'm the lucky one. I lost my family and now found a new one. One I'll love and cherish forever. You'll be the happiest woman on the earth if I can help it."

"I already am! I love you, Matthieu Sommer, and always will."

"Me, too," Alexandre said, smiling happily. "Now can you take me climbing again?"

ONE WEEK WITH THE FRENCH TYCOON

CHRISTY McKELLEN

This one's for my beautiful, witty and fiercely clever sisters-in-law, Kat and Buffy. Thank you for being the sisters I never had and welcoming me so warmly into your family. I love spending time with you. Here's to spending many more fabulous weekends in London together.

Formerly a video and radio producer, **Christy McKellen** now spends her time writing fun, impassioned and emotive romance with an under-current of sensual tension. When she's not writing she can be found enjoying life with her husband and three children, walking for pleasure, and re-searching other people's deepest secrets and desires.

Christy loves to hear from readers. You can get hold of her at www.christymckellen.com.

CHAPTER ONE

Arriving in Amalfi—a most lively and dramatic town in which to begin your journey...

WHEN INDIGO HUGHES had spent long hours daydreaming about her walking holiday along the Amalfi Coast of Southern Italy, *this* wasn't exactly what she'd envisioned.

Luggageless—after the airline had inexplicably sent her backpack containing her carefully organised walking gear to goodness knew where instead of Naples—and apparently dispossessed, because of a foul-up on the computer with her hotel booking, she was now facing the reality of spending the first night of her much anticipated holiday sleeping rough on the streets of Amalfi.

Whilst she wasn't averse to roughing it—she'd travelled to enough festivals and partaken in enough camping trips for that not to be an issue—she'd been looking forward to falling into a comfortable bed after a crazy week of late nights and early mornings, and was not in the mood to laugh this off.

'But my ex-boyfriend booked a room in this hotel

months ago,' she explained again to the receptionist, her voice now projecting the disconcerting characteristic of a crow with a sore throat.

The intimidatingly poised receptionist pursed her blood-red lips and tightened her arms across her impressive cleavage. 'I'm sorry, *Signorina.* As I said, I have no record of your booking and we are fully booked. If you had the documents to prove it, or even the credit card it was booked with, I could perhaps do something for you, but as it is…' From the look on her face, she clearly wasn't keen on having someone as scruffy as Indigo messing up her beautifully appointed five-star hotel reception desk whilst also challenging her competency.

Panicky heat rushed to Indigo's face. 'As *I* explained, my *ex*-boyfriend booked the room so I don't have the credit card or documents. I assumed a booking reference number would be enough.'

The woman's helpless shrug, then her overemphasised shift in eye contact to the next person in line, tipped Indigo over the edge of frustration into fiery indignation. But before she could draw breath there was a movement behind her and a tall man in a beautifully cut casual suit stepped forwards to stand next to her at the desk.

'Pardon, mademoiselle,' he interjected smoothly, his fresh, spicy scent hitting her nose at the exact same moment his eyes locked with hers.

Indigo had never related to the expression of being 'swept off her feet' by a man before, but that was exactly how she felt right now. As if the power of his presence had physically lifted her into the air, her internal organs quivering as if she were in free fall. She gazed up at him, his unusual combination of whisky-brown eyes and sandy-blond hair keeping her transfixed as her pulse beat an enthusiastic rhythm in her throat. But apparently she didn't capture his interest in the same way because, after giving her a curt nod, he turned sharply away, bringing her back down to earth with a thump.

'I have a reservation,' he said to the receptionist in a deep, smoky, French-accented voice, which made Indigo think of the actors in the Gallic art house films she'd been so in love with during her college days.

Lounging against the desk, he held up his smartphone so the receptionist could see the screen and type the booking reference into her computer.

Indigo looked from one to the other in disbelief. She seemed to have been well and truly dismissed.

Something she'd become rather too familiar with recently.

Before she could open her mouth again to point out that they were both being utterly rude and that she wasn't going to be ignored like this, the receptionist shook her head and looked up at the Frenchman, her expression projecting a lot more contrition than when she'd dealt with Indigo.

'I'm sorry, *Signor*, I don't have a record of your booking.'

'That's not possible. Check again, please,' the man replied in a tone that clearly brooked no argument.

Indigo watched with a sense of self-righteous vindication as the receptionist typed the number in again, then checked something else on another screen, her shoulders stiffening as she finally accepted there was a problem with the booking system.

She seemed a little pale when she looked back up at him. 'My apologies, *Signor*,' she breathed. 'I don't know what could have happened. It appears there was a glitch with the computer and I've given your room away. I only have the honeymoon suite available now, but it would be my pleasure to let you stay there tonight. We will correct the mistake by tomorrow and I will have your original suite available for you then.'

Indigo frowned as she twigged what was going on.

'Hang on a second. Why didn't you offer *me* the honeymoon suite? I was here first!' she protested, feeling a cocktail of humiliation and umbrage warm her face again.

The woman's gaze slid to hers. 'Because the gentleman booked a *suite, Signorina*, so this room is more in his...*category*.' She gave Indigo a tight little smile as if to say, *That's not the word I was grasping for, but you get the message*.

'Okay—' the Frenchman began in his smooth, lyrical accent.

But even the strength of his charisma couldn't keep the bubble of anger from rising through Indigo's body.

'Really?' she spluttered, taking a step back to run a critical gaze over his long, lean body. 'You're *really* going to take the room when you can plainly see that *I was here first*!'

He turned to look at her again, his expression giving nothing away as his heavy-lidded gaze swept over her face.

She felt exposed, almost naked under his scrutiny, and had to fight not to wrap her arms around her body for protection against it. Locking her jaw, she stared him out, knowing from experience that not backing down was the only way she was going to get what she wanted. Or, in this case, what she needed—a comfortable bed for the night. Which had already been paid for!

A muscle twitched in the Frenchman's jaw as he kept his gaze fixed on hers. He really did have the most striking face, with prominent high-set cheekbones and a broad masculine brow above those mesmerising eyes. What was it about French men that made them so unutterably sexy? The ones she'd met throughout her life had all had the same confident, direct gaze that made her feel simultaneously appraised and giddily unnerved. It was as though he was scrutinising the whole of her exterior whilst also looking deep inside her.

The feeling of being so thoroughly examined made her whole body tingle.

She stared harder at him to combat her dip in concentration.

Something flashed in his eyes and the corner of his mouth lifted fractionally. Was he amused by her determination to win?

Scowling as frustration pricked at her skin, she opened her mouth to restate her case—but he beat her to it.

'You're right,' he said bluntly. 'You must have the room.'

Indigo blinked at him in surprise, snapping her mouth shut. This, she had not expected.

'Oh! Okay.' She frowned, a little dazed by how easy that had been. 'Really?'

Sighing, he ran a hand over his clean-shaven jaw. 'To be honest, *mademoiselle*, I'm too tired to argue. It's been—' he winced, his expression turning troubled '—an *intense* day for me and I want to relax before starting my walk tomorrow.'

'Wait—you're walking the coast too?' she asked in surprise. Looking at him, standing there in his expensive suit with his designer bags sitting prettily at his feet, she'd imagined he was here to do some upmarket sightseeing in the town, or perhaps conduct a high-powered business meeting in the hotel.

His eyes crinkled at the corners as he half frowned, half smiled. 'Is that so unlikely?' he asked, his voice tinged with playful irony.

The bottom fell out of her stomach. 'No! No, I guess not.'

'Anyway, what kind of a man would I be to leave a lady stranded in a strange town in the middle of the night?'

Something about the way he said this, with a twist of wry humour, stopped her from telling him she didn't need a *man's* help—that she'd managed perfectly well on her own for the last three months without one, despite the challenges she'd faced.

'But, *Signor*, there are no other rooms available in Amalfi!' the receptionist cut in before Indigo could form a reply. 'It's a busy time and all the hotels in the town are booked up. I know this because I've already phoned around for another traveller.'

The Frenchman turned to face her. 'You're telling me you can't find me an alternative room for the night?' he stated with unnerving calm.

She shrank away from his gaze, suddenly seeming a lot less self-assured than she had a few minutes ago. 'Yes, *Signor*, I'm so sorry,' she said, her swallow appearing to catch in her throat. 'I'll be able to give you the suite you booked from tomorrow, but tonight there aren't any other rooms available—'

'This is unacceptable,' he said quietly, but with a girder of steel to his voice. 'I do not expect this level of incompetence from an establishment like this. Fetch your manager.'

The receptionist's shoulders tensed as if she'd balled her fists and her eyes widened. 'I can't disturb him—he is sleeping right now and has given strict instructions not to be woken—'

'I don't care. Get him.' He leant forward, pressing his hands against the desk. 'Now.'

'Please, *Signor*, I'll lose my job,' she whispered. 'I'm new here and I can't afford to make any mistakes.' Her brow tensed as her eyes took on a look of abject panic.

The desperation in her voice made Indigo's stomach tighten as a wave of pity washed over her. She could see by the way the young woman's eyes had pooled with impending tears that she was both terrified of her boss and totally inexperienced in dealing with this level of cold assertiveness from a customer.

'Describe the suite to me,' Indigo blurted to the receptionist before the Frenchman could respond.

The receptionist turned to stare at her in surprise

before recovering quickly, using the question as a lifeline to pull her professional self back to safety. 'There is a beautifully appointed bedroom with a super king-sized bed and an en suite bathroom—'

'Does the bedroom door have a lock?' Indigo asked.

Out of the corner of her eye she saw the Frenchman turn to stare at her in baffled disbelief. She ignored him.

'Yes, *Signorina*,' the receptionist replied, looking confused to have her patter broken into with such an odd question, 'and the separate living area has the latest entertainment system—'

'And a large sofa?' Indigo cut in again.

The receptionist blinked hard and frowned, then her expression softened with a mixture of relief and gratitude as she realised where Indigo was going with this. This time she didn't falter with her answer. 'Absolutely! It is very comfortable—large enough to fully stretch out on. There is also a separate bathroom with a whirlpool tub and a waterfall shower.'

Indigo nodded decisively. 'Okay then, we'll share it.'

'What?' The word jumped from the Frenchman's mouth as if he'd not been able to stop it.

She took a breath and turned to face his incredulous gaze. 'I'll take the sofa in the living room, you can have the bedroom; that way we both get to sleep tonight.'

The Frenchman's brow crinkled in disdain. '*Non.* Thank you, but I don't think that's appropriate.'

She raised an eyebrow. 'I don't bite, you know.'

His mouth twisted into a wry smile. 'I'm sure you don't, but it seems improper to ask you to share your room with a strange man.'

'You don't seem that strange to me.' She cast him a smile, which he begrudgingly returned, one eyebrow raised.

'But, seriously, it's fine,' she said. 'I don't mind sharing and I'd hate to feel responsible for this woman losing her job.'

He flapped his hand, dismissing her concern. 'It wouldn't be your fault.'

She looked him hard in the eye. 'But I'd still blame myself and it would ruin my holiday. Anyway, it doesn't sound like you have a better option.'

He gave a gentle snort and shook his head, wearily rubbing his hand over his forehead, as he appeared to give her suggestion some serious consideration. 'Are you sure you're happy to do this?' he asked, his eyes dark with indecision.

'Yes, of course!' she said brightly. 'When life throws problems at you, you have to do whatever you can to make the best of a situation.' She produced a firm smile. 'Anyway, what kind of a *woman* would I be to send an exhausted man out into the night to sleep on the streets in such a beautiful designer suit?'

He looked at her intently for another few seconds, as if giving her the chance to change her mind, and when she resolutely kept her mouth shut he gave a sharp nod.

'Okay, but you take the bedroom so you can lock the door; that way you have no reason to feel unsafe. I'll take the sofa. I'll be up and out early in the morning so I won't be in your way.' Without waiting for her response, he bent down to scoop up his luggage.

'I'm getting up early myself,' she said to the top of

his head, her cheeks heating a little as she realised how defiant that sounded. For some reason she didn't want him to think she was some kind of lazy slob.

'Then we'll each have to pretend the other doesn't exist,' he said with a flash of droll humour in his eyes as he looked back up at her, pushing a hand through his hair as he righted himself.

An impossible feat, Indigo thought, her eyes following the movement of his long fingers and the way his hair fell perfectly back into place, as if it didn't dare defy him. There was no way a man like this could ever be ignored.

Turning back to the receptionist, he held out his passport. 'If you'll give us two key cards we'll find our own way up to the room.'

With an air of sombre apology, the receptionist checked the passport, then picked up Indigo's—which was still lying on the reception desk—and tapped something into her computer. After swiping a couple of key cards through a machine, she handed everything back to the Frenchman. 'There are extra blankets and pillows in the wardrobes. I hope you will be comfortable,' she said sheepishly, before scurrying away to serve someone who had just arrived at the other end of the desk.

Handing Indigo her passport and key card, he turned abruptly on his heel and, without another word, strode away from her, bags swinging from his hand.

Clearly he was a leader, not a follower.

Indigo paused for a moment, staring after him, suddenly feeling a little unsure of herself.

Had she really just offered to share a suite with a complete stranger?

She was so used to figuring out quick fixes at work it hadn't struck her exactly what she'd committed to until it was too late to back out of it.

As she watched him reach the elevator and jab the button to call it, exhaustion from the mad scramble to get her community café in good shape so she didn't have to worry about it whilst she was away hit her like a wallop to the gut. The last three months had been tough, filled with worry about whether the funding she'd applied for in order to keep it running would materialise, and it all seemed to be catching up with her now.

Ironically, this week away was supposed to be a break from the stress of it. Initially it had struck her as ridiculous to come on holiday when she had the possibility of losing everything hanging over her head, but she'd dropped the ball and made a few silly mistakes recently that, while fixable, had meant she'd cost the café some money it could ill afford. As her friend Lacey had jokingly pointed out, it would probably do both her and the café some good to have some time apart.

Added to which, all the travel and accommodation for this week had already been paid for and was non-refundable, so it would have been a waste of money *not* to come.

Wastage was something she felt very strongly about.

Anyway, it was too late to change her mind now—even if she let the Frenchman have the suite to himself. She didn't have the money to pay for a room in another hotel, let alone the energy to face the monumental task of finding one.

This was her only option.

Hurrying after him, she caught him up just as the elevator door opened with a smooth *swish*.

'Okay, let's do this,' she said, her words coming out a little breathlessly after her dash across the room.

He just smiled in a perplexed sort of way that made the skin prickle on the back of her neck, and gestured for her to walk into the elevator before him.

'No, no, after you,' she said, sweeping her own hand in an exaggerated arc towards the centre of the car.

Shaking his head in amusement, he stepped inside and moved to the back to allow her plenty of room to follow him in.

Once she was safely past the doors, he hit the button for their floor and the doors closed on them with another gentle *swish*.

Heavy silence fell between them.

Indigo shifted from one foot to the other.

Well, this is awkward.

'Perhaps we should introduce ourselves, since we're going to be suite-mates,' she said, raising a questioning eyebrow at him. 'I'm Indigo. Indigo Hughes.'

'Julien Moreaux,' he replied, catching her off guard by stepping forwards and kissing her gently on both cheeks.

Being English, she'd forgotten about this traditional French greeting and almost jumped away in shock, only managing to hold her nerve at the last second. His scent hit her nose again, even more intensely this time due to his proximity, and instinctively she breathed him in, intuiting cool nights after hot days, the crisp tang of cold wine in the sunshine and the musky scent of warm skin.

Delicious.

After he'd stepped back it took her a full couple of seconds to pull herself together again. She gave him a friendly smile, but what she really wanted to do was pull him back towards her, bury her face in the scoop of his neck and drag his scent deep into her lungs again.

What was wrong with her? She'd never had this kind of visceral response to a complete stranger before, but there was something so commanding about this man. He made her feel safe, somehow.

Oh, get a grip, Indigo!

The honeymoon suite was exquisite, decorated in those amazing heritage colours that Italians employed so effortlessly, the furniture simple but refined, with an art deco theme tying the room together. Romantic aspiration seemed to ooze from the walls, as if they'd been infused with the happiness of all the newlyweds that had stayed there over the years. She felt sure this place had to have been included in every *World's Best Honeymoon Suites* article written for the glossy magazines she judiciously avoided buying these days.

After thoroughly investigating the suite with her eyes, she turned to look at Julien and realised that he hadn't even glanced around him and was instead staring down at the screen of his phone.

Clearly he was already *au fait* with the finer things in life.

Shaking her head at his lack of interest, she went to

explore the bedroom, which was just as overwhelmingly beautiful as the rest of the suite. This whole experience was like stepping into a fantasy.

Despite her protests about it being a waste of money, Gavin, her ex, had insisted on booking the first night of their stay in this expensive hotel—he'd wanted to start the holiday in style—before spending the rest of the week moving between smaller, more basic places. So this would be her only chance for luxurious pampering.

She was going to have to make the most of it.

After grabbing a blanket and pillow for Julien from the wardrobe, she floated back out of the bedroom and dumped them on the sofa before turning to find he was still staring down at his phone, lost in his own world.

'Stay in the honeymoon suite a lot, do you?' she asked, edging her voice with dry amusement.

He glanced up at her and for a split second a dark expression flickered across his face. 'Only once.'

His change in demeanour unsettled her. 'You're married?' she asked to cover her discomfort.

'Not any more.'

She could have sworn the temperature dropped a few degrees.

'Oh. Sorry to hear that.'

He flipped her his teasing grin again, breaking the tension. 'You English are always sorry for something.'

'I was just being polite,' she said, bristling.

His grin deepened.

She cocked an eyebrow back at him.

He looked at her for a moment longer with amusement in his eyes before turning away to drop his bags next to a mosaic-tiled coffee table in the middle of the room. 'Well, I'm going to—what do you English say?—*crash out*,' he said.

That was her cue to leave. And not a moment too soon. Her whole body felt hot and tingly with the awareness of being alone with him.

'Me too,' Indigo said, backing towards the bedroom. 'So I guess I won't see you in the morning.'

'Probably not,' he said, flopping down on to the sofa and stretching his arms above his head.

She came to a halt in the doorway and watched with fascination as he put everything he had into the stretch, the pleasure of it rippling across his face as he released the tension in his muscles. Forcing herself not to run her eyes up and down the powerful length of his body, she gave a stiff bob of her head, then turned to walk into the bedroom, shutting the door firmly behind her, pushing away the ridiculous urge to lie down on top of him—chest to chest, thigh to thigh—just to feel the solid strength of him beneath her.

It brought it home to her how much she'd missed being touched, being held, just being physically close to someone since Gavin had left her. Now she had the time and space to think about it, the after-effects seemed to be coming out in the strangest of ways.

She turned the key decisively in the lock, hearing it click.

Flinging herself at Julien was definitely not the way to deal with things.

Okay, time to put the sexy Frenchman out of her mind and get practical.

Striding purposefully away from the door, she dropped the small rucksack she'd used as hand luggage on to the bed. Thank goodness she'd had the forethought to pack a few essentials into it for just such an occurrence.

Even so, after spending a lot of time planning for this trip, it was unnerving to find herself without all her carefully thought-out trekking gear. She didn't even have her walking boots with her, so she would have to walk for at least five hours each day in the trainers she'd changed into at the last second at the airport because her feet were so hot. What an unfortunate decision that had been.

Hopefully the airline would find her bag soon and send it to one of the hotels on the route. She'd left her details and itinerary with the lost luggage desk at the airport and they'd promised—after what seemed like hours of form-filling—to send it on once it had been located.

The biggest problem she faced was that she'd put half of her money and her emergency credit card into the lost backpack too, not wanting to carry it all in her hand luggage in case that was stolen. At least her breakfasts were already paid for, so she could eat heartily in the morning and maybe skip lunch in order to eke out what little cash she had to feed herself in the evenings. Just until her backpack turned up. Which would be okay. She was used to budgeting and eating frugally.

It would all be part of the adventure.

Emptying out her rucksack on to the bedspread, she took an inventory of what she had with her: one extra pair of knickers and one pair of socks—that she'd have to alternate with the ones she had on and wash each day—a toothbrush and a tiny tube of toothpaste, a spare T-shirt and a short cotton skirt which she'd interchange with the shorts and vest she had on, a pack of mints, a mascara that promised to give you 'Hollywood eyes' and her trusty liquid eyeliner, a packet of painkillers, her wallet and passport and a book on walking the Amalfi coast. She didn't even have her mobile phone with her, she realised with a lurch, because she'd packed that into her missing luggage too, determined to only use it for emergencies on the trip so that she'd make the most of the scenery and social life and not be constantly diverted by the online world.

After packing everything carefully back into the bag, she took a refreshing shower in the floor-to-ceiling marble bathroom, lathering herself with the zingy-smelling complimentary shower gel, before sliding between the crisp cotton sheets of the bed.

What luxury!

Stretching herself into a starfish shape, she brushed her fingertips over the smooth mahogany headboard and sighed hard, painfully aware of how much empty space there was on either side of her.

The cruel irony of staying in the honeymoon suite had not been lost on her.

In a parallel universe—where Gavin hadn't fallen in love with another woman—she'd be tumbling into bed with him right about now.

What would he have said about staying in this room? She pictured them laughing about it, ribbing each other about how much sex they should be having to keep up with all the former inhabitants. Out of nowhere a feeling of utter desolation hit her right in the chest. It had been three months since they'd split up and she'd not allowed herself to fall apart since the day it had happened, keeping herself busy and using this holiday as a bright spot to look forward to when she felt glum. But the realisation that this was it—that she was here now, on her own, and this was the reality of her situation suddenly brought her low.

She thumped the mattress on either side of her. She was *not* going to let it get her down.

As she'd learnt from an early age, crying and whinging didn't get you anywhere. That was what growing up in an all-male household and having four smart, alpha, and now highly successful older brothers would teach you. She'd never won an argument or topped a challenge by turning on the waterworks or asking for special dispensation, and that was the way she preferred it. Everything she'd achieved had been on her own merits. She'd fought just as hard—if not harder—than her brothers for her successes and she was proud of what she'd achieved.

Unfortunately, Gavin hadn't understood that drive to succeed on her own, and had cited her desire to pour too much time and energy into making her café a success and 'excluding him from parts of her life where he wasn't necessary' as the catalyst for their breakup. According to him, she treated him like one of her projects and acted as if she had more love for the strangers who frequented the café than for him. That had been particularly gutting to hear because she liked to think of herself as a perceptive and caring partner.

Pushing away the threatening gloom, she sat up and punched her pillows back into shape before flopping back down and wriggling further into the sumptuous bed.

Well, from this point on she was looking after herself.

Whilst she was here she was going to get some fresh air and exercise, meet people outside of her small sphere of work and recharge her batteries before returning home feeling refreshed and more positive about her future.

As she lay there, willing away the lingering tight feeling in her chest, something about her earlier head-to-head with Julien suddenly occurred to her. He'd conducted his whole conversation, even the bit with the receptionist, in English. Had he done that so as not to exclude her? Or was he just better at English than Italian? From her experience with him so far, she got the impression he'd be good at everything he did—he certainly exuded that kind of confidence.

Except for that moment when he'd talked about how *intense* his day had been. There had been a vulnerability to his voice that hadn't been there for the rest of the time.

Whatever could have affected him so deeply? Could it have something to do with his failed marriage?

Perhaps he, too, was here to get a new perspective on life after a bad breakup.

She knew first-hand how demoralising it could be

going through a divorce. Gavin, her ex, had been an utter mess when he'd first moved into her spare room—which she'd offered to him as a favour to a friend of a friend after his wife demanded they separate. At that point it had been six months since her father had passed away and she was finding it very lonely living in their empty family home without him, so it had been nice to have the company.

She'd found comfort in taking care of Gavin: making him healthy meals when she discovered he wasn't eating properly and sitting with him, listening to him talk through his pain and humiliation for hours and hours.

At the time, she hadn't anticipated it turning into a relationship, but there it was. In retrospect, it seemed inevitable now that something more would have developed between them, especially when they'd grown so emotionally close.

A prickle of disquiet ran up her spine.

She really should have asked Julien if he was okay when he'd mentioned his divorce. In her experience, whenever people brought up things like that it was usually because they wanted to talk to someone about it, but she'd blithely ignored his prompt, more concerned about rebutting his teasing. It was possible she could use her experience to help him out in some way, though. As one concerned human being to another. Considering he was here on his own, she wouldn't be surprised to find he didn't have anyone at home he could talk to about what he was going through.

Turning over and letting out a huge yawn, she told herself that if she saw Julien again on the walk she'd make an effort to check that he was okay, just to set her mind at rest. But that would be it. The whole experience with Gavin had made her very wary of getting romantically involved with a divorcee again—she never wanted to be someone's rebound relationship ever again.

So for now, she was going to put the sexy Frenchman—unnervingly close on the other side of the door—out of her mind.

CHAPTER TWO

The Ravello Circuit. A tricky walk with lots of steps. We recommend breaking the walk at the magnificent Villa Cimbrone gardens before visiting Ravello, then stopping for a scenic lunch break in Pontone...

JULIEN MOREAUX AWOKE to find the sun streaming in through the large windows of the honeymoon suite. He rubbed a hand across his bleary eyes, forcing his thoughts into some kind of coherent arrangement.

He was here, in Amalfi. Finally.

It hadn't mattered to him exactly where he'd end up when he'd asked his PA to book this break for him—all he'd stipulated was that he wanted somewhere where he could move from one place to another so he didn't feel trapped into having to see the same people in the same place every day—and he was pleased with her choice.

This walking holiday had been marked in his mind for some time as the beginning of the return to the way things used to be, and he'd been looking forward to losing himself in the monotony of hard exercise and self-imposed solitude.

Not that the solitude part had worked out well so far.

He grimaced as the events of the previous evening came back to haunt him. Sharing his suite with a bohemian idealist with an overblown zeal for life had not been an ideal start, but after sensing Indigo's desperation to fix the situation amicably and seeing the earnest pleading in her eyes, he'd known there was no way he could refuse her suggestion.

And he was tired of being the bad guy.

A huge yawn hit him and he rocked his head back against the soft cushions of the sofa, giving his body a long, hard stretch to wake up his cramped muscles.

Considering the way he was feeling this morning, he suspected, if he allowed himself, he could easily spend the whole week sleeping. Not that he was going to do that. He'd come here for a change of scene and a reprieve from the pressures of life and there was no way he was wasting his time in Italy staring at four walls. Even if they were as magnificent as the ones in this hotel.

This observation led his thoughts back to Indigo's wry comment about him being familiar with staying in the honeymoon suite.

A cold prickle ran across his skin.

The last time he'd been in a room like this he'd thought his life had been on the up and up, but look at him now, barely two years later, holidaying alone only hours after signing his divorce papers, with the ink of his signature still drying in his mind.

Swinging himself into a sitting position on the sofa, he stifled another yawn behind his hand and rubbed his face hard to get the blood circulating.

He really needed to get up and out before Indigo emerged; he didn't think he had the mental energy this morning to deal with another awkward scene with her.

Glancing towards the bedroom door, he was surprised to see it standing wide open.

Huh, weird. He checked his watch. Seven o'clock. So she hadn't been joking when she said she'd be up and out early too.

Hauling himself off the sofa, he went to investigate further.

'Indigo?' he called gently, so as not to startle her in case she was still in there.

There was no reply.

Poking his head around the doorway, he saw that the bed was empty, with the sheets pulled haphazardly back and the door to the en suite bathroom flung open.

She was gone.

That was a relief.

Feeling the tension leave his shoulders, he went back into the living area and pulled out the clothes he was going to wear for his walk today, before heading off for an invigorating shower.

There had been something about her that intrigued him, though, he mused as he felt the soothing water cascade over his aching back—her determination and bolshie confidence perhaps. She certainly wasn't his usual type, with her leggy, voluptuous figure and short, feathery bobbed hair in a shocking shade of red, which had reminded him of the colour of the sea of poppy fields behind the house in Provence where he'd grown up. Historically, he'd always been attracted to petite women, usually blondes, with more of a delicate air about them, but there was something incredibly alluring about Indigo, with her wide, open smile and playful gaze.

She was sexy.

He shut off the water and reached for a towel, drying himself vigorously. If he was being honest, she'd probably only captured his interest because it had been refreshing to meet a woman who didn't want to take something from him and just walk away for once. He was used to being the one to sort out other people's problems, and it had been a long time since someone had done something benevolent for him.

It would be better if he didn't see her again, though, he told himself, flinging the towel into the bath. He wasn't in any state to be sociable at the moment.

After shaving off his morning stubble, he pulled on shorts, a light breathable T-shirt and the brand new walking boots that his PA had sourced for him, and gave himself a nod in the mirror.

Okay. Now he was ready to face the day and whatever it might bring.

He checked his email on his phone as he travelled down in the elevator ready to grab some breakfast in the restaurant, pleased to find there wasn't anything that needed his urgent attention. That was sure to change by the end of the week, though.

After dropping by the reception desk to confirm they'd have the suite that he'd booked available for him when he returned from his hike, he was about to walk away to get his breakfast when curiosity about Indigo's situation stopped him. He should probably check whether he was likely to come across her again, just so he could prepare himself for it.

He turned back.

'Did you find another room here for the woman I shared the honeymoon suite with last night?' he asked the receptionist.

Confusion flickered across her face, until recollection seemed to strike her. 'The lady from your suite checked out, *Signor*.'

That must mean she wasn't doing the Ravello circuit and coming back to Amalfi today, which meant there wasn't any danger of bumping into her again.

Good, that was good, because he'd feel compelled to acknowledge her if they saw each other again, which would encroach on his much anticipated alone time.

'Okay, thanks,' he said, giving the receptionist a nod before heading over to the breakfast room at the other end of the lobby.

Considering it was still pretty early, the place was already buzzing with guests, and he grabbed the only spare table near the back wall. After seating himself, he took a look around him, soaking up the animated vibe. Quite a few of the guests seemed to be dressed in walking gear, like him. Clearly the coastal walk was a big draw to the area. Hmm, perhaps it wouldn't be as solitary an experience as he was hoping, he reflected with a twinge of annoyance.

A flash of bright red on the other side of the room

caught his eye and, heart thumping, he quickly leant back, using the couple sitting at the table next to him as cover. Grabbing the menu in front of him and holding it to hide most of his face, he gradually leant forwards again to take another look. As he suspected, it was Indigo, standing at the breakfast buffet with her back to him, her hair damp and gleaming and her small rucksack slung over one arm.

She looked refreshed and energised this morning, her skin glowing with health and her posture relaxed. His gaze followed her as she moved smoothly along the buffet, seemingly checking over her options before making her choice. She grabbed an apple and a couple of bread rolls from the display and he stared in baffled amusement as she slipped them into the gaping opening of her bag. After a quick check around, she seemed to discern that no one was watching her and popped a couple of slices of Parma ham and a small bottle of mineral water from the cooler section in there too. Next went in a pat of butter and a little package of cheese.

Evidently deciding she had enough food stashed away, she strolled nonchalantly away from the buffet, slinging her bag over her shoulder and shoving her hands deep into the pockets of her shorts. He half expected her to start whistling *Food, Glorious Food* as she made her getaway.

She was staying in a five-star hotel, but she was too cheap to buy her own lunch? What was that about?

He allowed himself one last look at her long, shapely legs as she disappeared out of the room, then turned to gesture for the waitress to bring him some coffee.

And that, he guessed, feeling an odd twinge in his chest, would probably be the last he'd ever see of Indigo Hughes.

Indigo had thought she was in pretty good shape. She went to the gym at least a couple of times a week and opted to walk around London as much as possible instead of jumping on public transport, but by the time she'd climbed what seemed like a thousand steps leading away from Amalfi—pausing on her journey to walk through the ancient brick-walled walkways hung with canopies of vibrant greenery in the Villa Cimbrone gardens—then on to the quaint little town of Ravello, she realised her fitness levels were nothing like as good as she'd imagined.

Still, she'd made it here without incident, and after wandering around the quiet streets crammed with cool artisan shops and visiting the simple but atmospheric cathedral, it was a relief to walk downhill to the little village of Pontone and stop for a rest and to eat her lunch.

Sitting on a wide grassy viewpoint which looked out over the dramatic drop down to the coast, she was just about to take the final bite of the sandwich she'd made out of the food she'd filched from the breakfast buffet when she noticed a familiar figure making his way across the grass in the direction of the *trattorias* that, according to her guide, were favoured by walkers on the route because of the incredible views from their balconies.

After spending the whole morning trying not to think about the sight of Julien lying bare-chested on the sofa, looking utterly divine in repose as she tiptoed past him, she was disconcerted to see him again in the flesh. Not that she was going to let that stop her from being friendly. She'd made that promise to herself to check he was okay here on his own, so that was what she was going to do. Just because he was ridiculously sexy and ever so slightly intimidating it didn't mean she couldn't have a friendly chat with him.

'Hi there,' she called as he came level with where she was sitting.

He didn't appear to hear her.

'Julien! Hey, Julien, over here!' she shouted this time. She could have sworn she saw him flinch before turning to look over to where she was sitting. He raised a hand and gave her a nod of acknowledgement, before turning back and continuing on his journey.

Huh.

Perhaps he assumed she wouldn't want to be disturbed whilst eating her lunch. Yes, that must be it; he couldn't be deliberately avoiding her.

Could he?

No—she was being paranoid.

Jumping up and grabbing her daypack, she made after him, having to pick up her pace in order to catch up with him before he strode out of sight.

'Hey, Julien, wait!' she called, a little out of breath by the time she reached him.

He turned around and gave her a look of expectant concern. 'Are you okay?' he asked, his gaze flicking behind her as if he was worried she was being pursued.

'I'm fine,' she panted, 'just wanted to check you're

enjoying your day. You seemed a little—er—' she flapped a hand at him '—stressed yesterday.'

He took a small step backwards and let out a sharp snort. 'Yes, I'm enjoying it so far.' A small frown flickered across his face. 'Thank you.'

There was a pause while she waited for him to ask if she was having a good time too.

He didn't.

'Okay, good.' She clapped her hands together awkwardly. 'Well, I just wanted to say hi. So, hi!' she blurted, sincerely hoping he'd assume the blush travelling up her neck was a flush from the sun and her mad dash across the grass.

'Hi,' he replied flatly, folding his arms across his chest.

There was another heavy pause where he blinked at her, as if waiting for her to make her excuses and leave. Well, she wasn't going to. She'd learnt over the last year whilst working at the café that just because someone seemed unfriendly when you first spoke to them, it didn't necessarily mean they didn't want to talk to you. They were probably just distracted by something they'd been thinking about, or they were hungry, or concerned about the tightness of their trousers or something. Not that it appeared as though any of his clothes weren't fitting him perfectly. In fact, he looked as if he'd just stepped off a page in one of the hiking gear magazines she'd pored over whilst preparing for the holiday, before realising she could afford exactly none of the items in it.

'Did you like Ravello? All those steps up to it nearly

killed me!' she joked, cringing inside at the hint of desperation in her voice.

He didn't even break a smile. 'Yes, it was an interesting place.' His brow creased into a frown. 'They told me at the reception desk you'd checked out. I didn't expect to see you on this circuit today.'

She stiffened, wondering why on earth he seemed so irritated about her walking the same route as him.

'I have another hotel in town booked for tonight. A better organised one, I hope,' she said, shrugging off her discomfort and forcing a smile on to her face.

'Okay. *Bon.*' He took a deliberate step backwards, then froze as her words seemed to sink in. 'Do you mean you're staying in Amalfi again tonight?'

Another wave of warmth began to creep up her neck. 'Yup.'

His brow crinkled in confusion. 'Then why are you moving hotels after only one night?'

She shifted uncomfortably. 'I like to change things up. It keeps me on my toes.'

And I can't afford to stay in that hotel again, not that I'm admitting that to you, Monsieur Moneybags.

He nodded slowly, his gaze searching hers as if he was trying to rootle out a lie.

She just raised both eyebrows at him, determined not to give in and blurt out the truth, trying to ignore the way her pulse had sped up.

Letting out a sharp huff of a laugh, Julien broke eye contact and glanced behind him as if looking for an excuse to leave. Not that she could blame him; the conversation wasn't exactly flowing well and she was tempted to slink away herself. But she wasn't going to; she was going to see this through to the bitter end, as a matter of personal fulfilment.

'So, are you going to try one of those *trattorias* for your lunch?' she pressed, nodding in the direction he'd been heading.

He closed his eyes for a second and pulled in a sharp breath, then smiled politely. '*Oui*. I didn't have the forethought to bring any food with me.' He gestured towards the remains of her sandwich, which was still clutched in her hand. 'Where did you get your lunch today?' The dry irony in his tone suggested there was more to his question than a simple polite query.

He must have seen her take the food from the buffet. The realisation sent a prickle up her spine. Normally she would never have done such a thing, hating the idea of stealing anything from anyone, but with the limited funds she had available until her bag turned up, it was necessary to bend her rules a little.

'I purloined it from the breakfast buffet,' she admitted, forcing herself to keep her chin up and her gaze locked with his. 'I thought the least the hotel could do was gift me a lunch after their mess-up with the room last night. Anyway, a place like that always puts out more than is consumed. I was helping with their wastage problem,' she finished, aware that her tone was edged with defensiveness.

His eyes crinkled at the corners as his wry smile deepened. 'Don't worry; your secret is safe with me,' he murmured, leaning closer and enveloping her in his delicious scent.

It was all she could do not to take a great gulping breath of it through her nose. What was it that made his smell so enticing to her? Was this what people called the pheromone effect? She'd never experienced it before.

'Thanks,' she deadpanned.

He gave her a curt nod. 'Well, I'm going to go and eat.'

'Okay, enjoy,' she said, disappointed that he was leaving now. Despite his standoffishness, she'd enjoyed chatting with him after spending her morning alone. All the other English-speaking walkers she'd encountered on the route seemed to be part of a group, which she hadn't had the courage to try and break into yet.

She watched him stride away, trying not to stare at the way he moved his large, fit body with such powerful grace.

Judging by his troubled mood, she guessed he must be struggling with some serious emotional turmoil, which she knew from personal experience could make for a pretty lonely existence. She hated to see people in pain, especially if she thought she could do something to help.

Well, she'd just have to keep an eye out for him, just in case he fancied some no-strings company later.

CHAPTER THREE

Back in Amalfi. Make sure you take advantage of the wonderful selection of restaurants and eateries after visiting the imposing cathedral in the centre of the town...

AFTER THOROUGHLY ENJOYING the solitude of his walk earlier in the day, Julien had been looking forward to finding a place to grab a peaceful lunch when Indigo had run over and accosted him.

It had taken everything he'd had not to be rude and pretend he hadn't heard her calling out to him, then continue with their stilted conversation when it became clear she wasn't going to let him get away without extracting some kind of information out of him.

He wasn't sure why she'd been so keen to chat. Perhaps she was lonely and hadn't found any other English speakers to buddy up with. He hoped she'd got the message that he preferred to holiday on his own now though, and wouldn't bother coming over to talk to him should their paths cross again.

A niggle of shame twisted in his gut. He felt bad

about being so unfriendly, but she'd picked the wrong time to try and get to know him.

If that had been her objective.

Perhaps she was looking for something more. If that was the case, she was bang out of luck. After the train wreck of his marriage, he wanted nothing to do with women and relationships again for a very long time.

Even spirited ones with legs that went on for miles and eyes you could get lost in.

When he got back to the hotel, he took a long cooling shower then a refreshing nap before striking out for dinner, strolling through the centre of Amalfi on the way to the restaurants on the marina that the hotel receptionist had recommended he try.

Diverted by the magnificence of the *Duomo* in the town centre, he climbed the wide steps and walked through the Arabic style Cloister of Paradise, looking out through the grand archways at the panoramic view of the town, with its pastel-coloured stone buildings wrapped with iron balconies.

He knew what he was looking at should have blown him away, but ever since his life had fallen to pieces he'd had trouble finding pleasure in things. He felt desensitised to beauty, as if he was viewing it from inside a plastic bubble. Nothing seemed to touch him any more.

Shaking off the building tension at the base of his skull, he was just about to turn and walk back to the steps when a bright flash of red caught his eye.

Was that Indigo again?

Craning his neck, he tried to see past a crowd of tourists blocking his view and catch another glimpse of her so he could make sure to walk in the opposite direction, but she seemed to have disappeared. Was his brain playing tricks on him? No, it must have been her. That hair colour was so unusual it couldn't be someone else with the exact same shade—and he knew for a fact she was staying in Amalfi tonight.

Walking slowly down the steps, he forced himself to take a deep breath and relax, telling himself it was unlikely they'd cross each other's paths when it was so busy.

Reaching the Popolo fountain in the middle of the piazza, he sat down on the stone edge of it and ran his fingers through the water, enjoying the cooling effect on his skin. What was wrong with him today? His heart seemed to be racing and his palms felt sweaty.

The heat must be getting to him.

Someone sat down next to him and on impulse he glanced round to see who it was.

'Fancy seeing you here,' Indigo said, with a mischievous lift of her eyebrow.

He snorted and shook his head at his terrible luck. What was it about this woman that kept drawing them together?

'It's a small town centre; I guess we were bound to bump into each other at some point,' he said wearily.

She leant back on her hands and studied him. 'Are you off to forage for some supper?'

He raised his eyebrows, bemused. 'Forage?'

'Looking for a place to eat.'

'Oui.'

'On your own?'

'Oui.' He tensed, anticipating what was coming next.

'You're welcome to join me if you'd like,' she said brightly, confirming his fear. 'I was just about to grab a slice of pizza at one of those small family-run eateries just off the square.'

'You mean the cafés with the plastic tables? *Non*—' he began to say, but she cut him off.

'You'd be doing me a favour,' she said. 'I've been on my own all day and I'm beginning to have conversations with myself out loud, which is never a good sign. If you don't come and have dinner with me there's a good chance I'll be arrested by the end of the night and taken to a secure facility.' She sat up and folded her arms. 'Anyway, you owe me.'

He frowned, perplexed. 'What for?'

'For letting you share my room.'

'*Your* room?'

'I was there first, remember?'

He sighed, fighting a smile. 'How could I forget?'

'So what do you say? Can I tempt you with a slice of pizza?' She looked so hopeful it made something twist in his chest. But he needed to stay strong.

'I'm going to try out one of the restaurants down on the marina,' he said, giving her an apologetic look. 'Apparently they have fantastic à la carte menus with a good selection of locally caught fresh fish and seafood. Word has it the lobster spaghetti is not to be missed.'

Her eyes seemed to glaze over as if she was picturing the food he'd described. 'Sounds awful,' she joked, flashing an impertinent grin. 'Anyway, those places are a total tourist rip-off.'

'And the pizza joints aren't?'

Spreading out her hands, she gestured around the square. 'They're part of the local colour. You can eat overpriced gourmet food in Paris, or wherever you're from. Come and support the underdog for once.' She stared at him hard, like she'd done the previous night, dipping her head to one side and looking up at him through her thick black lashes, and something twisted again inside him—then broke.

Despite his earlier determination to keep to himself tonight, he realised he had no choice but to go and eat a huge greasy slice of pizza with this woman. Maybe then she'd leave him alone.

'Sure.' He threw up his hands in surrender. 'Pizza sounds good.'

'Great!' she said, breaking into a huge smile.

He hoped she wasn't going to read too much into this. Whilst he was prepared to spend the next hour with her, he didn't want her thinking he wanted to buddy up for the whole week.

As they walked away from the piazza towards one of the back streets that housed the pizza outlets, they passed a homeless person slumped on a filthy-looking rug next to one of the souvenir shops. Out of the corner of his eye, he saw Indigo reach into her pocket, then discreetly drop a handful of coins into an empty hat by the side of the man, before strolling on as if nothing had happened.

As soon as they'd ordered their slices of pizza and drinks from a very jolly waiter at a café with red plastic tables and chairs arranged out on the pavement, Indigo excused herself and went inside to find the bathroom and splash some cool water on to her face.

Maybe insisting on bringing Julien here had been a little extreme, she deliberated as she patted her face dry with a paper towel. He'd not exactly been enthusiastic about taking her up on the offer of company—but she couldn't shake the concern that it would have been a miserable experience for him, eating dinner on his own, and she was pretty sure if she was patient he'd thaw out eventually.

Sometimes people put up barriers for whatever reason and you had to coax them out of their shell. She'd seen it a lot throughout her time running her café and evening classes. People could appear to be confident on the outside, but when you dug a little deeper it became apparent they were dealing with some tough issues and putting a brave face on things. Often they just needed someone to ask if they were okay, then listen to them.

Which was exactly what she'd done for Gavin, she remembered with a lurch. Not that he'd appreciated it in the end.

Sighing, she rubbed a hand over her face. Was she setting herself up for more trouble here, getting involved in Julien's drama?

She stared into the mirror, looking deep into her own eyes. No. Because this wasn't going to turn into anything more than a brief encounter—hopefully just one of many connections she'd make during her week here. She was here to socialise and have fun, new experiences this week after all, but that was all it would be.

Pulling a face at herself, she smoothed down her hair then pushed back her shoulders, wishing she'd had something other than her walking clothes to put on tonight. It wasn't that she wanted to impress Julien exactly, but she felt scruffy next to his overt sophistication, and less confident because of it.

Returning to the table, she saw that the waiter had brought their slices of pizza, as well as a beer for Julien and a glass of tap water for her.

Julien looked so strikingly out of place—sitting there on his cherry-red plastic chair in his designer jeans and beautifully cut open-necked shirt, with his golden hair swept back from his face and aviator sunglasses perched on his head as he read something on his smartphone—that she couldn't help but smile.

Taking her seat, she gave him a friendly nod as he looked up to acknowledge her return.

'Great, the food arrived while I was away; I love it when that happens,' she said, picking up her glass and taking a sip of water to cover a sudden bout of nerves at being there with him.

He just looked at her as if she was slightly loopy.

Swallowing hard, she put her glass down and leaned forwards, propping her arms on the table. 'So, tell me, Julien, why did you choose to walk the Amalfi coast?' she asked brightly in an attempt to get the conversation started.

He took his sunglasses off his head and slid them on to his nose so all she could see now was her own reflection in the lenses. 'It seemed like a good place to get away from it all.'

'Apart from all the tourists.' She gave him a smile, which he didn't return.

'I didn't realise how popular this place was.'

'You mean you didn't do your homework? Somehow I find that hard to believe,' she said.

He frowned. 'Really? Why?'

'I don't know... You just seem very—*together.* Very—*businesslike.*'

He huffed out a dry laugh and picked up his beer bottle, taking a long pull. 'Why did you choose to come here?' he asked, gesturing to their surroundings with the neck of the bottle.

She paused, arranging her answer in her mind. 'I've wanted to do this walk for ages and I finally got round to booking it this year,' she said, uncomfortably aware of a jolt of sadness in her chest. She and Gavin had talked about coming here since they'd got together, when things had been good between them. Before he'd started to resent her.

Julien leant back in his seat and studied her. 'Do you often holiday alone?'

'No, just this time.' She took a breath, deciding she might as well be straight with him.

'Actually, I was supposed to come here with my boyfriend, but we split up three months ago. He didn't want to come with his new partner, so I figured, since it was non-refundable, I may as well use it as a chance to get away for a bit.' She was aiming for a breezy and upbeat tone of voice, but from the look on Julien's face she suspected she must have fallen well short.

Still, perhaps her confession would open up an opportunity for him to talk about his own situation.

'How about you? Were you supposed to come here with someone?' she asked, perhaps a little desperately.

He avoided her gaze, looking instead at the waiter who was busying about nearby. *'Non,'* was all he said, picking up his slice of pizza and taking a large bite.

'Oh.' She tapped her toe gently against the plastic leg of the table, then picked up her own slice and studied it, uncomfortably aware that she'd lost her appetite now.

'Well, it's really nice to be here, anyway,' she continued, to cover the now rather prickly silence. 'I haven't had a holiday in a couple of years—if you don't count the four days I spent at my oldest brother's house over Christmas, which wasn't exactly a relaxing break. Three of my brothers have kids—one of them has four boys—so it was more like staying in a soft play gym crossed with a zoo.'

Picking up his beer, Julien took another long pull. 'You don't have your own kids?' he asked.

There was a sharp spasm in her chest. She'd fantasised about her and Gavin having kids, once upon a time. Another thing to mourn the loss of. 'Not yet. Hopefully one day. I'm sure it'll happen when it's the right time.'

He grimaced as if he had a bad taste in his mouth. 'The right time,' he repeated flatly.

'Yeah, I firmly believe that kids turn up when you most need them to.'

Looking over the top of his sunglasses, he gave her a withering stare.

Irritation pricked at her skin. 'So I'm guessing you

don't have kids either?' she asked, determined to ignore his negativity.

'Non.' The word was terse and had a definite full stop at the end.

'But you'd like to, one day?'

'Can we change the subject?' he said levelly, but with an undertone of steel.

'Um, sure.' Clearly she'd hit a nerve.

Perhaps it was for the best that they talk about something else anyway. The subject wasn't exactly an inspiring one for her now that she was single.

Indigo nibbled at the crust of her pizza while she thought of a new topic of conversation.

'Your English is very good. Where do you live?'

'In Paris, but I conduct a lot of business in the English language.'

'Oh, yeah?'

For the first time that night he seemed to relax, pushing his sunglasses up on to his head again and sitting back in his chair. '*Oui*. My business acquires and renovates high-end holiday homes in France for clients all over the world. We also source and maintain corporate Parisian apartments for executives to live in whilst they conduct business in France.'

'Nice.'

'I enjoy it.'

'Lucrative.'

'Oui.'

'Good for you.'

'What about you? What do you do?' He took another large bite of his pizza.

'I run a café that uses mostly surplus and past *best before date* food from supermarkets and restaurants. We sell affordable meals for people on low incomes so they can come and get a square meal at least a couple of times a week. Since we opened, we've had a lot of elderly gentlemen come in who've lost their wives and have no idea how to cook, so I started running cookery lessons in the evenings aimed specifically at people like them, to give them a grounding in making basic, healthy meals for themselves at home. It's going well so far, but it's been hard work. We rely a lot on donations and public grants so there's loads of form filling and face-to-face negotiating, and quite a bit of pleading on bended knee.'

She took a large bite of her food to punctuate her monologue, not wanting to think about what would happen to the café if the next lot of funding didn't come through.

'I imagine you're very good at the negotiating part,' he said with a twist in his smile.

'Usually,' she said through a mouthful of pizza, smiling back at him with her eyes. It felt good to finally hit on a subject he wanted to talk about.

'It's hard work to keep a project like that adequately funded, though. There's a constant threat of grants being pulled or reduced, so I spend a lot of my time looking for new sources of cash. It's hand to mouth in every way, but we make it work.'

'Did you set it up by yourself?' The last of his pizza disappeared into his mouth.

'Initially, but I have a dedicated team of both paid

workers and local volunteers now.' She took another bite of her own food, aware that she needed to eat quickly now to catch up.

'That's impressive. No wonder you need a holiday.'

'Yeah, I've put in some very long days this past year. It's never going to make me rich, but it makes me happy.' At least it had, until her relationship with Gavin ended because of it.

Julien studied her again, this time with a small pinch between his brows.

'What?' she asked, swiping at her chin, worried that she had cheese strings dangling from it.

'I was just thinking it's good to meet someone with such drive and ambition.'

She smiled back in gratified surprise, feeling warmth pool in her belly. Putting her food back on the plate, she wiped her greasy fingers on the paper napkin next to it. 'Thanks. I've always wanted to run my own business—I hate the idea of working for other people for my entire life.' She took a breath. 'I think I was meant to do what I do.'

He snorted gently. 'You're a strong believer in fate. I suppose you're one of those people who think everything happens for a reason?'

'Sure am.' She stared at her pizza, wondering whether she could force down another bite. 'You've just got to keep positive and everything will work itself out in the end.'

When she looked up at him she was disturbed to see his expression had switched to a mixture of amusement and derision.

She frowned, riled by his change in attitude. 'What's so wrong with that?'

He shrugged and stared off into the distance. 'It's total claptrap.' He enunciated the word *claptrap* with some relish.

'It's not claptrap. It's called having a constructive outlook on life.'

Julien grunted and took another long sip of his beer. 'I suppose you believe in fairy tales too.'

'You must believe in happy-ever-afters if you got married,' she pointed out.

His gaze snapped back to hers. 'Maybe. Once. But divorce will knock that kind of naivety right out of you.'

She jumped as he thumped his beer bottle down on to the table between them, and there was an edgy pause as the word 'divorce' buzzed in the air between them like an irritating fly.

'Why did the two of you split up?' she asked gently, relieved they were finally getting to the crux of the matter.

He sighed and folded his arms. 'You know, I don't really want to talk about it. I came on this walk to forget about what went wrong in my life and look forward to a future on my own.' He over-enunciated the word 'own' this time.

Indigo bristled at his bluntness. 'That sounds kind of lonely.'

'Lonely sounds pretty good to me right now.'

The hollow look in his eyes disturbed her.

'You know, if you *did* want to talk about it, I'd be happy to listen,' she said.

His expression flashed with exasperation. 'I don't need some *amateur* psychoanalysing me this week, thanks.'

The stab of hurt she experienced must have shown on her face, because he gave a guttural sigh and shook his head.

Pushing his chair back from the table, he stood up and pulled a handful of notes out of his pocket, tossing them on to the table. 'I don't think I'm the kind of company you're looking for right now, Indigo,' he said tersely, dropping his glasses back down to cover his eyes. 'It's better if we don't spend any more time together. Enjoy the rest of your vacation.'

Without even glancing back, he strode away, his shoulders hunched and his arms hanging stiffly by his sides.

The whole surface of her skin felt hot and prickly with indignation as she stared after him, his words echoing cruelly through her head.

How rude! She'd just wanted to check he was okay here on his own.

Not feeling lost and alone and isolated.

But okay. Fine! If that was the way he wanted it she wouldn't bother trying to be friendly any more.

Swallowing down the painful lump in her throat, she rummaged around in her bag for her purse.

What was wrong with her? She didn't seem to be able to step away from other people's problems, even on holiday.

She shouldn't be spending her precious free time with someone who had such a cynical view about love either, she told herself, yanking the money out of the notes compartment. She needed to surround herself with positivity and optimism right now.

Slamming her money down on the table next to his, she got up from her chair, set her shoulders back and walked in the opposite direction of the one he'd taken.

From this point on she would do as he asked and make a concerted effort to avoid any further contact with Monsieur Julien Moreaux.

CHAPTER FOUR

On to Praiano. A tough day's walk and the first leg of your journey west...

JULIEN KNEW HE shouldn't have kept on drinking after leaving Indigo at the table, but he'd needed to do something to numb the mortification that had trickled through him like ice water when he thought about how bitter and miserable he'd sounded. The look of hurt on her face after his blunt rejection of her offer of friendship had stayed imprinted on his mind's eye till he'd finally managed to wash it away with his fourth beer.

This was exactly why he'd decided to spend the week on his own. The last thing he'd wanted was to let his frustration over the failure of his marriage ruin the first proper break he'd had in a very long time, let alone affect someone else's holiday.

He took another long pull on his water bottle as he slogged along the rocky coastal path towards Praiano, willing the throbbing pain behind his eyes to dissipate. Because of his hangover, he'd started the walk later than he'd intended, and was paying for it now by having to trek hard through the midday sun to make up for the time he'd lost.

According to the hotel receptionist, there should be a small *tratorria* about an hour's walk from where he was. He was looking forward to eating a nourishing, carb-heavy meal to pick him up and give him the boost of energy he needed to get through the rest of the journey.

He attempted to while away the time by thinking through the next stages of a new build he'd been over-seeing before coming here but, to his chagrin, Indigo's hurt expression kept popping back into his head. The worst thing, he finally accepted as he struggled along, was that he'd found himself beginning to like her as she'd revealed more about herself—particularly when she'd talked with such passion about the café and cook-ing classes she'd set up to cater for vulnerable members of her community.

He couldn't help but compare her to his ex-wife Celine, who, without even discussing it with him, had given up her job as a legal secretary as soon as they were married, spending her days shopping and watch-ing reality TV instead. He'd not made a fuss at the time, thinking she'd probably grow bored after a while, but she hadn't. Instead, she'd looked to him to provide all her entertainment and society, as well as supporting her financially.

Which had been fine for a time.

After years of having his nose to the grindstone and putting his business ventures before his personal hap-piness, meeting the beautiful, wild and carefree Celine had been like being caught up in a cyclone of desire, and his formerly work-orientated life had suddenly become a whirl of new experiences and unpredictable passionate moments.

Until the bad luck that had changed everything for them, and his once happy-go-lucky wife turned into someone he didn't recognise any more.

Pushing against the surge of discontent that continued to live within him, forever threatening to pull him under, he strode on, picking up his pace as the *trattoria* finally swung into view.

He trudged up the steps to the seating area inside, now desperate for some shade and sustenance, and managed to secure a small table near the door, slumping into the chair with a sigh of relief.

A loud squall of laughter floated over from the other side of the restaurant, and he turned around to see what was going on.

There was a large group of walkers all crowded around a table at the back, which heaved with the remains of what had obviously been a hearty lunch.

The only person who didn't have a large empty plate in front of her, but was instead nursing a glass of what looked like water, was Indigo. She was talking animatedly with a ruddy-cheeked middle-aged man sitting next to her, and the rest of the group were leaning in, listening to the story she was telling. There was another roar of laughter as she concluded her tale, and she sat back with a wide, captivating smile on her face, then drained the last of her drink and stood up.

His eyes were immediately drawn to her long, shapely legs as she stepped back from the table, and his heart rate picked up as his mutinous mind conjured up the impression of how they might feel wrapped around him.

He turned away quickly as she went to grab her bag, not wanting her to catch him watching her, aware of a heavy pull of disgust with himself in the pit of his belly.

What was he doing? This was ridiculous. He wasn't going to cower here like an idiot. He looked up as she walked past his table, readying himself to face the music, but she didn't notice him sitting there, her eyes looking a little glazed as she made for the door.

Had she eaten anything since breakfast? He suspected not, judging by what he'd just witnessed, and now she was about to walk for another few hours in the hottest part of the day.

He shifted in his seat, irritated by her foolhardiness, aware of an achy tension in his body. Not that it was any of his concern. She was a grown woman who could fend for herself. If she weren't, surely she wouldn't have come on this walking holiday alone?

Except that she wasn't supposed to.

The thought gave him pause.

But no, she'd made the decision to come on her own and just because they'd shared an association, it didn't mean he should feel responsible for her well-being.

He watched out of the window as she walked slowly away, then turned back to the matter in hand.

Looking after his own needs—in the form of lunch.

An hour later, he was back on the path, trudging towards a viewpoint where he planned to take another quick break and stare out across at the swell of the ocean while he caught his breath.

There was a long bench sitting proudly on the apex of the clearing, shaded by a fig tree, its branches heavy with fruit. And on that bench, stretched out with her head on her rucksack, was Indigo.

Julien came to a sudden halt and stared at her, his pulse rattling through his veins.

She looked exhausted, her face pink and the exposed part of her neck and upper chest glistening with perspiration in the heat.

His heart gave a jolt at the sight.

He really should keep walking and leave her alone to rest; she hadn't seen him standing there yet, so now would be a good time to turn around and keep on going. He could take a break another half mile or so on.

But he didn't move. Something was stopping him. Some misplaced sense of responsibility.

Sighing, he made his way over to her, resigned to checking that she was okay, thereby clearing his conscience.

She sat up quickly when she noticed him approaching, pulling her rucksack on to her knees and looping her arms around it, as if using it for protection against him.

Did she really have everything she needed for the whole week in that small bag? he wondered fleetingly. His own luggage was about three times the size of hers—hence getting it transported by courier from place to place as he progressed along the walk.

'Hi, Indigo,' he said as he came to a halt in front of her.

Her shoulders stiffened and she gave him a curt nod. 'Julien.'

'How are you today?'

'Fine, thanks. You?' From the tone of her voice she was clearly struggling to be polite.

'Hung-over,' he admitted, giving her a rueful smile.

She didn't smile back.

Tense silence crackled between them, and Indigo's stomach took the opportunity to rumble loudly.

'Have you eaten enough today?' he asked, aiming for an airy, upbeat tone but not quite pulling it off.

She tightened her arms around her bag and gave him a level stare. 'That depends on what you mean by enough.'

'Did you eat lunch?'

There was a pause, where she seemed to be arguing with herself about whether to answer him truthfully. 'No,' she said finally.

'Why not?'

'I wasn't hungry.'

There was an edge to her voice that told him she wasn't in the mood to be questioned any more about her choices.

'You mean you didn't manage to lift any extra food from the breakfast buffet?' he joked.

Her chin lifted fractionally and her shoulders tensed. 'That's right,' she said with a sarcastic bite to her voice.

It was the dismissive way she deliberately looked away from him into the distance that finally tipped him over the edge. 'You're crazy, you know that? You can't go walking for hours in this heat without eating enough.'

The look she gave him could have frozen water.

Sighing hard, he rummaged in the small rucksack he was carrying his provisions for the walk in and located his emergency energy bar. Striding over to the bench, he held it out towards her.

'Here, take this.'

She looked at the bar with some disdain. 'No, thanks. I don't need anything from you.'

From the tone of her voice, there was undoubtedly a lot more she wanted to add to that statement. Like exactly where he could stick his cereal bar.

Clearly he'd hurt her feelings last night, but, in his defence, he'd been doing her a favour letting her know right away that she was wasting her time if she was expecting anything more to develop between them this week.

Not that he was going to drag that up again right now.

Sighing with impatience, he dropped the energy bar on to the bench next to her, then stepped back, giving her a reproving look.

Okay, he'd done his duty now—he could walk away with integrity.

But, instead of picking up the bar, she stood up and shucked her rucksack on to her back, ignoring it completely.

'Well, it's time I got on with my walk and left you to enjoy the scenery on your *own*. Enjoy the rest of your vacation, Julien,' she said pointedly, echoing his words to her last night.

He watched her walk away from him, his jaw aching with tension as he fought the urge to go after her and tell her to stop being such a stubborn fool and at least stay and rest for a bit longer, the pressure of the denial restarting the throb of pain in his head.

Stomping into Praiano an hour and a half later, with aching legs and a decidedly damp T-shirt sticking to his back, Julien still hadn't shaken the feeling that he should have done more to convince Indigo to take the food he'd offered her.

His failure to persuade her to let him help had reminded him a little too keenly of the struggles he'd had with Celine at the end of their marriage.

Not that the two things could really be compared.

He'd not seen Indigo again on the route; he'd given her a twenty-minute head start after she'd stormed away, which he guessed must mean she'd made it to Praiano without collapsing. At least that was something.

It took him a couple of minutes to locate his hotel, which was in the centre of the small town, and he was about to stride into the glass-fronted lobby when his gaze caught on a familiar figure limping towards him along the pavement to his left.

Indigo didn't appear to notice him standing there and she stopped a few paces away, wrestling her bag off her back and dumping it wearily on to the floor by her feet to pull out her water bottle.

As his gaze followed the movement, he noticed that the trainers she'd chosen to walk for miles and miles in each day were beginning to fall apart, the rubber cracked and peeling away from the material at the sides of the shoe. Surely they couldn't be supporting her feet and ankles properly, and the soles had to be getting thinner and thinner from the rough ground.

Did the woman have *no* sense? Not only was she putting herself in danger of collapse from not eating enough, she was going to end up damaging her feet, or risk skidding off a cliff walking in such unsuitable footwear.

White-hot anger flashed through him at her stupidity, and he stalked towards her, not sure what he was going to say but knowing he needed to say *something* this time.

'Indigo, what are you doing walking in those running shoes over that kind of terrain?' he ground out, frowning hard and jabbing his finger down at her feet.

She took a small step backwards, the alarm on her face at his sudden appearance quickly changing to annoyance.

'What's it to you?' she asked archly, shooting up an eyebrow. 'For someone determined to spend his holiday alone you've got an awful lot to say about the way I spend mine.'

Julien found himself lost for words. She had a point—what was it to him? He wasn't responsible for her and she'd made it perfectly clear she didn't want or need his help.

But someone needed to point out her recklessness

to her. Apparently she had no idea how to look after herself.

'Trekking so far in those flimsy shoes is going to damage your feet.'

She took a tiny step towards him. 'I really don't need you to tell me what I should and shouldn't do, thanks very much.'

He matched her step with one of his own. 'You know, I think you're the most stubborn person I've ever met. It seems to me you need someone to point out the obvious or you're going to give yourself a serious injury.'

She let out a large huff of breath, her cheeks flaring with colour. 'Not that it's any of your business, but it wouldn't normally be my choice to go trekking in trainers. If you must know, the airline lost my bag which had my walking boots in it!'

He stared at her, perplexed. 'Why don't you buy yourself some more boots? Surely your insurance will cover it?'

There was a dangerous flash in her eyes. 'Just go and buy some more boots? With what? I know it's probably hard for someone like you to understand, but some people don't have extra money just lying around in their back pocket. I have nothing in my bank account at the moment and my emergency credit card and half my holiday money also happens to be in my lost bag!'

He could tell from the look in her eyes that she'd reached the end of her tether. Pain and hunger would do that to you.

It suddenly dawned on him what all her previous strange behaviour had been about: the change in hotel after only one night, the stolen lunch, the determination to eat pizza instead of à la carte cuisine.

Money trouble.

'Why haven't you asked your family for help?' he asked, gentling his voice now. 'Surely one of your brothers will lend you some money to tide you over?'

Sighing, she folded her arms and looked down at her feet, kicking at the ground and wincing. 'Because I don't want to.'

'Why not?'

She looked him directly in the eye again. 'I don't like to rely on other people. I need to know I can survive on my own without any help.'

He gave her a puzzled frown. 'That's impressive. But being able to accept help from others is a skill too.'

She opened her mouth as if to speak, then shut it again, shrugged, then flapped her hand around in an airy manner. 'It's an old habit. It was always do or die in the house where I grew up. Showing any kind of neediness to my brothers was deemed as a sign of weakness.'

This insight into her life disturbed him. 'What about your parents then?'

She paused before she spoke. 'My mum died from breast cancer when I was twelve and my dad passed away a couple of years ago—although, to be honest, he pretty much died when she did, at least his spirit did.'

Her whole posture seemed to shrink in on itself as she folded her arms across her chest. Clearly it was a difficult subject for her to talk about.

'He didn't cope well after she'd gone,' she continued, staring down at the floor, 'so I took over running the household. My brothers certainly didn't have a clue how to do it. Luckily, my mum taught me how to cook before she died and I found I was good at it.' She kicked gently at the ground. 'My dad suffered with bad depression so I ended up staying at home whilst I did my college courses, and then for a few years afterwards.' She shrugged. 'Tough times. But it taught me how to look after myself.'

There was a shadow of sadness in her eyes when she finally looked up at him.

Instinctively, he reached out, giving her arm a sympathetic squeeze. 'I'm sorry.'

'Ah, don't be. I'm okay.'

'That must have been really hard for you.'

She shrugged. 'I survived.'

'No wonder you're so driven.'

Taking a step back, she leant against the wall of the hotel. 'Yeah, well, I wanted to do something good with my life. I wanted to feel like my mum would be proud of me, had she survived. She only made it to forty-four before the cancer killed her. How can that be right? She was a good person. A kind and loving person.'

Her sadness hung thickly in the air between them.

'Some days, life seems anything but fair.'

'Ain't that the truth?'

The haunted look in her eyes broke him.

'Okay, come with me,' he ordered, scooping up her rucksack from the ground and slinging it over his shoulder, then setting off back down the street in the direction she'd come from.

It took a moment for her to come running after him.

'Where are you going with my bag?' she demanded, her breath coming out in short pants after her sprint.

'You'll see.'

'Julien, give it back to me!'

'I will, when we get there.'

'Where?'

'You'll see.'

She growled, low in her throat. 'Now who's being stubborn?'

Luckily, the shop specialising in walking gear that he'd walked past earlier was only another minute's walk away, down the next street, which was a good thing as Indigo was limping hard in her wrecked trainers now.

He ignored her exasperated sigh as he ushered her through the door and into the wonderfully cool air-conditioned interior.

She stopped dead just inside the shop and turned to give him a withering look. 'Julien, I told you, I can't afford to buy new boots right now.'

'I heard you. But you're not buying them. I am.'

Before she could even open her mouth to protest he held up a hand. 'Do not argue with me. I cannot let you walk any more in those monstrosities. It's offending my sensibilities.'

She shook her head. 'Julien, I can't—'

'Quiet, stubborn woman,' he growled in frustration.

Thankfully, she didn't take his tone as an insult, although he was a little perturbed when she burst into laughter instead.

In fact, he started to become seriously worried about her when the laughter seemed to overtake her, bending her double and shaking her whole body as she struggled to get her breathing under control.

When she finally managed to pull herself together, she looked up at him with tears of laughter still in her eyes. 'I'm sorry, I don't know why I'm laughing. I think I'm a bit hysterical. Today has just been a bit *much*, you know? In fact, this whole holiday hasn't exactly turned out the way I expected it to.'

'Yes, this wasn't what I had in mind when I pictured a break either. I was hoping for a little more peace and quiet and a lot less bickering with pig-headed women,' he said grumpily.

This only made her start laughing again, in great gulping gasps.

All he could do was stand there and wait for her to get a handle on it again.

'I have no idea why the state of my feet troubles you,' she said eventually, taking deep breaths to calm herself down, 'but if it means so much to you then I'll let you buy me some boots.' She swiped the tears from her cheeks and held up a finger. 'But you have to give me your address so I can reimburse you after I get home.'

He shook his head. 'There is no need to pay me back.'

This seemed to sober her up pretty quickly. 'Yes, there is, Julien.'

He could tell from the look on her face that the only way she'd let him help her out was if she felt she could even things out later. Which was fine by him. The cost of the boots meant nothing to him, but he knew this wasn't really about the money. It was about pride.

'Okay. Agreed,' he said, giving her a resigned smile. Catching the sales assistant's eye, he waved for her to come over.

'Now, let's get you sorted out.'

CHAPTER FIVE

Discovering Praiano—a simple town with a big heart. Check out the small pebbled cove, which is especially atmospheric in the evening...

THE NEW BOOTS felt wonderful on her feet.

Despite her protests, Julien had insisted on buying her some specialised walking socks and plasters too, in an attempt to protect her poor blistered skin from more damage. She was now wearing all the things they'd purchased and had dropped her ruined trainers into the shop's recycling bin with a huge sigh of relief.

The day was finally starting to look up.

After finally arriving in Praiano, footsore, disgruntled and almost faint with hunger, she'd hit rock bottom when she'd arrived at her hotel to find her bag still hadn't turned up.

She'd nearly cried, right there at the reception desk.

In fact, she was just on her way to grab the cheapest, most calorific meal she could find in the town centre to try and boost her morale when Julien had shown up out of the blue and marched her over to the hiking store.

Even though she felt hugely uncomfortable about him spending money on her, at that precise moment she hadn't had the strength to put up more of a fight.

That was why she'd given in so easily.

That and the fact she'd been acutely aware of something in his eyes when he'd argued with her—something that made her think he'd needed to win this small battle. Maybe it was just a macho male impulse to assert his authority, but for some reason she didn't believe that was the whole of it. Even though he'd made it clear he didn't want anything more to do with her, he hadn't been able to turn a blind eye when he'd seen how she was struggling.

Just the fact he'd noticed that she was in trouble made her feel like she wanted to cry again, only this time with gratitude. It felt like a long time since someone had looked out for her like that.

Argh! And now she was starting to like him again, when she'd told herself to stay well out of his way.

After exiting the shop with Julien hot on her newly shod heels, they stood awkwardly on the pavement, looking anywhere but at each other. She expected him to make some excuse any second now to get away from the strange tension deadening the air between them, but he didn't move, instead turning to look at her with that perplexed frown of his.

'Why don't you go for a short walk in your boots, to check they're fitting properly?' he said, breaking eye contact to glance down at her feet. 'Just in case you need to take them back. I'm guessing you're walking on to

Positano tomorrow, so you won't have an opportunity to swap them after today.'

'Yes, I am,' she said. 'That's a good idea.' Swinging her bag on to her back, she took a pace backwards. 'What are you going to do?' she asked, trying to make the question sound as casual as possible. What was the etiquette here? Should she invite him to come along? It felt rude to just stride off when he'd gone to the trouble of helping her out. But, then again, would she be putting him in an awkward position where he'd feel forced to reject her again?

'Why don't I come with you?' he said, surprising her. 'The assistant didn't seem to know much English and you might need me to translate again.' He frowned and shook his head. 'At least I'm assuming you don't speak Italian? I never asked.'

'You assume correctly.' It had pleased her to find out she'd been right about his linguistic skills. When the sales assistant had come over and they'd started speaking to her in English and she'd not understood the nuances of what they wanted, Julien had switched to Italian. To her untrained ear it sounded as flawless as his English. Which proved her theory that he'd been speaking her language for her benefit the night they'd shared the honeymoon suite. Something about this discovery gave her a little lift of joy.

'I can order a coffee and ask where the bathrooms are, but that's about the extent of my vocabulary without consulting a phrase book,' she said with a smile.

'*Bon*. I'll come with you then.'

'Don't you want to check into your hotel?'

He shook his head. 'Later.'

'Okay,' she said, shrugging, trying not to give away how pleased she was that he wasn't just going to abandon her now. 'I'm going to grab a sandwich from that shop over there before I die of hunger, but I can eat it while we walk.'

'We can sit down. I'm not in a rush.'

'Are you sure?'

'Yes. Sure.'

So, she bought a panini stuffed with prosciutto and nutty-tasting cheese and the sweetest sundried tomatoes she'd even eaten and sat at a long counter in the shop and consumed the whole thing in about two minutes flat. Julien stood next to her, drinking an espresso, not saying a word about her eating habits, though she could practically hear him thinking the words, *See? You were a fool not to take that energy bar when I offered it to you.*

Maybe she had been a little foolish, but she'd still been angry with him at the time for the way he'd spoken to her the night before, and had chosen her pride over her stomach.

After that they wandered out of the town centre and away towards the cliffs, enjoying the cool breeze coming off the sea. It was still hot, but much more bearable now that the sun had begun to slip down behind the horizon.

'Let's go and check out the beach,' she suggested, fully expecting him to say no and make his excuses to leave now.

He paused for a moment, his expression unreadable,

before nodding slowly. 'Sure,' he said, surprising her again with the warmth in his voice.

They made their way over to where a winding set of steps led down to the small pebbled beach. The sharp, briny smell of the sea hit her nose as they picked their way across to the centre of the deserted cove, the only sound coming from the rush of waves and the melodic tinkle of the stones as the water played back and forth over them.

She stopped near the water's edge and looked out towards the horizon, where the sun was disappearing from view, leaving the soft glow of dusk in its wake.

'Wow. It really is beautiful here,' she said as Julien came to a halt beside her.

They stood side by side and stared out at the gentle swell of the water in silence, listening to the faraway cries of the birds wheeling in the sky above them.

When she turned to glance at Julien, she was surprised to find he was looking at her with a strange little pinch between his brows.

A wave of tingling warmth washed from head to foot, pooling deep inside her as their gazes locked. She knew it was ridiculous to read anything into it, but something felt different between them now, as if a layer of armour had been peeled away.

Clearing her throat, she tore her gaze away and rummaged in her bag, desperate for something to distract her from the fizz of nerves in her tummy, producing her book on walking the Amalfi coast and her eyeliner. 'Here,' she said, thrusting them towards him. 'Write your address inside the front cover, will you? Then I'll know where to send the money.'

Without a word, he took them from her and, twitching his eyebrows at her choice of writing implement, wrote in the book.

She watched him move his strong, blunt-tipped fingers across the page, marvelling at how elegant his writing was.

He was a man of such contradictions.

'Why did you do this for me?' she blurted, unable to keep her speculation to herself any longer.

He glanced up at her, his eyes narrowing in thought. 'I don't like to see anyone in trouble, especially when I can do something to fix the problem easily.'

His choice of the word 'anyone' made her stomach drop a little with disappointment. 'You mean by throwing money at it?' she said, perhaps a little too snippily.

He raised an eyebrow. 'If that's what it takes.'

How lucky to have that luxury, she thought. But she didn't say it out loud. It would only have sounded petty and churlish.

'Well, thank you.' She took the book and eyeliner back from him and slid them carefully back into her bag.

There was an uncomfortable pause where they stood looking at each other again.

Indigo was aware of her heart beating hard against her ribcage as she tried to make sense of what was going on here. Why was he still here talking to her? Was it because he felt sorry for her? She hoped that wasn't it.

'Look, Indigo, I should apologise for being so rude last night at dinner.'

She couldn't meet his gaze, the memory of the humiliation she'd felt burning through her once again. 'Forget about it. It doesn't matter.'

'Yes, it does.' He moved his head to the side, then bent towards her, waiting until he'd caught her eye before he spoke again. 'Indigo, it does. I'm not normally so unfriendly; you've just caught me at a bad time.'

She gave him a shaky smile, cocking her head and splaying out her hands on either side of her. 'Okay, I accept your apology.'

There was relief in his eyes and something else.

Her lips tingled as his gaze dropped to her mouth and her pulse rocketed.

He looked like—

—he wanted to—

—*kiss* her.

The thought lit a fire inside her, burning through her veins and turning her nerve endings into a crackling mass of need.

Ever since she'd laid eyes on him she'd wondered what it would feel like to have those strong arms wrapped around her, holding her close, comforting and sheltering her. And those wide, firm lips pressed against hers, smoothing away her loneliness.

The air felt thick with longing as his eyes met hers again. They seemed to darken as she parted her lips to drag warm, salty air deep into her lungs in an attempt to calm her erratic heartbeat.

Something seemed to be pulling her towards him,

some strange magnetic instinct, and she took a microstep forwards to maintain her balance, raising her hand to his face.

He let out a low, rough breath as her fingers connected with the lightly stubbled skin of his jaw, and then suddenly Julien was no longer there in front of her, but far, far away.

Too far.

'What—?' She blinked in shock, stumbling forwards, dazed by the sudden desertion.

He was standing a few paces back from her now, shaking his head, his eyes a little wild. He held up a hand, his face a picture of remorse. 'That's not what I'm here for, Indigo.' He shook his head, his expression heavy with regret and frustration. 'I'm in no position to—' He waved a hand in her direction, his movements jerky and agitated.

'To what?'

'Do this.'

'I don't even know what *this* is, Julien.'

He took another step away from her and rubbed a hand across his face. 'I need my freedom right now, Indigo. I need to be alone.'

She snorted in angry frustration, every inch of her skin feeling hot and prickly. 'It was just going to be a kiss. A bit of fun. It didn't have to mean anything.'

If only that were true. Perhaps if it were then her voice wouldn't sound as if she'd just been picked up and shaken hard.

He screwed up his face in frustration. 'It's never just a bit of fun though, is it?' There was a look of admonishment in his eyes that made her stomach drop to the floor.

How embarrassing. She'd read the situation all wrong—though, to be fair to her, she hadn't come here looking for romance. She was just going with the flow, enjoying the adventure, seeing where the day took her.

Not that she hadn't considered the possibility of something more developing between them after he'd agreed to come down here with her. His change in mood had made her wonder whether there could be something more to this.

Something exciting. Something good.

But clearly she was wrong.

'What is it you're afraid of, Julien?' she asked, her tone a little defensive as she fought to maintain her pride.

He took another step away from her, rubbing a hand through his hair, messing up the neat waves. He looked back at her with such exasperation on his face it made her want to move towards him and smooth it away.

Which, of course, she couldn't.

Instead, she tried to smile as if it all meant nothing to her, which proved impossible because it felt as though the corners of her mouth were being dragged down by some kind of extreme gravitational force. 'I'm sorry. I didn't mean to pry.'

He looked at her for the longest time, his troubled gaze searching her face as if he wanted to say more but couldn't find the right words. Finally, he held up his hand, as if putting up a barrier between them. 'I'm going to go,' he said, taking a step away from her, his posture dipping a little as the pebbles gave way under his feet. 'It's for the best.'

And then he turned, his shoulders tense and his hands clenched into fists, and strode away from her until he disappeared into the inky-dark night.

CHAPTER SIX

Praiano to Positano—traversing the Path of the Gods. Be aware, this part of the walk includes vertiginous sections with breathtaking views...

JULIEN DIDN'T SLEEP well again.

Only this time his dreams weren't tangled with thoughts of his ex-wife and his failed marriage. Instead, they kept coming back to the intensity of the moment he'd shared with Indigo on the beach. Over and over again, as if the memory was stuck on repeat.

In his half wakeful state the next morning, he relived the overpowering instinct he'd felt to hold her close, to experience the strength of her wrapped around him, to taste her sweetness—only then to feel the wrench of guilt for almost indulging his cravings when he had no intention of following through on his physical promises.

There was no wonder she'd looked so wounded when he'd pushed her away. He'd practically accused her of being the one to lead their strange, lustful dance.

He'd been just as much to blame. More so, probably.

He'd wanted her.

But he had no right to indulge his wants. Not in the mindset he was in at the moment.

He'd known at the time that he was going too far—way too far—when he'd agreed to go down to the beach with her, but despite the warnings flashing through his mind, he'd not been able to walk away and leave her.

He'd been greedy for more time with Indigo Hughes.

It had felt so good to be able to take charge of her challenging situation and do something to help. After the sheer frustration of failing to save his marriage, it had fortified something inside him—given him the satisfaction that he hadn't lost his ability to take care of people when they needed help. Even if it had been for a near enough stranger.

Not that Indigo felt like a stranger to him any more. After hearing about how she'd lost both her parents and her struggles growing up in such a tough emotional environment, she'd become vividly real to him now. Which, of course, was part of the problem.

Standing on that beach in the quiet of dusk, watching the day change into another dark, solitary night, he'd wanted her to know what an incredible, impressive and attractive person he thought she was. At that moment making a connection with her had seemed important for some reason.

But, in doing so, he'd nearly stepped over the line and once again proved just how selfish he could be.

Giving up on getting any more sleep, he decided to set off early from the hotel in order to miss most of the other walkers on his way to Positano.

A couple of hours into the walk, he'd been enjoying

getting into the soothing rhythm of it, letting his mind wander freely, when he found himself on a particularly narrow part of the path which began to swing gradually out closer to the cliff's edge. It was only when he dragged himself out of his philosophical thoughts to take proper stock of what he was heading for that he realised the next part of the walk was going to take him past some unguarded sections where the exposed cliff edge fell steeply away from the path, straight down to the rocks below.

A bead of sweat trickled down his spine, followed swiftly by another as he carefully continued on the path, which, to his growing unease, was becoming narrower and narrower the further along it he walked.

He'd never been great with heights, but he'd never before experienced this dizzying horror as he took in the sight of the sea crashing against razor-sharp rocks below him. If only there had been a railing he could touch, to reassure himself there was no way he could stumble and fall down into what seemed in his unsettled imaginings to be oblivion.

His breath came fast now, scything in and out of his lungs and burning his parched throat as his pace slowed to a crawl. A gravitational force seemed to be pulling at him, attempting to draw him closer and closer to the edge as he picked his way along the path. Looking behind him, he wondered wildly for a moment whether he should go back, but the thought of even turning around on the narrow path caused a wave of pure terror to flood through his body and his stomach to lurch, bringing him to the edge of nausea.

It would be so easy to topple to the side and fall. He could picture the air rushing past him, feel the impending doom as he rocketed closer and closer to the jagged rocks, then the unforgiving suck of the sea as it pulled him into its fathomless depths.

His heart was pounding so hard he could feel it in his throat.

Closing his eyes, he grabbed for the foliage that rose to the right of him to steady himself and somehow managed to anchor himself enough to slide down on to his haunches with his back to the rough stone wall, pressing himself hard against it.

The solid feel of rock and earth steadied him and he opened his eyelids a crack to take stock of his situation.

Not good.

He was roughly halfway along the dangerously narrow path, with no easy way forward or back.

He was stuck.

Why the heck hadn't he bought himself a walking guidebook, like the last hotel receptionist had suggested? If he had, he'd have known what he was about to face and could either have taken a longer inland route or skipped this section of the walk completely and taken a bus to the next destination.

But then that hadn't been the point of the trip. He was here to challenge his endurance and push through any personal discomfort until he felt like himself again. Skipping part of it would have felt like cheating on the promise he'd made to himself.

But what a challenge it had turned out to be.

Adrenaline had raised his blood pressure, heating

his body as he fought the flight impulse so that he felt as though he was sitting in an oven—the fierce heat of the sun beating down on his head was not helping his cause.

What felt like an age later, the sound of voices floated towards him from the direction he'd come, and he turned his head to see who it was, humiliation already engulfing him at the thought of what he would look like, hunched over, clinging on to the rock face.

Pretty unheroic, he suspected.

A minute later a group of men that he'd not encountered before walked up to him on the path, all of them giving him an odd look as they picked their way carefully past him.

'Buongiorno,' he muttered to them, raising his head and forcing a friendly smile on to his face.

'Everything okay?' one of them asked in Italian as he passed, his brow crinkled with concern.

'Great, fine,' Julien muttered, flapping a hand in the air. 'Just taking a quick break,' he added, quickly lowering his hand again to grip back on to the rocky surface.

The man's frown deepened, but he didn't stop walking, giving a shrug and picking up his pace to catch up with his friends.

Letting out a low sigh, Julien pressed his head back against the wall again and tried to think himself out of his problem. This was ridiculous; he was a grown man of thirty-six, he should not be letting a bit of rock and air defeat him.

Blowing gently first up towards his forehead, then down towards his chest, he attempted to think cooling thoughts to regulate his heartbeat, then, when that didn't work, he tried distracting himself by thinking about work. But his mind kept leaping back to how close he was to the edge, which made him laugh out loud in a maniacal fashion because it occurred to him then that his whole world seemed to be full of edges that he was trying not to fall off at the moment.

Which inevitably made him think about Indigo. He shifted uncomfortably on his haunches as he thought again about the look of hurt in those beautiful eyes of hers—the look he'd caused—and he nearly toppled forwards.

That woman would be the death of him. Literally.

Another age passed while he tried to gather himself enough to stand up and force himself to walk along the rest of the path. It couldn't be that much further until it wound back inland. Could it?

Just as he was about to attempt to heave himself back to standing, the sound of more voices coming towards him made him freeze in dismay.

Taking a deep breath and cursing himself for picking such a popular walking route to be stranded on, he steeled himself to make polite conversation again until they'd gone. He really didn't want to have any witnesses to his humiliation, so he was going to wave them on and wait until they were well out of sight before he made his next attempt at getting off this damn cliff.

He readied himself, fixing a smile firmly on to his face and was about to turn towards the approaching group when he realised with a lurch that he recognised one of the voices.

Oh, no. Please, no. Anyone but her.

After counting to three, which did absolutely nothing to calm his raging pulse, he turned his head to watch Indigo walk towards him, followed by three women he didn't recognise.

His heart sank. Was this karma coming along to kick his butt? Or, since this was Indigo we were talking about—fate?

Her brow creased into a frown as she got nearer to where he was sitting, which wasn't entirely unjustified since he was taking up half of the path so that anyone wanting to journey on would have to step around him, putting themselves in even more danger of slipping off the edge of the cliff and into the sea.

'Julien, are you okay?' Indigo asked, her voice edged with unease. That would be due to the insulting I-want-you-no-I-don't debacle he'd put her through last night.

'I'm fine, Indigo,' he managed to rasp through a throat that had practically closed up with embarrassment.

Her frown deepened, but she kept on walking, stepping past him so that the women close on her heels could get by too.

Thankfully, none of the others spoke to him and he averted his gaze, willing away the raging heat in his face as he counted down the seconds until they'd be out of his sight line and he could make another attempt at standing up and leaving this godforsaken place.

There was a murmur of voices in the distance, which he assumed was Indigo filling the rest of her party in on the tribulations he'd put her through since they'd first clapped eyes on each other, and he dropped his head to his knees and let out a long, low breath.

So this was what payback felt like.

Indigo made it a few more metres down the path—after breezily explaining to the three women she'd made friends with at breakfast that Julien was just another hiker she'd met on the walk—when her conscience refused to let her take another step.

There had been something odd in Julien's expression when she'd walked up to him that had lodged itself in her head, and she couldn't shake the feeling that something had been very wrong, despite his assertions to the contrary.

After the humiliating episode last night she'd been determined to forget about him now and carry on with her holiday in the way she'd planned. She'd be coolly friendly, of course if—no, *when*—they bumped into each other again, but that would be it.

She wasn't going to put herself in a position where she made a fool of herself in front of him again. Because she didn't need an emotional roller-coaster ride like that right now.

She was supposed to be looking after herself this week.

But something about the way he was sitting there still niggled at her.

'I'm going to go back and check that Julien's okay,' she told her new friends, experiencing a dip of disappointment at leaving them when they'd all been getting on so well.

'Okay. Perhaps we'll see you in Positano,' the more senior of the women, Ruth, said, giving her a friendly smile. There was something else in her expression too, as if she suspected there was a little more to Indigo's about-turn than she was admitting to.

Not that it mattered what Ruth thought. Julien had helped her out by getting her the boots she was currently wearing, thus saving her holiday, and she owed him big for that.

He was probably fine anyway and would wave her concerns away in that arrogant way of his, so she'd be able to catch her new friends up again—but she just wanted to make sure.

Julien looked as though he was about to stand up as she made her way back to him along the rough, narrow path. She began to feel foolish for worrying and was about to turn round again when she noticed that the tendons in his hands were white with tension as he clung to the rock behind him, and a sheen of perspiration had broken out across his forehead.

What was going on here? Was he ill?

'Julien? Are you sure you're okay?' she asked as she came within striking distance of him.

He dropped his chin to his chest at the sound of her voice, as if he was exasperated with her for coming back and bothering him.

A sting of annoyance jabbed her, but she didn't back off. 'Are you feeling ill?'

He lifted his head to look at her and she could tell by the expression on his face that her instincts had been right. There was something badly wrong here.

There was a long pause where she worried whether he was even capable of answering her. Then she saw him swallow hard before letting out a long, frustrated sigh.

'I was fine with the first bit of this walk,' he said, his voice sounding strained, 'but then the path got narrower and I started to feel like the ground was sloping downwards towards the drop, which made me dizzy. Logically, I know it isn't doing that, but my brain keeps telling me otherwise. I've never been great with heights, but I haven't been affected this badly before.'

He was afraid of heights? No wonder he looked so distressed.

'Didn't you read about this bit in your guidebook?' she asked, wondering how the heck she was going to help him get out of here. It wasn't as if she could toss him over her shoulder and carry him the rest of the way.

He let out a huff of breath. 'What guidebook?'

'You don't have a guidebook with you?'

'*Non*. I'm—what do you English say?—*winging it*. I wanted to experience this holiday without any expectations.'

She couldn't help but laugh at the superior expression on his face. 'You are the most mercurial man I've ever met,' she said, unable to stop herself from teasing him. After the way he'd acted last night it was somewhat satisfying to get one over on him.

He gave her a rueful grin. 'I'm glad I amuse you.'

She could tell from the shake in his voice that he was genuinely rattled, though. It must be a terrifying thing, believing that you're stuck alone on the side of a cliff face, not able to go either forwards or back the way you came.

That thought galvanised her.

'Okay, this is what we're going to do. You're going to walk on the inside with one hand touching the wall or foliage and I'll walk next to you on the open side. You look ahead, but slightly inland so you're not looking at the drop the whole way along. I'll make sure we stay safely on the path. Okay?'

He stared at her for a moment, then blinked as if her words had taken a moment to sink in. 'Are you sure you want to do that?'

Once again she realised there was much more to his question than its face value. She knew what he was really asking.

Shaking her head, she put her hands on her hips. 'You think just because we had a minor disagreement I'm going to walk away and leave you here?'

His mouth twitched at the corner and he shook his head. 'No. That doesn't seem like the sort of thing you'd do.' He sighed, his exasperation with himself clear. 'Okay. Let's do it.'

'Okay then. Now, give me your hand.'

He looked up at her and frowned. 'What?'

'Don't worry, I'm not trying to seduce you,' she said, laying on the sarcasm. 'It will keep you grounded.'

'What if I fall and pull you over with me? I don't want to be responsible for tipping us both off a cliff.'

She let out a huff of breath at the doubt in his voice, but reined her irritation back in. 'That's not going to happen; I have fantastic balance. Now, give me your hand.'

Taking a breath, he let go of the rocks behind him and lifted his hand tentatively towards her.

She grasped it in one of hers. 'Okay, good. Now stand up slowly.'

He did so, wobbling a little as he righted himself and faced the direction in which they needed to go.

'Great, we're set,' she said, feeling the tension in his grip. 'Just keep looking at the wall and I'll guide us safely forwards.'

They set off slowly, Julien's steps hesitant at first, but becoming more sure as they made their way slowly along the pathway. Their clasped hands grew sweaty in the heat, but she didn't let go of him to wipe them on her shorts. She didn't think he'd appreciate that.

'Talk to me, take my mind off that thousand-metre drop just inches away,' he said when he wobbled a little at one point.

'I think a thousand metres might be a slight exaggeration—'

'It doesn't feel like it to me,' he cut in gruffly.

She bit back a smile. 'What do you want to talk about?'

'Anything. I don't care. Tell me about the people that you're teaching to cook.'

'Oh, my goodness… Well, there are some real characters in my cooking group.'

'I can imagine.'

'There's one guy whose wife left him six months ago after forty years of marriage because she was fed up with him being so insensitive and lazy. He's learning how to cook so he can woo her back.'

'Is it working?'

'It seems so.' She grinned at the memory. 'Apparently his spaghetti *sorry, babe* was a real hit and she's going back this week to sample his apple *turnover a new leaf*.'

She continued to tell him anecdotes about the people she'd come into contact with in the last year, actually starting to enjoy herself as she remembered things she'd not thought about for a while. It reminded her of how rewarding it had felt to make a difference in these people's lives. Even if it was only in some small way.

Julien listened intently, chiming in every now and again with a gruff question or comment, and by the time they reached the end of the vertiginous section and had come out into a wider, flatter path, his voice sounded almost normal again.

She was glad to have been able to help him, even though, as usual, he'd made it unnecessarily difficult for her.

The man was too proud for his own good—but she wasn't going to hold it against him. She knew all about pride.

It occurred to her that if she'd been here with Gavin and it had been her that had been scared of heights he would have lorded that weakness over her—even though he would have disguised it as teasing—and he wouldn't have let her forget about it for the rest of the holiday.

There was no way she was going to do that to Julien, and she felt sure he wouldn't have done it to her if the roles were reversed; he seemed too classy for that.

She awkwardly extricated her hand from his vice-like grip, somewhat disappointed now to let go. It had been nice having that connection with him as they'd talked.

He seemed a little surprised by the loss of her touch and turned to look at her with his brow drawn into a frown.

'Are you okay now?' she asked.

'Yes, I'm fine. My heart doesn't feel like it's going to explode in my chest any more.'

He looked away towards where the azure-blue ocean crashed noisily against the rocks far below them.

She gazed at his profile, taking in the strength of his jaw with its faint show of bristles, noting a small scar where the bone swooped up towards his ear. She wondered briefly how he'd got it, then pushed away the instinct to ask him. It was probably too personal a question and he might get snippy about answering it.

To be honest, she was a little hurt that he wasn't being friendlier to her after she'd just rescued him from certain doom. Not that she'd done it to be lavished with gratitude and praise, but to hear a simple thank you wouldn't hurt. Perhaps his alpha pride had been dented and this was his way of shutting the humiliation of it out.

But, even so—

He turned back suddenly, making her jump a little as the shock of the movement yanked her out of her reverie.

Taking a pace backwards, he folded his arms tightly against his chest.

She tried not to notice how this made the sculpted muscles in his arms bulge in a rather attractive way.

'So you should consider your debt for the boots paid off,' he bit out, his face dark with a frown.

Great. An acknowledgement. Sort of. It wasn't exactly a heartfelt outpouring of thanks, though.

'You do know there are more sheer drops on the next leg of the walk, don't you?' Indigo blurted with a reproachful lift of her eyebrow, unable to keep her annoyance at him spilling over.

His face seemed to pale. 'Really?'

'You know, I'd be happy to partner with you for that bit if you like,' she said loftily, 'just in case you need me to distract you with my witty repartee till we get past them.'

As soon as she'd said the words she regretted them. Not because she didn't want to spend more time with him, but because she knew, deep down, that it wasn't altruism that had prompted her to make the offer; it was because she enjoyed being around him. Even though there was a good chance she was letting herself in for more hurt and rejection here, she couldn't quite tear herself away from him just yet.

He captivated her with his strange mixture of gruff pride and compassion, not to mention the way he made her tummy flip when he looked at her with his impassioned, penetrating gaze.

She wondered again what could have happened to his marriage to make him so defensive.

'Why would you want to do that?' he asked brusquely.

'Because I'm the better person,' she joked, flashing him a grin, which he countered with a raised eyebrow.

She threw up her hands in exasperation. 'Okay, how about we say each day of walking pays off a boot? In my mind, that makes us even.'

'Okay,' he shot back. 'Fine.' He followed the word with a long, agitated sigh and glanced down once more at the sea beneath them. 'Now, let's put some more distance between us and this death trap and get to Positano before nightfall.'

They didn't speak again until they reached the outskirts of the town and checked the details of their lodgings for the night, which suited Julien just fine. After the humiliation of finding himself at such a disadvantage and having to rely on Indigo's goodwill to get him out of trouble, he'd just wanted to sink into his own head for a while.

Not that he hadn't been intensely aware of her presence beside him the whole way there. He'd been impressed with her fitness levels too—she'd not asked to stop once, even after a particularly steep ascent. No wonder she was in such good shape.

He forced the tantalising image of her lean, fit body that followed that thought right out of his head.

'We're staying on the same road,' Indigo said, throwing him an *it must be fate* smile. 'But I'm a bit further down the hill.'

'Bon,' he replied, desperate for some solitude now so

he could get a handle on these frustratingly conflicting feelings she'd stirred up in him.

He was intensely aware that in another life he would have jumped at the chance to make more of their connection—but that he couldn't act on his impulses, not here, not now. It wouldn't be fair to either of them. Despite the whispered demands of his body, his mind kept reminding him he couldn't offer her any kind of emotional commitment.

And from what he already knew of her, he could tell that wouldn't work for Indigo.

But the thought of saying goodbye to her now also twisted something inside him.

They reached the road they needed barely a minute later.

'Well, this is me,' she said, nodding towards the place where she was going to bed down for the night, with its simple crazy-paved stone frontage and garish sign that shouted: *cheap, but cheerful!*

'And that's me,' he said with a nod towards a much grander building sitting proudly a little further up the hill, with clear sea views and an elegant iron-railed terrace for every room.

Only a little further up the road, but worlds apart.

'Indigo—'

'Yes?'

'Thank you for not abandoning me to my fate today.'

He felt like a fool for saying it, but her expression lightened as if she was relieved to finally hear it.

His acknowledgement didn't stop her from winding him up, though.

'That wasn't fate trying to tip you off a cliff, it was just reminding you that you should be nicer to me.'

He rubbed a hand over his face and snorted. She was right, of course; he hadn't exactly been chivalrous about accepting her help. He'd been so embarrassed his manners seemed to have fled him.

'Okay, point taken.' Despite being desperate for some time alone, he knew he should at least attempt to show some appreciation for what she'd done for him today. She'd certainly gone above and beyond the call of duty. 'Can I buy you dinner tonight? To show my gratitude.'

She shifted on her feet, looking uncomfortable. 'You don't need to do that. I think we're even with the boots.'

She wouldn't meet his eye and her body language made him think about how she'd looked on the beach after they'd been so close—so dangerously close—to kissing. The sensory memory was so acute he could have sworn he caught the same briny scent on the air mixed with her sweet floral fragrance.

He shook it off and folded his arms. 'Look, Indigo, what happened last night on the beach—I never meant to lead you into thinking I was interested in a holiday fling. The truth is, I'm not in a good place right now. I've only just signed my divorce papers and, to be honest, I can't see myself wanting another relationship any time soon.'

She looked at him sharply, her brow pinched, and held up a hand. 'It's okay, Julien, I'm not interested in a fling either. I just came here for a break. To walk and see the magnificent scenery. That's all.'

He looked into her wide grey eyes and saw only steady resolve there. 'Okay then.' He cleared his throat, which felt strangely wadded and tight. 'Well, let's meet here at eight o'clock tomorrow,' he said. 'We should bring enough food to see us through to Nerano. Or, if you prefer, I can ask the receptionist where we can find a place to stop for lunch?'

She grinned at his rather clipped tone and rolled her eyes at him. 'Don't worry, I'll bring a packed lunch with me so you won't need to carry me past the finishing line.'

'Good,' he said, with one chastising eyebrow raised.

'Good,' she replied, pressing her lips into a pugnacious smile.

There was a voice in the back of his head warning him again about the wisdom of getting too friendly with her, but he pushed it aside. Neither of them were stupid; they knew what this was.

But, more importantly, they knew now what it wasn't.

CHAPTER SEVEN

Positano to Nerano via Sant'Agata. More vertiginous drops with a ridgetop walk and views for miles. Going for a reinvigorating swim in the ocean is a must at the end of this hard day's walk...

So, WALKING PARTNERS it was.

At least that would mean they could stop trying to avoid each other at every turn when it was clear they were destined to walk this path together, both metaphorically and physically, Indigo mused as she finished her breakfast the next morning.

She'd been really tempted to take him up on his offer of dinner last night, so much so that she'd had a physical pain in the back of her throat as she forced out her refusal, but she knew she had to be sensible here. There could be a danger she was reverting to type and turning him into a project, thinking she could help or even fix him without getting hurt—just like she had with Gavin—and that wasn't something she wanted to put herself through again.

Ugh! Was it going to be like this every time she met someone she was attracted to? Damn Gavin and his ability to make her feel so paranoid. So she liked helping people! What was so wrong with that?

Still, even if Julien had been willing to embark on a holiday fling with her, giving in to her attraction was a definite no-no. She'd be a fool to get entangled with him when he was so emotionally unavailable and she was still feeling sore after being given the boot by Gavin.

This holiday was supposed to be about looking after *her* for a change, she reminded herself for what felt like the millionth time.

After making sure she'd packed everything into her small rucksack, all the while giving herself a stern talking-to about keeping her fascination with him under wraps today, she checked out and left the hotel to meet Julien.

He was waiting for her where they'd agreed to meet the night before, looking just as perfectly turned out as usual, though his eyes were ringed with dark circles and he clearly hadn't bothered to shave. The sight of Julien with rough edges gave her a delicious little shiver of pleasure, which she quickly stamped on before it got the better of her.

Sighing, she tugged hard on her backpack straps to tighten them.

It was going to be a long day.

After a slightly awkward greeting they strode away from Positano, both a little quiet to begin with, but after a few false starts at conversation they fell into a comfortable rhythm, finding a surprisingly diverse array of subjects to chat about, including a somewhat heated discussion about whether London or Paris was the better city to live in.

'But we have amazing markets in London! Like Spitalfields and Notting Hill and the Columbia Road Flower Market,' Indigo interjected when Julien suggested that Paris was the best city in the world for street markets.

'Well, we have the best architecture,' he countered.

'London is full of great buildings, including lots of new ones,' she pointed out. 'The Shard, for example. It's way taller and more impressive than any of the buildings in Paris. Parisians seem to be totally averse to moving with the times and building anything new.'

'Ah, but we have the Eiffel Tower, which beats The Shard hands down for style,' he threw back, as if that answered everything. 'And I would hate to live in a place that was a perpetual building site.'

In fact, they were so engrossed in their back and forth banter about which city ruled supreme that Julien barely seemed to notice when she slid her hand into his as they reached the spot where one side of the path fell away to a sheer drop, as if it was the most natural thing in the world for her to do.

She thought he seemed a little less tense than he'd been the day before as they traversed the exposed section, moving their conversation on to debate the pros and cons of being part of the Euro. He seemed so engrossed, in fact, that Indigo found herself enjoying a sense of achievement at managing to distract him enough for his vertigo to not have been too much of a problem today.

Then later, chatting over lunch, it turned out they were both big fans of psychological suspense and they got into another animated discussion comparing the top writers of the genre, which took till they reached the fortress-like outskirts of Sant'Agata to conclude.

It had been so wonderful to talk about things they both felt passionate about that Indigo arrived in the town having really enjoyed her walk today.

Her hotel for the night was located on the outskirts, to the east of the town, which meant they walked straight past it once they'd left the trail.

'I'm going to use their bathroom to splash some water on my face before I leave you,' Julien said, following her up to the entrance and into the wonderfully cool interior.

'Okay,' Indigo replied, watching him stride away, feeling a mixture of apprehension and regret as she made her way to the reception desk.

Her insides felt twisted. Would this be the last they'd see of each other now that the more perilous parts of the walk were over? She couldn't imagine Julien wanting to continue holidaying with her now that she wasn't needed, not after what he'd told her about wanting time on his own to get his head together. Her stomach clenched with dismay. She'd so enjoyed getting to know him better today and had been surprised and excited by how much their tastes and beliefs had aligned.

They seemed to be kindred spirits.

Had he felt it too?

'Indigo Hughes—I have a reservation here for tonight,' she said absently to the receptionist when he looked up to greet her, her head still full of thoughts about Julien disappearing from her life now. She knew he'd think it was foolish, but she'd begun to wonder whether they'd been thrown together here for a reason. Ever since she'd met him she'd been filled with an unexpected buzz of hope and excitement for the future, which had been sadly lacking in her personal life for some time.

'Ah, yes, Signorina Hughes, I have a bag for you here,' the receptionist said.

She stared at him, her brain taking a while to switch gears and take in what he'd just said to her.

'Did you say you've got my bag? From the airport?' she asked, her voice trembling with excitement.

'Sì,' the receptionist said, leaving the desk to go into a small room behind reception and returning with her rucksack.

Indigo nearly fell to her knees with relief. After surviving with virtually nothing for half her holiday, it was absolute bliss to have her possessions returned to her. She took the large rucksack from his outstretched hands and hugged it to her like a lost child, then dropped it on to a nearby sofa in the lobby and yanked open the drawstring to check everything was still in there.

Julien returned from the bathroom to find her in a state of ecstasy as she rummaged through the bag, having pulled out first her money, then her phone and now her bikini.

'I can finally go for a swim! I've been desperate to get into the sea but I didn't want to scare the other holidaymakers by stripping down to my sensibly supportive but utterly hideous underwear,' she said, grinning at him.

He stood watching her with an amused smile as she continued to pull things out of her bag and hug them to her.

It felt a little like her birthday and Christmas had all come at once.

Except for the rather unsettling fact that she was about to say goodbye to Julien, of course. It seemed like such a shame when they'd just started getting on so well. Though there was always the possibility they might bump into each other again on the route.

'So, I guess you should be okay with the rest of the walk from this point on,' she said, forcing her mouth into a cheery smile. 'I don't think there are any more exposed paths to worry about.'

Crossing his arms, he leant his hip against the backrest of the sofa. 'Actually, I'm hiring a boat from Nerano. I'm going to sail north along the coast and stop off at some of the places of interest along the way.'

The hope she'd not wanted to fully acknowledge vanished in a puff of smoke and was replaced by a heavy thump of disappointment. So this really was it then. There would be no more opportunities to bump into him. She'd so enjoyed getting to know him today. It had been the most fun day she'd had since she got here. She'd loved the way he challenged and argued with her. Gavin had never stood up to her like that; he'd hated any kind of conflict, which, if she was totally honest, had made him rather dull company sometimes.

Julien, on the other hand, fired something inside her like no one else she'd ever met.

'Okay, well, I guess this is goodbye then,' she said, standing up on unsteady legs. 'It's been good getting to know you, Julien.' She held out her hand, hoping the tremble in it wasn't too obvious.

He stared down at it for the longest time, before clearing his throat and looking back up, straight into her eyes.

Her stomach swooped at the intensity she saw there.

'Listen, why don't you come out on the boat with me this evening? As—what do you English say?—a last hurrah? We can weigh anchor just off the coast, then you can swim away from the crowds. It would be good to have company for one more evening, to give me a chance to check out the boat before I set off on my lone voyage.'

She froze and stared back at him, excited by the invitation, but trying not to let it get the better of her. It was just a sail and a swim he was offering her, nothing more, she reminded herself sternly.

'That sounds like heaven, but are you sure you don't want some peace after having me chewing your ear off all day?'

He smiled, his lopsided grin shooting a disconcerting dart of desire through her. '*Non*. I enjoyed our discussions today. It was a nice distraction.' He didn't say from what, but then he didn't need to. He'd already made it plain why he was here. As an escape from bad memories. Just like her.

'Anyway, I need more time to convince you to give

my favourite thriller author another chance,' he continued when she didn't respond immediately. 'I feel I'd be neglecting my duty to you as a friend if I didn't give it at least one more try.'

The word 'friend' jolted her, reinforcing her resolution not to read anything more into this offer.

Despite her concerns, she couldn't bring herself to say no. Not if saying yes meant being around him for a little while longer. She loved the idea that he'd enjoyed her company today and right now she'd take gratification whichever way it came. After Gavin's accusations, it was nice to feel like she had more to offer than just a shoulder to cry on.

'Well, that would be amazing. I tell you what—since the rest of my money's turned up, I'll buy us dinner,' she suggested, needing to retain a modicum of control in their strange non-relationship relationship.

He smiled again, this time with real warmth, the action of it lighting up his whole face. 'Agreed. Then we're even,' he said.

This time she had to force herself to smile back, because, of course, the sad truth was that they wouldn't be.

Not even close.

A couple of hours later, they were sitting at a table in a beachside restaurant with views across its private golden-sand cove, groaning with pleasure after stuffing themselves full of what they both agreed was the best pasta dish they'd had since arriving in Italy.

'I have to try and persuade them to give me the recipe for this so I can teach my evening class how to make it,' Indigo said, looking round to see whether she could catch the eye of the waiter.

'Give it a go,' Julien said with a smile. 'Just widen those amazingly persuasive eyes at him and I'm sure he'll do anything you ask.'

He wouldn't be at all surprised if she managed to do it either. Indigo had such a lovely way about her it was almost impossible not to give in to her charms—as he himself had discovered time and time again this week.

'Ha! If only it were that easy,' she replied, her cheeks flushing.

Looking at her now, he realised that talking and bantering with her today had been the most fun he'd had in a very long time. She'd ignited something in him with her quick wit and ability to best his arguments, and he'd grown to like her more and more as the day had passed.

She was excellent company.

That was why he'd suggested she join him for a swim from the boat when he'd realised they were about to part ways back at her hotel. It didn't seem like the right way to end things after they'd had such a good day together.

And he hated loose ends.

They were both quiet for a moment as they watched the waiter bustling about between the busy tables.

'So where are we picking up this boat of yours?' she asked, turning to look towards where a number of them bobbed out on the open sea.

'Just over there.' He nodded over towards the other side of the cove where small rowboats and motorboats were being rented out to eager tourists.

'You know, I feel like this holiday has turned a corner,' she said, sitting back in her chair with a grin. 'Only a few days ago it was looking like I was going to have to sing for my supper and look at me now. I couldn't ask for more than this.'

When she looked round at him his heart nearly leapt out of his chest at the expression in her eyes. She looked happy. And the thought that perhaps he'd had something to do with that shook him to the core.

Get a grip, man.

'Anyway—' she cleared her throat '—I guess I'd better settle up.' She turned to catch the waiter's eye and make the international hand sign for the bill. 'Then we can go and cool off in the sea.'

That sounded like a very good idea to him right about then.

A short while after that they sat on a white sofa at back of the yacht that Julien had chartered, drinking from bottles of ice-cold beer.

Indigo leaned back against the plump cushions and stared up at the cloudless sky, barely able to believe where she was right now.

'You know, when you said *boat*, I envisaged something more like one of those,' she said, pointing towards a small rowboat being paddled back to the shore by a hot-and-bothered-looking young man while his girlfriend lay back, blithely trailing her fingers through the water.

'This is more like a luxury cruise liner, albeit a miniature one,' she added, flashing him a teasing grin.

She'd been speechless when they'd zoomed across

the water by motorboat towards this sleek, handsome yacht, which she'd assumed must belong to some millionaire playboy.

It had a kitchen aboard, for goodness' sake, and a full-sized bathroom.

And a bedroom.

That last discovery had thrown her for a complete loop.

'So are you going to sleep here tonight?' she asked, trying not to sound as covetous as she felt. It had to be wonderful to be lulled to sleep by the gentle rock and bob of a boat on the ocean. Especially if Julien was there in the bed too.

Don't go there...

'That's the plan,' he replied, taking another long pull on his beer. 'Don't worry, I can take you back to shore in the motorboat any time you want.'

'I'm not worried,' she said. And she wasn't. Not about him getting her safely back to shore anyway. She felt totally safe in his company; there was something very solid and steady about him—reassuring. But when it came to the way she felt about him, the way her heart leapt and her stomach plunged every time he looked at her...well, that was another matter.

And there was something disconcertingly intimate about the two of them being here, alone together, in the middle of the sea.

They sat back, admiring the view in silence, watching the seagulls wheel above them as the sun's final rays transformed into the warm glow of dusk.

'I can't believe they wouldn't give me the recipe for

that dish,' she said for the umpteenth time since leaving the restaurant, using her annoyance at not being able to charm the waiter as a way to disguise her twanging nerves. 'And I gave him a really big tip,' she added contritely.

'Ah, well, you can't blame them for keeping the secret of their success close to their chests,' Julien said, employing a full-on Gallic shrug, which made her smile.

'Yeah. I guess it's fair enough,' she grumbled. 'I could probably guess most of the ingredients anyway. I'm going to have to experiment when I get home.'

The thought of home made her chest contract. She didn't want to think about leaving here now that she was having such a good time. Or the fact that she'd probably never see Julien again once she left Italy.

'How's your beer?' he asked, breaking into her thoughts.

'Amazing. Best beer I've ever tasted,' she replied truthfully. She didn't often drink beer, usually opting for a glass of crisp, dry white wine when she went out, but it tasted perfect to her right then. In fact, thinking about it, everything tasted or felt or smelled that much more intensely satisfying when Julien was around. It was as if he made all her senses sit up and pay attention. Whenever she was near him she experienced this constant prickling frisson, as if she was plugged into a low-level electric socket, which made her heart race and her limbs twitch. It was as if her body was priming itself for something to happen. Something momentous and life-changing.

But she was a fool if she thought it would. The frustration of this awareness only made the restlessness worse. It made her want to leap around or jump off something, just to relieve the tension of her unsatisfied need.

'I've been meaning to ask—why the red hair?' Julien asked, reaching out and smoothing a piece of it between his fingers.

The tingle of awareness grew more intense. 'It makes me feel powerful,' she replied, desperately trying to latch on to some of that power to give her the strength to keep her wits about her.

'That figures. It suits you.' He smiled right into her eyes, making her breath hitch in her throat.

She gave a little cough to clear the tension. 'Thanks. I've wanted to do it for a while, but Gavin, my ex, wasn't keen, so I didn't until just before I came here.'

His eyebrows nearly hit his hairline. 'Really? I was under the impression you don't like to take orders from anyone.'

Huffing out a laugh, she pulled her feet up on to the sofa and hugged her knees to her. 'I don't normally. But whenever I brought it up as an idea he accused me of not taking his feelings into consideration and I felt bad about that.'

She looked away, remembering the frustration she used to feel when Gavin laid on the guilt to get his own way. It nearly always ended up with her giving in to what he wanted when he did that.

That was something she didn't miss.

Come to think of it, the hurt she'd been carrying around at the beginning of the week seemed to be greatly reduced now. Perhaps it had something to do with having something new and exciting to concentrate on.

Or someone.

Stop!

'Okay, I'm going for a swim before it gets too dark,' she said, springing up, unable to sit still next to Julien any longer, making him jerk in surprise.

Before he could say a word, she dashed down the steps to the diving platform, pulled off the towel she'd wrapped around her to cover her bikini and dived into the water.

The shock of the cold water was a delicious relief against her heated skin, and her heartbeat begin to calm as she swam steadily away from the boat, riding the gentle dip and swell of the waves, feeling a corresponding lift in her tummy.

In the distance, the cliffs rose majestically before her, the foliage vividly green against the soft grey of the rock.

It was so peaceful here, on her own in the middle of the sea with the vast sky above her and the undulating water disappearing into the horizon. This withdrawal was exactly what she needed right now to soothe the raging noise in her head.

It had been fine being alone with Julien when they were walking. The constant forward motion and changing scenery had kept her mind distracted from the intensity of his nearness, but now they were stuck in one place together she was afraid she wouldn't be able to hide how he made her feel when she was around him.

Deep inside her head she knew—she *knew*—that Julien wasn't emotionally available right now and that she should accept that as fact. He'd certainly warned her about it enough times, but it didn't stop her from wondering—hoping—*what if?*

When she finally forced herself to look back towards the boat, she saw that Julien was standing on the diving platform, his face turned towards her, shielding his eyes against the last low rays of the sun.

'Are you coming in? It feels wonderful!' she shouted, aware that her pulse had picked up again at the discovery that he'd been watching her all this time.

He paused for a moment and she got the distinct impression he was searching for an excuse not to join her, but apparently he thought better of it, pulling his T-shirt over his head in one deft move and stepping up on to the edge of the boat.

Indigo trod water, feeling her body being lifted and dropped by the gentle waves as she stared in rapt delight at his muscular physique, immensely glad of the cooling effect of the water as her body surged with nervous heat.

He dived in with the same grace he applied to every physical action and swam towards her, powering through the water. When he reached her, he stopped, barely touching distance away and gave her a wide grin.

'You're right; it does feel wonderful.'

She smiled back, wishing with all her heart that it was okay for her to reach out to him, to slide into his arms and wrap her legs around his waist, to ride the waves with him and laugh and play, then kiss him hard, so he'd know how much she was enjoying being here with him. How he'd opened up this whole new sense of excitement for life in her that she so desperately wanted to cling on to.

For this to be *their* holiday.

She longed to ask him how he'd feel about spending the rest of his week with her, but she knew she'd be on dangerous ground. This link between them was so tenuous it would snap as soon as she put any kind of pressure on it.

So instead, in an attempt to relieve her frustration and wipe that easy smile off his face, she drew back her hand and swished a sheet of water at him.

He didn't see it coming and got a face full.

'Right!' he said with an ominous growl after he'd recovered from the surprise of it, wiping the water off his face with an expression that promised retaliation.

She shrieked and swam away from him, turning back to find him in hot pursuit.

They laughed and played like a couple of kids, chasing each other through the water and sending great sprays of water back and forth until Indigo held up her hand in defeat, her eyes now stinging from the make-up she'd forgotten to take off before jumping into the water.

'Ow, ow, ow! My eyes! Wait, Julien, wait, I can't see.' Distracted by the smarting pain, she forgot to kick and dipped down into the water, sucking in a mouthful of it.

Kicking back up in alarm, she spluttered, coughing the water out and wincing at the revolting taste.

'Are you okay?' she heard Julien say, somewhere close by.

She nodded, but proved herself wrong by accidentally taking in another gulp of briny water when she drew in a breath to try and cough the sharpness out of her throat, starting to panic as she felt herself sinking back down beneath the waves again.

'It's okay, I've got you,' he said right next to her now.

She felt his arm slide around her waist and he pulled her securely against his chest, lifting her further out of the water. She clung to him, wrapping her legs around his hips to make it easier for him to swim, and he kicked hard, quickly taking them the few metres back to the boat.

Reaching to grab hold of the rail at the stern, he hauled them both on to the diving platform and they toppled backwards with the momentum, Indigo landing on her back beneath him.

He looked down at her, his face only inches from hers, his eyes dark with alarm.

'Are you okay?' he asked, the concern in his voice making her shiver.

She was suddenly acutely aware of how little clothing she was wearing and how solid and warm the boat's deck was under her back and how good the hard press of his body felt between her legs.

All she could do was nod in response.

'You look like a bedraggled panda,' he murmured, his voice sounding rough and deep as he ran his thumbs gently under her eyes, wiping the make-up away.

The simple tenderness of this action undid her and, from out of nowhere, an overwhelming urge to cry hit her, forcing the air from her lungs and tightening her throat. But she didn't want to let the tears come. Not like this, not with him looking at her like he was. He'd see it—her vulnerability and need. So, in the absence of a better idea, she raised her head those few precious inches and kissed him.

In her head, she'd meant it to be a kiss of gratitude, an apology to smooth away his worry, an acknowledgement of his act of kindness, but as soon as her lips touched his, she was lost.

She let out a small moan as she registered the firmness of his mouth, then a gasp as his lips parted so she could sweep the tip of her tongue against his.

He tasted so good: musky and seductive and sweet all wrapped up into one delicious essence. Pressing her lips harder against his, she tightened her grip and pulled his body closer to her, so she was hard up against his solid chest, revelling in the strength of him as she wrapped her limbs around him.

She was drowning again, only this time in his scent, turning into a bundle of nerve endings under his touch. Her whole body sang with joy as she felt the power of him surround her, drawing her down deep into the oblivion of the kiss.

Until something changed.

Her heart started to hammer as she realised he was withdrawing from her.

'Wait, Indigo, stop,' he muttered against her mouth, lifting himself away so she had to loosen her grip on him.

Misery sank through her in a heavy wave as she realised what she'd done.

Exactly what she'd been warning herself against for the entire day.

She'd given herself away again.

When she dared to open her eyes, he was shaking his head, his eyes squeezed tightly closed as if he was trying to will away what had just happened.

And then, like before, when laughter had overtaken her, something seemed to snap inside, only this time it was the tears that came, racking her body with brutal sobs.

'I'm sorry, I'm so sorry,' she managed to struggle out between gasps, wishing she was anywhere but there with Julien right then. She hated him seeing her break down like this.

'I guess I'm still feeling a bit raw and lonely after Gavin dumped me like he did. Not that that's much of an excuse.'

His dismayed expression told her everything she needed to know. She'd totally blown it with him now.

'Stay here. I'll go and get us some towels,' he said, getting up awkwardly.

She felt the cool movement of air on her skin as he left her, which was immediately replaced by the hot sting of humiliation.

Sitting up, she rolled on to her knees then carefully got to her feet, not entirely sure her legs were going to hold her up.

No way was she going to cower here like an idiot until he returned.

By the time she walked on to the main deck, he was coming back with two large, fluffy white towels. He handed one to her and used the other to wipe the remaining water from his face.

'Thank you,' she said, wrapping it tightly around her, unable to make eye contact with him.

'Indigo? Are you okay?' he asked quietly.

When she finally plucked up the courage to look at him his expression was dark with frustration.

'I'm just going to go and wash my face,' she said, tearing her gaze away and turning to make her way shakily down to the belly of the boat.

In the bathroom she sat down on the closed toilet seat and dropped her head into her hands.

What a fool she was. And she only had herself to blame. She'd thought she could handle being here with him—that it wouldn't mean anything to her, but it did. It did.

It meant the world to her.

After washing away the remainder of the make-up, she took a deep bolstering breath and left the bathroom, deciding to ask Julien to take her back to shore right now, before things got any more awkward between them—if that was even possible.

She found him sitting on the sofa when she shuffled back on to the deck, his elbows on his knees and his hands clasped in front of him. He hadn't bothered putting his T-shirt back on and his bare chest glinted with water droplets in the final dying rays of the sun.

Another tormenting rush of awareness made her skin tingle from head to toe.

She perched on the edge of the sofa next to him, readying herself to make some excuse about being tired or needing to get up early the next morning so he wouldn't have to feel guilty about getting her off his boat as soon as possible.

Acutely aware that this would be the last time she'd ever see him, she took a breath and turned to face him, her throat tight with sorrow.

'Tell me what happened with your ex,' he said before she had chance to speak, regarding her with a furrowed brow.

She stared at him, wondering whether she'd misheard.

He just looked back at her with an expectant expression on his face.

'Are—are you sure you want to hear it?' she stuttered.

'Oui.'

His genuine concern lit a fire within her, warming her both inside and out, but still she hesitated, not sure she wanted him to know the full humiliating story.

He held up a finger. 'Wait. I'll get us more beer.'

Returning a moment later with two more bottles of ice-cold beer, he handed one to her and sat back down, clinking the neck of his against hers before taking a long swallow and raising his eyebrows at her expectantly, waiting for her to begin.

She could *not* tell him, of course—could make up some general non-specific story about things not working out between her and Gavin—but she respected Julien too much to fob him off like that.

She took a long drink from her own bottle, then sat back and took a steadying breath, fighting back the nerves in her tummy before she spoke.

'Apparently my ex, Gavin, needed to be with someone who was more grateful to have him as a boyfriend.'

'More grateful?' Julien repeated slowly, looking thunderstruck.

She sighed and spread out her hands on her lap, staring down at them for courage.

'Yes, well, our relationship was a bit strange. We met when he needed somewhere to stay after his wife told him she wanted a divorce, and I had a spare room available, so I offered it to him as a stopgap—as a favour to a friend of a friend. He was an emotional wreck when he moved in and I made a huge effort to make him feel as welcome as possible.' She took a breath. 'We ended up getting really close and things sort of developed between us…romantically.'

She glanced at Julien but he just nodded.

'I really liked being the one he leaned on for support. I guess it fed into my need to try and fix people, or at least make their lives easier. I'd lost my dad six months before, after years of looking after him, and I felt a bit adrift. Gavin was the first serious boyfriend I'd ever had and I really threw myself into being with him.' She looked away, across towards the darkening horizon.

'I guess I feel drawn to looking after people. It's what I do. It makes me feel happy. Useful. In control—or something.' She knew she sounded defensive, but Julien didn't react so she kept talking.

'Everything was okay between Gavin and me until I started the Welcome Café,' she continued, wanting Julien to have the whole story before he judged her.

'He wanted to give me advice about how to run it—

he has his own catering business—and he used to get really offended if I didn't do what he suggested.'

Julien went to speak but she held up a hand, asking him to wait.

'To be fair to him, I'd started spending a lot of evenings working late and at the weekends, so I guess he must have felt neglected as well as ignored.' She sighed and rubbed a hand over her face, vaguely aware of how tight her skin felt after her dip in the sea.

'Thinking about it now, I can see the signs I missed. He'd been frustrated with me at the end of last year because he'd wanted me to go to parties and networking events with him, but I'd made commitments at work that I couldn't get out of so I hadn't been able to go to them.'

Balancing the bottle on her knee, she twisted the neck in her fingers. 'Then, three months ago, I found an engagement ring in the pocket of his coat and got all excited about it being for me.' The familiar tension began to build at the base of her spine.

'He walked into the hall while I was standing there with a goofy smile on my face, staring at it. He went totally white. Like all the blood had drained from his face. At first I thought it was because I'd ruined the surprise by finding the ring before he'd had chance to set up the proposal, but the look in his eyes told me otherwise.'

She realigned the bottle so that the label faced her square-on, unable to look at Julien now, humiliation burning her cheeks.

'He'd bought it to propose to the woman he'd been

cheating on me with.' She stared harder at the beer bottle, catching a drip of condensation on her fingertip as it made its way down the neck. 'He said he was going to tell me when he'd figured out the kindest way to break it to me, but I guess fate stepped in and forced his hand.'

She made an exploding motion with her hands. 'And that was the end of our relationship. They're getting married on Christmas Day, apparently. A winter wedding. Very romantic.'

Looking away, she tested the cool base of the empty bottle against the prickling palm of her hand to distract herself from how hot with mortification she suddenly felt.

'He didn't even give me a chance to fix what I was doing wrong—just found someone else and moved on.'

'It sounds like there wasn't anything for you to fix. He was a coward who used you to get back on his feet—taking advantage of your keen sense of compassion—then cheated on you because he's weak and selfish,' Julien said. There was a rough edge to his voice that she hadn't heard before.

Determined not to give in to the humiliation pressing at the edges of her mind, she sat up on the sofa and gave him a smile, which she hoped came across with sufficient sangfroid. 'Yeah, maybe that's how I should look at it.'

He was looking at her now with a strange expression on his face. Something like solidarity. Or affection.

Or perhaps that was just what she wanted it to be.

Oh, how she ached for it to be that. And more, so much more.

'According to him, it was my fault because I'd started to treat him like a project I'd grown bored with.'

'Had you? Grown bored with him?'

'No.' She shrugged, then sighed in exasperation. 'I don't know. Maybe. I never meant him to feel like that. But I guess once he didn't need me as much any more I took a step back. Perhaps he didn't like the fact I stopped doting on him like I had previously.'

'You mean you started concentrating on yourself and the café and he was annoyed that he'd lost your undivided attention.'

'I guess.' The mention of the café reminded her what was waiting for her to deal with when she got back home, making her stomach roll with unease. 'Ironically, I might lose the café soon anyway if we don't get the funding we need. It can't afford to pay me a living wage for much longer if we don't get the grant I've applied for, and there's no way I'm going to fire any of my staff when they've worked so hard to make it a success.'

Putting the bottle back to her lips, she was surprised to find she'd almost finished. Shrugging, she knocked back the last bit, then stared out towards the twinkling lights that had begun to appear through the velvety dusk in nearby Nerano, desperately trying to pull herself together and regain some modicum of pride.

Julien stared at Indigo's profile, transfixed, as she gazed off into the distance, the pain of her admission clear on her face. She looked younger and more vulnerable without the benefit of her make-up, and the sight of it touched something in his heart.

There was a tight pressure in his chest as he reflected on all that she'd told him. She blamed herself for the breakup of her relationship, which was patently ridiculous. It sounded like the guy hadn't been man enough to handle someone as headstrong as Indigo and, instead of having an honest conversation with her, he'd lied and cheated as a way to escape from a situation he couldn't control.

A raging sense of injustice made him move closer to her on the sofa and slide his hand under her jaw, gently urging her to turn back and face him. He wanted to say something, do something to take that look from her face.

'It never would have worked with Gavin, you know,' he said, shocked by the force of his words as they left his lips.

She blanched, her eyes widening, clearly surprised by the vehemence of his statement. 'You don't think so?'

'Non.'

'Why not?'

'Because you emasculated him.'

'What? What do you mean?' Pulling away from his touch, she stood up and took a step away from him.

He stood up too and held out a placating hand. 'I mean he sounds like the type of guy that needs his partner to dote on him to make him feel powerful.' He hadn't meant to alarm her, but he could tell from her body language that he had.

She blinked at him, hurt flashing in her eyes. 'You think I took his power away?'

'Not intentionally, I'm sure. Lots of men can't handle being with smart, assertive women.'

'Great. So what you're telling me is that, basically, if I want to run my own business I'm destined to be single forever.'

He made a move towards her, then stopped himself. 'I didn't say that.'

Her foot slid a little on the deck as she took another step backwards. 'I can't change the way I am, Julien.'

'You don't have to.'

He moved so he was standing right in front of her, barely inches away, and waited until she looked him in the eye again before he spoke. He felt a fierce, instinctive desire to let her know what an incredible person she was.

'Indigo, you're a very attractive woman. Clever, courageous, generous. You'll have no problem finding the right person to love you. Your ex was a fool not to appreciate you.'

She swallowed hard. 'You think? None of those things seem to impress you enough either. You can't even bring yourself to kiss me.' Folding her arms across her chest, she stared down at the floor.

He sighed and rubbed a hand over his face. 'That's because things are complicated for me at the moment.'

She raised a hand. 'It's okay, you don't have to make an excuse. I get it.'

'No, you *don't*, Indigo. You don't get it at all. You're the sexiest, most alluring woman I've ever met, but—'

Unfolding her arms, she flung her hands in the air. 'There's always a "but"!'

'Oui.' He lifted a hand to cup her chin again and force her to look at him so she could see the regret on his face. 'There is.'

His heart thumped heavily against his ribs as he stared into her striking eyes, her pupils so blown he could barely make out the dark ring of her irises in the sinking gloom.

It would feel so good to kiss her right now, to take away her pain. But he knew there would be no going back from it, but also no going forward. He shouldn't put her through that, not when she'd been hurt like she had.

So he just stood there like a fool, inhibited by a powerful sense of walking to the edge of a cliff and looking down into the depths, feeling an innate urge to jump.

'Take me back to shore, Julien. It's time we said goodbye,' she murmured, her eyes welling with fresh tears.

Taking a shuddering breath, she plucked at the end of the towel, which was still wrapped tightly around her, lifting up the edge and using it to dry her eyes before looking up at him again.

His heart gave a hard pulse in his chest at the sight of the pain and humiliation he saw in them.

Because of him.

Seeming to read his concern, she dropped her chin and stared at the floor. 'I'm sorry. I think I drank too much after being teetotal all week. And I'm tired. So tired.' She seemed to sag, as if all the fight had left her, and on instinct he pulled her into a tight hug against him, finding comfort in the scent of her that had become so familiar to him over the last few days. Strangely, he felt as if he'd known it forever.

And they fitted so well together. Like two pieces of a puzzle.

Relaxing his hold on her, he moved back a little so he could look into her face.

'Stay here on the boat tonight,' he heard himself saying.

'What?' Her expression was so full of wounded confusion he knew there was no way he could let her leave now. He had this fierce urge to protect and comfort her, even if it was only for one night.

'I want you to stay with me tonight. Let me prove to you exactly how attractive I find you.'

Without letting her utter another word, he bent to claim her mouth with his own, his body shivering with desire as he experienced the incredible soft sweetness of her again.

Now he'd made the decision he wanted her so much it hurt.

Before she could protest, he scooped her up into his arms, making for the steps to below deck where the bedroom was housed.

The sound of her giggle was music to his ears. 'Julien, you don't need to carry me. I can walk!'

He ignored her, striding down to the forepeak of the boat and into the bedroom, where he lay her gently on the bed.

'Let me look after you tonight, Indigo,' he said, brushing the hair away from her face and settling in next to her, dipping his head to claim her mouth once again.

She gave a small groan of need in the back of her throat. 'Yes,' she whispered against his lips, wrapping her arms around him.

And that was all he needed to hear to finally let himself go.

CHAPTER EIGHT

Nerano to Sorrento. Walking away from Nerano will be hard, but the cheering lure of Sorrento calls...

WHEN INDIGO WOKE up she couldn't quite place where she was. Opening her eyes a crack, all she saw was a plain white wall, which swooped up towards the ceiling like a roof in an attic room. Strange. She didn't remember going to bed in an attic.

Coming round a little more, she became aware of an unfamiliar rocking motion beneath her and a heavy weight around her waist that pressed gently into her tummy. Despite her disorientation, she felt curiously safe and protected.

Even so, something in the back of her brain told her that this wasn't where she was supposed to be, and as she shifted a little she felt a warm pressure behind her sink a little harder into her back.

Okay, that definitely wasn't right.

Holding her breath, she turned over carefully so as not to disturb whatever was behind her, only to find herself face to face with Julien. His eyes were still firmly shut and flickering slightly in REM sleep, his chest bare above the covers.

It all came flooding back to her in one long agonising rush.

She'd totally lost it last night after telling Julien all her sorry woes and he'd felt forced into taking her to bed to comfort her.

Ugh! What a fool she'd made of herself.

Poor Julien. He'd invited her for a sail and swim from his boat and she'd gone all melodramatic talk show on him.

Trouble was, she'd been holding in this guilt—this fear that the failure of the relationship with Gavin had all been her fault—for so long she'd not realised how close to the surface her pain and sadness really was. She'd just kept pushing it down in order to survive, and as soon as anyone had shown the slightest bit of interest in her she'd blurted the whole thing out in one long rambling splurge.

And he'd been so kind about it. In fact, he'd been more than kind, he'd been downright generous in his praise of her. Which had only served to heighten the emotion of it all.

It had been like catharsis, hearing Julien—someone she respected, revered and whose opinion she cared about—tell her it wasn't her fault. It had released something inside her. She'd finally been able to let the shame go and see the bigger picture.

It had brought it home to her what a fool she'd been thinking that Gavin could be someone she could spend the rest of her life with. She'd had a lucky escape when he left her.

Winter Wedding Woman was welcome to him and his inferiority complex.

But watching Julien now as he slept so peacefully, she felt like a fraud. She'd let him think she was distraught about Gavin leaving her, but that hadn't really been it at all. It was Julien she was most upset about. As she'd told him her miserable tale and seen the understanding and support in his eyes she'd known without a doubt that she'd lied to herself about their connection meaning nothing important to her.

She was in love with him.

Truly and desperately.

But of course she knew it was pointless to hope he felt the same way. He'd already backed away from her more than once, citing his need for freedom after his messy divorce, and one night with her wasn't going to change that.

After the pain of Gavin's cruel dismissal she couldn't put herself in a position where she'd be rejected like that again. Not unless Julien gave her a sign that he'd changed his mind about not looking for another relationship, which she was pretty sure he wasn't going to do.

He'd probably only slept with her last night because he'd felt sorry for her and didn't know what else to do when she'd blubbed all over him.

Her whole body flooded with prickly heat at the thought.

Was that all it had been? A kindness to her? Because he *was* kind—she knew that now she'd finally broken through his gruff exterior. But he'd probably regret what they'd done this morning.

She stared into his handsome face, wondering what it would be like to wake up every day and find him lying next to her. To be allowed to reach over and cup his face in her hands and plant a tender loving kiss on his lips. To be grateful every day for his presence beside her.

There was an ache deep inside her ribs that was making it hard to breathe. The hopelessness of the situation made her want to scream with frustration. Why did she have to meet him now? At the worst possible time in his life.

Perhaps because it wasn't meant to be, a small voice in her head warned.

If only he'd lower his defences enough for her to get through to him. But she understood why he was afraid to let her in; divorce could be a soul-destroying experience that could take months or even years to recover from. And with him living so far away from her there would be no opportunity to take things slowly, to try each other out for size, without making a major commitment.

It would be asking way too much of him.

And she wasn't prepared to be just some woman he'd had a fling with on the rebound.

She knew how these things went. He'd forget all about her once he returned to his real life, once the enchantment of the holiday had worn off. She'd just be some girl he once knew for a few days. An interlude. Barely even an anecdote.

Whereas for her, meeting Julien had been the best thing that had ever happened to her.

As if her last piercing thought had penetrated his dreams, Julien's eyes began to flicker open and he blinked hard, his pupils dilating as he stared into her face in confusion.

For just one heart-stopping second she thought he might lean forwards and kiss her, but he seemed to pull himself together and come fully awake, his brow creasing into a frown.

'Good morning, Indigo, how are you feeling today?'

God, she loved how he said her name, as if he was stroking every syllable with his tongue.

A telltale warmth crept up her neck at the rogue thought, continuing upwards to flush her face with heat.

'A little embarrassed if I'm honest,' she said, averting her eyes from his searching gaze.

He shifted back away from her and sat up, swinging his legs over the edge of the bed.

Realising how disrespectful that sounded, she put out a hand to touch the smooth skin of his back, but withdrew it quickly before she made contact. It felt like too intimate a gesture. 'I mean, I'm sorry for crying on you last night.'

Half turning back to face her, he exhaled in a rush of breath and shook his head.

'No apology necessary. I had fun.'

A bit of fun. That was all it had been.

A feeling of cold acceptance flooded through her, as if the remains of her hope was being washed away, leaving her thoughts clean and jagged.

Hardening the last piece of her heart, she leant down and plucked the towel that she'd been wearing last night from the floor and sat up to wrap it tightly around her.

'Well, I suppose I really ought to get back to shore. I want to get to Sorrento before the end of the day so I can have a good look around before setting off for Capri the day after. Could you take me back in the motorboat, please?'

Her words sounded so perfunctory she cringed with unease.

When she turned to look at him he was staring at her in confused surprise, then blinked and nodded as if coming out of a trance when he saw she was looking at him. '*Oui*. Okay.'

'Thank you.'

Not daring to look at him again, she strode quickly out of the room and into the bathroom, where she'd left her clothes the previous evening after getting changed into her bikini, trying to ignore the voices in her head that were urging her to turn around and tell him that she'd changed her mind and that she could stay for a little longer. Just till they'd eaten breakfast together.

Pull yourself together, Indigo, you fool! You're not a couple and you never will be.

Pulling on the dress she'd chosen with such care for their dinner together last night, she turned to the mirror to try and do something with her hair. It was sticking up in all directions after she'd slept on it wet and refused to play ball, so after a minute of fruitless fussing she gave up on it. She was desperate for a shower, but now that she'd made her mind up to go she didn't want to linger. It would only prolong the pain of leaving.

Giving her puffy face one last dismayed look in the mirror, she left the bathroom and made her way to the living area, where she found Julien sitting on the sofa waiting for her.

He stood up quickly when he saw her and walked with her towards the door to the upper deck, neither of them saying a word.

'Wait.' He put an arm across the doorway before she could walk through it, blocking her way out.

Her heart hammered hard in her chest as she looked up into his mesmerising eyes.

'You know, Indigo, if you don't mind missing that part of the walk I can sail you to Sorrento, then pick you up again the next day and drop you in Capri. I'm going that way anyway. You may as well come along for the ride.'

It was so tempting. But what a ride it would be. Just the thought of having to put a brave face on for him, pretending she was fine with them just being casual lovers for the next couple of days, made her shudder with horror.

No, she'd be better to cut her losses now and walk away while she still had some of her wits about her.

'No. Thanks. To be honest, I don't want to miss walking that bit of the track.' She couldn't meet his eyes. 'I only have a couple of days left here before it's time to get back to reality and I'm sure you don't really want me tagging along for the rest of your holiday.'

He was frowning at her now, which wasn't surprising as her voice seemed to have morphed into that of an ailing crow again.

'Are you sure you're okay?' he asked with real concern in his voice.

'Yes. I was just thinking about what you said about Gavin.'

'Oui?' He looked uncomfortable at the mention of her ex.

'I think you're right; it would never have worked out with him long term. I've been so distracted by the pain and humiliation of the way he dumped me I got the feeling muddled with missing him. I need to be with someone who's proud of me for what I've achieved, not jealous of my success. I've been beating myself up about the wrong things. It's time I stopped.'

'Oui.'

'Thank you, for making me realise that.'

'You're welcome. You deserve to be happy, Indigo.'

'As do you, Julien.'

They stared at each other, with the crackle of unsaid words in the air around them.

Say something more, Julien. Please.

But he didn't; he just nodded in a sage kind of way, as if he hadn't heard the underlying pleading in her voice.

So that was it; she had to leave right now, on her terms. It was important for her peace of mind that she kept her control, after having it so savagely ripped away from her in her last relationship.

For her own sense of self-confidence, she couldn't allow Julien to dismiss her too.

'Okay, well, I'm ready to go when you are,' she said overly brightly.

He didn't say another word as they walked up to the deck together. When they reached where the small on-board motorboat was housed, she hung back until he'd released it from its mooring and manoeuvred it down the small slope and into the water.

After climbing in he held out his hand to help her climb in too and she hoped to goodness he wouldn't notice how much she was shaking.

Neither of them said a word as Julien piloted the small craft back to the shore, sending waves of froth into the choppy water behind them.

At any other time she would have loved the feeling of powering through the waves at high speed, revelling in the adrenaline rush of something so alien and exciting, but the heavy tug of gloom in her belly cancelled out any enjoyment she might have felt.

Julien drove the boat straight on to the deserted beach and jumped out, pulling it further ashore so she could step out without getting her feet wet.

Hopping out, she turned to face him.

'So, I guess this is it then,' she said, turning to give him a smile that she knew must look incredibly fake.

'Probably not,' he said, dipping his chin and raising his eyebrow, his eyes holding a look she couldn't decipher.

Was he making a joke about their strangely magnetic connection, or was he about to ask to see her again after he'd concluded his holiday?

She drew in a shaky breath, anticipation making a pulse beat hard in her throat.

'Based on our luck so far, we're bound to run into each other on Capri,' he said with a playful lilt to his voice.

She nodded and waited—heart racing, breath stuck in her throat—for him to suggest they made a plan to meet up there.

But he didn't. Instead, he gave her a tight smile, then turned to look back towards where his yacht was anchored a mile or so off the coast. 'Well, I'd better get back and chart my course,' he said, his voice giving no suggestion at all that he was sorry to see her go. 'I only have the boat for three more days then it's back to real life.'

Real life.

Her stomach dipped and her eyes grew hot, but she refused to show him how much it was going to hurt her to leave him like this.

'Okay, well, enjoy the rest of your holiday,' she said, steeling herself as he moved towards her and placed a gentle kiss on each cheek, French-style.

'It was good knowing you, Indigo,' he murmured into her ear, before pulling back and giving her a firm nod.

'You too, Julien.' She was amazed she'd been able to get the words past her throat.

He nodded once more before turning abruptly on the spot and striding away from her.

It felt empty on the boat after Indigo had gone.

Julien paced up and down the deck feeling unsettled about the way she'd left so suddenly.

When he'd woken up to find her watching him with that perplexed expression in her eyes, he'd been worried that he'd made a huge mistake asking her to stay the night, that he'd hurt her more than helped her—and set himself up for more heartache too—and his first instinct had been to gently let her know that it had been a one-time-only thing for him.

He'd been relieved when she'd made the decision to go without him having to say anything, but he'd also been taken aback and a little perturbed by how vehement she'd been about it.

Something about the way she'd sprung out of bed didn't sit well with him.

After that he'd felt compelled to offer her a lift to Sorrento and had experienced a strange sting of hurt when she'd been almost cold in her refusal.

The memory of it disturbed him.

Perhaps she'd been embarrassed about what had happened between them after she'd fallen apart last night.

He wasn't, though. He'd loved the feel of her in his arms and the softness of her pressed beneath him. She'd been so responsive to him, making it clear she'd enjoyed his touch as much as he'd enjoyed hers.

Maybe she was just distracted by the thought of what awaited her when she got home after talking to him about it last night.

It made him so angry to think about how badly her ex had treated her because her strength and tenacity had intimidated him. And he hated the idea that she had to deal with the threat of the business she'd worked so hard to build from nothing being taken away from her all by herself.

She deserved better.

Needing a distraction from his thoughts, he went down into the galley kitchen and fixed himself some breakfast, raiding the ready-stocked cupboards and fridge, choosing sugar-free muesli and strong black coffee to satisfy his appetite. Not that he felt particularly hungry this morning.

After clearing away his crockery, he tried reading one of the books from a shelf in the living area, but he couldn't seem to concentrate on it. He was restless and twitchy. Perhaps Indigo had had a point about not missing today's walk. His body seemed attuned to doing that much exercise now and the lack of it today had left him with an abundance of energy.

Getting up, he went down to the bedroom and made the bed, pausing to skim his fingers over a small black smudge that the last of her eye make-up had left on one of the pillows.

It made him think of the way she'd looked at him through her thick black lashes when she wanted him to agree to something and a sudden, disorientating feeling of loss hit him straight in the solar plexus, taking his breath away.

Like the walking, he'd become so attuned to her presence he appeared to be missing her company.

Which finally brought him round to the real reason he'd felt troubled about her leaving so suddenly.

Waking up in the early hours of the morning to find her warm body snuggled up against his had shaken him.

Lying there under the heavy blanket of night he'd felt such a sense of calm—for the first time in as long as he could remember. He'd rested there, with Indigo in his arms, exulting in the rush and pull of the ocean beneath them, enjoying the gentle melody of the waves against the hull of the boat as he drifted in and out of sleep.

In his half wakeful state, he'd relived the feel of her long, long limbs wrapped around him, and the intoxicating scent of her as he dragged it deep into his lungs and the sweet taste of her in his mouth. He'd wanted her so badly he ached with it, and he'd just taken what he wanted even though he'd known it was a bad idea. An insight that had been reinforced when he'd seen the regret in her eyes the next morning.

It reminded him a little too keenly of all those gut-wrenching mornings, waking up next to Celine and seeing the shuttered look on her face. The cold, blank expression of a woman who despised him.

His failure to make things right between him and Celine still haunted him, even though they were divorced now and she was no longer his responsibility. He'd always been able to fix things before he met her—by finally earning enough money to buy his mother the kind of house she deserved and provide her with a lifestyle that made her happy, by finding jobs for friends who found themselves adrift and in money trouble—but with Celine he'd not been able to find a way to satisfy her. He'd given her everything he could think of and it still hadn't been enough.

It had eaten away at him.

And now he had a new regret.

He'd known, in his heart, that Indigo wasn't the sort of person who would be satisfied with a one-night stand, but he'd gone ahead and let it happen anyway. To satisfy his greedy need.

Slumping down on to the bed, he rolled on to his back and stared up at the ceiling, imagining the vast blue sky stretching out above him, feeling smaller and more helpless than he was comfortable with.

He really didn't want to have Indigo's suffering gnawing away at him too. He could have done so much more to make her happy, but he'd let her go, telling himself it was what she wanted.

She'd needed more from him than a kiss on the cheek and a metaphorical pat on the head.

His hands twitched at his sides as blood rushed through his veins.

There was no way he could leave things with her like this; it would plague him for the rest of his life.

Especially when he knew he could do something to really help and support her.

Sitting up, he took a deep fortifying breath, feeling his energy returning as purpose and resolve flooded his body with adrenaline.

He was going to find her and make things right.

CHAPTER NINE

Sorrento to Capri. It could be a rough ride between the mainland and the island, so be prepared for turbulence on your journey. Don't worry—once you're there it'll all be worth it...

HE'D NOT BEEN able to find Indigo in Sorrento.

It was ridiculous for him to feel miffed about the fact because the town had a population of over fifteen thousand, which no doubt doubled in high season. But after not being able to avoid her at the beginning of the week he'd fully expected to bump into her as soon as he set foot on dry land.

But after a fruitless search through the town, where he felt as if he'd visited every eatery and hotel that Sorrento had to offer, his heart lurching every time he caught so much as a flash of the colour red, he'd finally given up, deciding the best place to catch her would be the small port in Capri where the ferries sailed in from Sorrento on a regular basis.

Mooring the yacht in the marina just to the west of the main ferry port, he holed up early for the evening, determined to get up at the crack of dawn in order to meet the first ferry of the day in case Indigo was on it.

It felt good to have a purpose after spending the rest of the week in a state of disconnected limbo, occasionally checking his work email for news, only to find that everything was running smoothly without him. This had both heartened and distressed him.

He didn't like the idea of not being needed.

The early morning air felt fresh and cool on his skin as he made his way over to where the passenger ferries docked in the marina, armed with a bag full of food and beverages so he wouldn't have to run the risk of missing Indigo in between landings.

When he arrived, the place was only just waking up for business, catering for a few early risers who paced about waiting for the first ferry to arrive and take them back to the mainland.

He could tell from the intensity of the first rays of the sun burning through the low hanging clouds that it was going to be another hot day.

Settling down on to one of the long stone benches that faced out across the water, he took out a book he'd borrowed from his yacht's small library, made himself as comfortable as possible on a seat that wasn't really designed for people to sit on for more than a few minutes and prepared himself to wait until Indigo made an appearance.

Since leaving Julien on the beach in Nerano, Indigo had spent her time making good on her decision to continue the walk to Sorrento. In a stroke of pure luck, she'd bumped into Ruth and her group heading that way too, and was somewhat relieved to find herself warmly integrated back into the group.

She'd needed the distraction after spending the morning in a state of torment after saying goodbye to Julien.

It had taken Ruth a couple of miles' worth of small talk before she finally got round to asking about him, clearly sensing that there was something wrong in Indigo's world but that she wasn't going to bring it up herself.

Indigo had been preparing herself to talk about Julien, but even so, it was still hard to make her story of their walk to Nerano and subsequent night on the yacht sound as inconsequential as she'd wanted it to.

Ruth had not been fooled by her bluster though and had pressed her about their relationship until Indigo had given up on the pretence that he meant nothing important to her and blurted out the whole sorry tale.

'He sounds like he needs more time, love,' Ruth told her as they walked the last leg towards Sorrento.

'Yeah, I know,' she said with a sigh. 'It was just really bad timing.' They walked for another mile or so in companionable silence, with Indigo's thoughts spinning through her head until she couldn't keep it in any longer.

'I just felt like we were meant to meet,' she blurted. 'It was like some force kept dragging us back together. It felt right to be with him, you know?'

'I do,' Ruth agreed. 'My husband and I met in Western Samoa, of all places, after living only five miles apart for twelve years, never having crossed paths before. We kept missing each other, even though we now realise we'd attended quite a few of the same events. He was married to someone else at the time, though, who sadly died after a long illness a year before he and I met each other in Samoa, so it wouldn't have worked out if we'd bumped into each other earlier. It's funny how these things happen. You can't help but suspect there's some kind of benevolent force pushing you together at the right time.'

'Yeah, but if the other person isn't ready, there's only so much magic fate can weave.'

They'd come to a halt on the outskirts of the town at that point and Ruth put a comforting arm around her. 'If it's meant to be, you'll see him again, honey,' she said with a warmth in her voice that made Indigo think of the cuddles her mum used to give her when she was upset about something. From out of nowhere, she experienced a sudden and intense pang of loss. The grief of losing her mother never seemed to lessen, though it hit her less often these days, usually when she was feeling particularly low. This time it had the disconcerting effect of reminding her just how alone in the world she was right then.

Forcing back the tears that threatened to spill over, she hugged Ruth back hard, finally pulling away to give her a grateful smile.

'Thanks for taking me under your wing; I really needed the company today,' she said.

'You're welcome, sweetheart. We're flying back to England tomorrow so I'm afraid we won't be able to continue on your travels with you. I hope you enjoy your time in Capri, though—and that you find what you're looking for,' she said with a kind smile.

Indigo couldn't help but smile back, albeit with a twist of sad scepticism.

'Yeah, you never know,' she said.

And now here she was, stepping off the ferry in Capri into the bright morning sunshine and the first person she laid eyes on was Julien.

He appeared to have been watching the people getting off the ferry and as soon as he locked eyes with her he stood up and started walking towards her.

She came to a sudden halt in shock, feeling the other passengers push past her and hearing the odd 'tut' as she blocked part of the gangway. Her heart hammered in her chest, her senses on high alert as she watched him pushing his way through the crowd.

What was he doing here?

Pulling herself together, she started walking towards him again, feeling the tide of people drawing them ever closer together, until finally they were standing only feet apart, grinning as if they'd not seen each other for a year.

A gentle breeze whipped her hair around her head and she pushed it away from her face with a shaking hand.

'Julien—I thought I'd seen the last of you,' she said, hyperaware of a tremble in her voice. 'Were you waiting here for me?'

'Oui.'

She gazed into his eyes looking for a clue as to why, hardly daring to hope that he'd come to tell her he'd changed his mind about being ready for a new relationship, but his expression was inscrutable.

'I wanted to catch you before I leave Capri and sail on to Naples,' he said, taking her hand and leading her gently away from the crowd of people still mingling around the ferry and over towards the quieter side of the port.

So he wasn't staying on Capri? Was he here to try and persuade her to leave with him then? The idea of it made her stomach flutter.

When they reached a small stone bench next to a closed ticket office he let go of her hand and, reaching for her rucksack, lifted it from her shoulder and propped it up against the bench.

The anticipation was killing her. 'What's going on? Is everything okay?' she asked, hugging her arms around her. Despite her conviction they were meant to be together, something in the back of her brain warned her not to get her hopes up, just in case.

'I have something I want to give you.' He moved his hand around to his back pocket, glancing behind him as he removed whatever he had in there.

For one ridiculous, heart-thumping second she thought he was going to produce a ring and she drew in a sharp, shaky breath…

It was a large white envelope.

He held it out towards her, an expectant smile lighting up his eyes.

She tried hard not to let her disappointment show on her face as she stared down at it.

'What's this?' she asked.

'Open it and see.'

Her hands shook as she took the envelope from him and lifted up the flap at the back.

She stared at the contents, a heavy sinking sensation turning her stomach over.

It was money. Lots and lots of money. All in fifty euro notes.

'It's a donation to help with the running of your café. So you can keep working there,' he said, not appearing to notice her distress.

'I felt bad about the way we'd left things after what happened between us,' he said. 'I kept thinking about what a struggle you'll have when you get back to London. I wanted to do something to help you.'

'You came here to give me money?' she asked, her voice barely making it past her throat. Bitter disillusionment coursed through her, causing her eyes to burn with unshed tears and her skin to prickle as if she were being attacked by a thousand bees.

He frowned, looking visibly shocked by her lack of enthusiasm. 'What's wrong? I thought you'd be pleased.'

'Do you even know me at all? Did you really think I wouldn't be offended by you giving me money after I'd slept with you?' Her voice crackled with dismay. 'It's like you're paying me off to relieve your conscience!'

She knew it was a low blow, but she was so angry with him right now. Couldn't he see how humiliating this was for her?

'That's not why I'm giving it to you. *Mon Dieu!* It just means if your grant doesn't come through you can keep working there until you find another source of funding.' His shoulders tensed as he folded his arms across his chest. 'I wanted to do something to help you,' he repeated, in the same tone he'd used with the receptionist on the very first night they'd met, when he'd made it clear how disgusted he was with the lack of service she'd provided.

'I don't want your money, Julien.' This time the words came out loud and clear, thanks to a sudden surge of anger that came rushing up from the pit of her stomach.

He opened his mouth to speak, then looked away as if he'd thought better of it, frowning and shaking his head in confusion.

When he looked back, his expression was shuttered and a muscle flickered in his jaw.

'Where is this coming from, Indigo? Hmm? Why are you so angry with me for wanting to help? Can't you put your stubborn pride aside for a moment and let someone help *you* for once?' He shook his head, his eyes narrowed. 'I don't understand. What is it you want from me?'

How could he ask that? Didn't he know how she felt about him? Wasn't it obvious? 'I want you, you idiot!'

The silence after her outburst seemed to stretch on forever.

Finally, Julien closed his eyes and rubbed a hand over his face, letting out a long sigh.

'When you turned up here I thought you'd come back for me. *Me*, Julien!' Her throat felt painfully tight as she fought back the tears. 'But I guess that makes me the idiot!' A sob broke loose and she clasped a hand over her mouth to stop any more from escaping.

'Indigo—' His expression was full of regret now.

'I just want the opportunity for us to get to know each other better.' She took a deep, calming breath, not wanting to give in to her emotions and ruin any chance she had of making herself heard. 'To give a relationship a chance.'

He was shaking his head now, his eyes a little wild, as if she'd caught him in a trap and he couldn't see any way to escape. 'I can't, Indigo. I'm not ready for that.'

'So you'll just let this amazing connection that we have go? You feel it too, right? Please tell me it's not just me.'

There was another long silence where he stared at the ground. 'It's not just you,' he said finally.

'So why won't you give it a chance?'

'I *can't*, Indigo.'

'What are you afraid of?'

He rubbed a hand over his face. 'I've spent the last two years feeling like I was suffocating. I need my space—to begin to feel like I've got a grip on my life again.'

'And you can't do that and still have some space left for me?'

He spread his hands in mute apology. 'No. I'm sorry.' He gestured towards the envelope still clutched in her hand. 'That's the best I can do right now.'

'Well, I don't want it.' She thrust it back towards him and after a second's hesitation he took it from her.

From the intensity of his frown she could tell that he wasn't prepared to listen to any more of her entreaties.

She opened her mouth to try anyway, but he raised his hand to stop her.

'I can't ask you to wait for me, Indigo, because I don't know when I'll feel ready to have another serious relationship again—or if I'll ever be ready for one.

And, after what happened with your ex, the last thing you need is to embark on something so precarious with someone like me. I don't want to have any part in corrupting that amazing positivity that you have. I'm too bitter and messed up right now. I'd be a danger to you.'

'But you might feel differently one day?' There was a pleading tone in her voice now that made her cringe inside.

'*Oui*, I might. But I can't make that promise and it wouldn't be fair to ask you to wait in the hope things would change for me. I need my freedom right now and you need something I can't give you—stability. Don't wait for me. I'm sure the best person for you will walk into your life when you most need him to.'

'You already did, Julien.' Her voice broke on his name.

He shook his head and backed away from her, the expression in his eyes hard with determination. '*Non*, Indigo. I think you're an amazing woman and at another time in my life maybe we could have had something really special, but not now.'

She moved towards him, desperate not to leave things this way between them. 'You can't beat yourself up forever because of one bad relationship.'

'I'm sorry, Indigo, I have nothing else to offer you right now.' He held up the envelope, then dropped his hand again as if he felt frustrated to still be holding it.

The pause seemed to go on forever as she swallowed and swallowed and swallowed down the pain.

'Okay then, go, if that's what you think is best,' she finally managed to say.

He gave her one last nod, then turned and walked away, taking her very last hope for a future together with him.

She wanted to weep—for what could have been if only they'd met at another time.

How was it possible to feel like this for Julien after such a short amount of time? It seemed incredible that it was only a week since he'd come storming into her life with his reluctant heroism and inimitable strength.

But who you fell in love with wasn't something you could control.

And she had fallen in love with him. Desperately and completely.

But now she had to let him go.

There was something very fitting about the rough assault of waves against his boat, Julien reflected as he fought to keep the vessel on course through a sudden and ferocious storm that had swept in without warning the following day. It harmonised well with the raging confusion of emotions in his head.

This holiday was meant to punctuate a difficult and painful time in his life, to give him a definite end to the way it was then, but, to his utter frustration, it only seemed to have started a new chapter.

During his time with Indigo he'd begun to sense a difference in himself. Somehow she'd managed to pop the bubble that had been preventing him from feeling anything, bringing everything into razor-sharp focus.

The flip side of that was that he now felt everything. So acutely it made his chest ache.

He spent the next couple of days after the storm taking mental breaths whilst gliding slowly through the now peaceful waters, sailing past the looming greatness of Vesuvius, then onward towards his final destination, Naples, where he was to leave the boat and board a plane back to Paris.

Back to reality.

Not that this holiday hadn't been very real. In fact, it had probably ended up being more stressful than a week's work would have been, just for very different reasons.

Or, more precisely, one reason.

Not allowing himself to be with Indigo.

When he'd seen the look of appeal on her face, just before he'd turned away from her, he'd known in that split second what was causing the painful ache in his chest.

Love.

A fierce and irrepressible love for her.

It had shaken him to his core. Which was why he'd walked away and kept on walking until he was back on his boat, then back out to sea, putting a whole body of water between them.

He'd told himself at the time that he was leaving so she didn't get hurt, but he knew he'd only hurt her more. He'd seen it in her eyes and in the slump of her shoulders—the grief for something that could have been so good.

Thinking about it now, he realised he'd treated her with a total lack of respect by trying to buy his absolution.

How could he have thought that the way to make her happy was to give her *money*? How crass and unthinking he'd been. He knew now he couldn't buy her happiness or respect; he had to earn it with his actions, by giving her something of himself.

Which was a terrifying thought after what had happened with Celine. But then wasn't that the point? Real love was never easy; it was complex and sticky and downright rough sometimes.

He knew now that he hadn't been in love with Celine—in lust, sure—and he'd married her because he believed it was the right thing to do at the time. But the way he felt about Indigo wasn't wrapped up in sex or lust or duty; it was based on how he felt about himself when he was with her.

She'd made him come alive.

In the dark hours of the night, tossing and turning as sleep eluded him, he pictured her back in London, filling her days working at the café, laughing and joking with her colleagues, then perhaps going on a date with a man she'd met, the sparkle returning to her eyes as he lavished the praise and attention on her that she deserved.

The thought of someone else taking care of her made his stomach lurch with anxiety.

Indigo would be fine without him because she was a fighter. It was one of the things he loved about her.

But would he be all right without her?

Okay, so meeting Indigo right now wasn't great timing, but then what in life ever really was?

And at least this time being with her would be his choice.

Fuelled by the fervour of his revelation, he quickly plotted a course that would get him to Naples ahead of schedule, then picked up his phone, intent on getting himself out of Italy as fast as possible in order to set a new plan in motion.

He knew now that being here alone had been a pilgrimage to nothing. He'd thought he wanted his freedom—but it didn't feel the way he'd thought it would. It felt empty. And silent. And lonely.

A pyrrhic victory.

He'd thought he could go back to the way things used to be, before Celine, but trying to go backwards was a big mistake.

What he needed was a fresh start.

Finally, there was clarity in his mind. He missed Indigo. He loved her. He'd let her go.

And now he was going to get her back.

CHAPTER TEN

London is a vibrant and forward-looking city, ever evolving, with an exciting new encounter just waiting for you at every turn...

One week later

INDIGO WIPED HER hands on her apron and looked round at the eclectic gathering of local people who had turned up for her early evening cookery course, despite the torrential rain.

Her feet throbbed and her back ached from being on her feet all day, but her insides burned with satisfied warmth as she perused the table full of nutritious, delicious-smelling food that her class had produced in just half an hour—which they'd easily be able to replicate at home.

This made all her hard work worth it—the shine of pride on the faces of people who'd previously not believed they'd ever have the skills to cook anything vaguely edible for themselves, let alone something they'd be proud to share with friends or loved ones.

The kitchen at the back of the café wasn't stocked with enough culinary equipment to be able to teach more than five people at a time, but she was hoping that once the grant came through—she mentally crossed her fingers that it still would—she'd be able to afford to buy more so she could teach a larger group at one time.

'Well, I think you've all done a wonderful job today; it's great to see how much you've improved since you first started coming here,' she said, beaming at them all.

'It's good to have you back, Indigo; we missed your lovely smile while you were off gallivanting in Italy,' Ron, one of the gentlemen who had been coming to her for a couple of months, now called across the room, giving her a cheeky wink. He'd been a morose character when he'd first started coming, due to losing his beloved wife only a short time ago, but he'd slowly made friends and come out of his shell as, week by week, he'd allowed himself to be integrated into the group. She suspected there might even be romance blossoming between him and the only lady currently attending. They often had their heads together, chatting quietly as they worked.

Pushing away a sting of melancholy at the thought of the dire state of her own love life, he returned his wink and gestured towards the table.

'Okay, well, if you want to start tidying away, we're just about out of time. I don't know about you, but I can't wait to get home and eat after being tortured by the smell of your wonderful grub cooking for the last twenty minutes.'

It was hard keeping up a chipper tone of voice when

her heart was so heavy, but somehow she seemed to be managing it.

When the group had asked her about her holiday she'd worked hard to sound breezy and upbeat about it, telling them as much as she could whilst studiously avoiding mentioning Julien's name. She thought she'd pulled off making it sound as if she'd had a fun and revitalising time, though.

The bell of the café rang in the distance and she glanced over to her friend and kitchen assistant, Lacey, sharing a questioning smile with her.

'I'll go and see who it is and tell them we're closed,' Lacey said, already walking towards the door.

Grabbing some dirty bowls from the table, Indigo went to stack them in the dishwasher—wanting to pre-empt the tidy-up so she could get home a bit earlier tonight and have a soothing bath—and turned back to see Lacey walk into the kitchen, closely followed by a man.

A man who was tall, with blond hair and mesmerising whisky-brown eyes.

'Julien?' she gasped, not wanting to trust her vision. She hadn't been sleeping particularly well since she'd got back, her mind still whirling with thoughts about him, and she wondered for a second whether her addled brain had conjured him up to torture her a little bit more.

He walked slowly towards her, smiling in that wry way that she knew so well, making her heart beat a little faster with the comforting familiarity of it.

'What…what are you doing here?' she stammered.

'I hear you offer cookery courses to men who no longer have wives,' he said.

She blinked at him, confused by such a strange opening line. 'To widowers usually,' she said uncertainly. There was a beat of uncomfortable silence. 'But I guess we could make an exception for a divorcee,' she finished, not wanting to look rude and uncomfortable in front of her class.

'Is this the young man you met on holiday that you've been avoiding telling us about?' Margery, the lone woman in the group, piped up, her eyes twinkling with good humour.

The whole roomful of people seemed to shift at once as they all turned to look at each other, exchanging knowing glances.

Had they been talking about her behind her back whenever she left the room?

She sighed, feeling trapped and unprepared to deal with Julien's presence here in her kitchen—a place she liked to think of as her personal sanctuary. 'This is Julien,' she said, gesturing vaguely towards him. 'And yes, we met in Italy.'

There was a murmur of friendly greeting from the group.

Turning to face him now, she said with as much assertiveness as she could muster, 'I'm afraid we're just about to pack up for the evening, but if you'd like to come back at another time I'm sure we can talk about finding a place in a group for you.'

There was a glint of determination in his eyes. 'Actually, I was hoping I could walk you home tonight,' he said, moving closer. 'I have some things I need to say to you—and I'd rather not do it in front of all these strange people.' He held up an apologetic hand to the group. 'No offence.'

'None taken,' Margery called from the other side of the room, giving Julien a supportive grin.

'Yes, Indigo, you go,' Lacey said. 'I can supervise the tidy-up and make sure the place is locked up before I leave.'

Indigo opened her mouth to argue but, as one, the whole group shook their heads at her.

'Go and spend some time with your friend,' Ron said, flapping a dismissing hand at her.

Well, it seemed as if she didn't have much of a choice. Clearly, they weren't going to let her stay. So much for her being the one in charge here.

'Okay then,' she said with an exasperated smile, pulling off her apron and going to hang it up on one of the pegs on the wall. She gave her hands a quick wash, then went to fetch her bag and coat from the small office behind the kitchen, taking a moment to drag in some steadying breaths before she went back out there to face whatever was in store for her this evening. No way was she letting herself get excited about him being here. She didn't think she could cope with more disappointment when it came to Julien.

When she returned he was chatting comfortably with Lacey, who was leaning against the counter, looking up at him with big, friendly eyes.

Huh, trust him to charm everyone as soon as he walked in.

'Okay, I'm ready to go,' she told Julien as she approached the two of them, making sure to keep her voice emotion-free. 'Thanks, Lacey.'

'Have a good evening,' her friend replied, giving her a covert eyebrow-waggle.

Indigo scowled back, intensely aware of Julien's presence right there beside her.

'See you next week, everyone,' she called to the rest of the group, hoping to goodness her face didn't look as flushed as it felt. They all responded with a wave and a smile and continued to watch her with interest until she put her hand on Julien's back and ushered him towards the door. There was a gentle hubbub of noise as they walked out. No doubt tongues would be wagging once she'd gone.

Out in the damp night air, she turned to face him and crossed her arms in front of her. It felt so strange to see him here, on her patch. He was as immaculately dressed as always and her tummy tumbled as she fully took him in for the first time since he'd shown up. He looked so darn handsome, standing there as if he didn't have a care in the world. Which she guessed he didn't. She wondered fleetingly whether it was going to be possible to get through this without entirely losing her cool.

'So what's this all about? Why are you here?'

He let out a low breath and looked around him, as if gathering himself for what he was about to say. 'Let's walk, shall we?'

'Can't you just tell me here?' she said, grasping on to the only thread of power she had left.

He crossed his own arms and frowned down at the floor and she noticed for the first time that he had a black shopping bag swinging from one hand. She wondered what he could have in there. It was a strange receptacle for him to be carrying overnight clothes in.

'What's in the bag?' she blurted, unable to keep her curiosity to herself.

'You'll see,' he said, flashing her an enigmatic smile.

'Really? You're not going to tell me?'

'*Non*. You'll have to wait until we're back at your flat and I'm ready to show you. I'm not prepared to do this out on the street either.'

She bristled with frustration. 'And you think I'm stubborn!' Sighing, she took one more look at the determination on his face and gave him a resigned nod, knowing there was no way she could turn him away. Not if it meant she'd finally find out what was really going on with him. It had been eating away at her since she'd last seen him and she needed answers so she could move on.

'Okay, fine, you win.' She gestured for them to start walking. 'It's this way.'

It only took them two minutes to walk to her flat from the café and neither of them spoke a word as they made their way down the noisy main road, stepping around the puddles that the earlier heavy downpour had left in its wake.

'This is me,' she said when they reached the end of her road.

He followed her to her flat—the place she'd moved into after Gavin had left her. Hers was on the top floor of the converted terrace house, which she loved because she enjoyed falling asleep looking at the night sky through the skylight in the sloping attic ceiling.

'I'm at the top,' she said, letting them in through the main door and leading him up the stairs. It took her a moment to get the key to line up with the lock because her hands were shaking so much. He stood so close to her she could smell the wonderfully evocative scent of him and she had to take great gulps of air through her mouth so as not to become too distracted by the urge to turn around and wrap her arms around him and pull him close.

When she finally got the door open, she led him through to the kitchen diner and gestured for him to sit with her at the small dining table that she had set up in the middle of the room.

Blood pulsed in her ears as she waited for him to tell her why he was here.

'Have you heard about your grant yet?' he asked conversationally, throwing her for a loop.

Was he still cross about her refusing to take the money from him? She hoped he wasn't here to try and get her to change her mind. She didn't regret the decision she'd made, firmly believing that things would work out here without his help. Somehow.

She folded her arms. 'Not yet. Soon, hopefully.'

'That must be stressful.'

She shrugged. 'Yes, well, as you know, money and I aren't exactly on speaking terms at the moment.'

He smiled. 'That makes two of us.'

What did he mean by that?

'Are you having financial troubles too?' she asked, confused.

'No. But money seems to be my nemesis at the moment. It makes me do stupid things.'

There was a tense pause while she waited for him to elaborate.

He didn't. Instead, he jumped up and started pacing around the room, moving into the living area and running his fingers lightly over her things, as if wanting to learn them by touch.

'It's a great flat. Exactly the sort of place I imagined you living in. It's very you.'

'Me?'

He nodded, turning to look her in the eyes. 'Sophisticated, but welcoming.'

She couldn't stop the smile from breaking over her face. 'How very kind of you.'

He started pacing around again and she realised with a shock that he was nervous.

Standing up, she took a couple of steps towards him. 'Julien, will you please just spit out whatever it is you've come to say? You're killing me here!'

He stopped moving and turned to face her again, his expression apologetic.

Taking an audible breath, he walked closer. 'Okay, first of all, I wanted to say sorry, about trying to buy my freedom—and your forgiveness. It was a crass and selfish thing to do. I knew how much you needed that money and it wasn't fair to make you choose between that and me.' He snorted gently. 'Not that you did. In your inimitable style you turned your back on both options.'

'I couldn't feel like I was indebted to you, Julien, it would have destroyed any equilibrium between us.'

He nodded, his expression telling her he understood

what she was saying. 'It seems to have become a bad habit with me to throw money at things to try and fix them quickly and without pain. It was ignorant of me to do that and I can see now why you were offended. I apologise.'

A heavy weight seemed to lift from her chest. 'Apology accepted.'

Julien looked at the woman he loved and knew that if he wanted to repair things between them he had to tell her everything. He owed her an explanation after all the strife he'd caused. But now he was here he was having trouble finding the words he needed without making himself sound like the worst kind of low life.

This was exactly why he'd not talked to anyone else when it became apparent that his marriage was over. The shame had stopped the words—kept them lodged inside him, somewhere between his chest and his throat, like a cork pushed too far down to extract.

'I want to tell you why I was such a nightmare to be around in Italy,' he said. 'So you understand that my behaviour was never about something you did or didn't do.'

The apprehension in her eyes made his blood pump faster and he watched with concern as she walked further into the living area and sat down heavily on to her small red velvet sofa as if her legs had suddenly refused to hold her any longer.

'Okay. Go on,' she said quietly.

He sat down too and turned to face her, making sure he had her full attention before he started his sorry tale.

She looked back at him with such apprehension he hoped to God this wouldn't be the last time he'd ever see her after making his confession.

'My ex-wife's name is Celine,' he began, deciding to cover the basic facts first, hoping the rest would flow from there. 'We met at a mutual friend's wedding. Both of us were late and we snuck into the back of the church together and somehow managed to knock over a huge flower display and disrupt the service at a key moment. As you can imagine, that didn't exactly make us popular guests, but it banded us together as social fugitives.'

'Is your mutual friend speaking to you yet?' she asked with a smile in her voice.

He grimaced, too aware of the regret pulling at him to enjoy the gentle joke, but relieved that she felt comfortable enough to tease him still. 'Only just.'

She flapped a hand. 'Sorry to interrupt; do go on.'

'At that point in my life I'd been working so hard I'd not given any of my relationships—with perfectly nice women—a decent chance of surviving and it had begun to occur to me, as I watched all my friends get married and move on with their lives, that I'd put my career before my personal life for too long, and if I didn't do something about it I was going to end up a lonely old man.'

She shifted on the sofa, pulling her legs under her, and he took her cue and settled back, making himself more comfortable.

'Celine made me feel like there could be an exciting future ahead of me and, after our first meeting, we started seeing each other regularly—though when

I say "seeing" I mean we spent a lot of time in bed together. It was a crazy whirlwind of a relationship and she turned my entire world upside down. She had this energy that electrified me: she was wild and spontaneous and creative, all the things I'm not, but she was also highly strung and only seemed to thrive when all the attention was on her. I can see that now, with the benefit of hindsight, though I was blind to it at the time.'

He was quiet for a while as he relived the memory of what he'd thought was the most passionate and extraordinary interlude in his formerly routine life—until he'd met Indigo and realised what passion really was.

'So what happened?' she prompted gently.

He sighed. 'We jumped into getting married too quickly.' He took a breath. 'I thought I was doing the right thing at the time, but it was a huge mistake.'

'What do you mean, "doing the right thing"?' she asked with a careful tone to her voice, which made him think she'd already figured it out.

He turned to give her a sad, knowing smile. '*Oui*, she was pregnant.'

She looked at him steadily for a moment and he saw her throat bob as she swallowed hard. 'Ah. I see. Well, that was honourable of you.'

'Yes, well, my father left my mother after he got her pregnant and she struggled for money and support for years, raising me. It was very tough on her. I didn't want Celine to suffer like that and I wanted to be there for my child. I worked hard for years to be successful so I'd be in a good position to support a family, should

I have one. It didn't happen the way I was expecting it to, but I thought: *so what?* This was my child and I was prepared to make a go of the marriage so we could all be together.'

'So you *do* have a child?' she asked quietly.

He shook his head and averted his gaze, staring instead at a print of Monet's *Poppies* that she had on the wall behind the sofa, finding comfort in the vibrant colours. '*Non.* We lost the baby a few weeks after our wedding.'

When he turned back to look at her, the expression on her face was so full of sympathy it made his stomach drop.

'Oh, Julien, I'm so sorry to hear that.'

He nodded to acknowledge her commiseration. 'It wasn't just the failed pregnancy that wrecked our relationship, though,' he continued. 'It felt to me as though Celine gave up her individuality as soon as we got married, as if she didn't need to try at anything any more. She'd already handed in her notice at the place she worked and I became her whole universe. It was stifling. She wanted my undivided attention and I tried to give her as much as I could, but she'd phone me ten or twenty times a day and turn up when I had important meetings and make a scene if I didn't have time to see her.'

'Was this before or after the miscarriage?' Indigo asked.

'Before. It got even worse after it.'

Indigo didn't say anything, just nodded as if she understood.

'Then, when we lost the baby, she didn't want me to even leave the house. She became obsessed with trying to get pregnant again, to the point where there was no joy in our sex life any more. It was as if she only thought of me as a baby-making machine and would get angry with me if I said I was too tired or not in the mood. When I suggested we should wait a while before trying to get pregnant again, to give us both some time to recover, she was furious with me. So furious.'

He rubbed a hand over his face, feeling the familiar tension mounting.

'I tried to get her friends to talk to her, to give her the kind of support I couldn't,' he said, wanting Indigo to know he hadn't been totally heartless about it, 'but she froze them out, saying they couldn't possibly understand how she felt. She hadn't spoken to her parents in years—she and her father had had some kind of falling out when she was eighteen—so there was no support there either. And she refused to go to counselling. She wanted me to make things better, but I had no idea how to make her happy any more. It got too much. I started working later and later and ignoring her calls, just to get some space.'

The words seemed to be pouring from him now, as if the pressure they'd been stoppered under had finally found a release.

'Then she stopped talking to me, to punish me, I think, and my life outside work became one long, silent nightmare. So then I spent even more time away from the house so I didn't have to face what had gone wrong with my life.'

'Oh, Julien, that sounds horrendous.' She put her hand briefly over his and he found comfort in the warmth of her touch. But only for a moment.

'It wasn't the best year of my life, that's for sure.'

'So who ended it?'

'She did. She told me she wanted a divorce out of the blue one morning, then walked out and didn't come back.'

'That must have been difficult for you.'

'Honestly—I didn't try very hard to stop her.' He sighed and scrubbed a hand through his hair, making it stand on end. 'I didn't love her.'

'Oh, Julien—'

But he didn't want her sympathy right then, didn't feel as if he deserved it. 'She needed more from me. She needed my understanding. I knew she wasn't coping well with the miscarriage, but I kept pushing her away because I didn't know how to deal with everything that had happened either. I failed her.'

He felt Indigo move closer to him on the sofa. 'You mustn't think that. It must have been awful for both of you and it sounds like she fell apart and expected you to deal with everything. You shouldn't feel guilty for not trying harder. It sounds like you did everything you could think of.'

'I offered her a very generous divorce settlement to get it over with quickly. At least she'll never need to work another day in her life. I fixed her with money.' He let out a long, low rush of breath. 'And I feel relieved to be free of her. That makes me a terrible person, doesn't it?'

He glanced over at Indigo and was relieved to see understanding in her eyes.

On his way here he'd been terrified about how she'd take all this. He'd almost turned back a couple of times, but he knew if he wanted her he had to have the courage to tell her everything.

'It doesn't make you a terrible person. It makes you human,' she said, giving his hand a squeeze this time. 'And it doesn't sound like there was much of a relationship to save after you lost the baby.'

He picked up her hand from where it lay in her lap and linked his fingers through hers, feeling her shiver at his touch. The discovery that she felt the same way he did gave him courage.

'*Oui*. It became clear pretty quickly that we didn't have a lot in common after we got married. We thought and reacted to things in completely contrary ways. When we found out she was pregnant I told myself it wouldn't matter that we were so different because we'd have the child to hold us together.'

'It sounds like there was a good chance the marriage wouldn't have worked even if the baby had survived, and then you'd have felt guilty about depriving him or her of a stable family background instead.'

'Perhaps,' he said, letting her words wash though his mind. It felt good to have finally said all this out loud, after it had festered in his head for so long.

'Have you talked to someone? A counsellor or a friend?'

'Non.'

'Why not?'

'Because I'm fine.'

'But you lost a child too.'

'I'm *fine*.'

'So I get it now,' Indigo said, screwing up her face in sympathy.

He gave her a puzzled look. 'Get what?'

'The enforced solitude in Italy. You were making yourself walk the coast path alone as a penance—because you were punishing yourself for not doing more to save your marriage.'

'I didn't do a very good job of being on my own, though,' he said, forcing irony into his smile.

'Perhaps that's because, deep down, you know there was nothing you could have done to make things better, but you feel like you should punish yourself anyway.'

'Or I just couldn't keep away from you, no matter how hard I tried.'

'I'm glad you didn't,' she whispered, looking deep into his eyes, and he knew for sure. at that moment, it hadn't been a mistake to come here. She loved him as fiercely as he loved her. He could see it there, written plainly on her face.

And now he wanted to show her how much she meant to him.

'Are you hungry?' he asked. 'You must be after working with food all day.'

'A bit,' she said, giving him a baffled smile.

'Good, because I managed to get hold of the recipe for that pasta dish you liked so much in the beach restaurant in Nerano. I have all the ingredients in there.'

He pointed to the black shopping bag he'd left on the kitchen counter.

She stared at him, clearly shocked at this revelation. 'You persuaded them to tell you their secret?'

'Oui.'

'And you're going to cook it for me?'

'Sure I am.'

She raised an eyebrow at him, the expression in her eyes wary. Clearly, she still wasn't entirely sure what he'd come here for.

'Are you trying to woo me with your culinary skills?' she asked hesitantly, confirming his suspicions.

'You might want to taste my food before you decide whether it's woo-worthy. I'm not as experienced as you. To be honest, I very rarely cook.' He flashed her a smile. 'But I like a challenge.'

'I'm sure it'll be delicious,' she said, her eyes wide with badly concealed bewilderment, 'but I'm happy to lend a hand.' She started to get up from the sofa.

'Non.' He held up a finger, gesturing for her to stay where she was. 'You sit down and relax. I'll fetch you a glass of wine and you can watch me work.'

Indigo watched in baffled pleasure as Julien made a production of opening an expensive-looking bottle of wine, searching through her cupboards till he'd found her paltry selection of glasses, pouring a large measure into one of them and handing it to her, then going back to the counter to unpack the bag he'd brought with him.

There was something wonderful about watching him moving around her kitchen, preparing and cooking a meal especially for her. Being the one who was looked after for once.

'I'm moving to London, Indigo,' he said suddenly as he dropped pasta into a pan of bubbling water. 'I've decided to branch out and set up a new arm to the business that focuses on providing affordable housing for first-time buyers and low-wage families.'

She stared at him. 'Wow, that sounds amazing.'

He was moving? Here, to London? Her heart tripped over itself at the news.

He looked up at her, flashing her a smile. 'You inspired me.'

'Me?'

'Yes, you. After you told me about your community café it made me realise that I've been too profit-focused for too long. I want to make a difference in people's lives too. And that's the best way I can employ my existing skills and knowledge in order to do that.'

'Well, I think that's wonderful, Julien, but I thought you loved living in Paris?'

'I do, but you're not there.'

The shock of his words reverberated through her head, making her feel a little dizzy.

'You'd move here for me?'

'*Oui*. If we're to give a relationship a chance we need to be living in the same city, since we're both very busy people.'

She gaped at him, her mind reeling as a small but persistent bubble of hope pushed upwards.

'Anyway, you persuaded me whilst we were away that London could come a close second to Paris,' he continued, abandoning what he was doing at the counter and walking back over to her at the sofa. 'And it won't take long to travel back there for a weekend when I need a fix. I can introduce you to my favourite parts of the city. I'd like that.'

He sat down next to her, taking her hands.

'But what if it didn't work out between us?' she asked warily, unable to ignore the memory of how badly things had gone with Gavin. She didn't want to feel responsible for Julien giving up everything he loved if it made him miserable.

'Someone once told me that you've just got to keep positive and everything will work itself out in the end.'

'Someone once told me that was total claptrap,' she pointed out.

'That guy was an idiot.'

She closed her eyes and smiled. When she opened them again he was looking at her with an expression of utter seriousness.

'I've had enough time on my own to think about things. When we talked in Capri I was afraid—afraid that I couldn't give you the level of attention you deserve, that I couldn't be positive enough for you, that you'd come to resent me for my dour outlook and selfish moods. I didn't want you to think of me like that. I wanted to be ready and capable of showing you the real me. Not the shell of a man I was when we first met. It nearly killed me, walking away, but I had to be sure I could handle it.'

'And are you?'

'*Oui*. After panicking that I might have lost you, and

realising that would make me so much more miserable, I *know* I can now.'

Indigo swallowed hard, feeling a familiar tightness in her throat, only this time it was from overwhelming excitement.

He leaned forwards, stroking his thumbs over the backs of her hands. 'I've thought about you every single day since I left you, Indigo. Pretty much every minute of every day. What we had felt so right—no matter how much I tried to convince myself it wasn't—and in a way that it never did with Celine, or anyone else I've ever met. As soon as I met you I *knew*.'

'Me too,' she whispered.

He smiled, relief lighting up his eyes. 'I want to be near you so we can make a real go of a relationship. If you want that too. What do you say? Has fate kept my slot open for me?'

She was so excited by what he was saying, but she still couldn't stop a deep-seated worry from tugging at her.

'What is it?' he asked, clearly sensing her indecision.

'I'm worried that I get too argumentative around you and that you'll get fed up with it.'

'You mean your fighting spirit? I love that you stand up for yourself.'

She felt a smile pull at the corners of her mouth.

'But what if I become really self-centred again? I need to be able to concentrate on the café to keep it running and I might not always be around when you need me.'

'You mean you'd put yourself first for once? Instead, of always considering other people's feelings before your own? I think I could handle that.' He flashed her a wry grin. 'I want to be here to support you, Indigo. Not with money,' he added quickly when he saw the look on her face, 'but to be here when you need me. In fact, I'd live in a cardboard box if it meant I could be with you. The money, the possessions, they mean nothing to me; they're just noise. I have far more than I need to be happy and if me having money makes you uncomfortable then you can help me decide where it could best be donated in order to help other people.'

She stared at him. 'You'd be willing to do that?'

'Yes. For the woman I love.'

'Love—?' She could barely say the word as her throat filled with happy tears.

'Oui.' He nodded. 'I'm in love with you.'

'Oh, thank goodness,' she said in a rush, 'because I'm in love with you too.'

There was a look of acute happiness in his eyes as he lifted his hand and slid it into her hair, angling her head towards him and crushing his lips against hers, kissing her with such passion it took her breath away.

When he eventually pulled back she almost growled with frustration, until he cupped his palms around her jaw and looked deep into her eyes.

'Yes, I'm in love with you, Indigo. I love you for your strength and your determination. Your generosity when you have nothing left to give. Your kindness to a strange Frenchman who needed someone to take an interest in him and make him feel like he had something left to offer. That's why I love you. Because you remind me of all the good things about me that I'd forgotten about.

You're the person I'm supposed to have my happy-ever-after with. I believe that now.'

'I believe it too.'

'Good.'

He kissed her again, even more thoroughly this time.

'I want it all with you, Indigo,' he said, kissing her nose, her eyes. 'A home, a family…' He kissed her forehead, her cheeks. 'A future.' Her drew back and smiled, deep into her eyes. 'But mostly I want you.'

She experienced a surge of pure joy at his words, knowing for certain now that this was meant to be. That this was fate and she could give him everything he wanted.

And more.

Much, much more.

EPILOGUE

When pondering what to do for your next adventure, you might want to consider something that has it all: excitement, good society and a plethora of opportunities for personal discovery...

Two years later

INDIGO PACED BACK and forth, quickly covering the floor space of the home that she and Julien had bought together after he'd whisked her off to Paris to propose, just six months after moving to London.

They'd fallen in love with the bijou but funky flat situated in a warehouse conversion in Brixton as soon as they'd walked into it. Since moving in, they'd had great fun decorating it simply but stylishly, haunting the antique and flea markets in both London and Paris until they'd managed to put together a collection of furniture that suited and reflected both of their tastes.

With the two of them sharing the mortgage, Indigo had been confident she could comfortably afford her half of the repayment with her wage from the Welcome Café, and she loved walking through the door and knowing that this place was just as much hers as it was Julien's.

It seemed like a long time ago now that she'd been worried about having to give up working at the café, but she still felt grateful every day for the grants that had turned up just in the nick of time, allowing them to expand and, more recently, open up new branches in other parts of the city. Even though she'd known Julien would have stepped in and given her as much money as she needed had the grants not appeared, she would never have taken it from him, needing to maintain her financial independence for her own sense of pride.

As it turned out, he'd needed to invest a lot of it in his not-for-profit affordable housing scheme, which had already brought happiness and security to a large number of people who had previously believed they'd never be able to afford their own home.

She was so proud of him for what he'd achieved in such a short space of time. He'd worked tirelessly to make it all happen and was full of positivity for expansion in the future.

It made her heart swell to see him so fired up and happy.

Even though they both led very independent working lives, they'd made sure they were around for each other whenever support was required—either as a sounding board to bounce ideas off, or just to be there to listen to each other talk about the vexations or achievements of their day.

Since they were both incredibly busy during the

week, they made sure to take regular breaks away from the city at weekends, when they'd walk and camp and explore the most beautiful parts of England, and occasionally other European countries.

It was a solid and equal partnership, with both of them working hard to make sure they communicated any worries or frustrations they had well before they became an issue.

It worked.

But then she always knew it would. Because they both wanted it to.

Indigo could barely believe it had only been two years since they'd first met in Italy. It felt now as though she'd known him forever.

Their wedding, a year ago, had been a joyous affair, with family and friends travelling from far and wide to the beautiful rural estate just outside Paris—which had been loaned to them by a friend of Julien's—to celebrate with them.

Indigo had worried about how hard she might find it, not having either of her parents there to see her get married, and she'd shed a tear for their absence the night before, but she hadn't allowed it to taint her happiness during the day. She knew they were there with her, in her heart.

And she'd had plenty of people who loved her there, rooting for her. All of her brothers had come along with their families in tow, which had made for an entertaining and raucous gathering.

She and Julien had loved every second of it.

Walking into the kitchen, she gave the food in the

oven one last check to make sure it would be ready to serve as soon as Julien walked through the door. She'd been planning this special meal since this morning, wanting to mark the occasion with style.

Even though Julien had insisted on her teaching him how to cook so they could share the task and give her a break from it when she'd been on her feet all day, she still loved to make food for him, just to see the look of delight on his face when she presented him with one of his favourite meals. He was the perfect recipient, making sure to let her know just how much he appreciated her efforts, showering her with affection and love afterwards.

She couldn't have asked for more.

Except for one thing.

She twisted the much treasured wedding and engagement rings round and round on her finger as she waited impatiently for Julien to get back from work and walk through the door.

Since the wedding they'd tried and failed to conceive, each month bringing with it a sense of crushed excitement as the possibility of extending their family failed to come to fruition.

They'd stayed upbeat about it, but she could tell just how much Julien longed for it to happen. She knew exactly how he felt because she wanted it just as fiercely.

Her heart bumped hard against her chest as she finally heard the sound of Julien's key in the front door, and she rushed to meet him, her blood racing with excitement to finally have him home.

He'd barely made it through the door when she

launched herself at him, throwing her arms around his neck and hugging him tightly to her.

'Whoa!' he said, nearly losing his balance, only managing to keep them both upright by grabbing hold of the doorjamb. 'That's quite a welcome. What's this about?'

Pulling away from him, and without saying a word, she reached into the back pocket of her jeans and brought out the little bit of magic she'd been checking and rechecking over and over again all day with a ceremonial flourish.

'Ta-da!'

He stared at it, perplexed, until the penny finally dropped. 'What does it say?' he asked, his voice shaking with anticipation.

She held it closer so he could read the words on the little screen.

'You're pregnant?' he said, his voice lifting with excitement.

'Yes!'

'How long have you known?'

'I did the test this morning.' She could barely talk for excitement.

'Why didn't you call me?' he said, grabbing her around the waist and lifting her up so he could swing her round and round.

'I knew you needed to be able to concentrate on the meeting with your investors today,' she said, laughing with elation at his reaction. 'I was worried you might go to pieces and they'd think you were a bit loopy and refuse to give you the money.'

He laughed and put her down, holding on to her until

he was sure she had her balance, then flapping his hand in that Gallic way she loved so much. 'Go to pieces! Me! Never!' But there was a glint of tears in his eyes now.

Sliding her hands up to cup his jaw, she gently pulled him towards her so she could kiss his eyes, his nose, his mouth.

'You're a big softie really,' she murmured, kissing away a lone tear that had escaped from his eye.

'I'm just happy. I've wanted this so much.'

'Me too.'

He stroked her cheek, looking deep into her eyes.

'I'm so glad my child will have a mother like you.' He kissed her, his touch firm and possessive. 'Someone who is dedicated to bringing happiness to everyone she meets.' He kissed her again, the urgency of it reminding her how loved she was, how wanted. 'Someone who is full of love for others, no matter their situation.' This time the kiss went on and on until she was breathless with joy.

She couldn't believe how lucky she was to have him.

With each other's support and love they'd finally been able to close the book on the regrets of their pasts.

And now an exciting new chapter of their lives was about to begin.

* * * * *

IT HAPPENED IN PARIS...

ROBIN GIANNA

For my wonderful children, Arianna, James and George. You three are truly the light of my life. A big thank-you to good friend Steven J. Yakubov, MD, who has been conducting TAVI clinical trials overseas and now in the USA for years, and who inspired this story. I so appreciate it, Steve, that you called me to answer all my questions even after you'd had almost no sleep for three nights. Thanks bunches!

After completing a degree in journalism, working in the advertising industry, then becoming a stay-at home mum, **Robin Gianna** had what she calls her 'midlife awakening'. She decided she wanted to write the romance novels she'd loved since her teens, and embarked on that quest by joining RWA, Central Ohio Fiction Writers, and working hard at learning the craft. She loves sharing the journey with her characters, helping them through obstacles and problems to find their own happily-ever-afters. When not writing, Robin likes to create in her kitchen, dig in the dirt, and enjoy life with her tolerant husband, three great kids, drooling bulldog and grouchy Siamese cat. To learn more about her work visit her website: www.robingianna.com.

CHAPTER ONE

JACK DUNBAR STUDIED the map in his hand, trying to figure out where the heck he was in this city of two million people. He was determined not to waste his first hours in Paris, and never mind that he'd only had a few hours of sleep while folded into an airplane seat, couldn't speak French and had no idea how to get around.

But, hey, a little adventure never hurt anyone. Even getting lost would be a welcome distraction from thinking about the presentation he had to give tonight. The presentation that would begin the new phase of his career he'd worked so hard for. The presentation that would launch the newest medical device, hopefully save lives and change forever the way heart-valve replacement surgery was performed.

Before any sightseeing, though, the first thing on his list was coffee and a little breakfast. Jack stepped into the hotel restaurant and saw that a huge buffet was set up just inside the open doors. Silver chafing dishes, mounds of breads and cheeses, fruits and you-name-it covered an L-shaped table, but the thought of sitting there eating a massive breakfast alone wasn't at all appealing. He approached the maître d'. "Excuse me. Is there just a small breakfast I can grab somewhere?"

"Voilà!" The man smiled and waved his arm at the buffet with a flourish. *"Le petit déjeuner!"*

Jack nearly laughed. If that was the small breakfast, he'd hate to see a big one. "Thank you, but I want just coffee and something quick. What's nearby?"

"Everything you could wish for is right here, *monsieur.*"

"Yes, I see that, but—"

"I know a little place that's just what you're looking for," a feminine voice said from behind him. "When in France, eat like the French do. And that spread in there is most definitely meant for Americans."

He turned, and a small woman with the greenest eyes he'd ever seen stood there, an amused smile on her pretty face. He smiled back, relieved that someone might actually steer him in the right direction, and that she not only spoke English, but sounded like she was American, too. "That's exactly what I want. To immerse myself in French culture for a while. And soon, because I need a cup of coffee more than I need oxygen right now."

Those amazing eyes, framed by thick, dark lashes, sparkled as her smile grew wider. "Caffeine is definitely the number one survival requirement. Come on."

Leaving barely a second for him to thank the unhelpful maître d', she wrapped her hand around his biceps and tugged him toward the door and out into the chilly January streets of Paris. "Just down the street is the perfect café. We can get coffee and a baguette, then we'll be good to go."

We? Jack had to grin at the way she'd taken over. Not that he minded. Being grabbed and herded down the street by a beautiful woman who obviously knew a little about Paris was a pleasure he hadn't expected, but was more than happy about.

"I'm Avery, by the way."

"Jack." He looked at her and realized her unusual name went well with a very unusual woman. A woman who took a perfect stranger down the street to a coffee shop as though she'd known him for days instead of seconds. A red wool hat was pulled onto her head, covering lush dark brown hair that spilled from beneath it. A scarf of orange, red and yellow was wrapped around her neck and tucked inside a short black coat, and tight-fitting black pants hugged her shapely legs. On her feet she wore yellow rain boots with red ducks all over them, and a purple umbrella was tucked under her arm. Dull she most definitely was not.

"Nice to meet you, Jack." Her smile was downright dazzling. The morning looked a whole lot brighter than it had a few moments ago, despite the sky being as gray as pencil lead. "How do you like your coffee? American style? If you really want to be French, you'll have to drink espresso. But I won't judge you either way."

Her green eyes, filled with a teasing look, were so mesmerizing he nearly stumbled off the curb when they crossed the street. "Somehow I think that's a lie. And while I can handle being judged, I like espresso."

"I knew you were a man after my own heart."

He'd be willing to bet a lot of men were after her heart and a whole lot more.

The little coffee shop smelled great, and he followed

Avery to the counter. She ordered in French, and the way the words slipped from her tongue, it sounded to him like she spoke the language nearly like a native.

"You ordered, so I'm paying," he said.

"That's what I was hoping for. Why else did you think I brought you along?"

"And here I thought it was my good looks and sophistication."

"I did find that, combined with your little-boy-lost look, irresistible, I must admit."

He chuckled. Damned if she wasn't about the cutest woman he'd been around in a long time. They took their baguettes and tiny cups of espresso to a nearby tall table and stood. Jack nearly downed his cup of hot, strong coffee in one gulp. "This is good. Just what I needed. Except there isn't nearly enough of it."

"I know. And I even ordered us double shots. I always have to get used to the tiny amounts of espresso they serve when I'm in Europe. We Americans are used to our bottomless cups of coffee."

"Are you here as a tourist? With friends?" Jack couldn't imagine she was traveling alone, but hoped she was. Maybe they could spend some time together, since he'd be in Paris for an entire month. With any luck, she was living here.

"I'm in Paris to work, and I'm alone. How about you?"

"Me, too. Working and alone. But I do have a few hours to kill today. Any chance you'll show me around a little in exchange for me buying lunch?"

"We're eating breakfast, and you're already thinking about lunch?" More of that teasing look, and he found himself leaning closer to her. Drawn to her. "I've already proved I plan my friendships around who'll buy. So the answer is yes."

He smiled. Maybe this great start to his trip to Paris was a good omen. "Where to first? I know nothing about Paris except the Eiffel Tower, which I know is close because I saw it from the hotel."

"Paris is a wonderful city for walking. Even though it's cold today and may well rain. Or even snow. Let's walk toward the Seine and go from there. If we hit the tower early, we'll avoid some of the crazy lines."

"There are lines this time of year? I didn't think there would be many tourists."

"There are always tourists. Not as many in January and February as in spring and summer, but still plenty. Lots come to celebrate Valentine's Day in Paris. Romantic, you know?"

He didn't, really. Sure, he'd had women in his life, some briefly and some for a little longer. But, like his father in the past and his brother now, his life was about work. Working to help patients. Working to save people like his grandfather, who'd had so much to live for but whose heart had given out on him far too soon.

Avery finished her last bite of bread and gathered up her purse and umbrella, clearly ready to move on.

"I don't suppose they give little to-go cups of espresso, do they?" he asked.

"You suppose right," she said with a grin. "The French don't believe in multitasking to quite the same degree we do. They'd shake their heads at crazy Americans who eat and drink while walking around the city."

"I'll have to get a triple shot at lunch, then," he said

as they stood. He resisted the urge to lick the last drop from his cup, figuring Avery wouldn't be too impressed. Might even come up with an excuse not to take him to the Eiffel Tower, and one drop of coffee wasn't anywhere near worth that risk.

They strolled down cobbled streets and wide walks toward the tower, Avery's melodic voice giving him a rundown of various sights as they strolled. Not overly chatty, just the perfect combination of information and quiet enjoyment. Jack's chest felt light. Spending this time with her had leeched away all the stress he'd been feeling, all the intense focus on getting this study off the ground, to the exclusion of everything. How had he gotten so lucky as to have her step into his first day in France exactly when he'd needed it?

"That's L'Hôtel des Invalides," she said, pointing at a golden building not too far away. "Napoleon is buried there. I read that they regilded the dome on the anniversary of the French Revolution with something like twenty pounds of gold. And I have to wonder. Wouldn't all that gold have been better used to drape women in jewelry?"

"So you like being draped in gold?" He looked at the silver hoops in her ears and silver bangles on her wrist. Sexy, but not gold, and not over the top in any way.

"Not really. Though if a man feels compelled to do that, who am I to argue?" She grinned and grasped his arm again. "Let's get to the tower before the crowds."

She picked up the pace as they walked the paths crisscrossing a green expanse in front of the tower. Considering how cold it was, a surprising number of people were there snapping pictures and standing in line as they approached. "Are you afraid of heights?"

"Who, me? I'm not afraid of anything."

"Everyone's afraid of something." Her smiling expression faded briefly into seriousness before lightening again. "Obviously, the Eiffel Tower is super tall, and the elevators can be claustrophobic even while you're thinking how scary it is to be going so high. I'll hold your hand, though, if you need me to."

"You know, I just might be afraid after all."

She laughed, and her small hand slid into his. Naturally. Just like it belonged there.

"Truth? I get a little weirded out on the elevator," she said in a conspiratorial tone. "So if I squeeze your hand too tight, I'm sorry."

"I'm tough, don't worry."

"I bet you are." She looked up at him with a grin. "The lines aren't too bad, but let's take the stairs anyway."

He stared at her in disbelief. "The stairs?"

"You look like you're probably fit enough." Her green eyes laughed at whatever the heck his expression was. "But we don't take them all the way to the top. Just to the second level, and we'll grab the elevator there. Trust me, it's the best way to see everything, especially on a day like today, when it gets cloudier the higher you go."

"So long as we don't have to spend the entire day climbing, I'm trusting you, Ms. Tour Guide. Lead the way." The stairs were surprisingly wide and the trek up sent his heart beating faster and his breath shorter. Though maybe that was just from being with Avery.

For some inexplicable reason, she affected him in a way he couldn't quite remember feeling when he first met a woman.

They admired the views from both the first and second levels, Avery pointing out various landmarks, before they boarded the glass elevator. People were mashed tightly inside, but Jack didn't mind being forced to stand so close to Avery. To breathe in her appealing scent that was soft and subtle, a mix of fresh air and light perfume and her.

The ride most definitely would challenge anyone with either of the fears Avery had mentioned, the view through the crisscrossed metal of the tower incredible as they soared above Paris. On the viewing platform at the top, the cold wind whipped their hair and slipped inside Jack's coat, and he wrapped his arm around her shoulders to try to keep her warm.

"You want to look through the telescope? Though we won't be able to see too far with all the clouds," she said, turning to him. Her cheeks were pink, her beautiful lips pink, too, and, oh, so kissable. Her hair flew across her face, and Jack lifted his fingers to tuck it beneath her hat, because he couldn't resist feeling the softness of it between his fingers.

"I want to look at you, mostly," he said, because it was true. "But I may never get up here again, so let's give it a try."

Her face turned even more pink at his words before she turned to poke a few coins in the telescope. They took turns peering through it, and her face was so close to his he nearly dipped his head to kiss her. Starting with her cheek, then, if she didn't object, moving on from there to taste her mouth. Their eyes met in front of the telescope, and her tongue flicked out to dampen her lips, as if she might be thinking of exactly the same thing.

He stared in fascination as her pupils dilated, noting flecks, both gold and dark, within the emerald green of her eyes. He slowly lowered his head, lifted his palm to her face and—

"Excuse me. You done with the telescope?" a man asked, and Avery took a few steps back.

"We're all done," she said quickly. The heat he hoped he'd seen in her expression immediately cooled to a friendly smile. "Ready to go, Jack? I think we've seen all there is to see from up here today."

Well, damn. Kissing her in the middle of that crowd wasn't the best idea anyway, but even the briefest touch of her lips on his would have been pretty sweet, he knew. "I'm ready."

They crammed themselves onto the elevator once more, though it wasn't quite as packed as it had been on the way up. He breathed in her scent again as he tucked a few more strands of hair under her hat. "Thanks for bringing me up here. That was amazing." *She* was amazing. "So what now, Ms. Tour Guide? Time for lunch?"

"There you go, thinking about food again." She gave him one of her cute, teasing looks. "But I admit I'm getting a little hungry, too. There's a great place just a little way along the river I like. There will be a few different courses, but don't worry—it won't break your wallet."

He didn't care what it cost. Getting to spend a leisurely lunch with Avery was worth a whole lot of money.

They moved slowly down a tree-lined path by the river, and he felt the most absurd urge to hold her hand again. As though they'd known each other a lot longer than an hour or two. Which reminded him he still hardly knew anything about her at all. "Do you live here? You obviously speak French well," he said.

"My parents both worked in France for a while, and I went to school here in Paris for two years. You tend to learn a language fast that way. I'm just here for a month or so this time."

"What do you do?"

"I— Oh!" As though they'd stepped out from beneath a shelter, heavy sheets of rain mixed with thick, wet snowflakes suddenly poured on their heads, and Avery fumbled with her umbrella to get it open. It was small, barely covering both their heads. Jack had to hunch over since she was so much shorter than him as, laughing, they pressed against one another to try to stay dry.

He maneuvered the two of them under a canopy of trees lining the river and had to grin. The Fates were handing him everything today, including a storm that brought him into very close contact with Avery. Exactly where he wanted to be.

He lifted his finger to slip a melting snowflake from her long lashes. "And here I'd pictured Paris as sunny, with beautiful flowers everywhere. I didn't even know it snowed here."

"You can't have done your homework." Her voice was breathy, her mouth so close to his he got a little breathless, too. "It rains and snows here a lot. Parisians despise winter with a very French passion."

He didn't know about French passion. But hadn't Avery said when in France, do as the French do? He more than liked the idea of sharing some passion with Avery. "I'm not a big fan of winter, either, when snow and ice make it harder getting to and from work."

"Ah, that sounds like you must be a workaholic." She smiled, her words vying for attention with the pounding rain on the nylon above them.

"That accusation would probably be accurate. I spend pretty much all my time at work."

"I must have caught you at a good moment, then, since you're sightseeing right now. Or, at least, we were sightseeing before we got stuck in this."

"You did catch me at a good moment." Maybe the romantic reputation of Paris was doing something to him, because he lifted his hands to cup her cheeks. Let his fingers slip into her hair that cascaded from beneath her hat. After all, what better place to kiss a beautiful woman than under an umbrella by the Seine in the shadow of the Eiffel Tower? "I'm enjoying this very good moment."

Her eyes locked with his. He watched her lips part, took that as the invitation he was looking for and lowered his mouth to hers.

The kiss was everything he'd known it would be. Her sexy lips had tormented him the entire time they'd been together in that elevator and standing close to one another on the observation deck. Hell, they'd tormented him just minutes after they'd met as he'd watched her nibble her baguette and sip her espresso. He could still faintly taste the coffee on her lips and an incredible sweetness that was her alone.

He pulled back an inch, to see how she was feeling about their kiss. If she thought it was as amazing as he did. If she'd be all right with another, longer exploration. Her eyes were wide, her cheeks a deep pink as she stared at him, but thankfully she didn't pull away and he went back for more.

He'd intended to keep it sweet, gentle, but the little gasp that left her mouth and swirled into his own had him delving deeper, all sense of anything around them gone except for the unexpected intimacy of this kiss they were sharing. Her slim hand came up to cradle his neck. It was cold, and soft, and added another layer of delicious sensation to the moment, and he had to taste more of her rain-moistened skin. Wondered if she'd possibly let him taste more than her face and throat. If she'd let him explore every inch of what he knew would be one beautiful body on one very special, beautiful afternoon.

Lost in sensory overload, Avery's eyelids flickered, then drifted shut again as Jack's hot mouth moved from her lips to slide across her chilled cheek. Touched the hollow of her throat, her jaw, the tender spot beneath her ear. She'd never kissed a man she'd just met before, but if it was always this good, she planned to keep doing it. And doing it. And doing it.

His hands cupping her cheeks were warm, and his breath that mingled with her own was warm, too, as he brought his mouth back to hers. Her heart pounded in her ears nearly as hard as the rain on the umbrella. She curled one hand behind his neck, hanging on tight before her wobbly knees completely gave way and she sank to the ground to join the water pooling around their feet.

The sensation of cold rain and snow splattering over her face had her opening her eyes and pulling her mouth from his. Dazed, she realized she'd loosened her grip on the umbrella, letting it sway sideways, no longer protecting them. Jack grasped the handle to right it, holding it above their heads again, his dark brown eyes gleaming. His black hair, now a shiny, wet ebony, clung to his forehead. Water droplets slid down his temple.

"Umbrellas don't work too well hanging upside down. Unless your goal is to collect water instead of repel it," he said, a slow smile curving the sexy lips that had made her lose track of exactly where they were. Lips that had traveled deliciously across several inches of her skin until she nearly forgot her own name.

"I know. Sorry." She cleared her throat, trying to gather her wits. "Except you didn't bring an umbrella at all, so you would have gotten wet anyway."

"True. Not that I mind. I like watching the raindrops track down your cute nose and onto your pretty lips." His finger reached out to trace the parts he'd just mentioned, lingering at her mouth, and she nearly licked the raindrops from his finger until she remembered a few very important things.

Things like the fact that she barely knew him. Like the fact that they were standing in a public place. Like the fact that she wasn't looking for a new relationship to replace the not-good one she'd only recently left.

She stared at the silkiness of his dark brows and the thickness of his black lashes, all damp and spiky from the rain. At the water dripping from his hair, over a prominent cheekbone, down the hollow of his cheek and across his stubborn-looking jaw. The thought crossed her mind that she'd never, ever spent time with a man so crazily good-looking. Even more good-looking than her ex-boyfriend, Kent, and she'd thought at the time he was a god in the flesh. At least for a while, until she'd figured out the kind of overly confident and egotistical guy he really was. Until she'd found out he was actually the one convinced he was godlike.

Getting it on again so soon with another man was not something she planned on doing.

She drew a deep breath. Time to bring some kind of normalcy to a very abnormal day. "Let's go to the café, dry off a little and get some food. You being Mr. Hungry and all."

"I've realized there's only one thing I'm hungry for at the moment." His lips moved close to hers again as his eyes, all smoldering and intense, met hers. "You. All of you."

All of her? Was he saying what she thought he was saying? She tried to think of a quick, light response and opened her mouth to speak, but no words came out. Maybe because she could barely breathe.

He kissed one corner of her mouth, then the other. "What do you say we head to the hotel for a while? A little dessert before lunch. I want a better taste of you."

Her heart leaped into her throat. Never having kissed a man she didn't know also meant never having had a quick fling with one. Never dreamed she ever would. But something about the way he was looking at her, the way his fingers were softly stroking her cheek and throat, something about the way her body quivered from head to toe and heat pooled between her legs had her actually wondering if maybe today was the day to change that.

After all, her last two relationships had ended with loud, hurtful thuds. Didn't she deserve some no-strings fun, just this once? She'd only be in Paris for one month, busy at work most of the time. The perfect setup for exactly what he was suggesting. And what would be the harm of enjoying what she knew would be one exciting, memorable afternoon with an exciting, memorable man?

"I…um…" She stopped talking and licked her lips, gathering the courage to shove aside her hesitation and just say yes.

"I know. We've just met, and it's not something I usually do, either. Honest." He cupped her cheeks with his cold hands and pressed a soft kiss to her mouth. "But being with you here in Paris just feels right. Doesn't it? It just feels damned right."

She found herself nodding, because it did. For whatever crazy reason, it felt all too right. A no-strings, nothing-serious, no-way-to-get-hurt moment with a super-sexy man to help her forget all about her past disappointments.

Another drop of water slid over her eyelid, distracting her from all those thoughts, and she swiped it away. "Except I'm all wet, you know."

The second the words left her mouth his eyes got all hot and devilish, and she felt herself flush, realizing what she'd said. "That's a plus, not a problem."

A breathless laugh left her lips. Before she could change her mind she decided to give herself a little present to make up for what she'd been through with her past jerky boyfriends.

Silent communication must have zinged between them, because they grasped one another's hands and headed in a near run to the hotel. To her surprise, the closer they got, the more excited she felt. She was entering unknown territory here, and hadn't she always promised herself she'd live life as an adventure? Plunging into bed with Jack for an hour or two seemed sure to be one thrilling adventure.

With her heart thumping so hard she feared he could hear it, Avery followed Jack as he shoved open the door to his hotel room. Once inside, the nervous butterflies she'd expected to flap around earlier finally showed up. She stared at him, hands sweating, as he shut the door behind her, trying to think of what the heck she should say or do now that they were actually here.

"Wouldn't you know that the minute we come inside, it stops raining?" she said lamely. Why was she so suddenly, crazily nervous? A little fling was no big deal, right? People probably did things like sleeping with someone they barely knew all the time. Especially in Paris. She didn't, but surely plenty of women did.

"Maybe if we're lucky, it'll start raining again when we go out. I like kissing it off you." The brown eyes that met hers held amusement and a banked-down hint of the passion that had scorched between them just minutes ago.

He shut the door and flipped the lock, his gaze never leaving hers. The heat and promise and that odd touch of amusement in the dark depths of his gaze all sent her heart into a little backflip before he pulled her into his arms and kissed her.

Unlike their previous kiss, this one didn't start out soft and slow. It was hard and intense, his tongue teasing hers until she forgot all about what she should say or do. Forgot where they were. Forgot to breathe. His fingers cupped the back of her head, tangled in her hair, as the kiss got deeper, wilder, pulling a moan from her chest that might have been embarrassing if she'd been able to think at all.

His mouth left hers, moving hot and moist to the side of her neck to nuzzle there. "You feeling more relaxed now?" he murmured.

How had he known? Though relaxed probably wasn't quite the right word to describe how she was feeling. "Um, yes. Thank you."

He eased back, his fingers reaching for the buttons of her coat and undoing every one of them before she'd had a chance to blink. "I don't know about you, but I'm feeling a little warm," he said as he slipped it from her shoulders and tossed it on a chair.

"Must be from all that running to the hotel," she said, breathless, but not from their fast trek to his room. "I figured it was a good chance to start training for the spring marathon."

His lips curved. "I thought we were running for a different reason." This time, his hands reached for the buttons of her blouse, the backs of his fingers skimming her skin and making it tingle as he slowly undid them one by one. "The reason being that I can't wait to see what you're wearing under this."

Her lacy white blouse dipped low over her breasts,

and pure, feminine pleasure swept through her at the way his eyes darkened as he stared down at them. At the way a deep whoosh of breath left his lungs. His fingertips slipped down her collarbone and inside her bra to cup her breast at the same time that his mouth covered hers.

Oh. My. The man was certainly one amazing kisser. World class, really, and her bones nearly melted at the sensations swirling around her. His cool hand on her breast, her nipples tightening into his palm. His hot mouth tracking along her skin, her bra now slipping completely off her to the floor. Her pants somehow magically loose enough to allow his other wide palm to slide inside to grasp her rear before it moved to the front and touched her moist folds, making her gasp.

The loud patter of rain again on the window had him pausing his intimate exploration, and he lifted his head, his dark eyes gleaming. "Guess it's a good thing we came in here out of the rain."

"Good thing," she managed before he resumed kissing and touching her until she was trembling with the intense pleasure of it all.

"Avery." The way he said her name in a rough whisper, the way he expertly moved his fingers while kissing her mouth and face and throat, had her nearly moaning. It all felt so wonderful, every bit of nervousness evaporated, replaced by want and need.

How she ended up on the bed she couldn't say, but when his mouth left hers she looked at him, foggily realizing that she was somehow flat on her back completely naked, while he stood there, staring at her.

"You are every bit as beautiful as I'd fantasized you'd be," he said. "Looking at you takes my breath away."

If that was true, then neither of them had much of an ability to breathe at the moment.

"My turn to look at you. Strip, please."

Those bold words coming out of her mouth shocked her, but he just laughed. "Your wish is my command." His gaze stayed on her as he quickly yanked off his shirt, and her breath caught at his lean but muscular torso. As he shoved off his pants, his erection became fully, impressively but all too briefly visible before his body covered hers, hot and deliciously heavy.

"You didn't give me much time to look at you," she managed to say.

"Sorry. Couldn't wait to feel all your gorgeous, soft skin against all of mine."

Well, if he put it that way. She had to admit it did feel amazingly, wonderfully, delectably good.

Was she really doing this? Lying naked with a man she barely knew? The feel of his body on hers, his mouth pressing sweet kisses to everything within reach of it, his smooth, warm skin beneath her hands told her the answer was yes, but to her surprise she didn't feel tense or strange or regretful. All she felt was toe-curlingly excited and turned on.

His hands and mouth roamed everywhere until she found herself making little sounds and moving against him in a way that would have been embarrassing if she hadn't been so totally absorbed in the sensations and how he made her feel. Nearing orgasm more times than she could count before he backed off and slowed things down, she was close to begging him when he finally rolled on a condom, grasped her hips with his hands and pulled her to him.

Instinctively, she wrapped her legs around his waist, inviting him in, and the way they moved together made her think, in the tiny recess of her brain that could still function, that it seemed impossible they'd met only that morning. That this dance they danced hadn't been etched in both their bodies and minds many a time before.

And when she cried out, it was his name on her lips and hers on his as they fell together.

CHAPTER TWO

"JUST SO YOU KNOW...it's really true that I don't usually do this." Her pulse and breathing finally slowing to near normal, Avery managed to drag the sheet up to cover her breasts. She glanced over at Jack, whose head lay on the pillow next to hers, eyes closed, looking as sated and satisfied as she felt. She wasn't sure why the words had tumbled out, but once they had, she wasn't sorry. She didn't want Jack to think she routinely picked up men, showed them around, then dove into bed with them.

"Do what?"

The expression on his face was one of bland innocence, completely at odds with the amused glint in the eyes that slowly opened to look at her. She couldn't help but make an impatient sound. "You know very well what. Sleep with men I've just met. Heck, I've never even kissed a man I just met."

He rolled to his side, his warm body pressing against hers. "I believe it was I who kissed you. Figured it was a Parisian tradition. The city of romance and everything. And what's more romantic than a rainstorm in the shadow of the Eiffel Tower?"

"Well. There is that." Though she was pretty confident that if it had been any other man she'd invited to breakfast that morning, there wouldn't have been any kissing on their trek around town or any rolling around in the sheets, complete with a lovely afterglow. And, to her surprise, no feelings of regret at all. Maybe because she knew it would happen just this once.

The moment she'd stepped off the hotel elevator that morning, her attention had gone straight to him like a magnet. Tall, lean and obviously American, with an adorably befuddled expression on his handsome face as he'd spoken to the maître d', she'd moved toward him without thinking, inviting a stranger for coffee and breakfast as though she did it every day. Which he doubtless assumed she did.

"I hope you're not regretting it. Our kiss, and now this." He propped himself up on his elbow and slowly stroked his finger down her cheek. "I know I don't. Being so close to you under that umbrella, there was no way I could stop myself. And once I'd kissed you, all I could think of was kissing you more."

No way she could have resisted his kiss, either. Or the bliss that had come afterward. Not that she'd tried at all. "Well," she said again, as though the word might somehow finalize the whole crazy afternoon, "we've shared *le petit déjeuner*, walked a bit of the city and gone up the tower. Kissed under an umbrella and made love while it rained outside. I guess it's a good time to find out a little about each other. I hope you're not married?"

She said it jokingly, but a small part of her suddenly wondered if he possibly could be. If he was the type of man who philandered when working out of town. Her stomach clenched at the thought. After all, she knew that type way more intimately than she wished she did. Would Jack admit it if he was?

"Not married. Never have been. Remember, I told you, all I do is work. Which probably makes me pretty boring."

Whew. She looked at him carefully and managed to relax. Surely no one could lie about a wife so convincingly. "Don't worry, you're not completely boring." His twinkling dark eyes and devilish smile proved he knew he was darned exciting to be around. "Tell me something else about you. What's your favorite food? Besides espresso, that is."

"Sorry, coffee definitely is number one on my list of life's sustenance. Though I'm sure anything licked from your lips would qualify, too."

She laughed and shook her head. "I don't have to ask you about talents, because I already know a few of them. Blarney being one."

"And my other talents?" His eyes gleamed as his wide hand splayed on her back, pressing her close against him, and the heat of his skin on hers made her short of breath all over again.

"I'm not stroking your ego any bigger than it already is."

"How about stroking something else, then?"

"Already did that. And I see I'll have to watch what I say around you."

He chuckled as he kissed her shoulder, and she found herself thinking about his mouth and those talents of his and wasn't sure if it was that or his body heat making her feel so overly warm. Again. "So what are your hobbies?" he asked.

"I don't know if I'd call it a hobby, but I like to run. Helps clear my mind when it gets too busy. And I like marshmallows. A lot."

"Marshmallows?" He laughed out loud at that. "You're kidding."

"Unfortunately, no. I pop the little ones when I'm working on the computer. Which is why I have to run. Don't want to *become* a marshmallow."

"You're about as far from a marshmallow as anyone could be." His hand stroked feather-light up her arm and across her chest to slide down the other, making her quiver. "I'd like to run more than just on a treadmill, but my work just doesn't leave me that kind of time."

"So what is this work you spend all your time doing?"

"I'm a cardiologist."

Every muscle froze, and her breath stopped as she stared at him. A cardiologist? *Cardiologist?* Could this really be happening?

He was probably used to women swooning when he announced that, but not her. She'd worked with more cardiologists than she cared to think about, and being arrogant and egotistical seemed to be a requirement for becoming that kind of specialist. Something she'd allowed herself to forget for too long with her last two boyfriends.

Along with her shock came another, even more chilling thought, which now seemed all too likely since they were staying at the same hotel. Her heart thumped hard in her chest, her body now icy cold as she tugged the sheet up tighter around it. "What's your last name, Jack?"

"Dunbar." He smiled, obviously not sensing the neon "oh, crap" vibes she had to be sending off. "I'm working for the next month at the Saint Malo Hospital, testing a new heart-valve replacement device. I've worked damned hard to get the design finished and to get the arrangements for the trial finalized. Can't believe it's finally about to happen."

Oh. My. Lord. She couldn't quite believe it, either. Not the trial starting. This unbelievable coincidence.

How was it possible that the man she'd just slept with was Dr. Jack Dunbar? The Jack Dunbar she'd be working with and observing at the hospital? The Jack Dunbar who was testing the procedure many, including her, hoped would someday always be used, instead of open-heart surgery, to replace faulty heart valves? The Jack Dunbar who had helped develop the next generation of valve replacement catheter based on her original design?

A next generation she feared wasn't any better, or safer, than her own had been.

And if it became necessary to voice her opinion that the trial should be halted, he wouldn't feel like kissing her or making love with her again, that was for sure. Not that she planned on more kisses and lovemaking, anyway.

A cardiologist was the absolute last kind of man she wanted in her life. Again.

"How about you?" He lay back, reaching to grasp her hand, his thumb brushing against her skin. Just as it had earlier when they'd been walking in such a lovely, companionable way. This time the feeling it gave her wasn't electrifying and sweet. The sensation felt more like discomfort and dismay. "So, what kind of last name goes with Avery? And what kind of work brings you to Paris?"

She swallowed hard. "Funny you should ask. My work has a lot to do with your own, Dr. Dunbar."

"Your work is similar to mine?" Jack asked, obvious surprise etched on his face. "In what way? Are you a doctor?"

"No. I have a doctorate in biomedical engineering." She left it at that, which was absurd, since it was all going to come out sooner or later, and it might as well be now. Lying naked in bed with him.

That realization had her shaking off her stunned paralysis to leap out of bed and grab up her clothes.

"That's...impressive." He propped himself up on his elbow, obviously enjoying the view as she scrambled to get dressed. His dark eyebrows were raised even higher, an expression she was used to seeing when she told people what she did for a living. She was young to be where she was careerwise and being petite made her seem younger still.

"Not really. I just worked hard, like you. Then again, in my experience cardiologists are pretty impressed... with themselves." And was that an understatement, or what?

"I should be insulted, except it might be true." He grinned at her. "So what brings you to Paris?"

"Well, as I said, my work has to do with yours." And could there be a much worse situation? The very first time she had a one-time thing with a man, he turned out to be someone she'd be working with closely.

She still couldn't quite wrap her brain around this mess. With a nervous laugh threatening, she pulled on her shirt, relieved to be finally clothed. After all, being naked when they made their formal introductions would be all kinds of ridiculous, wouldn't it?

She smoothed down her clothes and took a deep breath as she turned to him.

"As you know, your company hired the designer of the first valve replacement catheter to come study and observe the trial of your new one. That designer would be me."

His mouth actually fell open as he stared at her. It seemed he shook his head slightly, and that jittery laugh finally burst out of her throat. Clearly, he was as shocked by this crazy coincidence as she was. Though maybe it wasn't so crazy or much of a coincidence—after all, the Crilex Corporation was putting them both up at the same hotel where they'd met.

"You can't be...Dr. Girard," he said, still wearing an expression of disbelief.

"I am. And I'm equally shocked that you're Dr. Dunbar." Awkwardly, she stuck out her hand. "Avery Marie Girard. Nice to meet you."

That slow, sexy smile she'd found all too attractive throughout the day slipped onto his face again before he laughed. He reached to shake her hand, holding onto it. "It's an honor, Dr. Girard. Obviously, I've read about all you've accomplished. Your designs for various medical devices. Studied them for more hours than I care to think about as I worked with engineers to design the one we'll be testing. I...can't believe that you're...her."

"Because I'm young?" Or more likely because he'd

already seen her naked, but maybe she could pretend it hadn't happened. As though *that* was possible.

"Because you're beautiful. And fun. And spontaneous. With silky hair you don't wear in a bun and crazy, colorful clothes instead of drab gray. Rain boots with ducks instead of orthopedic shoes." His eyes crinkled at the corners. "I'm obviously guilty of thinking of a very stereotypical brainiac scientist, and those stereotypes don't include any of the things you are."

"Jack Dunbar!" She shook her head mockingly, having heard it all before. "You shouldn't admit any of that. The Society of Women Scientists will publicly flay you if you say that aloud. Maybe mount your head on an energy stick and parade the streets with it, denouncing stereotypes of all kinds."

"And I'd deserve it." The eyes that met hers were warm and admiring. That admiration would doubtless change into something else if he knew about her true role in his project. A slightly sick feeling seeped through her. Why, oh, why, hadn't she learned who he was before she'd slept with him?

"Glad you admit it. Scientists come in all ages, sizes, genders and personalities."

"You're right, and I'm sorry." He got out of the bed as well, and she averted her gaze from his glorious nakedness. "Sounds like you buy into some stereotyping, too, though. That cardiologists are all egotistical and impressed with themselves."

Guilty. But she had good reason to believe that, and it wasn't based on a stereotype. It was based on personal experience. And then, today, she'd dived into bed with another one. How stupid could she be? "Let's agree to set those preconceived ideas aside, shall we?"

"Agreed." He shook his head as he pulled on his own clothes. "Wow. I'm just blown away by this. I'd been interested in meeting the famous Dr. Girard and pleased to have her participate in the trial with me. Little did I know she'd be an incredible tour guide, have the greenest eyes I've ever seen and..." he paused to look at her, speaking in the low, deep rumble that did funny things to her insides "...the sweetest lips on either side of the Atlantic Ocean."

Oh, my. And his were beyond sweet, as well. "Except you realize this was a bad idea. Now that we know we'll be working together."

In fact, he didn't have any idea exactly how bad an idea it had been.

Robert Timkin, the Crilex CEO, had spun to Jack and everyone else involved that Avery would be there just to observe the trial for her own education. But the company knew she had concerns about the new device and had really hired her to evaluate the data, giving her the power to stop the rollout of the next trials if she thought it necessary.

Jack had worked on designing the new device and organizing the trial for over a year, and he'd doubtless flip out if the data forced her to shut it down.

"Working together." His warm smile faded and his brows lowered in a frown. "I guess you're right. That is a problem."

"It is." She drew a calming breath. "Listen. This afternoon was wonderful. A lovely day in a wonderful city between two strangers. But now we're not strangers. And I have to be an objective observer as I gather data on the trial. From now on, we're just working colleagues, nothing more."

He stared at her silently for a moment, his expression serious, before he nodded. "You're right. Business and pleasure never mix well."

"No. They don't." Not to mention that she'd sworn off cardiologists for good.

He stepped forward and pulled her close, pressing his lips to hers in a soft, sweet kiss. Despite her words and thoughts and conviction, she found herself melting into him.

"That was from Jack to Avery. Thank you for an unforgettable day," he whispered against her lips before he stepped back. "Dr. Dunbar will be meeting Dr. Girard tomorrow in the cath lab as we both concentrate on why we came to Paris. Okay?"

"Okay."

He dropped one more lingering kiss on her mouth before he picked up her coat and draped it over her arm. She stepped out to the hall and the door clicked quietly behind her. She lifted her fingers to her lips, knowing with certainty this had been the only one-time fling she'd ever have. That she'd savor the memory, and pray that over the next thirty days it didn't come back to sting her in more ways than one.

CHAPTER THREE

AVERY STOOD BEHIND a wall of glass to one side of the operating table in the hospital's cath lab, watching the procedure on the X-ray fluoroscopy viewing monitor. She'd gowned and masked like everyone else in the room, but unlike anyone else, she held a tablet in her hand to record the notes she'd be taking.

"The prosthetic valve is made from cow tissue," Jack said to the nurses and doctors assisting or observing the procedure, as he and Jessica Bowman, the nurse he'd brought with him from the States, readied the patient. "This version doesn't require a balloon to open it as the previous one did."

He continued to explain, as he had last night during his presentation, how a transcatheter aortic valve implantation, TAVI, worked. The details of how the catheter was designed, and why the stent and valve were in an umbrella shape, designed to push the diseased valve aside before the umbrella opened, seating the new valve in its place. With the procedure not yet started, Avery had a moment to watch him instead.

Today, he was all business, his dark eyes serious above his mask, his voice professional and to the point.

In stark contrast to yesterday's amusing and witty companion. As they'd laughed and walked through Paris, his eyes had been perpetually filled with interest and humor, his mouth curved in a smile, his attention on her as much as it had been on the landmarks she'd shown him.

A very dangerous combination, this Dr. Jack Dunbar. So dangerous she'd thrown caution off the top of the Eiffel Tower. Thank heavens they'd agreed that no more hot, knee-melting kisses or spontaneous sex could be allowed.

Though just thinking about those kisses and their all-too-delicious lovemaking made her mouth water for more.

She gave herself a little mental smack. Date a cardiologist? Been there, done that. Twice. Fool me once, shame on me, fool me twice, shame on me again. Fool me three times? Well, her genius status would clearly be in question.

Then there was the other sticky issue. Obviously, the best-case scenario would be for the device to work fabulously, for the trial to be a success and for it to be further rolled out to other countries and hospitals. After all, in the U.S. alone over one hundred thousand people each year were diagnosed with aortic stenosis, and a solid third of them were high risk who might not do well with traditional open-heart surgery or weren't candidates at all.

But, from studying this stent and catheter, she worried that it didn't fully address the significant problem of postoperative valve leakage and subsequent pulmonary edema, which her own design had not solved and was something she was trying to fix in her new prototypes.

"I'm going to establish a central venous line through the right internal jugular," Jack said as he made an incision in the patient's neck. "Then insert a temporary balloon-tip pacemaker. Both groin areas of the patient have been prepped, and I'll next insert an introducer sheath into the femoral artery."

Avery watched as his steady hands worked. After completing the first steps, he made another incision in the patient's groin, moving the guide wire inside the artery. "Contrast dye, please, and monitor the heparin drip," he said as he watched his maneuvering of the wires on the overhead screen. "You'll see that it's important to puncture the artery with a high degree of angulation to minimize the distance from the artery to the skin."

The man was an incredibly skilled interventional cardiologist, that was obvious. She quickly focused on the careful notes she was taking to squash thoughts of the man's many skills he'd thoroughly demonstrated to her yesterday. Why, oh, why, would she have to be around him every day when the whole reason she'd given in to temptation had been because she'd thought she'd never see him again?

Finally, he finished stitching the access sites and the patient had been moved to Recovery. Jack shook hands with all those in the room congratulating him.

"Thank you, but I'm just one cog in this wheel that will hopefully change valve transplantation forever," Jack said. "One important cog is right here with us.

The designer of the first catheter-inserted replacement valve, Dr. Avery Girard."

Taken off guard, she felt herself blush as Jack turned, gesturing to her with his hand, then actually began to clap, a big smile on his face, as the others in the room joined him. She'd been keeping a low profile, and most of the hospital had just assumed she was a Crilex representative. Most cardiologists she knew—most definitely both of her old boyfriends—loved to play the big shot and preen at any and all accolades. Neither one of them would have shared the glory unless they had to.

"I appreciate your nice words, Dr. Dunbar," she said, feeling a silly little glow in her chest, despite herself. "I have every hope that the new design you've helped develop will be the one that works. Congratulations on your first procedure going smoothly."

"Thank you." His warm eyes met hers, reminding her of the way he'd looked at her yesterday, until the doctors observing converged on him to ask questions and he turned his attention to them.

Avery took off her gown, mask and hat, and caught herself watching Jack speak to everyone. Listening to his deep voice and the earnest enthusiasm there. She wanted to stay, to listen longer, but forced herself to move quietly from the room to go through her notes. Limiting her interactions with him to the bare minimum had to be the goal, and since there was just one surgery scheduled today, there was no reason to hang around.

Satisfied that her notes were all readable, in order and entered correctly into her database, Avery walked toward the hotel, feeling oddly restless. She'd planned to work in her room, but a peculiar sense of aloneness came over her. Since when had that ever happened?

Still, the feeling nagged at her, and she stopped to work for a bit at a little café, which seemed like a more appealing choice. After a few hours she headed to her room and settled into a comfy chair with her laptop. Projects on her computer included ideas on how to fix her previous TAVI design if the one Jack had in trial had significant issues.

That unsettled feeling grew, sinking deep into the pit of her stomach, and she realized why.

If she had to recommend the trial be discontinued, would Jack think it was because she wanted Crilex to develop one of her designs instead? That her concerns would be from self-interest instead of concern for the patients?

She'd been doing freelance work ever since abruptly leaving the company that had funded her first TAVI design. They'd insisted on continuing the trials long after the data had been clear that the leakage problems had to be fixed first, which was why she'd been glad to observe this trial before that happened again.

If only she could talk to Jack about it, so he'd never think any of this was underhanded on her part. But her contract with Crilex stated she was to keep that information completely confidential.

She pressed her lips together and tried to concentrate on work. Worrying about the odd situation didn't solve anything and, after all, Jack knew she'd designed the original. Wouldn't he assume she was likely working on improvements to it and observing his with that in mind?

She couldn't tell Jack the power she had over the

trial. But maybe she should tell him she had concerns with the design. To give him that heads-up, at least, and maybe nudge him to look for the same issues she would be as the trial continued.

Avery caught herself staring across the room for long minutes. With a sigh she shut the lid of her laptop and gave up. Clearly, she needed something to clear her head. Fresh air and maybe a visit to somewhere she hadn't been for a while. A place popped into her head, and she decided it was a sign that it might be just what she needed to get back on track.

A half hour later, jostling with others passengers as she stepped off the metro, she saw the sun was perilously low in the sky. She hadn't torn out the door in record time to miss seeing the Sacré Coeur at sunset and headed in that direction in a near jog, only to bump into the back of some guy who stepped right in front of her.

"Oh, sorry!" she said, steadying herself.

"No, my fault. I'm trying to figure out how to get to the Sacré Coeur to see it at sunset, and I..."

She froze and looked up as the man turned, knowing that, incredible and ridiculous as it was, the man speaking was none other than Jack Dunbar. Saw his eyes widen with the same surprise and disbelief until he laughed and shook his head. "Why is it that whenever I need a tour guide, the best one in Paris shows up to help me?"

Fate. It was clearly fate, and why did it keep throwing her and Jack together? Should she even admit that was exactly where she'd been going? "I wish I had the answers to the universe. But somehow I don't think you'll be surprised to learn that's where I'm headed, too."

He looked at her a long, serious moment before he gave her a slow smile, his eyes crinkling at the corners, and the warmth in them put a little flutter in her chest. "You know, somehow I'm not surprised. And who am I to argue with the universe? Guess this means we're going together."

A buoyant feeling replaced the odd, unsettled feeling she'd had for hours. Bad idea? Yes. Something she could walk away from? Apparently not.

"Then we've got to hurry." She grabbed his hand, knowing she was throwing caution away again. But how could she say no to the happy excitement bubbling up inside her? And after all, it was just a visit to the Sacré Coeur, right? "The sun's setting soon, and we don't want to miss it."

"Lead on, Ms. Tour Guide. For tonight I'm all yours."

CHAPTER FOUR

JACK LOOKED AT the adorable woman dragging him through the streets and wondered, not for the first time, how he could have gotten so lucky to have met her before they'd started working together. A personal connection before a professional one got in the way of it.

The professional part was unfortunate, since he'd vowed he'd never again get involved with a woman at work. For just one more night, though, he'd let himself enjoy being with Avery. After all, here they were, together. And, smart or not smart, he just couldn't resist.

"A lot of people think it's really old, but did you know the Sacré Coeur was consecrated after World War I in 1919?"

"I didn't know. Are you proving again to me that female scientists are well versed in many subjects?"

"I don't have to prove anything about women in science," she said in a dignified tone, "seeing as I'm not wearing orthopedic shoes."

He laughed. "True. And they're even bright green, which I've never seen in leather ankle boots."

"Clearly, you live a sheltered life. Maybe you should get yourself some brightly colored shoes."

"Somehow, I think my patients would worry about my skills if I dressed that way." His eyes met her twinkling ones, an even more vivid green than her boots, and just looking at her made him smile. "You get to hide in your lab and behind your computer. I don't."

"You could wear them while your patients are under anesthesia." She had that teasing look in her eyes that he'd found irresistible yesterday when they'd gone up the Eiffel Tower, then spent that magical time in his hotel room. That he'd found irresistible since the moment she'd grabbed his hand and led him to breakfast. That he had to somehow learn to resist, starting again tomorrow.

"Except most of my patients are awake during procedures, so I'll stick with black or brown."

"Where's your sense of adventure?"

"Here with you tonight."

She looked up at him, an oddly arrested expression on her face. "Mine, too." She stepped up their pace. "We're almost there, and since January's off season, hopefully there won't be big crowds. Good thing the sun's peeking through. I think it just might be a beautiful night."

"It already is."

A blush filled her cheeks as she realized what he was saying. And maybe it sounded hokey, but he meant it. His intense focus on work usually didn't allow him to notice things like a beautiful sunset or, though he probably shouldn't admit it, even a beautiful woman sometimes. But she'd grabbed his attention from the second he'd met her, and he didn't know what to do about that.

She led him around a corner then suddenly stopped,

turning her full attention in front of them. "*Voilà!* We made it! And, oh, my gosh, I think it's about the most spectacular I've ever seen!"

His gaze followed hers, and the sight was beyond anything he'd expected. At the end of the street behind a beautiful old building with large columns, the Sacré Coeur rose high above everything else. Its numerous cupolas and spires were bathed in pink and gold from the sunset, emerging from the pale sky and looking for all the world like a stunning mural in the mist.

"That's...incredible."

"It is, isn't it?" She took her hand from his, moving it to clutch his arm, holding him closer. He looked down to see her eyes lit with the same wonder he was feeling and that strange sense of connection with her, too, that had prompted yesterday's memorable interlude. "I haven't seen the basilica for a long time."

He moved his arm from her grasp and wrapped it around her shoulders, wanting to feel her next to him. They stood there together a long while, staring as the pastels changed hue and darkened. Eventually, the sun dipped low, taking the color and light with it, and Jack turned to her, pulling her fully into his arms without thinking. "Somehow, I don't think it would have seemed quite as beautiful if you hadn't been here with me."

She smiled and lowered her head to rest her cheek against his chest as she gazed down the street at the now shadowed church, and he couldn't believe how natural it felt to hold her like this. Like they'd been together a long time instead of one day. Like there weren't good reasons not to.

He stroked his hand up her back, sliding it beneath

her thick hair to cup her neck. "How about we take the funicular up to see the city below?"

She lifted her head and leaned back to look up at him. "How do you know about the funicular?"

"What, you think you have all the dibs on tour guiding?" He tucked her hair under her cute hat, a yellow one this time, letting his fingers linger on the softness of her locks before stroking briefly down her cheeks. "I read a Paris tour guide book because I didn't know I'd have a personal one tonight."

"And yet here I am."

"Yeah. Here you are."

For a moment her green eyes stared into his until, to his surprise, worry and utter pleasure, she lifted herself up on tiptoe, slipped her arms up his chest and around his neck and pressed her lips to his. The touch was instantly electric, surging through every cell in Jack's body as he tightened his arms around her. Until he forgot they worked together. Until he forgot they were standing near any number of other sightseers who were snapping photos and admiring the church. On the side of a busy street where cars and motorcycles and scooters veered all too perilously close.

Just as had happened yesterday under that umbrella, Avery managed to make him forget everything but the drugging taste of her mouth as it moved softly on his.

The roar of a scooter zooming by had him breaking the kiss. He leaned his forehead against hers, their little panting breaths creating a mist of steam in the cold air between them. "Wow. That was nice."

"What, you think you have all the dibs on initiating a kiss?"

He chuckled at her words, mimicking his. "Believe me, I'm more than happy to share the dibs. But as much as I'd like to keep kissing you, I don't want either of us sent to the hospital by one of the crazy drivers around here." Or get into a sticky situation because of their jobs. "Let's go on up to see the view."

She pulled away and something, maybe embarrassment, flickered in her eyes. He reached for her chin and turned her face to his. "Hey, what's that look for?"

"I don't know why I kissed you. Why I keep kissing you, even when we agreed not to." She shook her head, a little frown between her brows. "It's like something comes over me and I lose all common sense."

"If you have to lose your common sense to kiss me, I hope you don't find it," he teased, earning a small smile. He took a few steps backward, bringing her with him, until he came up against the wall of a building. Even as he knew he shouldn't, he lifted his hand to cup her cheek, gently stroking her beautiful lips with his thumb. "You taste damned good to me."

"Except we need to work together. So kissing or… anything else…isn't a good idea."

"I know. It's a hell of a bad idea." He kissed her again, and the sigh that slipped from her lips, the way her body relaxed into his nearly had him going deeper, and to hell with the risk of being struck by a car. But he forced himself to let her go, reaching for her hand. "Come on. Your funicular awaits, princess."

They rode to the top and enjoyed the incredible views of the city as he held her close to shelter her from the colder air and wind. They meandered along the cobbled streets of Montmartre as Avery filled him in on some of the history of the village that had long been a haven for artists, including Picasso, Monet and Van Gogh. Today it attracted young artists who peddled their work on the streets.

"I don't know about you, but I haven't eaten," Jack said as they passed a restaurant with an appealing exterior. He looked at the posted menu and laughed when he realized it was, of course, in French. "I don't know what this place serves, but you want to grab something to eat?"

"My parents and I lived right here in Montmartre the two years we were in Paris, but I've never eaten here," she said, looking at the menu. "It's pretty expensive."

"We deserve something besides hospital food, which we'll be eating a lot of. Come on."

The food turned out to be good, and they enjoyed a lively conversation and occasional debate about medical devices like stents and implants until they both laughed about it.

Jack grabbed the bill when he saw her reaching for it, handing his credit card to the waiter. "My treat. I like a woman who eats all her food and talks about something besides shopping," he said to tease her.

"You treated me yesterday, so it should be my turn. And it sounds like you've been dating the wrong kind of women."

"No doubt about that." In fact, she didn't know how right she was, and it was a good reminder why he couldn't date Avery, no matter how attractive she was. No matter how much he wanted to.

"I don't always practically lick the plate, though," she said with a grin. "Thank you. The food was amazing, but you spent way too much."

"You forget I'm a rich, egotistical cardiologist. When I'm not working like crazy, I like to throw money around to impress beautiful women."

"You're right. Somehow I'd forgotten."

Her smile disappeared. He had no clue why and tried for a joke. "It's my pleasure to shower money on gorgeous scientists who wear colorful shoes."

Still no smile. In fact, an odd combination of unhappiness and irritation had replaced every bit of the pleasure that had been on her face.

Well, damn. But it was probably just as well, considering everything. "Time to head back to the hotel," he said, shoving back his chair to stand. "We have two surgeries tomorrow I need to get ready for."

She nodded and they headed toward the metro. It felt strange not reaching out to hold her hand, and a pang of regret filled him. But wishing their circumstance could be different didn't change a thing.

"Oh! I think that's Le Mur des Je T'aime! I've never seen it."

"What's Le Mur...whatever you said?"

He followed her as she moved closer to look at a wall of tiles with words scrawled all over it and splashes of red here and there in between. "It's the Wall of I Love You. An artist named Baron conceived of the wall, with 'I love you' written in something like three hundred languages. As a place for lovers to meet."

A place for lovers to meet? That bordered on overly sentimental as far as Jack was concerned. "Sounds like something from a chick flick, with a gooey happily-ever-after."

After he'd said it he thought maybe he should have

kept his opinion to himself, and was relieved when she laughed. "Typical man. Not that I know much about lasting relationships and happily-ever-after."

"That makes two of us."

"Nobody you'd meet here at the wall? Old flame or old pain?"

"I've been too busy." The only woman who qualified as an "old pain" was the medical device sales rep he'd dated who, it had turned out, had used him big-time to advance her own career. He hadn't come close to being in love with her, but it had been damned embarrassing. Which was why he never dated anyone remotely connected to his work. And he needed to remember that.

She began walking toward the metro again, and they were mostly quiet on the way back to the hotel. Another sudden shower burst from the night sky that had them wet in an instant and nearly running the last blocks, intimately tucked beneath Avery's little umbrella.

Finally sheltered under the overhang in front of the hotel doors, she shook the rain from it. "Clearly, I'm going to need to get a bigger umbrella," she said, her voice a little breathless. "This one isn't nearly big enough for both of us."

Except, after tonight, they wouldn't be touring Paris together anymore. "I could invest in a big, yellow rain poncho and leave the umbrella to you. That would be pretty masculine and sexy, don't you think?"

"I don't know. People might mistake you for a giant lemon."

He loved her laugh and the way her eyes twinkled. Fortunately, other people loaded onto the elevator with them or he just might have found himself kissing that beautiful, smiling mouth of hers again. He grasped her elbow when they arrived on her floor and moved into the hall.

"What are you doing?" she asked. "You're staying on the eighteenth floor."

"I always walk a lady to her door."

"I don't think hotels count."

"Why not? There are so many doors in this huge place, you might get lost." He thought she'd smile at his teasing tone, but she didn't, and he sighed. "If that look on your face means you think I'm planning to jump your bones again, I'm not. Much as I'd like to, I get that it's different now. And agree it needs to be. Okay?"

"Okay."

She smiled, and it was her real, sunny smile. So real he had to kiss her one last time. She tasted the same as she had before, an intoxicatingly sensual mix of chilled, damp skin and warm mouth. The smell of rain and a slight, perfumed scent from her hair filled his nostrils, and the feel of her body through her coat filled his hands. He wanted to strip it off of her so that barrier wouldn't be between them.

A little sound came from her throat, and the sound inflamed him, his own low groan forming in response as he deepened the kiss. Damned if this woman didn't knock his socks off in every way a woman could.

She pulled back, her gloved hands a softly fuzzy caress on the sides of his neck. Her eyes were wide, her mouth wet from his kiss, her breathing choppy. "What is it about you?"

"Funny, I was just thinking the same thing. About you. Except I know the answer. You're amazing, and we have chemistry about equal to a nuclear explosion. Which makes it nearly impossible not to kiss you, even when I know I shouldn't." He pressed his lips to hers for another long moment before looking into the deep green of her eyes again.

She stared at him a moment longer before her beautiful mouth curved in an answering smile. "I guess we need to think of this as one last time Avery and Jack meet one another."

"I like that. A kiss dictated by the universe."

"By the universe." She rose up and kissed him again. Just as he was trying, in the midst of the thick fog in his brain, to mentally calculate how many hours it was until he had to be at work and alert, and how much longer he could enjoy the taste and feel of her, she drew back.

Her eyes were lit with the same desire he felt, and he was glad one of them had enough presence of mind to stop while they still could.

"There's something I want to be honest with you about," she said, clasping her hands together in an oddly nervous gesture. "And when you hear it, it'll probably help us keep our distance from one another."

"That sounds ominous. Is it that you're actually the one who's married?"

She smiled and shook her head. "No. It's about your TAVI device. I'm worried it doesn't address the flaw mine had. Leakage resulting in pulmonary edema."

He stared at her in surprise. "Why? We've barely begun the trial."

"I know. But I'm just not sure the corrections you've made will be enough, and feel it should have been tested longer on animals before a human trial."

What the hell? "The bioengineers and I worked hard to improve it. It's more than ready."

"I just wanted you to know I believe we should both pay extra attention to that aspect of the data."

Maybe this was how people felt when someone said their baby was ugly, and it wasn't a good feeling. "Duly noted. Good night, Dr. Girard."

He headed to his room, still reeling a little from her announcement. He was damned proud of the new device and would never have guessed she had any bias whatsoever about it. Surely she would remain scientifically impartial as she collected the data. Her announcement, though, did seem to make it easier to step away and keep his distance, which he tried to see as a positive development.

But as he attempted to sleep, he was surprised and none too happy to find himself thinking about Avery nearly as much as he was thinking of the work waiting for him early in the morning.

CHAPTER FIVE

JACK SAT AT the small desk the hospital had given him to use and finished his notes on the procedures they'd just completed. Now that surgery was over for the day, he let himself think about Avery and this uncomfortable situation.

For the first time in his entire career he'd had trouble getting one hundred percent of his focus on the patient and surgery in front of him before the procedure had begun. To not notice Avery standing behind the glass, ready to watch the TAVI procedure on the monitor, taking her notes. He'd finally managed, but somehow, some way, he had to keep Avery Girard and her premature concerns about the device from invading his thoughts.

He shoved himself from the chair to concentrate on what he'd come here to accomplish. He pulled up the patient records and headed toward the room of the second patient they'd done the procedure on.

Simon Bellamy was eighty-six years old and had been referred to them because of his severely diseased aortic valve. Although reasonably healthy otherwise, his age put him at high risk for open-heart surgery. He'd been doing well the past two days, and Jack expected he could be released tomorrow.

The satisfaction he was feeling as he looked at the patient's chart disappeared the instant he walked into the man's room.

Short, rasping gasps were coming from his open mouth, and he sat bolt upright in his bed, eyes wide. Jack grabbed his stethoscope from his scrubs pocket as he strode to the bedside. "What's wrong, Mr. Bellamy? Are you having trouble breathing?"

The patient just nodded in response, his chest heaving. Jack listened to the man's lungs, and the obvious crackling sounds were the last thing he wanted to hear. "Ah, hell." He pushed the button for the nurse, then got the blood-pressure cuff on the man. He stared at the reading, his chest tightening at the numbers. While it had been normal earlier today, it had soared to two hundred and twenty over one hundred.

The nurse hurried into the room. Jack kept his attention on his patient as he spoke, checking oxygen saturation levels, and was damned glad almost everyone in the hospital spoke English. "We need to reduce his heart's workload by getting his blood pressure down immediately. Also administer furosemide and get a Foley catheter placed, stat."

The man's oxygen level proved to be very low, which was no surprise. It was disturbingly obvious what was happening here. "I need to get a chest X-ray. Can you...?" He glanced at the nurse, who was busy getting the Foley placed. "Never mind. I'll call down to have the portable brought up."

And damned if the minute he finished the call to

X-Ray, Avery walked in with her tablet in hand, stopping abruptly.

"What's wrong, Dr. Dunbar?"

For a split second he didn't want to tell her, after her revelation to him last night. Which would be childish and unprofessional, not to mention pointless, since she'd figure it out anyway. "Acute onset aortic insufficiency. Getting a chest film to confirm."

Just his luck that she was witnessing exactly what they'd just talked about. A significant complication from the valve leaking. He knew her being there or not didn't change the reality and told himself he was mature enough and confident enough to handle it. For a small number of patients it wasn't an unusual complication, anyway, and Jack discussed with everyone all the risks and potential side effects.

Avery gave a single nod and stepped out of the way as the tech rolled the X-ray machine into the room and got the patient prepared to get the picture of his lungs. To her credit, there was no sign of I-told-you-so smugness on her face, just concern.

"Have you given him a diuretic and blood-pressure meds?"

Had she really asked that? He nearly let loose on her, until he saw the deep frown over her green eyes and the genuine worry there. He managed to bite back the words he wanted to say, which was that he knew what he was doing, for God's sake, and to butt out. Did she really think he was a lousy doctor? "Having a Foley catheter placed and gave him furosemide and BP meds. With any luck, he'll be more comfortable shortly."

She nodded again, moving farther away to one side

of the room as she opened her tablet. Her head tilted down and her silky hair swung to the sides of her cheeks as she began to tap away at the screen.

Frustration surged into his chest and he stuffed it down, a little shocked at the intensity of it. His years of practicing medicine had taught him how to remain calm even in critical situations, and he was fairly legendary for being cool under fire.

He inhaled a deep, calming breath and turned away from her to check on Mr. Bellamy. Already the man was breathing a little easier and able to lean back against the raised bed. The X-ray tech ambled off with the films, and Jack hoped they'd be done fast, though he didn't expect them to show anything he didn't already know. There was no doubt in his mind this was pulmonary edema, the patient's lungs full of fluid from the valve leakage.

"Feeling slightly better now, Mr. Bellamy?"

The man nodded, still mouth-breathing but not nearly so labored as before. Jack reached for his hand and gave it a squeeze. "I know that's a scary thing, when you can't get a breath. You've been given a water pill to get your lungs clear, and we're going to keep the Foley catheter in to catch the fluid. It will have to stay there until we get the volume of fluid we want to see and make sure it's nice and clear. Okay?"

The man nodded again, giving his hand a return squeeze before Jack headed out of the room to check the X-ray.

"Dr. Dunbar."

Avery's voice stopped him in the hall and he turned. He folded his arms across his chest, wondering if this was the moment for an *I told you so.* Which he absolutely would react calmly and professionally to, damn it, if it killed him.

"Yes?"

She stepped close to him and, to his surprise, placed her cool palm on his forearm. He couldn't figure out exactly what her expression was, but it didn't seem to be self-satisfaction. More like…remorse?

"I owe you an apology."

He raised his eyebrows. That was about the last thing he'd expected to come out of her mouth, and he waited to hear what she was apologizing for.

"It was completely inappropriate of me to ask if you'd administered blood-pressure meds and furosemide. You're the doctor in charge and far more knowledgeable about patient care than I am."

"Yes, I am."

A little laugh left her lips. "There's that egotistical cardiologist finally coming out. I knew he was in there somewhere." She dropped her hand from his arm and gave him a rueful smile. "During the clinical trial on my original device, I was often required to give instructions to nurses post-op when the doctors weren't around. I guess it's an old habit that's hard to break. Sorry."

She bit her lip, and damned if the thought of how incredible it had been kissing her came to mind.

How could he be thinking about that now? He looked into the green of her eyes, filled with an obvious sincerity, and felt his frustration fade. "Just don't let it happen again, or everyone in the hospital might start to wonder if you know something they don't. Like that I bought my MD online."

"It would take more than me blurting something dumb to tarnish your awesome reputation, Dr. Dunbar. Everyone here thinks you walk on water." Those pretty lips of hers curved. "But, believe me, I'll do my best to keep my trap shut. You know that old saying about how if looks could kill? Seeing the expression in your eyes at that moment, if that was true, I'd be lying on the floor lifeless."

In spite of everything, he felt himself smile, and how she managed that, he didn't know. "Cardiologists do have superpowers, you know. Better not test me to see if that's one of mine."

Her smile widened, touched her eyes and sent his own smile even wider. They stood looking at one another, standing there in the hallway, until Jack managed to shake off the trance she seemed to send him into with all too little effort.

He couldn't allow himself to fall any further for her obvious charms. Her work was too tangled up with his, and he'd promised himself never again.

He brought a cool, professional tone back to his voice. "I'm going to check on Mr. Bellamy's X-ray. I'll put the notes in his chart for your database."

He turned and strode down the hall, fighting a stupid urge to look over his shoulder to see if she was still standing there. When he stopped at the elevator he glanced back up the hall, despite his best intentions not to, and his heart kicked annoyingly when he saw her backside as she moved in the opposite direction. Riveted, he stared at the view. Her thick, shiny hair cascading down her back. That sexy sway of her hips, her gorgeous legs with their slender ankles, her delicate profile as she turned into a patient's room.

And found himself powerless against the potent memories of how she'd felt held close in his arms, the taste of her mouth on his, the feel of his body in hers.

Damn.

He focused on the gray elevator doors. This just might prove to be the longest month of his life.

CHAPTER SIX

"SO, LADIES AND GENTLEMEN," Bob Timkin said, smiling at the group attending the late dinner meeting at the hotel, "we are encouraged at the success so far after a full week of the clinical trial. Patients and their families are pleased with the results, and I have great optimism as we look forward to the rest of the month."

The forty or so attendees clapped, a number of them turning their attention, smiles and applause toward Jack. He shifted slightly in his seat, wondering why it felt a little awkward. Not long ago he'd felt pleased with the media attention he'd gotten for his role in the development of the prototype device and the work involved in getting it finished and the trial set up. Happy that his mother, father and brother—all doctors—were proud of him and what he was trying to accomplish in memory of his granddad.

A large group effort had made it happen. The biomedical engineers had taken his suggestions to heart when they'd created the device. Crilex had funded it. French officials had seen the value of conducting the first trials here. He'd always been sure to include every one of them in his presentations and mention them in interviews.

But when it came down to it, the focus of others had been primarily on his work and his skills.

Avery's gaze met his across the room, and damned if he didn't have to admit she was probably why he felt this sudden discomfort. Her original design was the whole reason he had a new TAVI device at all. And while a slight valve leakage in a small percentage of patients was normal, he didn't like it that now three of the patients in this trial so far had experienced that complication. Statistically, that was far higher than the expected six percent, and that knowledge, along with Avery's announcement of her concerns, added to his unease.

He and Avery had managed to be simply cordial and professional to one another for the remainder of this first week. She also hadn't said anything to him about the latest patient with the valve leakage, which he'd been surprised but glad about. She must have finally seen it was still way too early to become truly concerned.

Jack nodded in acknowledgement of the recognition being sent his direction, but as his gaze again met Avery's he knew he couldn't stand her believing he was egotistical enough to think he alone merited the applause. Why what she thought of him mattered so much, though, wasn't something he wanted to analyze.

About to get to his feet and give a little speech about all the people deserving credit for the trial, Jack saw Bob moving from the lectern. Discomfort still nagged at him, but he figured it would be ineffective and even weird to start talking as the crowd began to stand and disperse.

Next thing he knew, he was looking at Avery again, and, disgusted with himself, quickly turned away. He would not allow himself to wonder what she was doing the rest of the evening. Would. Not.

He should go to his room and look over the history of the patient he'd be doing surgery on tomorrow. But an odd restlessness left him thinking he needed to do something else first, so he could concentrate later. Maybe a little downtime, listening to music in the lounge, would help him relax.

He moved toward the table where Jessica was sitting with some other nurses, yakking away like they'd become best friends. "Hey, Jess. How about a drink at the bar? We only have a single surgery tomorrow afternoon, so I think we can stay up one night past ten p.m."

"You don't have to ask me twice." She smiled at the women she was with. "Anybody want to join us?"

One by one they shook their heads. "I need to get home to get my little ones ready for bed," a young woman said. "Their papa will let them have crazy fun all night if I'm not there, then they will be tired and crying in the morning before school."

Another nodded in agreement, rolling her eyes. "*Oui.* My Raoul thinks that, if Maman's not home, dinner can be a chocolate croissant."

Jack smiled as everyone at the table laughed in agreement. It sounded just like his sister-in-law's gripes on the rare occasions his brother took over with the kids. If he was ever a dad, he'd try to remember this conversation and be more responsible.

That the random notion came to mind at all took him

aback. Since when had he even thought about having a family? The answer was never. Work consumed his life.

For the first time, he wondered if that was all he wanted. If work could always be everything.

He shook his head, trying to shake off any and all peculiar and unwelcome notions. Paris was clearly doing strange things to him and had been since day one. He'd be glad when the month was over and the clinical trials continued elsewhere. Maybe he should consider talking to the Russian government about a winter trial in Siberia—if that didn't freeze some sense into him, nothing would.

He moved into the hotel lounge with Jessica, passing the dance floor as the heavy beat of music pulsed around them. "I can't believe I've worked with you for three years, but don't know your tipple," he said to Jess as they settled into a round, corner banquette.

"Like that's a surprise?" she said with a grin. "I don't think we've ever been out for a drink before. Ever. You're always still at work when I leave."

"We haven't?" He thought back and realized with surprise that was the case. "It bothers me to realize you're right. Though I'm pretty sure a big part of that was you falling for Brandon. And the two of you getting married thing was kind of a big deal."

"Okay, maybe that's true," Jess said, chuckling. "A cosmopolitan makes me pretty happy. Sounds extra-good after the constant demands you've put on me this week."

"Cosmo it is."

He ordered from the waitress and was just about to ask Jess a few of the questions he realized he'd never bothered to ask her before when, out of the corner of his eye, he saw Avery walk into the lounge. Not alone.

Every ounce of the relaxation and good humor he'd managed to feel for the past five minutes died when he saw the guy who accompanied her.

Jack recognized him as a doctor from the hospital, though he didn't know him. A urologist, maybe. French. Well dressed, like most Parisians, and good looking to women, too, he supposed.

Jack watched the guy laugh at something she'd said. As she gifted him with her amazing smile in return, he pressed his palm to Avery's lower back and led her to the dance floor.

The way she moved, the way she smiled, the way she rested her hand on the man's shoulder made it hard for Jack to breathe, reminding him of the moment they'd first met. Every muscle in his body tightened at the way the guy was looking at her as they moved to the beat of the music. Like she was first on his list of desserts.

"Earth to Jack. Should I call the bomb squad before it goes off?"

Jessica's words managed to penetrate his intense focus on Avery and the guy, and he slowly turned to her. "What?"

"You look like you're about to explode. Which I don't think I've ever seen from you. Jealous a little?"

"Jealous? That's ridiculous."

"It may be ridiculous, but I hate to break it to you. It's all over your face."

Somehow he managed to control his accelerated breathing. To school his expression into something he hoped was neutral. "I don't date women I work with. You know that."

"Uh-huh. Except this one's making you rethink that, isn't she?" Jack hadn't even realized the waitress had brought their drinks until Jessica took a sip of hers, studying him over the rim of her glass. "Listen. I get it. She's smart and pretty and, other than me, you're alone here in France. But acting on your attraction to her? That's just trouble calling your name."

Trouble with a capital *T.* Unfortunately, he'd felt that trouble calling his name ever since he'd arrived in Paris. Trouble in the form of a small woman with soft skin, smiling eyes and a mouth that tasted like bright sunshine on a gray day.

Had she joked with the guy that she chose dance partners based on who would buy her a drink? The thought squeezed his chest so tight he had to force out his response to Jess.

"Since when are you my guardian angel? Believe me, I know all of that, and you don't have to worry. I'm keeping my distance." At least, he'd managed to for the past week or so.

"Guess you'd better run, then, because she's heading toward our table."

He stiffened and turned. Then couldn't help the relief he stupidly felt when Dr. Frenchman wasn't with her. And hoped like hell he wasn't looking at Avery the same way that guy still was, watching her from a corner table.

"Dr. Dunbar, may I speak with you for just a moment?" Avery asked when she stopped in front of them, her gaze flicking from him to Jessica and back.

He sat back, trying to pretend she didn't affect him in any way, which stretched his acting skills to the limit. "What's on your mind?"

She stood silently for a moment. Jack took in how perfectly the yellow shift dress she wore fit her slim body. How she folded one hand over the other in a nervous gesture before she stilled them against her sides. How her silky eyebrows twitched the way he'd noticed before when she pondered what to say.

"I wanted to suggest that, when you have a day off soon, you let me show you—"

As though pulled by a string from some invisible puppeteer, he reached out to grasp her wrist, tugging her down onto the bench seat. Her hip bumped into his as her eyes widened in surprise. Jessica's presence had nearly helped him resist the urge but, God help him, the hot jealousy that had grabbed him by the throat took control. Wanting to send a message to the guy still sitting across the room. Prompting Jack to say what he couldn't stop thinking about, and before he knew it the words were coming out of his mouth.

"Show me the correct way to use an umbrella?" Of its own accord, his voice went lower as he dipped his head, his lips nearly touching hers. "Or explain the mysteries of chemistry and spontaneous combustion? In which case, we can find a more private place to talk."

She stared at him, and even through the darkness of the bar he could see the surprise and confusion on her face. "Um, no. I wanted to talk to you about the trial."

"What about it?"

"With three patients already experiencing valve leakage, I'm sure you see why I'm concerned."

He watched her lips move, thinking about how good it was to kiss her. Let his gaze travel to the V of skin below her throat, which he knew was soft and warm. "The trial's barely started. We haven't had nearly enough patients to come to any kind of conclusions yet."

"I know. But as I said before, sometimes there are red flags right away." Deeply serious, her green eyes locked with his. "I want to introduce you to a patient who underwent one of the first TAVI procedures with my original device. I'd like you to see what he's living with."

He laughed, disgusted with himself. While he couldn't stop thinking about the taste of her mouth and the softness of her skin, she didn't seem to be having any trouble focusing on work.

He realized he was still holding onto her wrist, and dropped it. "I know what people with postoperative complications live with, Avery. I treat them every day."

"Just think about my offer." As she lifted her hand to his shoulder, a part of him liked having it there, while the saner part reminded him she'd just had that same hand on Dr. Frenchman's shoulder. "You might find it enlightening to meet this man and his family."

She slid from the seat and walked away. To Jack's surprise, she didn't sit with Dr. Frenchman. Instead, she exited the bar entirely, and he was glad he didn't have to watch her cozy up to the man, at the same time annoyed as hell that he felt that way.

What was it about this woman? First he'd grabbed her and pulled her down next to him like he had a right to. And in spite of it being a beyond-bad idea, every time he looked at her, all he could think of was how much he'd enjoyed being with her and kissing her and having sex with her. How much he wanted more of all of it.

"Boy, you've got it bad." Jessica shook her head. "I hope you can keep from getting so tangled up with her that you lose perspective on what we came here to do."

As he watched Avery's bright yellow, curvy behind disappear into the hotel foyer, he could only hope for the same thing.

CHAPTER SEVEN

AVERY STEPPED OFF the hotel elevator to head to the front doors, then stood frozen when she saw Jack standing right where she wanted to go. An absurdly handsome Jack, wearing a pale blue dress shirt, necktie and sport coat.

She and Jack had been friendly but professional over the past two days of surgeries and patient follow-ups, and she hoped it could stay that way. Without the uncomfortable attraction that remained in a low hum between them. The attraction that had clearly prompted Jack to do the caveman thing and pull her down next to him after she'd danced with the French doc she'd met. Jessica was walking toward him, and Jack's mouth tipped into a smile when he spotted her. Normally wearing scrubs all day, Jessica had dressed up tonight, looking very attractive in a black dress with a coat slung over her arm. Obviously, the two were going to dinner somewhere, and when Jessica reached Jack she said something that made him laugh.

Could there be something going on between them, now that she and Jack had agreed to keep their professional distance?

The thought twisted her stomach in a strange little knot, which was ridiculous. Must be just a residual reaction to the shock of her ex cheating on her.

Still, the thought of walking past Jack and Jessica to leave the hotel made her feel uncomfortable, though that wasn't very mature. Hoping they'd move on to wherever they were going, she saw Jack pull his phone from his pocket. In just seconds his expression went from relaxed to a deep frown, and the sudden tension in his posture was clear even from all the way across the room.

Jack shoved his phone back into his pocket, spoke briefly to Jessica, and pushed open the doors to head out into the night. Was there a problem with a patient? Without thinking, Avery hurried to talk to Jessica, to see if there was anything she could help with.

"Jessica?"

The woman turned, and when she saw Avery the concern on her face morphed into a neutral expression. "Yes?"

"I couldn't help but notice that Jack ran out of here quickly. Is something wrong?"

Jessica seemed to study her before she answered. "One of the patients we performed surgery on today is experiencing slurred speech and weakness in one arm."

Obviously, a possible stroke. "Which patient?"

"Henri Arnoult."

"All right. Thanks." Avery took a step toward the doors to head over there, but Jessica's hand on her arm stopped her.

"There's nothing you can do, Dr. Girard. He'll either make it or he won't, and you know as well as I do that stroke is one of the major risks of any kind of surgery involving stents."

"I do know. But it's my job to record every bit of data on every patient, whether it's a normal complication or not, and whether it's a good outcome or a bad one."

"Jack told me you have some concerns about this TAVI device. I hope your personal bias wouldn't interfere with—or influence—that data."

"I don't have any personal bias. Concerns, yes. Bias, no." Jessica regarded her with clear skepticism, and Avery sighed. "Listen. I appreciate that you support Jack, and I assure you that any and all data I record and analyze will be done carefully and scientifically. I'd love for this trial to be a success as much as you do."

"Good. Jack is the best surgeon I've ever worked with, and this groundbreaking work is extremely important to him. Important to heart patients, too."

"I know."

"Okay," Jessica said, nodding. "Please ask Jack to let me know how things go. Even if it's in the middle of the night."

"I will." As soon as Avery pushed open the door, cold wind whipped down her neck and up her dress. She closed her coat as tightly as she could and hurried the two blocks to the hospital.

She found Jack in the patient's room in the ICU, talking to the house doctor who had likely been the one to call him in. Avery hung back, not wanting to intrude inappropriately. It seemed like forever before the house doctor finally left the room. Avery inhaled a fortifying breath before she entered. Jack stood there, his back to the door, his hands in his pockets, looking down at the patient lying in the bed. She moved to stand beside him, her heart sinking when she saw that Mr. Arnoult was unconscious and connected to a breathing machine.

Without thinking, she tucked her hand through the crook of Jack's arm and his elbow, pressing it close against his side. "These are the tough days, I know, Jack," she said softly. "Do you know what's wrong?"

"He seemed fine when I saw him this afternoon. But I'm told his blood pressure soared and his speech became slurred, so they quickly got a CAT scan. Which confirmed he's had a large hemorrhagic stroke."

"It's not impossible that his condition could improve."

"No. Not impossible. We've given him meds to try to control the brain swelling, among other things, but I don't know. It's a big bleed."

"Have you...checked to see how the TAVI looks? Is it still in place?"

"Not yet. I just ordered an echocardiogram. I hope to God it hasn't moved, because there's no way he could survive open-heart surgery on top of this. Hell, he wouldn't have survived that kind of surgery before this." A deep sigh lifted his chest. "I suppose this is more confirmation to you that the trial might be premature."

He turned to look at her as he spoke, his eyes somber with concern. Her heart filled with the certain knowledge that it was for this ill man and not concern for himself or for the future of the trial.

"Will it shock you when I say no?" She pulled her hand from his arm to rest it against his cheek. "Risk of stroke is an unfortunate complication of any procedure like this. Give an elderly patient with serious underlying health problems the blood thinners necessary for this kind of surgery, and sometimes it doesn't go the way everyone hopes it will. It's no one's fault. It's not your fault or the device's fault. It just is."

He stared down at her for a suspended moment before, to her surprise, he gathered her in his arms. Another deep sigh feathered across her forehead as he rested his head on top of hers. She pushed aside his necktie before pressing her cheek against his chest, and she wrapped her arms around him, too, since he clearly needed that connection right now. He smelled wonderful, just as he had on their first day together, holding her close beneath that umbrella, and she found herself closing her eyes at the pleasure of it as she breathed him in.

"I'd hoped we wouldn't have any catastrophic events," he said as his hand stroked slowly up and down her back. "But you're right. It is a reality that this happens sometimes. And I appreciate you not making it even worse by stomping up and down and yelling about it."

"Wow. Sounds like you think I'm a troll or something."

"A troll?" She could hear the smile in his voice. "That, I've gotta say, never occurred to me."

It took great force of will for Avery to lean back and break the close contact between them. She glanced at Mr. Arnoult and the steadily beeping monitors and figured they should continue their conversation elsewhere.

"I could use some coffee. You?"

At his nod, she took his hand and they walked to the nearly empty coffee shop on the first floor. Sitting at a round table so tiny their knees kept bumping,

Avery sipped her espresso before asking the question she needed to know the answer to. “Jessica seemed to think I might skew the data based on what she called my bias about the device. Do you, too?”

“Honestly?” He quirked a dark eyebrow. “I’d be lying if I said it hadn’t crossed my mind.”

Her chest ached a little at his words. Obviously, there’d be no friendship between them if that was how he felt. And she realized, without a doubt, that she very much wanted that friendship. More than friendship, but under the circumstances friendship was all they could have.

And even friendship was probably a bad idea, considering Jack didn’t know all that Crilex had hired her to do.

“I find, though, that for some damned reason,” he continued as he leaned closer, his mouth only inches from hers, “the uncertainty seems to turn me on.”

A startled laugh left her lips. “And my wondering if you’re different or the same as most other cardiologists apparently has kept me interested, as well.”

He leaned closer still, so close his nose nearly touched hers. “Or maybe it’s that we just have this undeniable chemistry that refuses to be snuffed out by little things like that.”

The timbre of his voice, the expression in his dark eyes made her a little breathless. “Well, I did get straight As in chemistry. It’s something I’m good at.”

“Now, that I already knew.” He closed the tiny gap between them and gave her the softest of kisses. “I’m going to go check on Mr. Arnoult again and see if the echocardiogram’s been done. You might as well go on back to the hotel, or wherever you were going to go tonight, and collect his data tomorrow. Unless your plan was to go out with Dr. Frenchman. He's a total player, and even more egotistical than I am."

"You mean the man I danced with?" Was it wrong of her to be pleased at the tinge of jealousy in his voice, to know that he'd noticed and had obviously been bothered by it? Was it also wrong of her that she'd secretly hoped he would, even though she'd been disgusted with herself when the thought had occurred to her? "I didn't realize you knew him."

"I don't. I just know his kind."

"Uh-huh. Aren't you the man who told me I shouldn't judge you negatively just because of what you do for a living?"

"That's totally different. Trust me, I know how guys think and saw the way he was looking at you."

"What way?"

"Like I do." She'd never known something like a hot twinkle existed, but there it was in his eyes as he stood. "I'm going to spend the night here so I can keep tabs on Mr. Arnoult."

A sudden desire to stay right here with him, supporting him, came over her, but she knew it didn't make a lot of sense. She wasn't Mr. Arnoult's family, she wasn't a medical doctor, and she and Jack needed to keep a professional distance. Though, at that moment, as her gaze stayed connected with his, she knew with certainty that was getting more difficult every day.

Concern for Mr. Arnoult and thoughts of Jack staying up much of the night, working, left Avery unable to sleep well, either. Up early and in the hospital just after 7:00 a.m., she stopped in the hospital coffee shop to get double shots of espresso for both her and Jack, knowing she'd find him there somewhere.

She checked Mr. Arnoult's room first, relieved to see Jack was there, able to drink his coffee while it was still somewhat hot. Her heart squeezed the second she saw him standing next to the patient's bed, his dark head tipped toward the nurse and another doctor as he spoke to them.

Mr. Arnoult was still connected to the ventilator, and from her distance by the door it appeared he was still unconscious or heavily sedated. The squeeze in her chest tightened when she saw his head was thickly bandaged, which most likely meant they'd decided to try draining the hemorrhaging blood from around his brain.

Jack glanced up as she entered the room, and his gaze held hers for a moment before he finished his conversation and walked to meet her in the doorway.

"I could smell that coffee all the way across the room," he said. His hair was uncharacteristically messy, dark stubble covered his cheeks, and the lines at the corners of his eyes were more pronounced. "Nothing better than a woman who understands a caffeine addiction."

"I nearly got you a triple, but thought maybe I could get you to go to the coffee shop I took you to that first day. It would be good for you to get out of the hospital for a breath of air."

He shook his head. "Not yet. Maybe later."

"How is he?"

He grasped her elbow and led her down the hall to

the little office he'd been working from, pulling the single chair from behind the desk for her to sit on.

"No, you sit," she said, perching on the side of the desk. "You're the one who's been up most of the night."

"If I sit, I might fall asleep." He set down his coffee, giving her a shadow of a smile as he took hold of both her shoulders and gently lowered her into the chair. "A woman who brings coffee deserves not only the chair but being draped in gold, like you said women should be."

"Well, coffee is worth its weight in gold." She sipped her espresso and resisted the urge to ask again about Mr. Arnoult. Forced herself to be patient and wait for him to speak when he was ready.

With his body propped against the side of the desk and long legs stretched out, he drank his coffee and stared out the door. Just when she thought she couldn't keep silent another second, he put his cup down and turned to her. "Things aren't good. We couldn't control his brain swelling, so the neurosurgeon drained the blood from his brain about two this morning. I had hoped that releasing the pressure would work, but the swelling continued. Tests show there's now severe, irreversible brain damage—his pupils are fixed and dilated. No movement of his extremities, no gag reflex. Just received CAT scan images that confirm it. Which I'm going to have to share with the family when they get here."

"I'm so sorry, Jack." She stood and moved in front of him to hold both his hands in hers. "I know this is never the outcome anyone wants. But as I said yesterday, we both know this risk exists in a patient like him.

He was extremely ill before the procedure. You'd hoped to give him a new lease on life, which he had no chance of having without replacing his valve, and he wouldn't have made it through open-heart surgery for that. You tried your best."

He released her hands, his tired eyes meeting hers. "Thanks for all that. I do appreciate it. I know it, but it still feels crappy."

Without thinking, she slipped her hands around his neck and kissed him. Just like she had in front of the Sacré Coeur. This time, it was to comfort him, soothe him. But the moment her lips touched his, the moment his arms wrapped around her and held her close, the moment his warm, soft mouth moved against hers she nearly forgot the goal was comfort and not something entirely different.

But they were in an office attached to a busy corridor, which both of them seemed to remember at the same time. Their lips separated, and she rested her head on his shoulder as she hugged him, working on the comfort part again, stuffing down the other feelings that wanted to erupt.

It felt good to hold him. Felt good to try to offer him comfort. But as the moment grew longer, warmer, she reminded herself that she was there for another reason, too. She should ask him about the prosthetic valve and if he'd checked it or not, but she didn't want to break the closeness they were sharing. Not quite yet, anyway. The valve wasn't the reason the man had had the original stroke, and she'd find out soon enough if it had moved or leaked after the brain had begun to bleed.

Apparently, though, this connection between her and

Jack seemed to include mind reading. "I already know you well enough to guess you're dying to know about the valve," he said, loosening his hold on her to lean back. "We've done two separate Doppler echocardiograms, neither of which showed any fluid flow around it. It's fitting tight as a drum, which makes me all the sadder that he stroked before he could enjoy his life a little more."

She nodded. "That's encouraging for other patients but, yes, it's very sad for Mr. Arnoult. Would you like for me to join you when you talk to the family?"

"No. This is a part of what I do. The hardest part, but the buck has to stop with me."

She nodded again, and instantly pictured the caring and sympathy that Jack would show the man's family when he shared the bad news, because it was obvious that was simply a part of who he was.

"Then I'll leave you. How about letting me give you a little TLC later? I'm good at that." As soon as the words came out of her mouth and a touch of humor lit his eyes, she knew how he'd interpreted it. And found her heart fluttering, even though that wasn't how she'd meant it.

"I bet you are. And despite us agreeing we shouldn't mix business with pleasure, I can't seem to keep all that in the forefront of my mind when you're around." He tipped up her chin. "Something else seems to take over instead. Like serious anticipation of some TLC from you."

He gave her a glimmer of a smile, his dark eyes connecting with hers for a long, arrested moment. Then he kissed her in the sweetest of touches. The rasp of his beard gently abraded her skin, and he tasted of coffee and of deliciousness, and she could have kept on kissing him for a long, long time. But his lips left hers to track, feather-light, up her cheek and linger on her forehead before he drew back. “Thanks for being here. I’ll find you later, okay? Maybe dinner?”

She’d barely had time to respond before he left the room, his posture proud and erect despite the exhaustion he had to be feeling. And at that moment she knew with certainty that Jack was nothing like her old boyfriends. He had an integrity and warmth and depth they couldn’t even begin to match.

Avery concentrated on seeing all the patients who were still in the hospital after their procedures, carefully recording their vitals, test results, state of mind and comfort levels. But throughout those hours she often found herself thinking of Jack having to continue on and do his job. How he’d still operated on the patient scheduled for early that morning, his focus never wavering throughout the procedure as she’d watched, despite the obvious fatigue in his eyes.

She’d bumped into him once, rounding on patients, spending a long time talking with each of them, recording his own notes. She wondered if he’d spoken with Mr. Arnoult’s family yet, and her chest tightened at how tough that was going to be on all of them.

As she moved down the hall to see a different patient, she heard the rumble of his voice in Mr. Arnoult’s room and the sound of quiet weeping. Her stomach clenched, and when she glanced in she saw two middle-aged men standing, flanking an elderly woman who sat in a chair, dabbing her face with a crumpled tissue. Jack was crouched in front of her, one hand patting her shoulder, the other giving her another tissue he'd pulled from the box on a chair next to her.

Avery found herself pressing her hands to her tight chest at the sweet and gentle way Jack was talking with the woman, the deeply caring expression on his face. A part of her wanted to go into the room and stand next to him for support, but she knew he wouldn't want or need that. It wasn't her place to spy or eavesdrop, either, and she quickly moved on to the last patient she needed to see.

At that moment, she knew she wanted to somehow help him feel better about it all. While she knew this was far from the first time in his career he'd had to deliver bad news to a family, and certainly wouldn't be the last, giving him a reason to smile suddenly became her priority for the day.

How, though? They'd already been up the Eiffel Tower and seen the Sacré Coeur at sunset. Her mind spun through her favorite places in Paris, but many of them were more fun to go to in the summertime, when you were lucky enough to enjoy some sunshine and the gardens were glorious. Still, there was something to be said for just walking the city on a cold night, cuddling to stay warm on a bench in one of the gardens or by the Seine.

Cuddling? Her plan for the evening was about cheering Jack up, not kissing him or having sex or anything like that.

Except she'd be lying to herself if she pretended that she hadn't thought about throwing aside the very good reasons they shouldn't be together for one more memorable night. A night to help him forget a very long and difficult day. Knowing it would be more than memorable for her, too, would be the icing on the cake.

CHAPTER EIGHT

AVERY'S HEART, WHICH only moments ago had felt all bubbly at the thought of spending the evening with Jack and finding ways to make him happy, stuttered, then ground to a halt.

Standing stock still now just outside the doorway to Jack's office, she stared at what seemed like a reenactment of her warm and intimate time in that room with him earlier. A woman had her arms wrapped around his waist, and he held her close with his cheek resting on her head.

But unless Avery was watching some holographic image of that moment in time, Jack was not holding her. He was holding a different woman.

Jessica.

Barely able to breathe, Avery backed up a few steps, then turned to hightail it out of there.

She'd become completely, utterly convinced he wasn't at all like the last two doctors she'd been involved with, which proved how incredibly bad she must be at judging character. Clearly, every one of them charmed, lied and cheated as easily as they breathed, and she thrashed herself for forgetting. For thinking Jack was different.

She stalked down the hall, her throat tight with embarrassment as she thought of the really good fantasies she'd been dreaming up about their night together. Gullible idiot. Fool. IQ genius with no brains.

"Avery." Jack's voice and footsteps followed her, and she walked faster. "Avery, stop, damn it!"

His fingers curled around her arm, turning her toward him. She yanked her arm from his hold. "What is it, Dr. Dunbar? It's been a long day, and I have a date." A date with herself and her computer and her work, which she'd just remembered she'd promised herself would be her only focus until she'd let a certain man change her mind about that.

"Your date is with me. And if you're running off in a huff because I was hugging Jessica, you know damned well that she's married."

"Like that matters to some people."

"It matters to me. And to her. We've worked together for three years. She's my coworker and my friend. And as my friend, she felt bad about Henri Arnoult. Just like you did. That's all." He grasped both her arms this time, tugging her closer. "It's been a hell of a bad day. Mr. Arnoult's family had to make the hard decision to take him off the ventilator. We had to let him go. And, yeah, that's one damned difficult part of being a doctor, and I'm tired inside and out. The last thing I want is for you to be upset and thinking things that are all wrong."

She stared into his dark eyes, which were filled with frustration and exhaustion and worry. Could she have been wrong? Jumped to conclusions too fast? And hadn't she wanted to comfort him, not add to his stress, if she was wrong?

She definitely didn't want to make his day any worse

than it already had been. But her heart didn't feel up to being exposed to more punishment, either. "Listen. I think it's a good idea for you and Jessica to be together tonight. She knows you better than I do, and you'll have a nice time, I'm sure."

"Except that, even though I shouldn't, I want to know you better." He glanced down the hall, which was fairly quiet this late in the day, before turning back again, lifting his hands to cup her cheeks. "After the great time we've spent together, how could you even think I might have something going on with Jess?"

She stared up into his eyes and could see he really wanted to know. But she didn't feel like sharing her past. Her embarrassment that she hadn't seen her exes for who they were.

"I didn't. Not really. I was just being weird."

His eyes crinkled at the corners in a smile. "The only way you're remotely weird is the odd color combinations you sometimes favor." His thumb stroked along her cheekbone before he bent his head and kissed her. Maybe it was stupid, but the soft warmth of his lips managed to sap every ounce of the worry and self-deprecation she'd felt just moments ago. The feel of his mouth slowly moving on hers sent all of that to the outer reaches of her brain and her thoughts back to the fantasies she'd been having before she'd seen him with Jessica and freaked.

He broke the kiss, and the eyes that met hers were so sincere she knew she couldn't let what had happened with her stupid exes mess with her mind anymore. No way did she want to live her life suspicious of people and their possible agendas, backing away from potential pain instead of exploring all the wonderful things the world had to offer.

That Jack just might have to offer, if their potentially disastrous professional relationship didn't ruin everything before they had a chance to spend more time together.

"It would sure be nice to kiss you without knowing there are hundreds of people who might be spying on us at any moment. Which is pretty much the only times we've kissed so far. Let's get out of here."

She wanted that, too, but felt she had to ask about Jessica's plans. After all, the woman probably had nothing to do, and maybe she shouldn't hog Jack all to herself. Even though that was all she wanted, darn it. "Shouldn't we ask Jessica to join us for dinner?"

"One of the reasons she was happy to come and assist me in the trial here is because she has a cousin with three little kids living in Paris. She's enjoying spending time with them. And even if she wasn't," he added, his eyes gleaming, "I wouldn't ask her along. Three's a crowd, and you're the one who said you're good at TLC and offered to comfort me, right?"

"I did make that offer, though you probably don't need it. You're pretty tough, I know."

"Tough or not, a guy always appreciates some TLC from a beautiful woman. Looking forward to being with you tonight is the only thing that made today bearable." He placed his mouth close to her ear, and his words, the rumble in his voice, made her shiver. "I know you don't back out on your promises. And I can't wait to be on the receiving end of some tender, loving care from the talented Dr. Girard."

* * *

Chilly wind nipped what little skin they had exposed, and Jack watched Avery tug her blue and purple scarf more tightly around her neck. Figured it was the perfect excuse to hold her even closer to his side as they walked through the Palais-Royal gardens. Though gardens would be an overstatement at the moment, since everything was dormant from winter, and the only things remotely green were the carefully trimmed evergreen shrubs.

"I love this park in the summertime, when all the roses are in bloom and you can sit and enjoy the quiet and seclusion from the busyness of the city," Avery said, smiling at him, her cute nose very pink from the cold. "And the trees are trimmed in an arching canopy that's fun to walk beneath on the way to the fountain. I'm sorry it's not all that pretty right now."

"You're sorry because you could do something about it being the end of January? Are you a magician as well as a scientist?"

"Wouldn't that be nice?" She laughed. "Sadly, no. I just wish I could show you the Paris I love all year round, but we'll have to settle for now."

Her words struck him with a surprising thought, which was that he wished for that, too. For more than just these brief weeks with her. But that wasn't meant to be. He had his work and his TAVI trials, which would take him to various parts of the world, and finally, assuming all went well, to trials back in the States. He didn't have time in his life for any kind of real relationship and felt a pang of regret about that reality.

"I'm enjoying the now with you," he said. "What's the next part of now, Ms. Tour Guide?"

"Let's pop into a few of these boutiques. Anything in particular you like to look at? Or want to buy?"

"Yes. The one thing I particularly like to look at is you." Which had been true from the moment he'd met her. He tugged her close enough that her steamy breath mingled in the cold air with his own. "And I'd like to buy a thin gold chain to slip around your neck, except you'd accuse me of being an egotistical player again. When the only reason would be to please you. Okay, and touch your skin, too. I'm definitely looking for ways to make that happen."

She blushed cutely, and he loved the humor that shone in her green eyes. "You don't have to buy me gifts to make that happen."

Maybe she saw exactly where his thoughts had immediately gone, because she stepped out of his hold to walk through the doorway of a little shop.

"In truth, I'm into this kind of thing more than gold," she said as she picked up a delicate, inlaid wooden box.

"Music boxes? Any special kind?"

"I love old ones. But any kind makes me smile. Like lots of little girls, I had one with a dancing ballerina and fell in love with them after that." She opened the lid and a tune began to play. An adorable smile lit her face and eyes, making him smile, too. "Isn't it beautiful?"

"Beautiful." He damned near took it from her hand to buy it for her, but was sure she'd protest. It would probably make her feel uncomfortable to receive a gift from him at that point in their relationship—or whatever you'd call the powerful force that kept drawing him to her.

They stared at one another, and the hum in the air between them was so strong it nearly drowned out the soft tune tinkling between them. She put the box down and, to his surprise, grabbed his hand and trotted quickly out of the store, the sexy blue ankle boots she wore clicking on the pavement.

"Where to now?" he asked.

"I just thought of something that would be fun to do with you."

He hoped that "something" was her hauling him off to the hotel to get naked for the TLC she'd promised, but had a feeling that was wishful thinking. "And that would be?"

"This." They ran until they got to a carousel, the music filling the air around it not all that different from the music box, except a lot louder. She jumped onto its platform, turning to him with the bright eyes and brilliant smile he'd come to see in his dreams. "Come on! Which horse do you want?"

"Whichever you're on."

She laughed and walked between the rows of wooden animals, finally straddling a white horse with a bright green saddle and carved mane that looked to be flying in the wind. Jack swung himself up behind her. As her rear pressed against his groin, as he wrapped one arm around her waist and one hand on top of hers on the pole, as he breathed in the scent of her hair and her skin, he knew he'd never see another carousel without remembering this moment with her.

"I never knew I loved merry-go-rounds until this moment," he murmured in her ear.

"Doesn't everybody?"

"Everybody lucky enough to have a gorgeous woman sharing their horse."

The music grew louder, and as the carousel began to turn, their horse rose and fell, pushing his body into hers, rubbing them together. And damned if even through their clothes and jackets it wasn't just about the most erotic thing he'd ever experienced outside a bedroom.

He tried to scoot back, away from her a little, so she wouldn't feel exactly how aroused he was, but had a feeling she already knew. He dipped his head and let his lips wander over what skin he could reach, which wasn't nearly enough. Her cheek and jaw, her nose, her eyebrow. Her soft hair tickled his face as he nibbled her earlobe, tracing the shell of her ear with his tongue until her sexy gasp, the shiver of her skin he could feel against his lips, took every molecule of air from his lungs and sent him on a quest for her mouth.

The arm he had wrapped around her tightened as he lifted his hand from the pole to grasp her chin in his fingers, turning her face so he could taste her lips. Her eyes met his, a dark moss green now, full of the same desire he knew she could see in his.

Her head tipped back against his collarbone, and he covered her mouth with his and kissed her. Kissed her until he wasn't sure if the spinning sensation he felt was from the earth turning, the carousel revolving, the horse rising and falling or his brain reeling from Avery overload.

The sound of people laughing and talking seeped into his lust-fogged brain, and apparently Avery's, too, as they both slowly broke the kiss, staring at one another, the panting breaths between them now so steamy he could barely see her moist, still-parted lips. He brushed his thumb against her lush lower lip, and it was all he could do not to kiss her again.

"Didn't I say I'd like to kiss you, just once, without people standing around, watching?" he said when he was able to talk. "I don't think this accomplishes that."

She gave him a breathy laugh. "No. So let's accomplish it now."

As the carousel slowed to a stop, he slid from the horse, then helped her down. "Any ideas on how?"

"Oh, yeah." Her lips curved, and the only word to describe her expression would be *sensual*, which kicked his pulse into an even faster rhythm than it was already galloping in. "They don't call me the 'idea gal' for nothing."

CHAPTER NINE

JUST LIKE THE first time—the one she'd been sure would be the only time—Jack had her coat and blouse off before she'd barely drawn a breath. Time to get with the program and get his coat off, too. Her fingers weren't quite as swift as his talented surgeon ones, and she wrestled to get it unbuttoned.

He shrugged it off and tossed it on top of hers before reaching to touch his thumb to the top of her bra as he had before, slowly tracing the curve of it, and her breath backed up in her lungs at the expression in his eyes, at the low, rough sound of his voice. "Bright blue lace this time. Hard to decide if I like this or your pretty white one better."

"I have matching panties on. Does that help?"

His eyes gleamed in response. "Don't care if they match. I can't wait to see you in them." He lowered his mouth to hers, softly, sweetly, before moving it across her jaw, down to her collar bone, slipping farther until his tongue traced the lacy top of her bra. Sliding down to gently suck her nipple through the silky fabric until her knees wobbled. Avery clutched the front of his shirt, hanging on tight, wondering if she just might faint from lack of oxygen and the excruciating pleasure of it all.

She wanted to see his skin, too. Wanted to touch him and lick him, as well. "No fair that you're ahead of me," she managed to say, reaching for the buttons of his shirt. "No more distractions until I get your shirt off."

He lifted his head, ending his damp exploration of her bra, and his dark eyes gleamed into hers as she attempted to wrangle his buttons. "Happy to assist, if you'd like."

Oh, yes. She'd like. Mesmerized, she stared as he flicked open one button at a time, slowly exposing the fine, dark hair on his smooth skin, before finally pulling the shirt off entirely. About to reach for him, she lifted her gaze to his. Saw that his focus was on her breasts, and the hunger in his eyes sent her heart pounding even harder.

"You have one beautiful body, Dr. Girard."

"Funny, I was just thinking the same about you, Dr. Dunbar."

With a smile, he closed the gap between them, reached behind her, and in one quick motion had her bra unhooked, off her arms and onto the floor. His hand cupped her breast and his thumb moved slowly back and forth across her nipple until her knees nearly buckled.

"As I said before, those are some quick fingers you have, Dr. Dunbar. Should have known you were a surgeon or guitarist or something." She pressed her palms to his hard chest, sliding them through the dark, soft hair covering it. On up to wrap her arms behind his neck, holding him close, loving the feel of his body against hers as she moved backward, bringing him with her.

"You haven't seen anything yet," he said in a gruff voice so full of promise she found herself mindlessly touching her tongue to his jaw to taste him as she pressed her body to his. His mouth moved to capture hers as they continued their slow meander to the bed. She didn't even realize he'd unbuttoned her pants, too, until she felt his hands moving on her bottom, inside her silky underwear and on down her thighs until every scrap of clothing was pooled at her feet.

She gasped in surprise, which sent the kiss deeper. Until the backs of her legs hit the bed, and the impact jolted her mouth from his. He stared at her a moment before he slowly kneeled, pulling her undies and pants off her ankles as he nipped and licked her knees, making her jerk and laugh.

"Stop that," she said. "My knees are ticklish."

He grasped her calves as his tongue slipped across the inside of one knee, then the other, interspersed with tiny nibbles. "How ticklish?"

"Very." She gasped and wriggled, the sensation of his teeth and tongue on her bones and skin both sensitive and exciting. "And if you don't stop, it's not my fault if my reflexes send one up to crack you in the jaw."

"Risk noted." His hands slipped up to widen her legs as his tongue moved on in a shivery path to her inner thighs. "But I think we already agreed that life is full of risk. If it's potentially dangerous to taste you all over, then, believe me, that's a risk I'm more than happy to take."

Her breath coming in embarrassing little pants now

as he moved northward, she knew it was time to change direction. While part of her wanted, more than anything, for his mouth to keep going to the part of her currently quivering in anticipation, it seemed that mutual pleasure was more in order.

"Come up here and kiss me." She placed her hands on his smooth shoulders, trying to tug him back up.

"I am kissing you." And, boy, he sure was. His lips were pressing inch by torturous inch against her shivering flesh.

"My mouth. Kiss my mouth." She tugged harder at his shoulders. If she didn't get him away from where he was headed, she knew she just might combust. "I'm the one who's supposed to be administering TLC here, remember?"

He lifted his gaze to hers. His eyes were heavy-lidded with desire, but touched with amusement, too, and the smile he gave her was full of pure, masculine satisfaction. "For some reason, I forgot. Probably because I'm already feeling much less stressed. But if it will make you happy, who am I to argue?"

With one last kiss so high on her inner thigh she nearly groaned, he got to his feet. Which reminded her he still had his pants on, while she was sitting there utterly naked. His gaze traveled across every inch of her skin, hot enough to scorch, and she was a little surprised that his perusal was exciting instead of embarrassing.

She reached for his pants and undid them, happy that he took charge and quickly finished off the job. Then stared at the now very visible confirmation that he was every bit as aroused as she was.

"So now what, Dr. Girard?" He placed his hands on

the bed, flanking her hips, and leaned close. "The TLC ball is in your court."

She gulped. All the things she'd fantasized about seemed to have vacated her mind, along with every rational thought. Except how much she wanted to grab him and pull him on top of her and feel him deep inside.

"I...I can't remember exactly what I had in mind to soothe you and make you feel better. Give me a minute."

"That's okay," he said between pressing soft kisses to her mouth. "As I said, I already feel a whole lot better. Expecting to feel even better real soon."

His strong hands wrapped around her waist and he lifted her up to him, nudging her legs around his waist as he kissed her again. She was vaguely aware of the sound of the covers being yanked back and the cool sheets touching her skin at the same time Jack's hot body covered hers.

"I've realized the one thing that will soothe me the most," he whispered against her lips.

"What?"

"Making you feel good." He kissed her again. His body was deliciously heavy on hers as his hands stroked her everywhere, exciting and tantalizing. Their kiss grew deeper, wilder as his talented fingers finally delved into her moist core until she feared he might bring her to climax with just his touch.

Then the sudden, harsh ring of her hotel phone startled them both, sending their teeth clacking together. "Holy hell!" Jack frowned. "Are you okay?"

With her breath still short, she slid her fingers across his moist lips. "No blood, I don't think. You?"

"Fine. More than fine." His eyes gleamed into hers.

"Except for the damned interruption just when things were getting very…soothing."

She chuckled breathily as they both turned their heads to the still-ringing phone.

"Do you need to get that?" he asked.

Was he kidding? Even if it was the French president, she wasn't about to talk on the phone at that moment. "Whoever it is will leave a message. Or call back. Now, where were we?" She reached for him, squeezed, and the moan he gave in response sent her heart pumping faster and her legs around his waist in silent invitation.

He quickly ripped open a condom. "About to get to the next step in making us both feel good," he said, grasping her hips as they joined. Slowly, wonderfully, but as the tension grew she had to urge him to move faster, deeper. The room seemed to spin dizzily like the carousel had, but this time there were no barriers between them. She held on tight, loving the taste of him and the feel of him, until she cried out in release, wrenching a deep groan from his chest as he followed.

Jack buried his face in her neck, their gasping breaths seeming loud in the quiet of the room. Until another sound disturbed her bone-melting, utter relaxation and tranquility—the muffled ringing of a cell phone.

Jack lifted his head and looked down at the floor with a frown. "Who the hell keeps bothering us? I hope nothing's happened at the hospital."

He dropped a kiss on her mouth, lingering there, before he got up and dug his phone from the pocket of his discarded pants. Avery enjoyed the very sexy view of him, standing there comfortably naked, his skin covered with a sheen of sweat.

"Dr. Dunbar."

She watched his frown deepen and sat up, beginning to get alarmed. Hopefully this wasn't a crisis with a patient.

"And you can't give me some idea what this is about now?" he asked. "Fine. I'll be there."

"What is it?"

"I don't know." His warm body lay next to hers again, propped on his elbow. "Bob Timkin wants to meet with me—with both of us—tomorrow morning at eight. Says he has to talk to me right away about something to do with the trial."

"What? Why?"

"He wouldn't say. You don't happen to know, do you?"

The pleasure of the evening began to fade at the expression on his face. Beyond serious. Maybe even a touch suspicious? She couldn't even imagine how he'd react if he knew Crilex had given her the power to shut down the trial if she deemed it necessary, and the thought chilled her formerly very toasty body. "No. I don't. If I did, I'd tell you."

"Did you tell him you were concerned about the number of patients who've had the valve leak? You know I feel strongly that we haven't treated nearly enough patients to make any kind of judgment on that yet."

"Of course I didn't speak with him about Mr. Arnoult. For one thing, I haven't had a chance to finish compiling the data on his...situation. And I also told you I know the valve design was not why he died."

A long sigh left him before his mouth touched hers with a sweet, tender connection at odds with the tense tone of his voice. His finger tracked down her cheek before he slipped from the bed and got dressed, his expression impassive when he turned to her.

"I wish mixing…this…with work didn't create a hell of a complication for both of us. But there's no getting around it that it does." He stepped to the bed and took her chin in his hand, tilting her face up for another soft kiss. "Thank you for the TLC tonight. Sweet dreams."

And then he was gone, the door closing behind him with a sharp click. A whirl of emotions filled her chest, and she didn't know which one took center stage in her heart. Frustration that he still clearly didn't completely trust her to report the data scientifically and not emotionally? Disappointment, even sadness, that this obvious "thing" they had between them was a huge problem because of their jobs? Anxiety, knowing he would definitely not like having been kept in the dark about her authority to decide if the trial was rolled out further or not?

She flopped back onto the bed, her body still feeling the remnants of their lovemaking, and remembered how wonderful every second of it had felt.

Now, instead of stealing a kiss or two with him tomorrow, she knew the smart thing to do was go back to a strictly professional friendship. And she also had to wonder what in the world Bob Timkin had planned.

CHAPTER TEN

JACK SWALLOWED THE last of his morning coffee, wishing it didn't make him think of Avery and how her mouth always tasted after they'd shared espresso. Made him think of that first morning they'd spent together, that entire, magical day, and how beautiful and adorable she'd been. Realizing, from that moment on, he'd been fascinated by her in every way. Her looks, her brains, her personality.

He couldn't shake that fascination and attraction. An attraction that had grown even deeper after their time together last night, making love again to her beautiful body. Except his heart rate had barely slowed when the phone call had come, bringing a lot of questions with it. A harsh reminder of what he kept forgetting whenever he was with her. Which was that mixing business with pleasure was always one hell of a bad idea, no matter how incredible that pleasure was.

He thought he'd learned that painful lesson all too well. A lesson that had come in the form of doubt cast on his professional character and integrity, resulting in some very personal questions from a hospital ethics board. A lesson in why he should never get involved with a woman connected in any way with his work. Except he knew Avery was nothing like Vanessa. She wasn't the kind of woman who would advance her own career at the expense of someone else's.

He took the elevator to the hospital's administrative offices on the top floor, where Bob had a nice, cushy office that someone had clearly given up for him. About to knock on the doorjamb, he was surprised to hear Avery's voice speaking through the partially open door, then the rumble of Bob's voice in answer.

He knocked on the door and didn't wait to be asked in before pushing it all the way open to step inside. Timkin looked up, then stood, a broad smile on his face. "Jack. Thanks for coming. Have a seat."

"I'm good standing, thanks."

"Dr. Girard was just updating me on the patient data from the trial so far."

"Seems impossible to have any kind of real report, considering we've operated on all of twelve patients so far."

"Well, yes. But all of them came through it nicely, I see."

"Actually, that's not entirely true," Avery said. "Several of the patients have had significant paravalvular regurgitation, as Dr. Dunbar and I have discussed."

"And in that discussion I noted that a certain percentage of patients are expected to have that complication and can live fine with it." His chest began to burn a little. Was she about to tell Timkin she thought there might be a flaw in the design? He was confident that Bob was completely behind this trial and the next phase of the rollout to other hospitals.

"We do know that is a normal, and expected, complication, Dr. Girard," Timkin said. "While I'm aware the numbers of patients experiencing that are currently slightly higher than we would have wished, the procedure hasn't been done on nearly enough patients for those numbers to be meaningful."

Jack relaxed a little, and he waited to hear why Timkin had called the meeting. Avery's brows were lowered in a frown, and he could practically see the wheels spinning in that brain of hers, probably coming up with various data she wanted to spout.

"Which is why I asked you both to come here this morning," Timkin said. "We've decided to significantly increase the number of patients in this clinical trial, which I'm sure will please you, Jack."

"What do you mean, you want to increase the number of patients in the trial?" Avery asked, her eyes wide.

"It seems logical to me that we get as many patients in the trial as we can for these last two and a half weeks," Timkin said. "We need as much data as possible before we decide how many hospitals to roll this out to next. I have a few of my people looking for good patient candidates and screening them as we speak, and of course I'd like your nurse to work on finding some, as well."

"Frankly, I don't think that's a good idea," Avery said. Her gaze flicked to Jack, then away, before she continued. "With the comparatively high percentage of the prosthetic valves experiencing leakage, I think the trial should be conducted on a smaller number of patients so we can keep our eye on that until we know more."

"I respect your opinion, Dr. Girard. But increasing the numbers can't be anything but good, giving us the conclusive data we all want."

Jack smiled at this great news. "I appreciate the vote of confidence, Bob. Dr. Girard is, of course, the leading expert on this device but isn't as familiar with patient care. Those in the trial experiencing the valve leakage are all doing well as we manage their situation."

As he turned to leave, his gaze paused on Avery, and he was surprised to see the look on her face was completely different from that of a moment ago. Instead of concern, her green eyes held deep disappointment. He'd even call it hurt. Was it because of what he'd said when he'd reassured Bob he had the leakages under control?

This trial was beyond important to him, the patients it was helping and the future of interventional cardiology. Avery knew that as well as anybody. Why she was so overly concerned about the valve leakage, he didn't understand and refused to worry about yet.

But as he headed to the cath lab, the image of the hurt in her eyes went along with him.

Jack headed for the hotel fitness room, needing a physical release from another long day at the hospital, his muscles tense from hours of standing on his feet doing surgeries. He had to give Crilex credit—they'd gotten additional patients lined up incredibly fast, and he and Jessica had been working flat out. Which he welcomed for the clinical trial and welcomed for himself.

The busy pace had left him with little time to think about Avery. During the brief moments he'd had free, though, she'd been on his mind. Thinking about all the great things he'd learned about her over the past weeks. Knowing she wasn't the kind of self-interested person who would skew data to benefit her career, and feeling bad that had even crossed his mind. They might not always agree, but the woman had absolute integrity.

That it seemed he'd accidentally hurt her made him feel like crap. Made him want to head to her room and apologize, then grab her to explore more of Paris and laugh together. Kiss and make love together. That desire was so strong he could only hope that running hard on the treadmill would somehow blank it all from his mind.

At 9:00 p.m. there were only two other people in the exercise room, and he was glad he wouldn't have to wait around for any of the machines or weights to become available. He slung a towel around his neck and started out jogging on the treadmill, increasing the pace until he was running, breathing hard, sweating. To his disgust, even that didn't stop his thoughts from drifting to Avery. To the softness of her skin and the taste of it on his tongue. To her laugh and the amazing green of her eyes.

Which made him one damned confused man. He adjusted the treadmill settings and picked up the pace, noticing out of the corner of his eye that the middle-aged man who had been lifting crazily heavy weights was now sitting strangely sideways on the bench, leaning on one hand.

Jack looked more carefully at him, realizing the guy didn't look like he felt very well. He slowed to a stop, quickly wiped the sweat from his face and walked over to the man, concerned at the ashen color of his face.

"You okay?"

The man shook his head and laboriously said a few words in French. Jack hoped like hell he could at least understand a little English, even if he couldn't speak it. "I'm a doctor. I'm going to check your pulse."

Thankfully, he nodded, and Jack pressed his fingers to the man's wrist to see if his heart was in a normal sinus rhythm. It was fast, very fast, and he'd begun to sweat buckets, too, neither of which were signs of anything good. Just as Jack was about to ask the man if he thought he might be having a heart attack he slumped sideways and started sliding clear off the bench.

"Whoa!" Jack was able to grab him midway, managing to keep him from cracking his head on the hard floor.

"What is wrong, monsieur?" The other person in the room had come to stand next to him, staring.

"Get the hotel to call the medical squad."

The guy ran off just as the man opened his eyes again, thank the Lord. His brows lowered as he blinked at Jack, saying something Jack wished he could understand. Pressing his fingers to the man's wrist again, he grimly noted his pulse was thready, which meant his blood pressure was high, which again meant nothing good.

"Good God, Jack, what's wrong?" To his surprise, Avery crouched next to him, deep concern on her face as she looked from the ill man to him.

"I think he's having the big one. Going in and out of V-fib, and his pulse is really tachy." He looked up at her, relieved she might be able to communicate with the man. "Ask him how he's feeling, where it hurts."

She quickly spoke to the man in French and he managed to answer her back. "He says he's nauseated and his chest feels strange."

"Damn. The chances of this not being a heart attack are slim to none." He scanned the room and didn't see what he'd hoped for. "I wish this place had a defibrillator. His arrhythmia is bad, and if he crashes, I don't think CPR's going to do it."

"They do. Over here." She ran around the other side of the L-shaped room and returned with exactly what he needed if the man went into true V-fib.

"How did you know that was there? I've been in this gym ten times and never noticed."

"It's by the plié bar, which I'm guessing you don't use."

She gave him a quick grin, and he grinned back before turning to place his fingers against the man's carotid artery. "You'd guess right. I—"

With a sudden, strangled sound the man, who'd been lying on his side, flopped onto his back, obviously unconscious again. Jack shook him, then rubbed his knuckles against the man's sternum. "Hey, buddy! Wake up. Can you hear me? Wake up!"

But the guy just lay there like he was dead, and Jack cursed. "We've got to get his shirt off so I can check his heart rate with the defib."

They wrestled the T-shirt off the man as quickly as they could, then Jack grabbed the defibrillator. Both moved fast to get the paddle wires untwined as he pressed them to the man's chest. Then stared at the EKG monitor on the paddle in disbelief.

"He's code blue. I'm going to have to bust him." He looked up at her tense face. "Can you set it at three hundred joules while I get it placed? Then get the hell out of the way."

She nodded and her fingers got it adjusted impressively fast.

"Okay. Ready? Clear!"

She jumped up and backpedaled as Jack sent the electricity to the man's heart.

Nothing.

"Clear again." His own heart pounding like he'd just jumped off the treadmill, he busted the man once more. When the man's chest heaved and his eyelids flickered, then opened, Jack exhaled a deep breath he hadn't even realized he'd been holding in his lungs.

"Thank God," he heard Avery say devoutly as she came back and kneeled next to them, reaching to hold the man's hand.

"Yeah." Jack pressed his fingers to the man's throat. "Pulse is down to ninety. And his color's even a little better. I think we did it, Dr. Girard."

Their eyes met briefly across the poor, supine guy, and a wordless communication went between them. Relief that they'd been able to help and joy that he was hopefully out of the woods.

The man weakly said something in French, and Avery smiled and answered before turning to Jack. "He asked what happened. I told him his heart stopped, and you saved his life."

"We saved his life. You were awesome."

Her smile widened before she turned back to speak to the man again, and Jack could see her squeezing his hand. Now that he could take a minute to breathe, he had to marvel at how calm she'd been through the whole thing, and how comforting him obviously came as second nature to her. Doctors and nurses were trained how to react to this kind of crisis, but he doubted there was a lot of that kind of education in biomedical PhD school.

The door to the fitness room clattered open as several emergency medical techs wheeled in a gurney. The guy who'd run from the room to get help followed, along with several people Jack recognized as hotel management. He stood and updated the med techs on what had happened and where the man's heart rate was now.

The hotel guys talked with Avery. She handed them the defibrillator, and he heard her saying what a hero Jack was. Part of him absolutely hated that, since he was no hero. He was a doctor who'd been in the right place when he'd been needed.

But another part of him couldn't be unhappy about Avery praising him that way. The hotel staff pumped his hand and thanked him, and he repeated that it was just lucky he'd been in the right place and gave them credit for having the defibrillator there for him to use. If they hadn't, he was certain the outcome would not have been good for the man.

It seemed the room went from full of people to empty in a matter of minutes, and he noticed what he'd missed before in all the excitement. Avery wearing tiny, sexy exercise shorts that showed off her toned legs and a tank top that revealed a whole lot more of her skin than he'd ever been able to see before, since she was always dressed for the cold or the hospital.

Well, except for their two blissful moments together, when he'd been privileged to see every inch of her body.

His heart went into a little atrial fibrillation of its

own at the memories and the current vision standing right in front of him.

"That was one lucky man," Avery said. "How many people have a cardiologist around when they're having a heart attack? Were you in here working out when it happened?"

"I was running on the treadmill. Trying to loosen my muscles." *Trying to forget about you.* "He was lucky all right. Lucky that you came in when you did and that you knew where the machine was. I've got to tell you, I'm pretty impressed at how calm and cool you were, helping with what needed to happen without freaking out."

"Believe me, I was freaking out on the inside." She grinned. "But that's a sweet thing for you to say. Much better than the stinging barbs you've thrown lately."

"Listen." He rubbed his hand across the back of his neck to loosen the knots there. Hoped she'd accept his apology. "I'm sorry I said you didn't know much about patient care. I'm sure you do. I just wanted Bob to know the leakages so far are minor, but I shouldn't have implied you're clueless about postoperative treatment."

"No, you shouldn't have. I may not be a medical doctor or nurse, but gathering the data teaches me plenty, believe me."

"I'm sure it does." He cupped her chin in his hand because he wanted that connection. Wanted to show her he truly cared how she felt. "Did it hurt you when I said that?"

"Honestly? To my core." Her words pricked his heart, but the sweet smile she gave him soothed the wound. "Though I just might have not very nicely accused you of certain things, as well. Like maybe you were sleeping with a married woman the same week you were kissing me."

"You know, you're right. That wasn't nice of you at all." He caught her elbows in his hands, tugging her against him. "So we're even."

"Even."

As he looked into the green of her eyes he tried hard to conjure all the reasons he had to keep a professional distance from her. But he couldn't. All he could think about was how much he enjoyed kissing her and making love with her, and how he wanted more of all of it.

"What is it about you that makes it impossible for me to keep a professional distance? Even when I try?" he asked, genuinely baffled.

"Maybe because we share a love of espresso?"

"Maybe," he said, dipping his head down to speak against her lips. "Or maybe it's just you."

"No." She shook her head, her lips slipping back and forth across his mouth as she did, and that simple touch nearly made him groan. "It's us. That mysterious and unexplainable chemistry, whether we like it or not."

"Sometimes not," he said. "But I find I can't help that, way more often, I like it very much."

Knowing he damned well shouldn't, he kissed her, loving the way she instantly melted against him, her arms sliding around his back to hold him tight. Their mouths and tongues moved in a slow dance that already felt seductively familiar. A tiny little sound came from her throat as the kiss deepened, a sound so full of desire it sent his blood pumping and nearly had him slipping his hands into those tiny shorts she was wearing, not caring at all about the consequences.

Somehow, though, he managed to summon every ounce of inner strength he had to break the kiss, dragging in a few desperate breaths to clear his head. Not only were they in a public place, which seemed to always be a problem whenever he kissed her, but nothing had really changed.

The chemistry—hell, more like a nuclear reaction—was most definitely there. But so was the inescapable conflict in their jobs. And that situation was one harsh reality.

"Right now, there's nothing I'd like more in the world than for us to head upstairs and take up where we left off a few nights ago," he said, and the truth of that statement nearly had him grabbing her hand, hightailing it to his room and acting on exactly what he wanted. "But that would just make our jobs more difficult. The work I'm doing here is damned important to me. And I know your work is important to you."

"It is. Which is why I'm going to stretch on the bar, then get running. Good night, Jack." She rose on her toes to give him a quick peck on the cheek and turned to walk to the plié bar.

The sight of her sexy rear in those shorts and the thought of how she might contort herself around that bar practically made him groan. A mini war raged in his chest, with the part of him that wanted her yesterday, today and tomorrow fighting with the cool, rational part of his brain that seemed to short-circuit every time he was around her.

He thought about pretending to continue his workout while really watching whatever she was about to do, but he managed to move to the elevator instead. Giving work one hundred percent of his focus was something he'd been good at for a long time. Time to get with that program and somehow forget the vision of Avery's shapely butt cheeks peeking from beneath those shorts.

Yeah. Like that was going to happen. Which made him wonder. How cold, exactly, could he get the shower in his room?

CHAPTER ELEVEN

JACK STARED IN frustration at the Doppler echocardiogram. The paravalvular regurgitation from the prosthetic valve was more than obvious. The valve looked like it was fitting tightly, but there was no denying the image of the fluid seeping slightly from around it. Why had the past two patients experienced this problem when it hadn't been an issue with the last ten?

"What do you think, Jack?" Jessica asked, peering over his shoulder at the echocardiogram.

"I don't know what to think. I'm trying to figure out if I somehow did something different with these two patients. Maybe I'm not being careful enough as I insert the cath to remove the diseased valve. Or when I place the new one."

Jessica shook her head. "I'm watching almost every second you're working, and if I'd noticed you doing anything different at all, I'd say so."

His mind spun back to past procedures, wondering if the increased patient load had made him hurry in any way. He didn't think so, but he would be extra careful from now on to be sure to take his time and triple-check the monitor as he was putting the prosthetic valve in place.

Jessica glanced around, then leaned close, speaking in a near whisper. "Do you think it's a design flaw, like Dr. Girard has been worried about all along?"

His chest tightened. He'd have to be as stubborn as a mule to not have wondered exactly that. "I don't know. It's possible. The percentage of patients with medically manageable leakage is more than we expected, but not dramatically more. We're just going to have to wait and see the numbers as the trial unfolds."

Jessica nodded. "This patient's pulmonary edema is improving nicely, and the liquid from her Foley is crystal-clear now. She's going to be fine, I think."

"Good. I'll check on her again this afternoon."

"Dr. Dunbar!"

He and Jessica both turned to the nurse who'd run in. "Yes?"

"Madame Belisle is having trouble breathing. I fear it may be another aortic insufficiency."

He stiffened. Another one? Damn it to hell. "We'll be right there."

Jack grimly strode to Mrs. Belisle's room, with Jessica right behind. When he saw that Avery was in there, standing by the patient's bed, his heart knocked hard in his chest. He wasn't sure if it was from seeing her, or if it was because he knew she was taking notes on the third patient with this problem in a matter of days.

He took the woman's pulse, checked her blood pressure and went through the process to confirm the diagnosis, but it was pretty clear. Same song, different verse, and he hated that they had no idea why this kept happening at this rate.

As he gave orders to Jessica and the other nurse, he

was painfully aware of Avery observing all of it, tapping away at her tablet. Watching as the patient received the medications needed to reduce her blood pressure, the diuretic to clear her lungs and the Foley catheter to catch the fluids. Continued tapping away as the portable echocardiogram was brought to the room to get images of Mrs. Belisle's heart activity.

He resolutely ignored her presence, concentrating on the situation. A half hour later, relieved that the patient was breathing a little easier, Jack let himself glance up at Avery, surprised to see her green eyes staring straight into his. This time there wasn't a hint of the humor he loved to see there. They were beyond serious.

"I'm going to look at the echocardiogram," he said to no one in particular. He knew his voice was gruff, but he couldn't help the slightly sick feeling in his gut that maybe this clinical trial was heading downhill fast.

"I'd like to look at it with you, Dr. Dunbar," Avery's voice said from behind him as he moved down the hall.

Of course she would.

His gut tightened a little more. No matter how disturbing all this was, though, he knew he couldn't blame her or feel ticked at her. She was doing her job and, ultimately, if it turned out she'd been right all along, he had to accept that. Should welcome it, really, because if the device was truly flawed, he wouldn't want to put patients at risk any more than she did. If he had to spend another year working with Crilex's biomedical engineers to improve it before testing it on humans again, then that's what would have to happen.

Way premature to be thinking like that, Jack fiercely reminded himself. This clinical trial was only half over, and it was very possible they'd just had a run of bad luck and the next twenty patients would all do fine.

"What are you thinking, Jack?" Avery asked quietly as they studied the Doppler echocardiogram of Mrs. Belisle and the obvious, slight leakage from around the valve.

He looked at her, measuring his response. He trusted her. He did. But loose lips sank ships, as the old saying went, and there was too much riding on this trial to jeopardize it by being too forthcoming with the woman who'd been concerned about this risk all along.

"I'm thinking that I will carefully examine how I'm inserting the catheter and device. As I do that, we'll continue to compile the data. We're also going to perform the procedure on all the very sick patients who've lined up to receive it. Even those with this complication will be better off than they were before the surgery, you know."

"So you're not worried that this is clear evidence the device design just isn't yet where it needs to be?"

The expression on her face showed loud and clear that's what she thought, with maybe a little contempt thrown in. Or was it disappointment? Either way, he didn't want to see it and turned his attention back to the monitor. "Too soon to say. There's not enough evidence, and worrying about it when we don't have the data from a full study is pointless."

She was silent for so long, with such an odd, thoughtful expression as she studied him, it made him jittery. When he couldn't stand it any longer, he abruptly turned. "I have some other patients to see."

"Jack."

He paused and looked back at her, bracing himself for a lecture, willing himself to not let his frustration over all this send his temper flaring. "Yes?"

"I have a great idea," she said, her voice suddenly, surprisingly, light and playful. The same voice she'd used that first, very memorable day they'd spent together.

"Sounds scary."

"Not scary. I think you'll like the proposal I have in mind."

That mischievous smile that usually made him smile back was in her eyes once more. Right now, though, it made him wonder why her demeanor had changed so abruptly. He folded his arms and waited.

"You've been working long and hard and don't have any patients scheduled this weekend. You're looking pretty haggard, which is going to worry your little old lady patients who think you're the most handsome thing in the world."

"You think?" He actually did smile at that, and how she managed to change the entire atmosphere of the room in one minute, he didn't know. "Is that what's called a backhanded compliment?"

"Maybe. So here's my proposal." She moved closer to him and pressed her hands to his chest. He felt some of his stress seep away at their warmth through his scrubs, at how good they felt there.

It made him realize how much he'd missed her touch. Missed touching her.

He let himself cup her waist with his hands because he wanted to, and she was the one who'd started the touching after all. "Does it have anything to do with espresso? If it does, a triple sounds pretty good right now."

"It might." Her smile could only be described as flirtatious, which ratcheted up Jack's interest tenfold. At the same time, he felt even more perplexed. "I promise some serious espresso consumption if you agree. Wine consumption, too."

"Wine consumption? You sure know how to intrigue a guy. What other guilty pleasures might be included in this proposal?"

"You'll find out, if you just say, 'Yes, Avery.'" Her coy words were accompanied by the sparkle in her eyes he'd fallen for the first day they'd met, oddly mingling with a tinge of seriousness.

"I never say yes until I know what I'm agreeing to. What's the catch, and is it going to hurt much?"

"It might hurt, but you're tough enough to handle it," she said, the sparkle fading a bit. "I'd like you to come to Alsace with me, to a little village northeast of Paris. Not too far and easy to get to by train. It's beyond beautiful, so I'll get to show you more of France, and you'll get to shake the dust of this place from your feet and be all refreshed when you come back to work."

He tipped his head to study her, trying to figure out where she was going with this. "Despite the wine consumption promise, I suspect you're not inviting me there for a weekend of sightseeing and wild sex." Though just thinking about spending two days alone with her sent a hot zing through every nerve ending, which he quickly tamped down. Hadn't he sworn off sex or anything else with her?

Yeah, right. If that was her proposal, he'd be saying yes in half of one second and to hell with the consequences.

"Maybe it is about wild sex," she said, giving him the adorable teasing look he'd missed almost as much as her touch, and his heart pumped harder. "Along with meeting the patient I mentioned before, who was one of the first to receive my original TAVI device. I'd like you to hear his story."

"Uh-huh." Here was the damned big letdown he'd known was coming. "How about we go for the wild sex and forget the rest?"

"It's a package deal. We'll be out of Paris and away from the hospital to relax."

"You want me to meet this guy so much you'll risk more of us mixing business with pleasure?" The part of him that wanted his hands and mouth on her again was already yelling yes, but going there with her would be one bad idea. "I know the problems patients with leaky valves live with, Avery. And much as I'd like nothing better than to go on a weekend away with you, it'd just complicate an already complicated situation."

To his shock, she reached up to wrap her arms around his neck and kissed him. Kissed him until his knees nearly buckled and his heart raced. Kissed him until he couldn't breathe and his stress had completely evaporated. Kissed him until he'd say yes to pretty much anything she asked.

When she finally stopped, he could see in her eyes the same delirious desire he felt pumping through every cell in his body. Even though she was obviously using her all-too-irresistible feminine wiles to get him to see that guy, it was also clear she was every bit as turned on as he was.

"How about it, Jack?" she whispered against his lips. "I know you need a break. And meeting this man will just add to your data, so there's nothing to lose. Except, maybe, your virtue."

"Pretty sure I lost my virtue that first day we met." He had to chuckle, but he shook his head, not quite believing her tactics. "You drive a very hard bargain, Dr. Girard."

She pressed closer against him, and when his erection pressed into her stomach she gave him the wickedest smile. "Very hard, Dr. Dunbar. Which I hope means your answer is yes."

In a sign that this trip just might go as well as Avery hoped, the gray clouds parted and the sun cast its golden fingers across the vineyards and snowy mountains that surrounded Riquewihr. Jack parked the little rental car outside the town's ancient walls and turned to her with a smile.

"This place is amazing," he said. "I can't believe that one minute we're driving through endless vineyards, then all of a sudden here's this beautiful old medieval town parked right in the middle of it all."

"You should see it in the summertime, when everything's green and flowers are everywhere," she said, glad he already seemed to like this place. "Wait till we get inside the walls. The town itself is every bit as amazing and lovely."

She smiled, pleased that he again looked like the upbeat man she'd met in the hotel that very first day, and not the cardiologist whose tense and tired expression the past week had made her want to gather him up and hold him and give him more of that TLC she'd promised him before. It wasn't good for his patients or for Jack if he worked endless hours under stress, and in a sudden decision not too different from the moment she'd first met him in the hotel, she'd wanted to do something about it.

For days, a disturbing feeling had nagged at her. As the number of patients in the trial had more than doubled, the problems had increased, too. She knew Jack was as concerned about it as she was. But she also knew him well enough to guess that his fatigue and worry would turn into defensiveness if she suggested again that he ratchet the trial back to its original numbers, or even fewer.

Inspiration had struck on how she could accomplish two things at once. Get him to come here to Riquewihr for a much-needed break—and to meet Benjamin Larue. A lovely man with a lovely family, whose life had been damaged irreversibly during the first TAVI trials.

Jack's loose stride already seemed much more relaxed than the fast pace he kept in the hospital, moving from surgeries to patients to various test results and back. They headed toward the old clock tower, walking through the gate beneath it in the ancient wall.

"How many times have you been here?" he asked. "Just in the summertime?"

"I've been here twice. Once in winter and once in summer. Totally different things to do, of course. I love to hike the mountains, but the snow cover at the moment requires a different approach. So I figured maybe we'd cross-country ski or snowshoe. Have you ever tried it? I made a reservation for us just a half hour from now, so we'll have to hurry to get there. Unless you'd rather do something else."

"I haven't tried either one." He leaned closer, the devilish smile that had knocked her socks off—among other things—back in full force and electrifying the air. "But I'm all for any kind of exercise you might think up to get our blood pumping."

Her blood was already pumping just from looking at him and thinking about the kind of physical exercise he obviously had on his mind.

The curve of his lips, the light in his eyes as he looked at her and the various landmarks they passed reminded her so much of the Jack she'd shown around Paris that first day. The Jack she'd tumbled into bed with, before she'd thought long enough about it. Before she'd found out exactly how ill-advised that decision had turned out to be.

But pretending that hadn't happened, and deciding not to let it happen again, had come to seem pretty pointless. When the trial was over and she'd studied the data, her recommendation to Crilex would be the same no matter whether they were sleeping together or not. She knew Jack wanted what was best for the patients, and she had to believe, either way it went, that he'd come to the same conclusion she did.

She smirked at herself. Like before, she seemed to have a much easier time talking herself into being with him than the other way around. Probably because he looked sexier in scrubs than about anybody she'd ever seen, and asking her to not think about stripping them off him to see that lean, muscular body of his was like asking her to give up coffee.

She glanced at him out of the corner of her eye, smiling at the memory of his shocked expression as she'd coerced him to come on this trip. She'd never tried seducing someone to get them on board with a different agenda. Now she knew it was pretty exciting to know how well her sex appeal apparently worked on the man.

They walked down a cobbled street flanked by beautiful medieval buildings, with Jack commenting on all of it in amazement, before they checked into their small hotel. From the moment she'd first seen the place she'd been awed and delighted by the beautiful pastel blues, yellows and mauves of the buildings, like something from a fairy tale.

"Some cities in France had to rebuild after World War II, so a lot of the buildings are really replicas rather than the original medieval structures," she said. "I'm told that only two bombs dropped here, though, so it's nearly all original. Isn't the whole place incredible?"

"It is. I've never seen anything like it."

Pleasure fluttered inside her at the fact that he liked it as much as she did. As they made their way down the narrow, stone-lined hallway, Jack smiled at her. "Gotta tell you, the whole town reminds me of a Hollywood movie set."

"I know what you mean." The first time she had come here, she had thought the Renaissance-style stone and half-timber homes were almost too enchanting to believe. "I've always wondered if the animators who did *Beauty and the Beast* came here for inspiration."

"I confess I haven't watched that movie and also

confess I hope that's not part of your agenda for the weekend." He shoved open their room door and looked down at her with the teasing humor she'd enjoyed that first day they met. Humor that had been in short supply the past week. "Or watching *The Sound of Music*. Have to wonder if that's the plan, though, considering the dirndl that you're wearing."

"Dirndl?" She set her suitcase on the floor and fisted her hands on her hips, giving him a mock glare. "My dress is not a dirndl, Dr. Dunbar. It's a blouse beneath a corduroy jumper."

"If you say so." He reached to unbutton her coat, pulling it apart to look at her dress. "No need to get defensive, though. I like it. A lot."

He ran his finger along the lacy top of her blouse that dipped low to just above her breasts. Avery looked down, watching the track of his finger, her breath growing short. Vaguely, she pondered that maybe the skirt did look a little like a dirndl. Her main thoughts, though, were that his touch felt wonderful, that she'd missed it, and that, unlike the first two times they'd briefly shared a hotel room, she didn't feel at all nervous. All she felt was a delicious anticipation of the day and night they'd be spending together.

She looked back up at him, and a warm flush crept through her body at the way he was looking at her. The small smile was still on his face, but his eyes were filled with something entirely different that told her he, too, was feeling that same breathless anticipation.

"Bonjour, monsieur...mademoiselle."

They both turned to the open door and saw an older gentleman with a wide, curled mustache smiling at them. “I wanted to suggest that you join us this evening at five o’clock for a wine tasting from our local vineyards. There will be complimentary hors d’oeuvres as well, in our wine cellar.”

“Thank you,” Jack said. “We haven’t made any plans yet, but that sounds great.”

He shoved the door closed behind the man and turned to her again. “Are you sure Riquewihr isn’t just some elaborate Hollywood hoax? I mean, how often do you see a guy with a mustache like that outside the movies?”

Her laugh morphed into more of a little hiccup when his fingers tugged apart the lapels of her coat again. “So,” he asked in a low voice, “are we staying in or going out?”

“I…um…” She struggled to decide, wanting to show him the amazing and wonderful things about Riquewihr during the daylight hours of this single Saturday that they had. Wanted to enjoy the same delight she’d felt, that she was sure they’d both felt, seeing the Eiffel Tower and the Sacré Coeur. Have those kinds of lovely moments before they stopped at the Larue family winery to meet Benjamin.

But she also wanted that heady give and take they’d had before. The overwhelming sensations when they let go of all the external problems, shared their bodies and simply let the chemistry between them ignite into a searing, physical passion like none other she’d ever experienced.

She drew a breath to try to finish her sentence, but it was a shaky one at best. Because it was clear he could read exactly what she’d been thinking, and she nearly caught fire just from the look in his eyes before he lowered his head.

His lips covered hers, teasing, tasting, as his hands moved to her waist. Slid up to cup her breasts, his fingers again brushing the filmy top of her blouse as he deepened the kiss, the sweep of his tongue so delicious she had to bite back a moan.

When he broke the kiss, his eyes were so heavy-lidded she could barely see the gleam in the darkness of his eyes. “Didn’t you say we have a time schedule to hit the mountain for a little skiing or snowshoeing?”

She nodded, knowing any verbal answer she gave at that moment would just come out as a whisper until she caught her breath. “Yes,” she finally managed. “I thought you’d enjoy the fresh air and how gorgeous it is up there. But we don’t have to. We have the day off to do whatever makes us happy.”

“Just being with you makes me happy,” he said, and she was surprised the words didn’t hold a sensual tone. They sounded beyond sincere, and her heart tripped in her chest. “And since we have only so many hours of daylight, I think we should do what you’d already planned for us. Because I sure haven’t been disappointed in any of our activities in France so far, Ms. Tour Guide.”

She stared at Jack and realized he was being utterly genuine. He truly enjoyed just being with her, here or in Paris or wherever they happened to be, and hadn’t come here with her just for the “wild sex” she’d teased him with. As she thought back to her two previous relationships, she realized that the physical part of them had been the primary element.

Which wasn't at all what she had with Jack. What they had between them went deeper than the sexual chemistry they'd talked about, which was thrilling and scary at the same time. Because she knew his job was not just his priority, it was his life. She was a brief interlude in that life—an interlude he'd made clear he felt uncomfortable participating in.

And if it became necessary to halt the trial, she could only hope and pray he understood why.

Her heart giving an odd little twist, she gave him a soft kiss before grasping his hand and smiling into his beautiful eyes. "Then let's head to the Vosges mountains. I think you'll love it, and afterward we'll both be more than ready for a little après-ski."

"Lead on, Dr. Girard. I'm all yours."

CHAPTER TWELVE

"EVEN WITHOUT THE potential for wine and wild sex, I'm glad I agreed to this trip," Jack said, looking handsome as all get-out with his cheeks flushed and his dark hair poking from beneath his knit hat. "Growing up, a few of my friends went skiing in the winter with their families. Both downhill and cross-country. We never went places like that, but now I wish I'd tried this kind of thing at home."

"I knew you'd like it." The crisp mountain air was filled with the rhythmic crunch of their snowshoes and Avery's heavy breathing from tromping practically straight up for the past fifteen minutes. "Also knew the only thing that would convince you to take your mind off work by coming here was the potential for sexual favors."

"Already, the woman knows me well." He sent her his most devilish smile, and she was pretty sure it was his expression and not the cold air that made her insides quiver.

"So, where did your family go on vacation?" The tracks of the cross-country ski course had been grooved into the snow next to them, and they followed that line to be sure to not get lost. A straight uphill line, and Avery's lungs and legs sure hoped for a downhill slope soon.

"We didn't, much." He shrugged. "Both my parents are workaholic doctors, with my dad being the worst. We mostly took the occasional short trip to New York or the beach. Just for a few days, so they wouldn't be gone long."

"Ah. So you took after them?"

He flashed her a grin. "Probably. My brother, too. But I'm beginning to see the value of a little vacation time."

The path curved in a C shape to finally slope slightly downhill, thank heavens, but it was one long way down. Avery had thought she was in pretty good shape, but the burning in her thighs and lungs after the uphill climb told her maybe not so much. "Let's cut through here. Catch the path on the other side."

"I may not be a skier, but I've heard you shouldn't go off the trail. What if we fall into a crevasse?"

"You're such a rule follower. Come on."

She grabbed his hand and veered to the right near a line of trees that went all the way down the mountain.

He slid her a look that said she was crazy, but his lips were tipped into an amused smile. "There are times to follow the rules and times when it makes sense to break them. Wandering around on a mountain doesn't seem like the best time to me, but you're the tour guide. Lead on."

Even though the snow was deeper there, going downhill made it easier to breathe. And she was glad she wouldn't be panting when she asked the question she'd been wondering about. "Was there some bad situation in your life that made you not want to spend time with me after we found out who each other was? When I said it wasn't good to be involved with someone you had to work with, you were very quick to agree, and I thought there must be a reason."

"First, there was never a moment I didn't want to spend time with you. I just knew it was a bad idea." She relaxed at his teasing expression, glad he wasn't going to get all stiff again now she'd brought up the unsettling back and forth between them. "But your observation is very astute. And here I'd always heard genius types were book smart but not people smart."

She rolled her eyes. "Again, the stereotype. I thought we were done with that."

"Sorry." He took a sideways step, his shoulder bumping into hers as his eyes got that wicked glint in them. "Learning that female scientists wear lacy, colorful underwear has changed my perspective forever. Don't think I'll ever be able to see techs with their test tubes and not wonder what they have on under their lab coats."

It was utterly stupid, but his words pricked at her heart. It wasn't like they were a real couple. One that would be together after the trial was complete in just over a week. He was a career-driven man who liked women in small doses, and fantasizing about lingerie and wild sex was part of that package.

"Hey." He must have seen something in her expression because he stopped walking and tipped her chin up. "I was teasing. There's only one woman whose underwear I wonder about."

She forced a laugh. "And I just might have to keep you wondering. But you haven't answered my question."

They continued their trek as several cross-country skiers slid by in the tracks above them, and the sound of his deep sigh mingled with the swish of the skis. "When I first found out who you were I was amazed. Well, I was amazed a whole lot of ways that day." He aimed that glint at her again.

Warmth crept into her cold cheeks at his words, remembering exactly how she'd behaved and how she'd never done such a thing in her life before. "I'd prefer you didn't remind me I slept with a man I'd just met. I'm embarrassed by that, and you know it."

"You shouldn't be." He wrapped his arm around her and tugged her close to his side. "The romance of Paris and our chemistry together made it inevitable. If it hadn't happened that day, it would have happened another day. From the second I turned to see the knockout woman talking to me in the hotel, I knew it was meant to be."

His words, his low voice and the expression in his eyes caught her breath. "Maybe it was," she replied softly. "And you're still doing a darned good job of avoiding answering me."

"You just want to gloat when you hear I made a stupid mistake. Because you know I never do, and admitting I made one once isn't something I like to do."

"I know, Dr. Dunbar, that you think you're perfect."

"Hey, my mom calls me Prince Perfect. What do you expect?" That quick grin flashed again, almost as dazzling as the sunshine on the snow, and Avery had to admit he just might be as close to perfection as a man could be.

A minute went by, silent except for the crunch, crunch

of their shoes, and she'd begun to think he'd never tell her when he finally spoke. "My crown slipped a few years back, though. I dated a medical supplies rep who sold, among other things, stents for angioplasty. I switched to the stent she repped because I honestly thought it might be superior to the ones I'd been using. You can imagine how many stents we use a month, and because it was more expensive, the hospital bean counters questioned it. When it came out that she and I had a personal relationship, all hell broke loose. Hospital bigwigs accused me of behaving unethically, and as it all unfolded, a whole lot of dirty laundry spilled out."

She couldn't imagine Jack having a whole lot of dirty laundry. "Like what?"

"Turned out the beguiling Vanessa was sleeping with numerous docs, in multiple hospitals, who used high-end surgical and biomedical products. She was trying to get a big promotion at her company and used me, and the other saps, to get the sales record and promotion."

He shook his head, his lips twisted into a grimace. "What a fool I was. My relationship with Vanessa was pretty much strictly physical, but knowing the truth, that she'd used me, made me feel sick. I hated answering to the ethics board, having them question my professionalism. I was cleared of any wrongdoing, but vowed I'd never so much as look at a woman involved in any way with my job."

"Wow." His story might even be worse than her former boyfriend mistakes. And explained why the wall between them had been wider even than she'd thought their situation warranted.

"Wow?" He raised his eyebrows at her. "Maybe I shouldn't have confessed. You think I'm an idiot now?"

"No, of course not. But I've gotta tell you. While I feel bad you went through that, you've made me feel a little better about my own poor judgment."

"Which would be what?"

Part of her didn't want to share something so embarrassing, but he'd shared with her, so it was only fair. "I dated a couple of cardiologists for a while. The first one traveled a lot, teaching his specialized procedures. Turned out he had a woman in every port. Or every hospital, to be more accurate."

He stopped walking to stare at her. "I can't believe there's a human alive who could be stupid enough to not hang onto you with both hands when he had the chance."

He looked genuinely astonished, and what woman wouldn't feel pretty good about his words? "The second one started talking down to me, saying disparaging things."

"What kind of disparaging things?"

"Oh, like when people asked me questions about angioplasty and stents, which happened sometimes because that's what he did, he'd say I was the 'equipment' girl and wasn't qualified to talk about medical procedures."

"You've got to be kidding me." The astonishment was still there on his face, along with anger. "No wonder you wrote off cardiologists as being total jerks. But he was probably jealous of your amazing smarts. That kind of guy isn't worth having, and you know it."

"I do know. But I guess that whole experience has

made me hypersensitive. Which is why I was suspicious of you and Jessica. Sorry. But there are some real winners out there."

"Yeah. There are." His eyes and voice warmed and he stopped, turning to wrap both his arms around her and draw her close. Her own arms slipped around his back, and the sizzle between them could be felt all the way through their coats and hats, warming her from the inside out. "The kind of winner that makes a man do something he swore he wouldn't do. So maybe I'm still a fool. But I can't seem to keep you out of my head."

His cold lips touched hers, and in an instant both their mouths were toasty warm as they shared a slow, sweet kiss. Just as Avery angled her head, inviting him to delve deeper, the swishing sound of skis on snow came from above them. They pulled apart and looked up the hill to the trail they'd abandoned to see nearly a dozen skiers following one another in single file on the trail.

"Are you kidding?" Jack said. "Even out here in the middle of a mountain we have an audience?"

She wasn't about to let a few strangers ruin the heavenly moment. Of all the places she'd kissed Jack, holding him close on this wild, beautiful mountainside, his cold nose touching hers and his mouth so hot and delicious—this place was her very favorite. "Who cares? We're in France."

She tried to go up on tiptoe to kiss him again, but found it pretty difficult with snowshoes on her feet. Luckily, the superheated gleam in his eyes showed he knew exactly what she wanted and he kissed her again, sending her heart pounding even harder. Her legs wobbled, whether from the kiss or the hiking or both she wasn't sure. She hung onto Jack's coat as his mouth moved across her cold cheek and beneath her earlobe in a shivery path that made it very hard to breathe.

Frigid wind swept the cheek not currently covered by Jack's warm one and at the same time clumps of snowflakes dropped onto her face. She opened her eyes to see Jack lifting his head, a slow, sexy smile curving his lips as his finger swept the snow from her eyelashes.

"Guess we should have thought to bring your umbrella up here on the mountain with us." His hat and shoulders were covered with snowflakes, too, and she looked behind him to see the wind catch more of the snow loaded on the evergreen trees and swirl it onto them, like Mother Nature was playing a joke and tossing it with her hand.

"Who knew?"

Their steamy, breathless laughter flitted between them as they separated, her gloved hand in his, to trudge on down the mountain in a companionable silence. She pulled in a deep, satisfied breath, realizing she felt as comfortable and relaxed as she'd felt in a long, long time, and hoped Jack was feeling the same.

Except he probably wouldn't be much longer.

"So here's the other thing we have scheduled today," she said, hoping her announcement wouldn't ruin the beautiful, quiet mood between them.

"Dare I hope it's the wild sex or the wine consumption? Or both combined?"

"Not yet. That might come later, if you're good."

"Oh, I'm good. You know I'm good."

She hated to squash the teasing heat in his eyes and

sucked in another breath, this one no longer relaxed. "After we turn in our snowshoes, we're going to take the car out to the Larue family vineyards."

Something in her expression obviously told him this wasn't just another pleasure excursion. "Your TAVI patient?"

"Clearly, I'm not the only astute one." Suddenly she felt nervous. Would meeting Benjamin make Jack go all defensive again? Snuff out the smile on his face, the relaxed posture, the teasing looks? Make it difficult for them to enjoy the hours together in this beautiful place?

Maybe it would. But with the complications that patients were experiencing increasing, her gut told her Jack needed to step back from how deeply he was wrapped up in the trial and think about it objectively. If meeting Benjamin didn't do that, probably nothing would. "Are you...okay with that?"

"I told you this morning, Dr. Girard," he said, his gaze steady on hers, "I'm all yours."

The house looked to be hundreds of years old, though at the same time it was still in pristine condition. Proof that most people had been shorter long ago, Jack had to duck beneath the ancient beam above the thick, wooden front door when he followed Avery, who was being kissed on both cheeks and warmly greeted by a woman who was probably in her early forties. Both were yammering on in French, and since he couldn't understand a word, he took time to look around the cozy room. A welcoming fire burned inside a huge stone fireplace, and a wooden table was covered with so many plates of finger foods you'd have thought every guest at the hotel was stopping by.

He blew out a breath. He'd known all along this was the catch to an otherwise great weekend with Avery, but now that he was here, dread began to seep into his gut. What did Avery really want from him? And what could this man have experienced that he hadn't seen before, anyway?

It wasn't as if he didn't know all too well about the challenges people with bad hearts faced every day. He stood by his statement that a less-than-perfect outcome was still better than what most had lived with before the procedure. This TAVI trial was doing important work, critical work, work that might have helped someone like his own grandfather, who had died with so much left to live for. Help a lot of people who couldn't get a new heart valve any other way.

Benjamin Larue must not have had luck on his side. Sometimes bad things happened to good people, and every doctor experienced days when it felt like a shower of bricks came down on everyone's head. When it did, it hurt like hell and left bruises that lasted a long time.

"Jack, this is Vivienne Larue. Vivienne, Dr. Jack Dunbar."

"Welcome, welcome! Please sit and make yourself comfortable while I get Benjamin. He is very happy you've come to visit."

Jack wasn't sure *visit* was the right term—why did he suddenly feel a little like he was standing in front of a firing squad? The feeling persisted, even though he sat in a comfortable chair by the flickering fire. Maybe it was the way Avery's green eyes were focused on him—*expectantly* would be the word—and that fueled his discomfort.

"So were you telling secrets about me in French?" Maybe making a joke would lighten up the awkward mood that hung like a cloud in the room.

"I don't know many of your secrets, though that one you shared on the mountain was a doozy. Can't wait to hear more and spread them all over the hospital."

Damned if the woman couldn't make him smile in the midst of an avalanche. "I might have to make up some juicy ones, just to surprise you."

"You've been surprising me since the minute we met." A sweet, sincere smile accompanied her words, and he felt himself relax a little.

"Likewise, Dr. Girard."

"Vivienne makes the best cheesy puff pastries," Avery said as she put a few things on her plate. "You should try one."

Before he could answer, he heard a sound behind him and turned to see Vivienne pushing a man in a wheelchair into the room.

It wasn't an ordinary wheelchair. It was semi-reclining, the kind someone who couldn't breathe well would use, and the man sitting in it had a prosthetic leg. His head was raised to look at his guests as introductions were made, and a friendly smile didn't mask his pallor or the thin, drawn look to his face.

So much for feeling less tense. His gut tightened all over again when he saw how young the man was to have this kind of disability. Probably only in his early forties, like his wife. It was damned unfair that sometimes a guy drew the short straw, and medical science just wasn't advanced enough to replace it with a longer one.

And wasn't that exactly why the work he was doing was so important? Advancing medical science to help patients was the critical goal.

"*Bon après-midi*, Dr. Dunbar. I'm honored to have you visit," Benjamin said in a hoarse, rasping voice as he extended his hand. "Avery tells me you have developed a new prosthetic valve device. I wish you well with it."

Jack stood and leaned over to shake his hand. "Thank you. Avery thought that speaking with you might help me do the best I can for other patients as we move forward."

Benjamin's smile broadened. "And I hope that you will taste our latest wine vintages to help me with those, as well. We make the finest wines in France right here, you know. Pinot Gris, Pinot Noir and Rieslings are our specialties."

"I didn't know. I don't pretend to be a wine expert, but I'm more than happy to lend my palate to you."

"Excellent." Benjamin beamed, then turned to talk to Avery. As Jack watched them banter, the room seemed to lose its claustrophobic feeling and he relaxed, taking a bite of the cheese Vivienne offered. Which made him realize he'd been prepared for criticism or attack or who knew what from all of them.

"So, Dr. Dunbar. Avery is determined that I tell you my story. Why she continues to take responsibility for God's hand in my life, I do not know. It is what it is. So I will recite it quickly, then we can enjoy more important things." Benjamin looked at her with an expression similar to that of a fond uncle, and her emotions were right there on her face, visible to anyone who wanted to look.

Warm friendship. Caring. Heartache and guilt.

She'd been through tough times with this man, he saw, surprised at that revelation, though he shouldn't have been. She had obviously had her own days where bricks had fallen all too hard on her head. She might not be a medical doctor, but she cared about the patients using the devices she'd designed as much as any of them. Cared about them deeply enough to forge this bond that obviously both hurt and soothed.

"I'd like to hear your story, Benjamin," he said. "More than anything, I want to help people like my late grandfather, and like you, with challenging heart valve problems."

He thought he was focused on Benjamin, but realized he was glancing at Avery, too. At her smile, and the softness in her eyes that told him she liked his response. He'd always thought he didn't care what others thought, that he worked for his patients and for the goals he'd set for himself, and that was all that mattered. But at that moment her approval brought a smile to his own face and made his chest swell a little, even though he knew that was absurd.

"At the age of nine I was diagnosed with diabetes," Benjamin said, staring at the swirl of red wine in a glass his wife had poured. "As the years went on, I was one of the less fortunate. Many complications, and eventually I lost my leg."

"Juvenile-onset diabetes can be a difficult disease to manage." Jack saw all too many patients with terrible complications from diabetes and hoped like hell researchers would eventually find a cure.

"It is." Benjamin nodded. "Then, when our boys were only seven and nine, my kidneys began to fail. We fit weekly dialysis into our schedules somehow. Along with caring for the vines and harvest and crush and all the other things that must happen for a winery to survive. For me to survive." His hand reached to Vivienne and she clasped it tight. "My beautiful wife has stood by me through all of this, and why that is I do not know. I only know that I am blessed."

"It is your stubbornness, Benjamin Larue. Your irresistible stubbornness."

Jack saw tears fill Vivienne's eyes, and he glanced at Avery to see hers had filled, as well. In her line of work she probably didn't often work with sick people. He dealt with it every day, but that didn't make it any easier. "When did you begin to have heart problems?"

"Not long after my dialysis began. When I worked with the grapes or played with my sons, I tired quickly, becoming very short of breath." His eyes met Jack's. "Do you have children, monsieur?"

"No."

"Then you do not know the joys and frustrations of their abundant energy. Energy I wanted to keep up with."

Jack might not know about wanting to play with his own children, with any children, but could easily imagine how that inability could cut away at your soul. "So you and your doctors decided a valve transplant would help. Except you weren't a candidate for open-heart surgery because of your other health issues."

"*Oui*. I was pleased to think a new procedure might help me breathe easier, work longer and play ball with my boys for more than five minutes." He grinned. "You may look at me and wonder, but I got pretty good at kicking with my pretend leg, which amused my children."

"Amused everyone," Avery said, smiling, too. "When his doctor and I came here to talk about the risks and benefits of the TAVI trial, I couldn't believe how Benjamin could practically do spin moves. His boys joked that he was Iron Man and had an unfair advantage. Tiring quickly was his primary problem, which we'd hoped to fix."

"But the surgery didn't go well." Jack wanted to get to the crux of the matter, though he already knew.

"Non." Benjamin's smile faded. "Afterward, I was much worse, not better. Now if I lie flat, my lungs fill. I cannot kick the ball with my boys at all anymore or work in the vineyard. My kidney problems make it impossible for me to take a diuretic to lessen the fluid buildup, and my body is not strong enough to handle open-heart surgery." He gestured at himself. "So this is it for me. I accept it, but hurt for my family that they must do all the things in the vineyard and at home that I no longer can."

"Bottom line, Jack? It was an utter failure," Avery said, her eyes intent on his. "We wanted to make Benjamin's life better, but we made it much worse instead. I know you see patients with bad outcomes. But you've been convinced that those with leakage from the prosthetic valve are medically manageable and still better off than before. Benjamin's situation proves that's not always the case. The percentage having this problem must be very small to justify the risk."

What was he supposed to say to that? All procedures carried risks. Every single one of them, from the simplest to the most complex. But he understood the frustration and deep disappointment. Benjamin may not have had the exercise capacity he'd wanted before the procedure, but now he had none at all and couldn't even sleep in a bed with his wife.

"Papa! Papa!" Two boys careened into the room, nearly skidding to a halt next to the wheelchair, speaking fast in French until he held up his hand.

"English, please. Our guest does not speak French, and it is good for you to practice."

Both boys took a breath, and Jack was impressed at how polite they were during a brief introduction, before launching into their story again.

"*Les chevreuils* got through the fence that has a hole and into the berry bushes. They were eating up the brambles before we chased them off! Why do deer eat thorny things like that, Papa?"

"The same reason you like your mother's macaroons, I suppose."

"Are you saying that eating my macaroons is like swallowing thorns, Benjamin Larue?" Vivienne said in faux outrage, her hands fisted on her hips.

"*Non, non*, my dearest, I am saying the brambles are like a delectable delicacy to *les chevreuils*, as all your wonderful dishes are to me." His chest filled with a deep chuckle that morphed into a horrible coughing fit that immediately swept all amusement from everyone's face.

Jack tensed, wishing there was something he could

do to help Benjamin breathe more easily, but there wasn't. The fluids had to work loose on their own, and he was sure everyone was as relieved as he was when the poor man's coughing finally subsided. Benjamin took a moment to catch his breath, then spoke to his sons, telling them where to get materials to repair the fence. Pride lit his eyes as they kissed both his cheeks, said their goodbyes and ran off as fast as they'd run in.

Jack thought of his own brother and how the two of them had always looked up to their dad. The man hadn't done much around the house, always busy working at the hospital. On the occasions they'd tackled a project together, though, he still remembered how he'd admired his father's smarts and physical strength. Not having that physical strength had to hurt Benjamin like hell, but thank God he still could guide and mentor his boys in other ways.

"You have a fine family, Benjamin," Jack said. "Think they'll continue the family tradition of wine making?"

"If they do not, we will disinherit them." His eyes twinkled. "Now it is time for that wine tasting, *oui*? I cannot walk down the stairs to the cellar, so we will have to enjoy it here. Vivienne, will you uncork them, *s'il vous plaît*?"

Jack saw the closeness between husband and wife just from the way they smiled at one another, and he found himself looking at Avery. Thinking about sharing that kind of lifelong bond with a woman had never been on his list of things to accomplish in his life. Wasn't sure it ever would be. But he had to admit there just might be something good about having that kind of steady love and support in good times and bad.

The Larues had managed to keep that through plenty of bad times.

Jack didn't have to know them well to hurt for them. He got why Avery wanted him to see what Benjamin lived with, but at the same time he felt she was being naive. If he counted the number of patients living less than optimal lives, he'd spend all day doing it. Life wasn't fair, that was for sure.

The clinical trial he was working so hard on was all about trying to level the playing field just a little. Trials existed for a reason, and that reason was to test new procedures and devices. If everyone threw in the towel halfway through because potential questions arose, nothing good would ever get accomplished from most of them.

Did Avery think meeting this great family that had to live with adversity and challenges would change his goals, or make him question what he wanted to accomplish? He damned well had plenty of his own patients who had to endure a life with far less than optimal physical ability. Surely she knew that.

Improving the lives of patients was all he wanted to accomplish. If she didn't understand or believe that, their time alone together this weekend wouldn't turn out the way he hoped it would.

CHAPTER THIRTEEN

SEEING THE LARUE family always left Avery with a tumble of emotions. Pleased about spending time enjoying the closeness of their family. Grateful for her own health. Sad for what they had to deal with every day. Guilt that she hadn't done a better job designing the TAVI device before it had gone to human trials.

At that exact moment she wasn't sure which emotion was winning.

Jack's arm wrapped around her waist, holding her close, might not be helping much with the guilt and sadness, but it did feel good there. Warm and comforting. Despite their height difference, their bodies seemed to fit perfectly together as they strolled through the village in search of a *biscuiterie* and the coconut macaroons Riquewihr was famous for. The shop she usually went to was closed for the winter, and she peered hopefully at dimly lit signs, trying to find another one that was open.

"There's one," Avery said, pointing down a crooked little street. "I don't remember it, but I'm sure every one of the *biscuiteries* are good."

"So you claim these cookies are the best things in the whole world?"

"The best. I guarantee you'll love them."

They went into the tiny shop and selected a few macaroons and espresso before sitting at a small table. Avery felt pretty much sapped of small talk and nibbled her cookie, hoping its deliciousness would cheer her up and make her a better companion, which she knew she couldn't claim to be at that moment.

"I have a confession to make," Jack said, looking extremely serious.

She paused with her macaroon halfway to her mouth. "A confession?"

"Yes. I'm not a big fan of coconut. In fact, I usually avoid it like flesh-eating bacteria. But if sharing coconut macaroons with you banishes the melancholy in your beautiful eyes for even a split second, I'll gladly choke one down."

As he said it, she could swear he actually shuddered, and she managed a laugh. "You believe it would cheer me up to watch you eat something you liken to flesh-eating bacteria? What does that say about the kind of person you think I am?"

"That you are caring. And that you obviously feel all beat up right now."

"There's that astute thing again."

"Don't have to be astute to see it, Avery. How you're feeling is written all over your face."

"Good to know." She closed her eyes and swallowed at the sudden lump in her throat. "I do feel beat up whenever I see them. Who wouldn't? I designed the prosthetic valve, and that valve is why his life is awful now. It's hard for me to see that wonderful family dealing with what they deal with. See Benjamin barely able to walk, when I saw him running with the boys before my TAVI device destroyed that."

"For all you know, his heart might have gotten worse anyway. The man's been dealt a bad hand of cards, and I feel for him, too." He reached for her hand, and its warmth had her holding it tight. "But if I blamed myself for every patient who didn't do well, or who died, like Henri Arnoult, I'd never be able to function and do my job. Medicine is both rewarding and damned difficult. The only way to help people is to forge on and do the best you can. Would it help people if you just stopped designing biomedical devices? Never came up with an improved stent or something no one's invented yet?"

"No. But I should have insisted it be tested further on animals first." Not that the manufacturer and sponsor would have listened anyway. "I'd hoped you'd come to see you should consider that, too, for yours."

"I am listening to you, Avery. Hearing you loud and clear, and paying attention to the reason for your worries. I want you to know that." Seeing how deeply serious and sincere he looked brought her hope that he truly meant it. "While it's impossible to know how Benjamin's health would be right now without the TAVI, I understand your point about possibly making it worse for some patients than others. This trial is already under way with patients who have no other options. I still believe we're doing far more good than harm. But since we have more than double the number of patients now giving us additional data, I will keep him in mind as we look at how things are going."

The weight in her chest lifted at the same time it squeezed even tighter. Not only did Jack respect her opinion, it sounded like this trek had accomplished her goal. How could she have thought he might be too narrow focused, too hell-bent on success, to at least listen? She'd already seen what a committed and caring doctor he was.

"Okay, for that you don't have to eat the macaroon," she said, managing a smile. "I can't believe you were going to, if you don't like coconut. Though I admit I'm incredulous that's even possible."

"Maybe I'd like it after it's touched your lips." His finger gently swiped her bottom lip and she could see bits of cookie on his finger just before he licked it off.

Had she really been yakking away with crumbs all over her mouth? Her embarrassment at that realization got shoved aside by serious body tingling at the oh-so-sensual look he was giving her.

"You know what?" He sounded genuinely surprised. "It is better. Definitely. Sweet and delectable, in fact."

"Not like flesh-eating bacteria?" She found herself staring at his mouth, and to keep herself from diving in there and tasting for herself the crumbs and espresso on his tongue, she tried for a joke. "I'm not a big fan of escargots, which I saw you gobbling up at the hotel hors d'oeuvre party. Maybe you could hold one between your lips and I'll nibble it from there. Just to see."

His laughter made her grin and realize he'd managed to squash much of the sadness she'd been feeling. Had also managed to blast away every negative thought her former relationships had stuck in her brain nearly from the first day she'd met him. Had managed to prove himself the complete package of what a sexy man should be. At that moment she knew the attraction and lust she'd felt when she'd first met him had evolved into very much more.

The thought both scared and thrilled her, and she wasn't at all sure what to do with the realization that had just slammed her between the eyes.

"Somehow, nibbling snails from my lips doesn't sound nearly as appealing as licking cookie crumbs from yours. I think we need further research on this, Dr. Girard."

"I think we need further research on why talking about flesh-eating bacteria and nibbling snails hasn't at all dulled my desire to kiss you, Dr. Dunbar." Further research on that, and on the tender emotions swirling around her heart as she seriously considered pressing her mouth to his right then and there.

"Then I definitely want to find out what will happen if I suggest you nibble *chocolat* from my lips. Which you can bet I'm pulling from the minibar in our room the minute we get there." His voice had gone so low, his expression so wicked that her belly quivered in anticipation of any and all nibbling action.

He tossed back the last of his espresso and stood, grasping her hand and leaning down to speak close to her ear. "Bring your cookies back to the hotel so I can see how they taste licked from your lips. After I lick off the chocolate. In fact, I like the idea of keeping a database of how all kinds of things taste from your lips and other beautiful parts of your body."

Whew, boy. She felt so hot she nearly didn't bother putting on her coat before they moved out into the chilly night. Jack walked fast, and because he was holding her hand she had to nearly run to keep up.

"Slow down a little. My legs aren't as long as yours."

"Having a hard time slowing down, thinking about our future data collection." His eyes glittered in the darkness. "And I figured the pace would keep you warmer."

No need to worry about her being warm. At all. About to skirt the ornate fountain in the center of a square, she found herself, ridiculously, wanting to make a wish like she always did when she was here. She tugged his arm so he'd stop. "Let's make a wish in the fountain. I always hope it's like the Trevi Fountain in Rome."

He pulled a couple of coins from his pocket and handed one to her. "What are you going to wish for?"

"It won't come true if you tell." She looked skyward to make her wish, surprised to see how remarkably clear it was for a winter night in France, which made her think about how wonderful it would be to make love to Jack outdoors deep in the vineyards when it was warmer, which briefly sidetracked her from her mission.

She yanked her thoughts back to ponder her wish as the stars seemed to twinkle down on them. She closed her eyes and tossed the coin into the fountain with a satisfying plunk.

"Your turn."

He tossed his coin. It landed just a millimeter from hers, and she wondered if that meant something. Which was beyond silly—it was just water in a fountain, and what would she want it to mean anyway?

"Maybe you'll get lucky and your wish will come true," she said.

His expression as his eyes met hers was odd, almost serious. It was too bad it wasn't really a magic fountain, because she'd love to ask it what his wish was.

"I'm already feeling lucky. Though I very much hope I'll get even luckier."

Her insides went all quivery again, as there was no mistaking the superheated gleam that returned to his eyes as he spoke. If the two of them making love again was what he'd wished for, he'd wasted his wish. Her breath caught just looking at his handsome face and sexy smile, and she fully intended to enjoy these hours with him before the stress of work faced them once again. Before he moved on to his next trial and she went wherever her job took her.

This time, it was Avery setting the pace, giving a quick greeting to the hotel manager before running up the two flights of stairs to their floor and into the room.

"For some reason, I'm feeling a little déjà vu," Jack said as he shoved the door closed behind them. "If it was summertime, I'd be sneaking into one of the vineyards and feeding you grapes while making love to you under the stars."

Did the man have mind-reading powers, too, or was it just part of this electric connection they seemed to have? "Funny, I was just thinking the same thing. We could add grapes to the database." Breathlessly, she wrangled off her coat and tossed it on the chair. "It does seem like we've done the same dash into a hotel room several times since we met, wearing an awful lot of heavy clothes."

"Not exactly the same dash. For one thing, it seemed like you weren't too sure you wanted to unbutton your coat before. This time you're ahead of me." He reached for her and pulled her close. "Not to mention that, each time, it's gotten even sweeter. I'm betting tonight will be also, not even counting the macaroons you brought."

"Know what? You do taste sweeter than any cookie." She stood on tiptoe and slid her hands behind his head before she kissed him. Deeply, deliciously, pouring herself into it, wanting to show him how much she'd come to care for him. To tell him without words how impressed she was that he'd shared his honest view about Benjamin and medicine, while still listening to her, respecting her, caring what she thought. To enjoy the connection they shared that was of both mind and body.

He kissed her back. And kissed her. Until her breath was choppy and her knees nearly stopped holding her up. Figuring she'd like to be sitting or something before that happened, she backed them both toward the bed, but he stopped the movement and broke the kiss. He stood there just staring at her with eyes that were peculiarly serious behind the obvious desire shining there.

"What?" she whispered.

"When I came to Paris I was keyed up and couldn't think about anything but how all my work was about to pay off. Being with you that first day seemed like a great way to take the edge off before the trial started." He slowly shook his head. "But it didn't quite work out that way. Instead, you've added another edge."

"What do you mean?"

"I hate not having complete control over how I feel about you." He pressed her body so close to his it was hard to breathe. "I've spent my adulthood being in control of my life and my career. Not having that makes me damned uncomfortable."

Her heart constricted into a cold little ball at the fact that she was the one who had control over this current phase of his career that was so important to him. And he'd be very angry and upset that she hadn't shared that reality with him, if he ended up finding out. Or if she had to wield that control and power.

And yet somehow her heart swelled, too, at his words and the way he looked at her. Like she'd come to mean as much to him as he had to her. "Is being in control all the time important? Because right now I wouldn't mind you losing control a little."

"Yeah?" She thought he was about to resume their motion toward the bed, but he veered sideways toward the bathroom. At the same time he somehow managed to slip her blouse over her head, unzip the back of her skirt, yank off his own shirt and pants, and throw a condom onto the floor until they were standing naked just outside the tiny shower.

"I've heard the verse 'Jack, be nimble, Jack, be quick,'" she said, amazed and more than excited as she stared at his all-too-sexy physique. "Was that written about you?"

"You make me want to be quick. For some things, not everything." His lips curved. "Not jumping over any candlesticks, though. Wouldn't stay lit for what I'm planning next."

"And what are you planning next?" Avery quivered at the superheated gleam in his eyes, knowing whatever it was would be a whole lot better than any snail nibbling.

Jack turned the faucet on, then tugged Avery's

breathtakingly naked body into the cubicle and closed the door.

"My plan is to lick water from every inch of your skin," he said. The closeness of the space sent her pink nipples nudging against his chest and his erection into the softness of her belly, making him groan. Still-cold water rained onto his back as he shielded her from it until it warmed, but it didn't do a thing to cool the heat pumping through every one of his pores.

"It's small in here, I know. But I don't care. I liked kissing the rainwater from your face and mouth so much I've been fantasizing about getting you in the shower ever since."

"Should I get my umbrella? I kind of liked kissing you under that before we got all wet."

"Maybe next time." God, she was adorable. "I'm already all wet, and soon you will be, too."

He kissed her, letting one hand palm her breast while the other stroked down her soft skin and between her legs to make his last statement come true. The little gasping breaths and sexy sounds coming from her mouth into his nearly had him diving into her right then and there, but tonight was about slow and easy. Being together just this once without work and patients and the trial hanging around with them.

The water pounding on his back had finally warmed, and he pulled her under it to join him. He shoved her wet hair back so he could see her beautiful face and started with her forehead, sipping the water from her skin as it tracked down her cheek, her throat, her breasts.

Her fingers dug into his back as he tasted as much of her as her could reach, and the feel of her tongue licking across his shoulder, too, up his neck and around his ear, made him shiver and burn at the same time.

"You taste so delicious," he murmured against her damp sternum as her other slick wetness soaked his fingers and the scent of her touched his nose, making him want to taste her there, too. Probably not possible in the tiny shower, but later? Oh, yeah. "The best dessert any man could ask for."

"This water doesn't taste as good as the rain, though." Her chest rose and fell against his mouth. "Maybe we should try bottled water, since I don't think they drink tap water here."

"Too late for that." He chuckled and looked up at her, then paused in mid-lick. Arrested by the look on her face. It was filled with the kind of intimate connection between them he'd only felt with her—a humor and euphoria and something he couldn't quite define. He wanted to see more of it, wanted to look into her eyes as he kissed her mouth. Every bit of her tasted beyond wonderful, but that delectable mouth of hers was his absolute favorite of all.

Grasping her rear in his hands, he wrapped her legs around his waist, then realized he had to get the condom from the floor. He crouched down, juggling her on his knees as he reached for it, but she slid sideways. Mashing her close against him so she wouldn't crack her head on the tile wall, he fell back on his tailbone, his erection nearly finding home base as she slid forward on top of him.

"Well, hell. Note to self. Even the best idea can be ruined by poor planning." He steadied them both, resisting the urge to massage his sore butt, and saw she was stifling a laugh.

"Not ruined. Altered." She grabbed the trouble-making condom and tore the wrapper, and he thought he might come unglued as she opened it and rolled it on, then slowly eased herself onto him.

"Is this a good alteration to the plan?" she asked in a sultry voice as she moved on him, her eyes all smoky green, her beautiful lips parted, and he had to try twice before he could manage a short answer.

"Yes. Good." The back of his head was against the hard tile wall, his neck all kinked, and he was practically folded into a pretzel as the water still flowed and pooled on the shower floor, but none of that mattered.

All he could feel was her heat wrapped around him. All he could see was the vision that was her—her breasts, her hips, her face, the total goddess that was Avery Girard. He reached up to touch all of it, all of her, pulling her to him for the deepest kiss of his life as she increased the pace. As he felt her orgasm around him and followed her there.

Warm and bonelessly relaxed, Jack held Avery close beneath the sheets and down blanket. Round two in bed with the promised *chocolat* from the minibar had been every bit as good as the shower, which he'd never have believed until he'd experienced it.

"You were right, you know," he murmured against her silky hair.

"I usually am." He could feel her lips curve against his arm, and he smiled, as well. "What was I right about this time?"

"I did need a break. I needed to relax so I have a clear mind when I get back to work tomorrow. So thank you for that."

"Thank you for coming to meet Benjamin and listening to my worries with an open mind. That's all I wanted."

"All you wanted? Not me licking water and chocolate from you?"

"Okay, I wanted that, too."

He loved that little gleam in her eye and got distracted for a few minutes from something he'd been wanting to ask, having to kiss her again. When he finally came up for air he slipped her hair from her eyes and refocused his attention from the libido that kept leaping onto center stage around her.

"I've been wondering why you haven't come up with a next-generation TAVI device," he said. "You had to have heard through the biomedical grapevine I was working with Crilex on one. Is it because of Benjamin?"

"No. I can't quit trying to come up with a design to help people like him. I have a couple I'm working on. But I want the most promising device to be tested on animals until we're as sure as we can be of a positive outcome for patients. If I let a trial get started too soon, it's out of my hands after that."

"You didn't have much say during your first one?"

"No. Even after the percentage of patients with aortic insufficiency was too high and then Benjamin had his catastrophic problem, the sponsor insisted on finishing the trial."

Finally, he got why she wasn't working for that

company anymore, doing freelance work instead. "So you quit."

"I quit. I know trials carry risks, and patients know those risks. But for the cardiologist and corporation to ignore them when things have obviously gone wrong? That's unacceptable."

"And you think that's what I'm doing?"

"No." Her lips pressed softly against his arm, and he pulled her closer against him, glad that was her answer. "I don't think this trial is there yet. But it might get there, and if it does, I hope you'll do the right thing and shut it down."

"I want to finish the trial and study the data for the rollout, because I think we have to do that to come to any real conclusion." He hoped she understood his perspective. "If there was an extreme and obvious high risk, though, I wouldn't put patients' lives in harm's way to accomplish that."

"I know that now." Her teeth gleamed white in the low light. "That's why I'm lying here in bed with you, sticky with chocolate."

"Happy to lick you more to clean it off, if you like."

"Need to record the current data first. Macaroons, wine, espresso, chocolate." She pushed up onto her elbow. Her soft hand stroked across his chest, and he captured it in his, kissing her fingers and sucking the chocolate still clinging to one until she laughed and yanked it free. "So, you know my dirty little secret about the failure of my device and the failure of the people in charge to abort the mission. Tell me how you became so passionate about a second TAVI device."

He sighed. The subject of his grandfather still had the power to bring an ache to his chest. So much knowledge and grace had died with the man.

"My dad, my brother and I all decided to become cardiologists because of my granddad. I wish you could have met him—he was just a great guy and a great doc. Always seemed ironic that he had a heart attack when he was only in his fifties and suffered for years from a faulty valve afterward. He eventually had open-heart surgery, but he was one of the small percentage who didn't make it through."

"I'm sorry, Jack."

Her hand slipped up his chest to cup his cheek, and he liked the feel of it there. He turned his face to kiss her palm. "The more I worked with various stents in interventional cardiology, the more convinced I got that we could solve that problem. Help patients without other options and someday have the TAVI procedure completely eliminate the need to perform open-heart surgery for valve replacement. I want that to happen. And I want to be a part of it."

"You already are. No matter how things end up, this step you've taken is a huge one. Mine was, as well. Unsuccessful, yes, but each time, no matter what, we learn something that will help us do it better next time."

"Is that the biomedical engineering creed?" While he admired the hell out of her attitude, and agreed with it, he couldn't help teasing her a little, wanting to bring a smile back to her now somber face.

"My creed. Yours, too, I bet."

"Yeah. Mine, too." He wasn't even close to giving up

on this device. He was still convinced, even if Avery wasn't, that rolling it out to other hospitals remained the ultimate way to study it.

CHAPTER FOURTEEN

"AH, DR. DUNBAR, you will promise I can tend my garden after you fix me, *oui*?"

"No promises, Mrs. Halbert. But I'll do the best I can. What do you like to grow in your garden?"

The smile Jack was giving the woman, the way his eyes crinkled at the corners and how he seemed genuinely interested in her garden all made Avery's heart feel squishy. It wasn't the first time that organ had felt that way around him. In fact, he'd made it squish a little their very first day together, and it had gotten to the point where it became pretty much a melted mess whenever he was around.

That she'd ever believed the success of this trial was important to him for his personal fame and fortune—more important than the success of the patients' health—made her cringe now. It was so obvious he was doing this to help people with no other surgical option. To someday change valve replacement surgery altogether, as she had wanted to do. To honor the memory of his beloved grandfather.

"I know I cannot dig my leeks from the ground. But grow chard and cucumbers, *oui*? My grandchildren love it when I fix them. And to prune my roses. *Est-ce que je serai capable de la faire?*"

He glanced at Avery, and she quickly translated. "She wants to know if she'll be able to do that after the surgery."

Jack placed his hand on the woman's gnarled one. "I hope so, Mrs. Halbert. Maybe I'll be here when you come for checkups this summer. I'd like it if you would bring me one of the roses you've pruned, to see and smell what you love to grow."

"Oui, oui." The woman beamed and patted his hand resting on hers. *"Quelle couleur? Rose? Blanche? Rouge?"*

Avery was about to translate again, but he was obviously able to figure it out as he smiled first at the woman, then at her in a slow perusal from head to toe. "I'm fond of every color, Mrs. Halbert. Preferably enjoyed all at once."

As his eyes met hers, that squishy feeling rolled all around in her belly. When he turned back to the patient she glanced down at herself and the yellow blouse and red shoes she wore. She decided she just might have to buy a new scarf in multiple hues to go with them for the next time she and Jack went out together.

The thought surprised her. Since when had she ever dressed for anyone but herself? Apparently the answer was, *not until she'd met Jack.*

Nurses came in to prep Mrs. Halbert for surgery, and as Jack spoke with them Avery quietly left the room. She pulled up the data from the past three days of surgery after she and Jack had returned from their weekend together. The weekend that had left her with the unsettling yet exhilarating knowledge that, for good or bad, her heart was in Jack's hands.

She hadn't planned on falling for him. For anybody. And she was pretty sure Jack was in the same boat. But since it was too late to keep it from happening, she fully intended to see just where these new feelings she hoped he shared might take them.

Yet there was that one potentially huge, very worrying issue with that, and she felt a little queasy just thinking about it. More than a little queasy, as she studied the information she'd gathered onto her tablet.

The dramatically increased patient load in the trial and the resulting data had waving red caution flags written all over it. If it continued like this, she would have to try to convince Jack to halt the trial. If that couldn't be accomplished, she'd have no choice at that time but to recommend to Bob it be halted and that future trials be discontinued.

Her stomach churned more, even as she hoped against hope that things would improve with the surgeries scheduled over the next couple of days. But if they didn't, if that's what had to happen, would Jack understand and agree?

She didn't know. But one thing she did know. No matter how much she'd come to care for him, those feelings would not get in the way of her professional integrity.

"Breathing better now, Mrs. Halbert?" Jack asked. It felt like he'd said those words a dozen times in just the past eight days, and it took a major effort to keep his voice calm and steady when he wanted to slam his fist into the wall and kick something.

"*Oui.* Better."

This déjà vu wasn't the great kind he'd shared with Avery, running to hotel rooms together. This was a recurring nightmare for both his patients and himself.

After taking the weekend off with Avery, Jack had returned to work feeling ready to take on the world. That feeling of energy and optimism had been quickly replaced by stress and anxiety as no fewer than three patients from last week and two from this one were already suffering with leakage from their new valves.

He studied Mrs. Halbert, very glad to see that her hands had loosened their grip on her chest and each inhalation seemed more even and less labored. He checked her vitals, asked the nurse to look at the fluid in her Foley and listened to her lungs, which were definitely clearer. Blood pressure improved, oxygen improved. Crisis hopefully over, and she'd be okay.

"Sorry you got that scare." He reached for her hand. "I know it feels bad when you can't catch your breath. But I believe you're going to feel pretty good by the time you go home to prune those roses."

"Merci beaucoup." She gently patted his hand as she'd done every time he'd talked with her. If the woman had been in an advertisement playing a dear, lovely grandma, people would have bought whatever she was selling, and his chest felt a little heavy as he wondered if the sweet woman would be thanking him in a few months.

Think positively. He checked her pulse again and reminded himself she'd likely do just fine with meds to control the leakage, which was thankfully minor. But as he looked at the smile on her wrinkled face he saw someone younger. Benjamin Larue, who couldn't even sit upright without drowning in the fluid that collected in his lungs.

"I'll be back to check on you later, Mrs. Halbert." He shoved to his feet, spoke again to the nurse and said his goodbyes. Then saw Avery standing in the doorway.

Her expression bore no resemblance at all to the flirtatious, fun Avery he'd spent the weekend with. The woman looking at him rivaled a grimly stern principal about to haul a student off to her office, and Jack braced himself for the lecture she'd given before that he absolutely did not want to hear again at that moment.

He walked past her into the hallway, and she followed. He closed his eyes for a moment, trying to find his calm, before he turned to her and held up his hand. Needing to stop whatever she was about to say before it started, because it had been a damn long day and week and he knew his nerves were worn thin enough that he just might say something he regretted. He liked her—hell, more than liked her—and respected her, and getting into an argument with her was the last thing he wanted to do.

"I know the percentage of patients with problems is higher than we expected," he said. "I know you're worried that some won't be medically manageable, and I know you think we should perform the procedure on fewer patients as we finish the trial. I know, Avery."

"So what are you going to do about it?"

What *was* he going to do about it? Very good question, and one he didn't have a clue how to answer. He scrubbed a hand over his face, and when he looked at her again, saw her beautiful green eyes were somehow both soft and hard as they met his.

"Last week I was worried, but still watching. This week, in just ten surgeries, you've had two major leakages, and now Mrs. Halbert, which makes it thirty percent. Sweet Mrs. Halbert, who just wants to be able to prune her roses." She shook her head. "I think you know what you should do. The real question is whether or not you will."

"First, Mrs. Halbert's original valve was so diseased she could barely walk twenty steps. Second, thirty percent of patients in three days isn't thirty percent over the entire trial, which you may not be aware is how data must be collected."

Her mouth dropped open. "That's a nice insult. Reminds me of another cardiologist I used to be involved with."

Damn it. "I'm sorry, that was just frustration talking. You know I admire and respect you and your expertise." The disappointment he saw in her eyes made him want to punch himself the way he'd wanted to punch the wall. Saying something he shouldn't was exactly why he'd wanted to avoid the whole conversation. "But you think it's black and white. It isn't. If we reduce the number of patients, there might be fewer with problems, but there will also be fewer who get the help they need. Some who might die soon because their aortic valve barely works. Have you taken the time to talk to any of them or their families? Because I have."

He knew his voice was rising, and he sucked in a breath to control it, walking farther down the hall away from the rooms. He turned to her again, and she had that damned tablet clutched to her breast like a shield. "I've told them exactly how the trial is going, good and bad, and asked if they still wanted to participate. And you know what? They do. For almost all of them this is their last shot at a decent life. Or life at all. We won't have the conclusive data we need until trials are conducted over the next year at various hospitals."

"The data is screaming at you, Jack, but you're not listening."

"I am listening. I'm hearing the patients talk and the data talk. After it's rolled out everywhere it's scheduled to be, we'll listen to the entire conversation and go from there." He dropped a quick kiss on her forehead, knowing even that connection would ease his frustration with her and the situation. "I've got to get to my next surgery."

He scrubbed, then headed to the cath lab, working hard to bring his focus where it needed to be. Jessica was already there, arranging the last items needed for surgery, and she handed him his lead apron.

"Can I talk to you privately for a minute before surgery gets started?" she asked, glancing around at the doctors and nurses starting to filter in behind the glass wall in the cath lab to observe. Then she focused a laser look at Jack that was odd enough to grab his attention. He nearly asked why before just giving her a nod and moving to a quiet corner where he didn't think anyone would be able to hear them.

"What's up?"

"I found out something this morning that you're not

going to like." Jessica's lips were pressed into a tight line and a deep frown had formed between her brows. In the three years they'd worked together she hadn't been a woman prone to drama. Big drama was written on her face now, though, and he felt a little fissure of concern slide down his spine.

"This sounds ominous. We're getting started soon, so make it fast, please."

She glanced behind them again before speaking, keeping her voice low. "I was in the back room finishing up some things after your last surgery yesterday evening. Bob Timkin was there, talking to a hospital administrator type from a different French hospital who had just arrived in Paris to observe the trial. Timkin was showing him the TAVI device and talking it up. But when the guy asked him about conducting a trial at his hospital in Nice, I was surprised when Timkin put him off. Said we had to finish this trial first and see what the results were before they considered any rollout."

Jack frowned. "That can't be what he said. The whole reason French interventional cardiologists have been here observing how the procedure is done is so they can conduct their own trials. The trials at other French hospitals are about ready to begin."

"How long have we worked together, Jack?" Jess fisted her hands on her hips. "I heard him say it with my own ears. Are you implying I'm confused?"

"I believe you heard something. But it just doesn't make sense, so I have to think you missed some important part of the conversation." He trusted that Jessica must have heard a conversation that had been out of the ordinary. But it didn't add up. "Crilex has poured money into the development of the device and this trial for that exact reason—to conduct additional trials elsewhere for the next year. We've just begun to collect the data."

"I know. But, believe me, I didn't misunderstand. So, when he left to take the guy to dinner, I was glad he left his Crilex binders behind. He must have gotten them later, though, because this morning they were gone."

"You were planning to snoop through them?" Jack nearly smiled despite concerns about this conversation they were having. Jessica was the queen of snooping into things around the hospital she ordinarily wouldn't be privy to. "Must have ruined your morning that they were gone."

"A little." A small, return smile flitted across her face before that deeply serious expression came back. "But I did get a chance to snoop through them some. Quite a bit, actually, until a couple of people came in. Enough to surprise and worry me. I didn't call you about it then, because I'd hoped to look more this morning, to make sure I wasn't reading it wrong. So here's the other part you're not going to like."

Her expression was so dark and downright grim his chest tightened and the alarm bells rang louder in his brain. "Spill it, Jess. We don't have all day."

"Genius biomedical engineer Dr. Girard isn't here to just observe and possibly use ideas from this device on a new one she might design in the future. Crilex hired her to give her evaluation of your device regarding its safety and effectiveness. At the end of the thirty days, if she gives them the green light, they'll roll out the trials elsewhere. If she doesn't, Crilex won't fund any more clinical trials with it."

Jack stared at her in utter disbelief. "There's no way you can be right about that. No one can make any kind of final judgment call on a device's success or failure after just one month of clinical trials. That's ridiculous."

"It may be ridiculous, but I'm telling you it's true. And there's more." She stepped even closer, speaking in a conspiratorial whisper. "I wanted to make sure you knew before the procedures today, so you could watch your back and be careful what you say and do. Here at the hospital and before you get in any deeper with her."

The numb shock he was feeling started to take over his whole body. "Make sure I knew what?"

"The whole reason Dr. Girard is here is because she approached Crilex after seeing, in all the medical journals, details on the new design for the upcoming trials. And articles about you, working together with bioengineers to develop it. She told them, just like she told you, that she believes your design hasn't fixed the valve leakage problem hers had. Crilex decided they should listen. They don't want to pour millions more into something if it has an obvious defect. They'd rather put that money into a new design, then conduct trials with that one. I don't know about you, but I'm thinking she'd rather design her own for them, which is why she's 'concerned' about yours."

The numbness faded, morphing into a hot, burning anger. Could any of this possibly be true? That, all along, Avery had withheld from him the fact that she had full control of the future of this trial? That she'd told the product developer and sponsor of these trials she thought the device he'd worked on for over a year was bad?

He sucked in a calming breath. Jessica hadn't had time to read through all the binders. Maybe she was wrong. Maybe there was a mistake.

One thing was certain, though. After this procedure, he was damned well going to find out.

Avery stood in Bob Timkin's office, waiting for him and Jack. After the last surgery, Jack had asked her to meet them here in such a tense voice she wondered if he might be coming around to her suggestion to halt the trial.

Except when he walked into the room her stomach clenched when she saw the hard look on his face. It didn't seem to be a "you might be right" expression, but who knew?

He folded his arms across his chest and stared at her. "I've been trying to figure out how to ease into this, but I'm just going to ask. Did you go to Crilex with your concerns that I thought you'd only shared with me about the new TAVI device? And did they then hire you to evaluate the device and give your opinion on its safety and effectiveness? To decide if more trials should be conducted or not?"

Avery felt like she'd swallowed the big bomb he'd just dropped. How had he found out? And what should she say? She was contractually bound to secrecy on the subject.

"I've been here to observe the new device and the clinical trial. You know that." Which was true. Just not all of it.

"Cut the crap, Avery." Anger flared in his eyes. "I may have only known you a few weeks, but I can tell when you're lying. So tell me the damned truth. I think you owe me that."

"I like you a lot, Jack, and I respect you and the work you do. But I don't owe you anything." She breathed deeply before forging on. "The people I owe are the patients who went through the trial with my first device. People like Benjamin Larue. The people I owe are the patients going through this trial now."

"So it is true," he said in a rough, disbelieving voice. He shoved his hand through his hair. Stared at her like he was seeing her for the first time. "So you get to decide if it works or if it doesn't? If it's worth putting money into the next trials? That while you've feigned interest in how I think it's all going, you haven't really given a damn because you're calling the shots?"

Her hands felt icy cold and she rubbed them together. Wrung them, really, before she realized what she was doing and flattened them against her stomach. "Yes." She braced herself for whatever reaction he was going to have to what she had to say. "After I voiced my concerns Crilex management decided that if patients have significant problems during this trial, it might make more financial sense to put their money into a next-generation device. They don't want to spend millions on multiple and extended clinical trials only to have to redesign the device and start all over again."

"You know damned well that this trial, even with the increased patient load, won't provide close to enough data to make any kind of final judgment." The anger rolling from him now was nearly palpable. "Who do you think you are? Just because you designed the first device, it doesn't make you qualified to make that kind of call on a procedure like this. You're not the cardiologist doing detailed study of the patients' history. You're not the doctor performing surgery on the patients, taking their vital signs and carefully monitoring them post-op. Taking notes from the charts the *doctor* has written isn't even close to the same thing as medically caring for them."

Her own anger welled in her chest. Here it was. The same kind of insult her old boyfriend had liked to give her—that she'd been so sure Jack would never throw at her. "I may not be a cardiologist or a medical doctor but, believe me, I am more than qualified to know whether the device is safe or not and effective or not."

His eyes narrowed at her. "This whole thing smacks of unethical self-interest to me. You collect data on the trial, tell them the device is flawed and the roll-out should be stopped, and suddenly Crilex hires you to design the new one. No more messing around doing freelance work. You'll have a nice steady job and pay-check for a long while."

"That's beyond insulting." How had she thought he might be different from other egotistical, jerky cardiologists? "I have no expectation of being hired by Crilex. They have a great team of bioengineers, which you know very well since you worked with them to get this catheter designed. I resent you questioning my ethics and integrity."

"And I resent that you kissed up to me. Now I know why you approached me in the hotel and invited me out for the day, ending up in bed. You knew who I was and hoped I'd let slip some concerns of my own about the device or trial that you could use against me." He pointed his finger at her. "Stay out of my cath lab, Avery."

"For the record, I had no idea who you were. But it doesn't matter. You may be the brains and brawn behind this trial, Jack, but Crilex is the sponsor, which means they're running this show, not you. And they have given me authority to decide the next act."

Jack's heart was pounding so hard he thought it might burst from his chest. He'd thought the déjà vu with Mrs. Halbert had been unpleasant? This reenactment of the way Vanessa had used him to advance her career stunned him. Avery had pretended to like him when, in reality, she'd used him and the situation to snatch the reins of the trial from him, design a new catheter and run with it in her deceiving little hands.

"Doctors." Timkin came into the room to stand between them, frowning. "What's the disagreement here?"

"I've just discovered you gave her the authority to evaluate this TAVI device. Behind my back, keeping me in the dark. I've worked almost two years on this damned project, but you leave its future to someone else?"

"Jack. We simply wanted her expertise to contribute to the data collection. While it's true we asked her to give her opinion at the end of the trial, we have always fully expected there to be a full rollout when it's complete."

"Why didn't you tell me?" He wouldn't have let himself get so wrapped up in her if he'd known. He found himself looking at her beautiful, lying face, and wanted to kick himself. Wrapped up in her? Damn it, he felt so entwined with Avery he knew the pain of all this would twist him in knots for years to come.

"It seemed best to not have you distracted by any concerns about the future trials. You had enough on your plate getting everything set up for this one."

"I think you deemed it best for *you* not to have me go off on you. I don't appreciate my sponsor not being up-front with me, hiring someone to collect data behind my back and report to you."

"You knew I was collecting data for the study, which I've encouraged you to look at, so don't accuse me of doing it behind your back," Avery said, her eyes flashing green sparks. "Except you haven't wanted to really look at it."

"Tell me this." He turned to Timkin. "If Dr. Girard claims the device is unsafe, will Crilex hire her to design the next-generation one?"

"I already told you," Avery said hotly, "that Crilex's own biomedical engineers—"

"Yes," Timkin interrupted. "We would offer that position to Dr. Girard, should that be the case."

Jack could hardly breathe. He'd known it and had to believe she'd known it, too. "Funny, these self-interested concerns of yours, that you said you wanted to be 'honest' with me about. What a joke."

"My concern now is that thirty percent of patients have had serious to mild valve leakage just this week," she said. "Fourteen percent overall so far, which is more than double the expected number. The trial should be stopped and the data analyzed before any more procedures are performed."

"How do you feel about that, Jack?" Timkin asked.

How did he feel about her deception and the way she'd used him and her wanting to stop the trial right now so she could get started in her new, cushy job? Shocked and furious barely covered it. "It's a normal risk. All patients are being medically managed, and we've barely begun to have any kind of big picture here. You've already invested a lot in this device, and we need the year's worth of data," he said to Timkin. "Are you going to listen to her or to me?"

"Both. We'll decide on the rollout after everyone in this trial has received the TAVI. I need sufficient data to give shareholders as we decide to fund either this device or the next one."

"Now, there's some impressive corporate talk. Numbers instead of lives." Avery stared at them both, slowly shaking her head. "You told me, Jack, that you wouldn't put patients in harm's way if the risk became obvious."

"I said extreme risk. Fourteen percent isn't extreme."

She didn't rebut his statement, simply looking at him like he'd disappointed her ten times as much as her past boyfriends combined.

He told himself he didn't care. She'd used him and lied to him. He'd screwed up big time, believing in her, but that was over with. "Is this meeting done? I have work to do."

Slowly and carefully, she held the tablet out to him. "Good luck and goodbye. I can't be a part of something I no longer believe in."

She was quitting? Jack couldn't analyze the burning sensation in his gut, but he wasn't sure it was relief.

He watched the sway of her hips as she walked away, hating that he still wanted to. Watched as she moved all the way to the end of the hall and out the door, because he knew it was the last time he'd get to enjoy the view he never should have enjoyed to begin with.

He squared his shoulders. Work was what he did and who he was—always had been. It was past time to remember that.

CHAPTER FIFTEEN

AVERY WANDERED THROUGH Montmartre on her way to the apartment she'd been lucky enough to find available to rent for a few months.

She'd always loved this neighborhood. Loved walking the cobbled streets, window shopping in all the art stores and seeing the Sacré Coeur, which was beautiful any time of day.

Today, though, her soul wasn't filled with the pleasure of it all, bringing a smile to her face. Instead, it felt hollow and empty, because all she could think about was Jack. How angry and shocked he'd been, as she'd known he would be. How obviously beyond disappointed in her that she'd kept the secret she'd been asked to keep. Maybe she should have handled it differently somehow, but it was too late now.

There was plenty of disappointment to go around. She just didn't understand him. How could he be so blind to the fact that there were simply too many patients having problems to go on with business as usual?

She knew he was an excellent, caring doctor. An incredible man. But it seemed he cared more for his career and the future of the trial than he did for his patients. Or maybe his determination and narrow focus was keeping him unrealistically optimistic when it was clearly time to look at everything more objectively.

Out of the corner of her eye she saw a couple kissing and realized she was standing at the Wall of I Love You. It was the day before Valentine's Day, which hadn't been her favorite holiday anyway, but now was a day she wished would forever disappear from the calendar.

Her heart ached, thinking of being here in Montmartre with Jack. Thinking of their time together all over Paris, and in Riquewihr, and how much she'd come to care for him.

How she'd come to fall in love with him.

Her throat clogged, and she sniffed and swallowed hard, quickly moving away from the wall. There'd be no reunion with Jack, here or anywhere. The universe had gotten it wrong somehow, and it just wasn't meant to be between them the way she'd come to think maybe it was.

Time to get back to her computer and back to work on a new TAVI device that maybe some company would want to fund. And tomorrow, on Valentine's Day?

Tomorrow she'd load up on tissues and romantic movies and marshmallows and coconut macaroons, giving herself a whole day to cry.

Jack stared at the X-ray fluoroscopy as he seated the prosthetic valve into the patient's heart, surprised and none too happy that in the midst of it a thought of Avery flashed through his mind. The thought that he wished she was watching. That she could see she'd been wrong to quit. Wrong to want to shut down the trial since, so far, not a single one of the last eight patients had had any problems with their new valves.

He told himself it didn't matter whether she was there or not. That he should be glad. But he couldn't deny that, without her behind that glass wall, the cath lab felt empty. The air flat and dull. The woman brought an effervescence and energy everywhere she went, and even though he hated that he did, he missed it.

"Valve looks like it's fully in place and seating nicely, so I'm withdrawing the catheter and guide wires," he said to those watching. There were some new docs there today from outside France, interested in bringing a trial to their own hospitals, and he was damned glad things were finally going more smoothly.

Except, suddenly, they weren't. The wire wouldn't release from the valve the way it was supposed to. With a frown, he gently pushed, pulled, and twisted it, but it was stuck like a damn fish hook in rocks on a riverbank.

"Get the patient's feet up in the air to see if a change in position helps the wire release."

Jessica did what he asked, and he worked at it a few more minutes, but nothing. "Try helping him roll onto his right side. If that doesn't work, roll him to the other side." More minutes, more tugging and jiggling, more nothing.

Damn it to hell. "Jess, grab my cellphone and get Toby Franklin on the line. The bioengineer from Crilex who helped design the device. Quick."

Jess hurried to make the call, explained the problem, then held the phone to Jack's ear.

"Toby. I've been trying for ten minutes to get the guide wires loose. Any ideas?"

"Put the patient in the left lateral decubitus position," Toby said. "See if having him take a deep breath to increase the pressure in his chest cavity helps. Then give it a good twist to the left, pull, and pray like hell."

Sweating now, Jack did what Toby had suggested and nearly shouted *Hallelujah!* when the wires finally released from the valve and he was able to slowly withdraw them. "Okay. We're almost done. Get ready to clamp the artery so I can close the access site."

He dragged in a deep, relieved breath as Jessica and the other nurse put a weight on the artery in the man's leg, then clamped it. Able to take a brief break, the thought of Avery flashed into his brain again. This time he realized he was glad she hadn't been there to see the problem, though he shouldn't feel that way. He couldn't take every damned thing that went wrong as a personal failure. But the fact that it had happened at all would suggest a design flaw different than any they'd seen so far. He didn't want to talk about it with her, but definitely planned to discuss it with Toby.

"Dr. Dunbar, patient's pressure is dropping."

He looked up from closing the access site in the man's leg to see Jessica frowning at the monitors. "What is it?"

"Was one twenty. Now it's one hundred—no, ninety—and his pulse is dropping." Her eyes were wide with concern as she looked at him over her mask. "Oxygen saturation is falling, too."

What the hell? "Give him a liter of fluid and get an echo."

Jessica quickly rolled over the echo machine and got a picture. Jack stared at the image of the man's heart.

The valve looked snugged in right where it belonged. He peered closer and his own heart practically stopped when he saw the one thing he dreaded to see.

"Oh, no," Jessica whispered. Obviously, she'd seen it, too, and they stared together for a split second before Jack snapped himself back into action.

"We have a large, pericardial infusion," he announced to the room, his throat tight. "Jess, page Anton Maran. He's the thoracic surgeon on call. Somebody get in touch with Anesthesia. Everybody move to get the patient to the OR fast. We don't have a single second to spare."

The room became a flurry of activity as they got the patient ready, running down the hall with Jack as he pushed the gurney, because saving the man's life would require fast work and a lot of luck.

Breathing hard, his mind spun back to the whole procedure. How could he possibly have perforated the man's ventricle? There was just one, obvious answer. Somehow, when he'd had to twist and pull the wires to get them to release from the valve, the catheter had torn it.

"Is he going to make it?" Jessica asked as she ran along beside him.

"Stitching the cut will be easy for Anton. Getting him to the OR on time will be the hard part. The other part of the whole equation is whether or not he can recover from the open-heart surgery we were trying to avoid."

Jack said a prayer of thanks that Anton Maran and the anesthesiologist were already scrubbed up and in the OR when they wheeled the patient in. He briefed

Anton, but they'd already spent time going over each patient just in case there was an emergency like this one, so he was able to get to work fast.

Jack watched throughout the whole procedure. The shock of the man's ventricle getting perforated had worn off, leaving a stabbing ache behind. An ache of disappointment that the trial had ultimately not been the success he'd so wanted and expected it to be. An ache for the patient having to recover from this intense surgery, if he did recover.

An ache for Avery, who was long gone to who knew where. And all because he'd refused to listen to her.

Avery not being there, standing next to him through this thing, felt all wrong. How had that happened in a few short weeks? He had no idea, but somehow her absence felt like a huge, gaping hole in his life. In his heart.

All he'd wanted or needed in his life had been his work. Something he loved and was damned good at. Until Avery had shown up. Avery, in her colorful clothes with her beautiful green eyes, a teasing smile on her face and every bit as strong a work ethic as he had.

He'd wanted just a day or two of fun with her. To his surprise, she'd given him that and so much more. And what had he given her? Not a damn thing. Not even the respect he'd slammed her old boyfriend for not giving, either.

He shook his head at himself. What a damn fool.

Hours later, the surgery was over and a success, and Jack could only hope that the man remained in a stable condition. Feeling wiped out, he changed out of his scrubs and went to his hotel room. The thought of going out to eat without Avery sounded miserable, and he didn't feel like hashing out the day's events with Jessica, either. As he pondered room service, a knock at the door sent his heart slamming against his ribs.

Had Avery heard what had happened? He moved toward the door, wishing it would be her standing there, ready to give him another lecture that, for once, he'd be happy to listen to.

But it wasn't. "Jessica."

"Wow, my ego's gotten even bigger at how excited you sound to see me," she mocked. "Can I come in for a minute?"

"I'm always glad to see you. I'm just tired."

"Of course you're tired. I don't think you've rested for more than a few hours all week, and today was rough."

She sat on the side of the bed while Jack perched in the wooden chair by a small table and looked at her. "I've decided to stop the trial. I'm telling Timkin tomorrow morning."

He hadn't even realized he'd made that final decision, but now that the words had come out of his mouth, he knew without a doubt it was the right one.

Jessica nodded. "I figured you would. But that's not what I want to talk to you about."

He raised his eyebrows at her, hoping she didn't have some marital problem with Brandon. He wasn't up for that kind of conversation.

"Are you interested in where Avery Girard is?"

Hell, yes. He sat up straight. "I might be."

"Might be. Right." She snorted. "You've been glum

and cranky ever since she quit the trial, even before today's scary event. Which I guess proved maybe she was right, which means maybe you should find her and apologize and kiss her and then we can all be happy again."

If only it were that easy. "I don't think she has much interest in my apologies." Or in his kisses, and the thought made his chest ache all over again.

"I bet she does. But there's only one way for you to find out." She dug into her purse and pulled out a piece of paper, leaning over to wave it in his face. "Her address in Montmartre. She's rented an apartment for the month."

"How did you find that out?"

"Nurses at any hospital know everything." She stood and patted him on the head like he was a little kid. "Now, go. I'm heading to dinner with my cousin and expect a full report tomorrow."

He stared at the door closing behind her as adrenaline surged through his blood.

He knew he'd disappointed Avery, but he could fix that. Tomorrow was Valentine's Day, and he had to admit he didn't know much about romance. But the woman who'd held his clinical trial in her hands held his heart now instead, and she'd given him a few ideas about what just might work on her.

Avery frowned at the knock on her door, wondering who the heck could be bothering her at 9:00 p.m. in an apartment few knew she'd moved into. While she was eating marshmallows and macaroons and crying over movies. Cautiously, she peeked through the peephole and the shock of who was standing there stole her breath.

How had Jack found out where she was? And why? She knew it couldn't have anything to do with it being Valentine's Day. The man probably wasn't even aware of the holiday.

She took a moment to wipe her nose and eyes, smooth down her skirt and conjure the frustration and deep disappointment she'd felt the last time she'd seen him. Except the sight of his handsome, tired face made her want to wrap her arms around him and hold him close instead.

Disgusted with herself, she opened the door. "Lost in Paris?"

A small smile touched his mouth, but didn't make it to his eyes. "I am lost. Looking for a tour guide. You available?"

"No, I'm not."

"Can you give me just ten minutes? Please?"

She willed herself to resist the entreaty in his beautiful brown eyes, but felt that darned melting sensation inside her chest that seemed to happen whenever he was near. She sighed and figured she may as well spend ten minutes with him. Who knew? Maybe it would help heal the huge hole he'd left in her heart.

"Ten minutes."

She grabbed her coat from the rack by the door, and the feel of his fingers touching the back of her neck as he gently tugged her hair from inside made her eyes sting again. Lord, if she'd known what a heartbreaker the man was, she'd have avoided him that first day in the hotel like flesh-eating bacteria.

A little half laugh, half sob formed in her throat as she thought about their ridiculous conversation about that and snails and about the magical time they'd spent in Riquewihr. Which hadn't accomplished a thing, except to make her fall even harder for the man.

She was a little surprised he didn't touch her the way he always did as they walked to wherever it was they were going. Clearly, this must be a business visit and nothing more. Which, of course, she'd known anyway. Tears again blurred her eyes, and she forcefully blinked them back, getting really annoyed with herself now. Why would it even cross her mind to think it might be anything else?

When her vision cleared, she glanced at her watch, noting the time and fully planning on only ten darned minutes of torture with the man. Then realized they were standing by the Wall of I Love You. As she looked at him in surprise, the memory of kissing him there clogged up her breath.

"Someone told me this was a special place created just for lovers to meet. And this day, of all days of the year, seems like a good one for that to happen." He reached for her hands. "At the time, I thought that was a little hokey. I didn't realize how important such a place could be until my lover left me."

His lover. She closed her eyes at how wonderful that had been. But it wasn't meant to be. "We were supposed to be lovers just that one day. We should have left it that way."

"If that was all it was supposed to be, it would have been. But it was more than that. A whole lot more, at least for me. You brought a joy into my life I didn't even know was missing."

His words, the intense way he was staring at her squeezed her heart. But what was she supposed to say to that? He had his work and she had hers, and trying to combine that with being lovers had created nothing but conflict and pain.

"I love you, Avery." His hands tightened on hers. "I thought my work could be everything. But now I know. Even if I never see you again, it will never be enough. There would always be an empty place where you belong."

He loved her? Stunned, she stared at him as he drew her close, wrapped his arms around her and kissed her. So sure she'd never feel his lips on hers again, the pleasure of it had her melting into his chest and sighing into his mouth.

He pulled back slightly to look at her. "Remember when we made a wish at the fountain? I got my wish."

"I know. I figured you wished for sex, except I was going to give you that anyway."

"No, though I wasn't counting on that. Just hoping." A small smile touched his lips before he got serious again. "I wished for the wisdom to know when to keep at something and when to quit. It didn't kick in any too soon, but thank God it finally did."

"You're stopping the trial?"

"Yes. I'm sorry I didn't listen to you, because I should have. But that's not what I got the wisdom for. My wish kicked in when I knew I had to find you and tell you how much I love you and ask you to forgive me for all the things I've done wrong."

"You...you're not still mad about me not telling you the truth?"

"I wish you'd been honest with me, but who knows? Maybe we would have really kept our distance from one another, and we wouldn't be standing here tonight, kissing, on Valentine's Day."

"Maybe you're right. Who knew you were such a romantic?" Swallowing back tears, she reached to cup his face in her hand, barely believing this was really happening.

His lips curved in his first real smile of the night, and he gave her a long, delicious kiss that wobbled her knees before he let her go and reached into his pocket. To her shock, he pulled out the music box she'd looked at with him. The little tune tinkled when he opened it, and she started to shake all over when she saw what was inside it.

"Jack. What—"

"You said you wanted to be draped in gold." His fingers grasped the ring tucked into the red velvet folds of the box and held it up. A diamond flanked by sapphires, rubies and emeralds. "I thought a plain diamond was too dull for you, and I'm not sure this qualifies as draping, except around your finger. But I hope it's good enough for now. Will you marry me and be my forever Valentine, Avery?"

"You're asking me to marry you?" She stared into the intense brown of his eyes, barely breathing.

"I'm asking you to marry me. Begging. And since I'm about to have a heart attack because you haven't said you love me, too, please tell me. One way or the other."

"The answer is yes. *Oui, oui, oui.* And I do love you. Crazily love you. Wildly love you."

"Insanely love *you.*" He pulled her close and pressed his face to her hair. "I don't deserve you, but I'm keeping you anyway." He held her for a long time before sliding the ring onto her shaking finger. She sniffed at the tears stupidly popping into her eyes again and wished she could see it better.

He held her hand tight as he pressed soft kisses down her cheek. "What do you say we team up to create a new TAVI device, Dr. Girard?" he whispered against her skin. "Sound like a good idea?"

"Une très bonne idée." She tunneled her hands into his hair and tipped his face so she could look into his beautiful eyes. Eyes that looked at her with the same kind of love she felt all but bursting from her chest. "I think we'll make a very good team, Dr. Dunbar. One very good team."

* * * * *